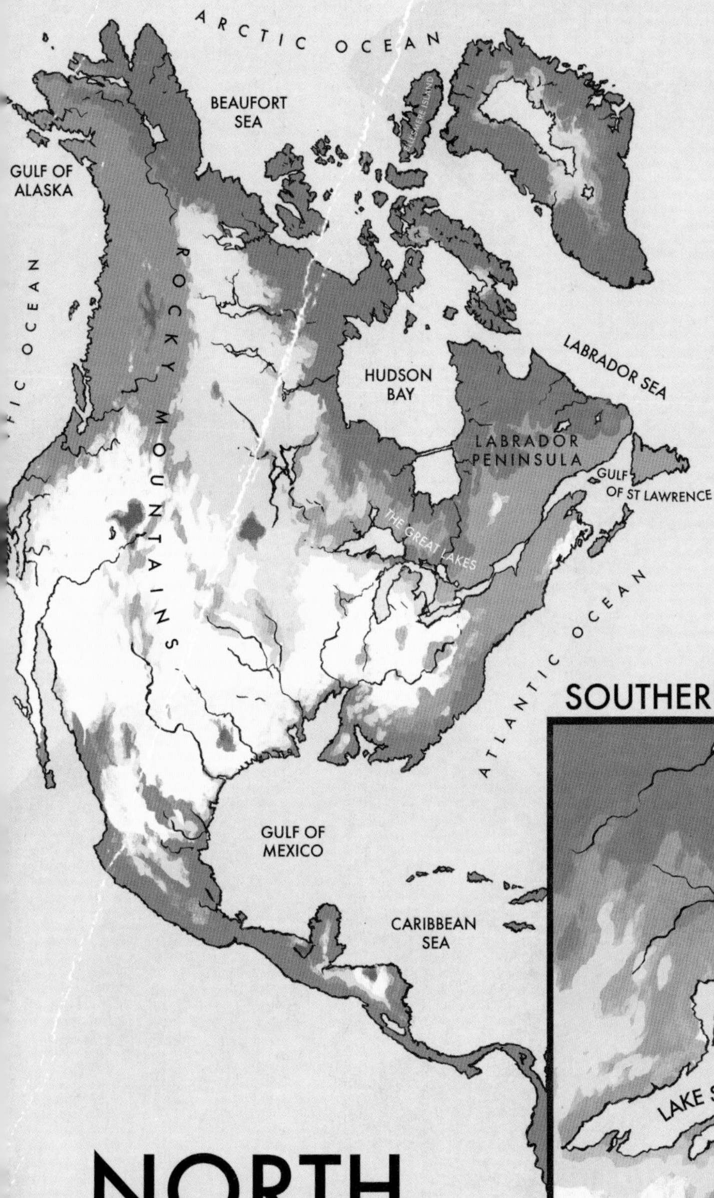
ARCTIC OCEAN
BEAUFORT SEA
GULF OF ALASKA
ROCKY MOUNTAINS
HUDSON BAY
LABRADOR SEA
LABRADOR PENINSULA
GULF OF ST LAWRENCE
THE GREAT LAKES
ATLANTIC OCEAN
GULF OF MEXICO
CARIBBEAN SEA
FIC OCEAN

BIOMES OF NORTH AMERICA

- BOREAL FOREST
- PRAIRIE
- TEMPERATE FOREST
- DESERT
- TROPICAL FOREST
- UNKNOWN BIOME
- RAINFOREST

SOUTHERN HUDSONI TERRITORIES

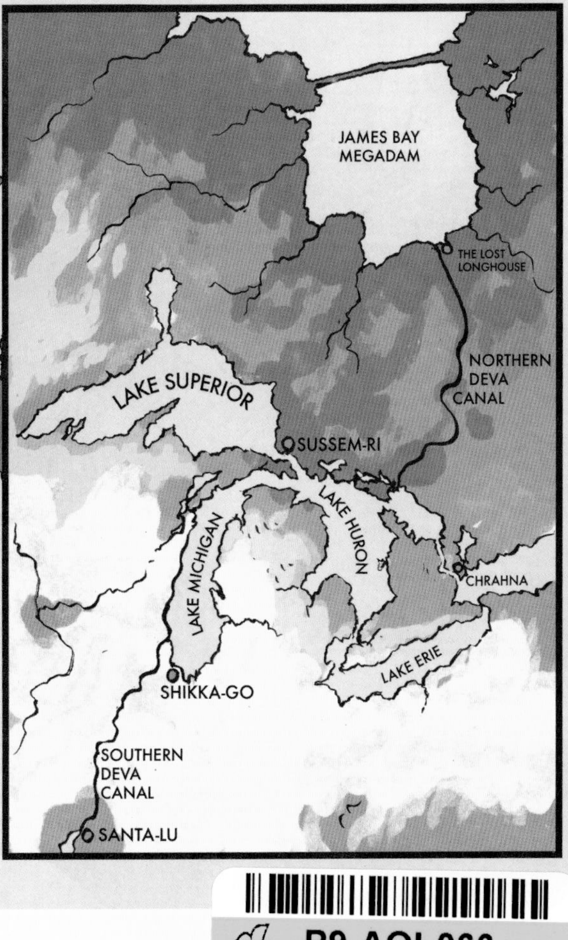
JAMES BAY MEGADAM
THE LOST LONGHOUSE
NORTHERN DEVA CANAL
LAKE SUPERIOR
SUSSEM-RI
LAKE HURON
LAKE MICHIGAN
CHRAHNA
LAKE ERIE
SHIKKA-GO
SOUTHERN DEVA CANAL
SANTA-LU

NORTH AMERICA
IN THE THIRTY-THIRD CENTURY

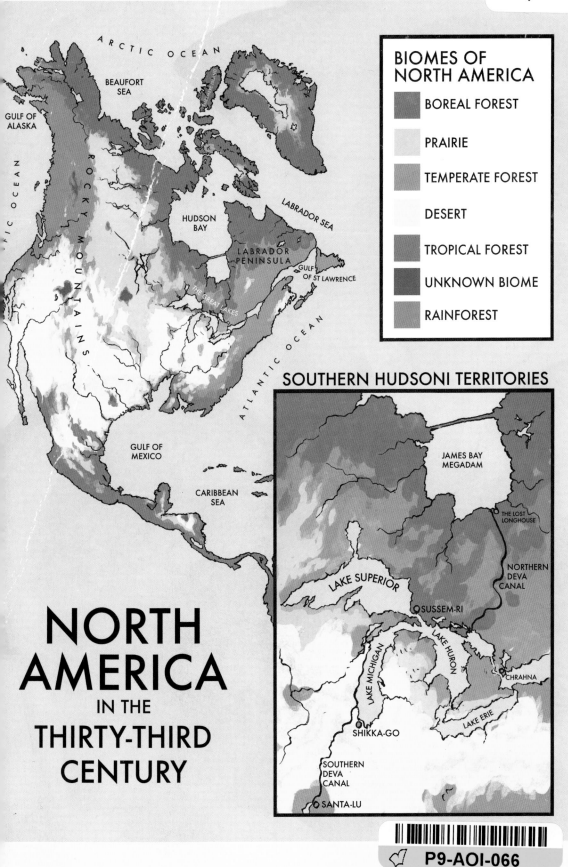

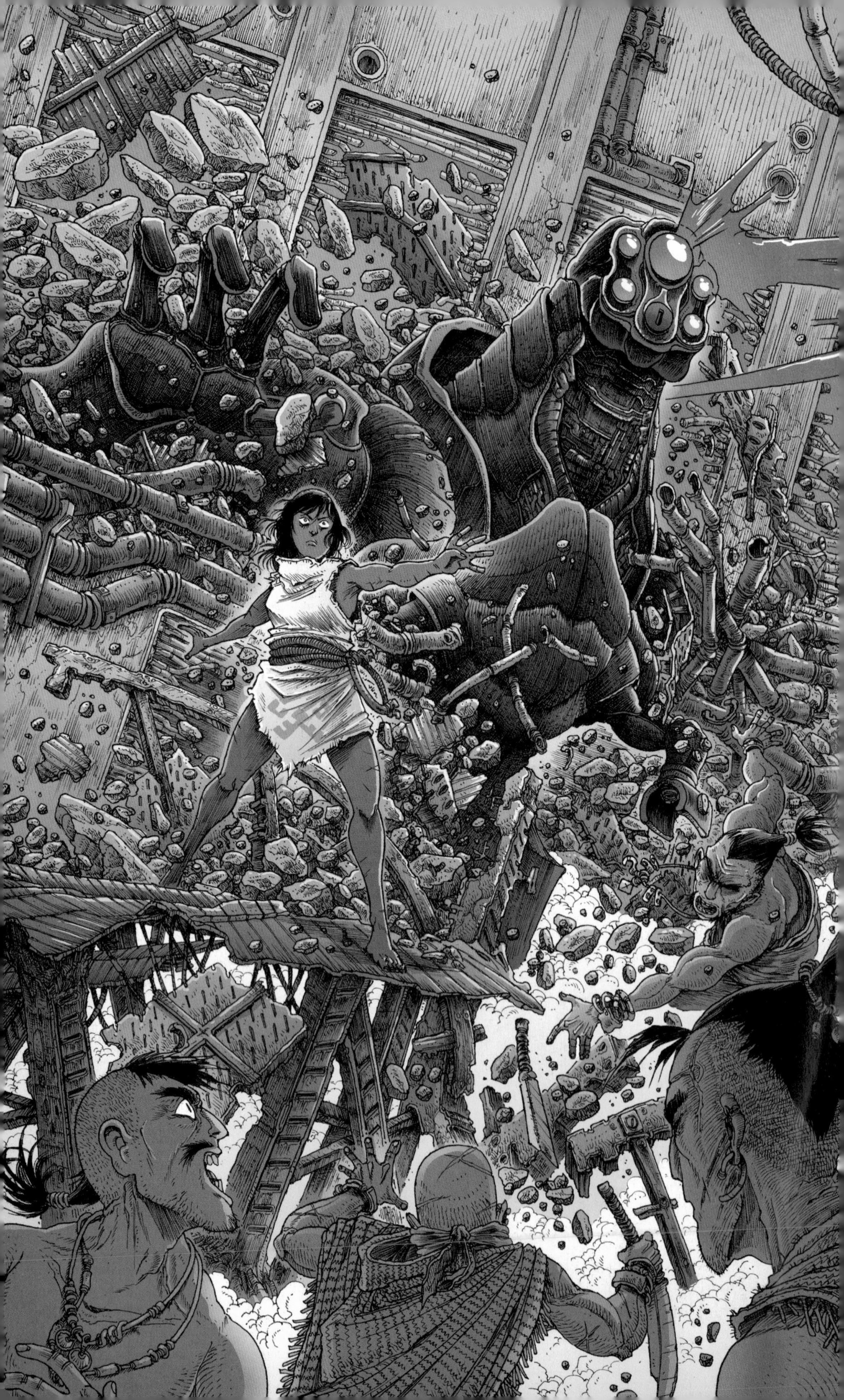

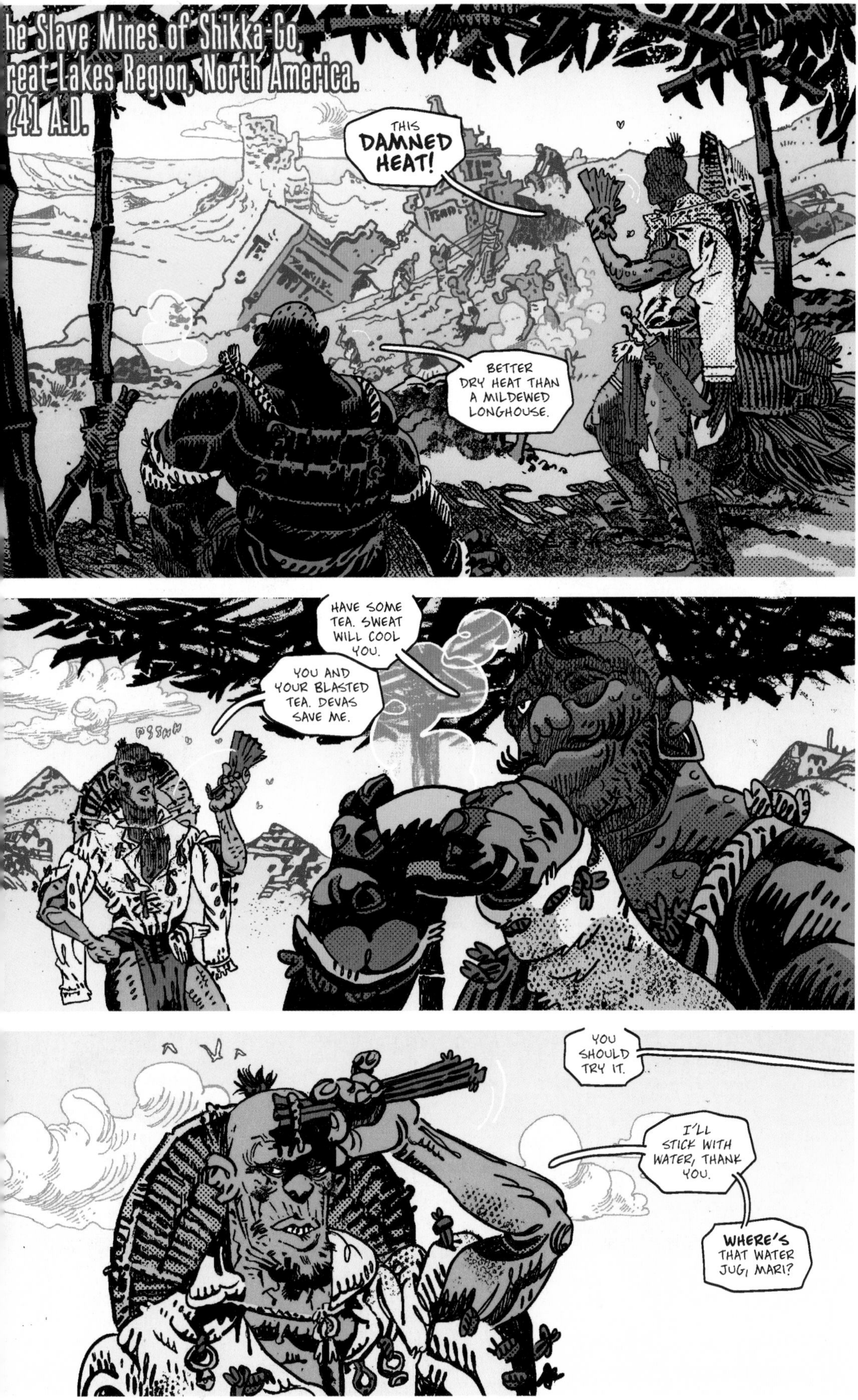
he Slave Mines of Shikka-Go,
reat Lakes Region, North America.
241 A.D.
THIS DAMNED HEAT!
BETTER DRY HEAT THAN A MILDEWED LONGHOUSE.
HAVE SOME TEA. SWEAT WILL COOL YOU.
YOU AND YOUR BLASTED TEA. DEVAS SAVE ME.
YOU SHOULD TRY IT.
I'LL STICK WITH WATER, THANK YOU.
WHERE'S THAT WATER JUG, MARI?

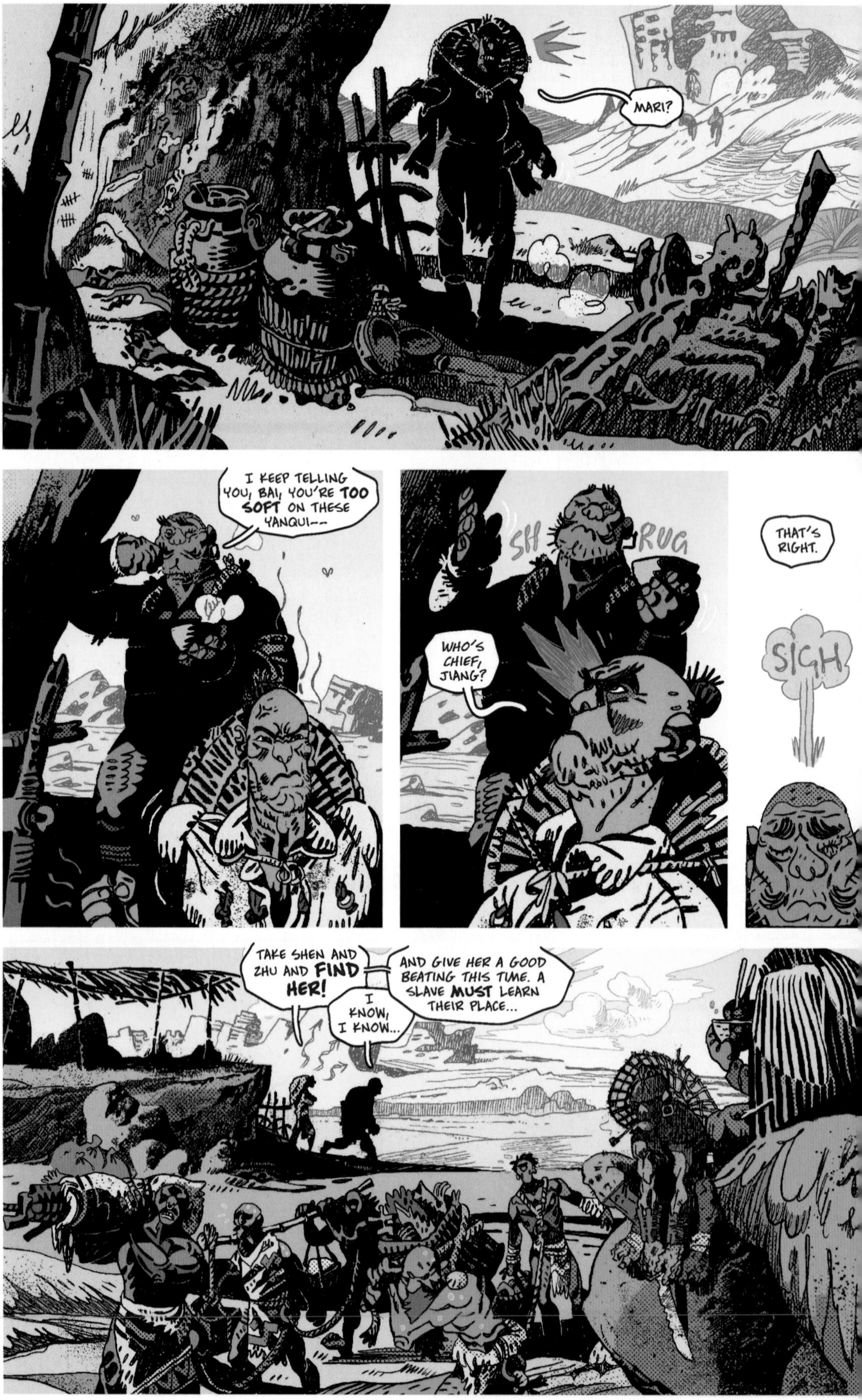
MARI?
I KEEP TELLING YOU, BAI, YOU'RE TOO SOFT ON THESE YANQUI--
SH RUG
WHO'S CHIEF, JIANG?
THAT'S RIGHT.
SIGH
TAKE SHEN AND ZHU AND FIND HER!
AND GIVE HER A GOOD BEATING THIS TIME. A SLAVE MUST LEARN THEIR PLACE...
I KNOW, I KNOW...

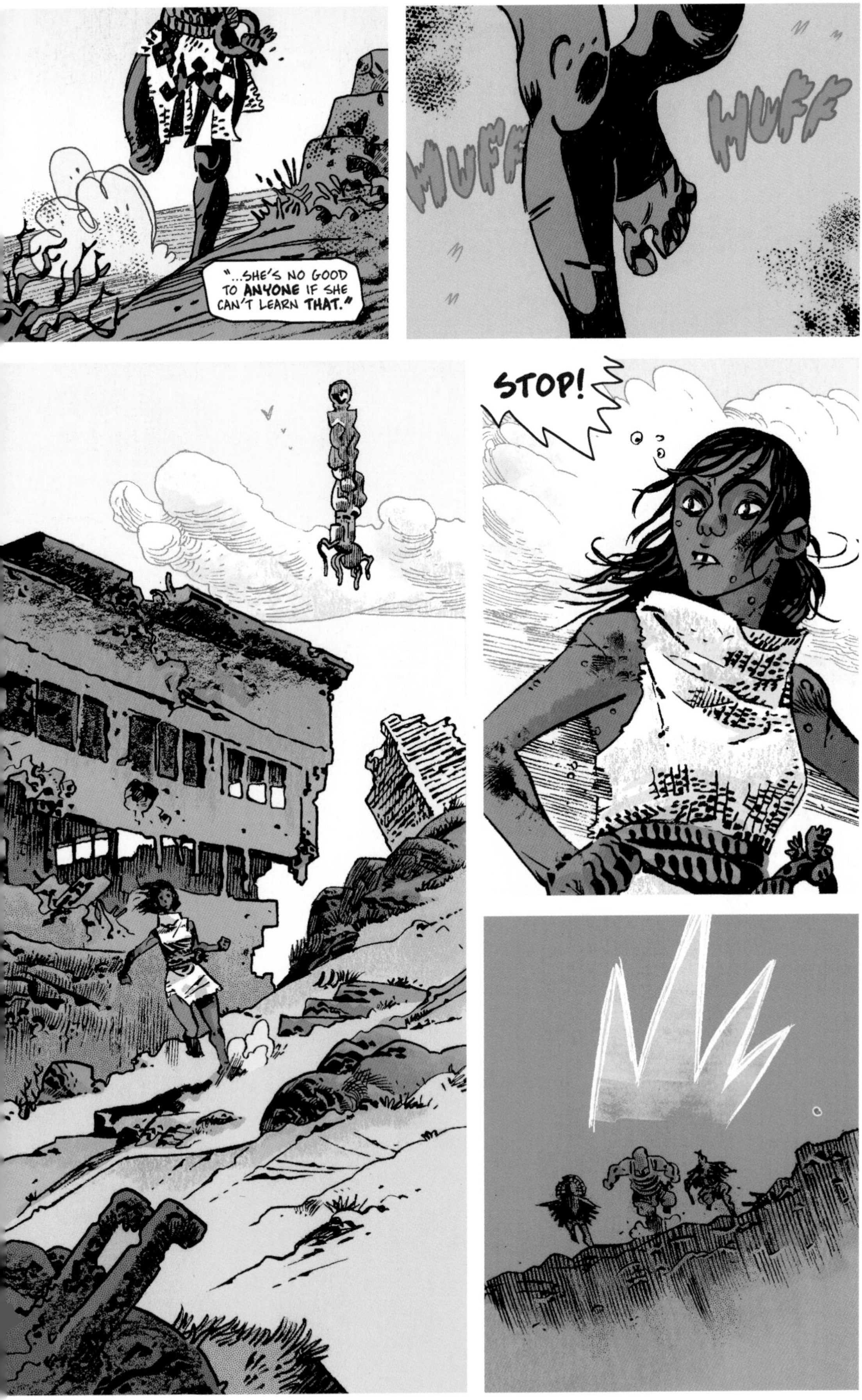
"...SHE'S NO GOOD TO ANYONE IF SHE CAN'T LEARN THAT."
HUFF HUFF
STOP!

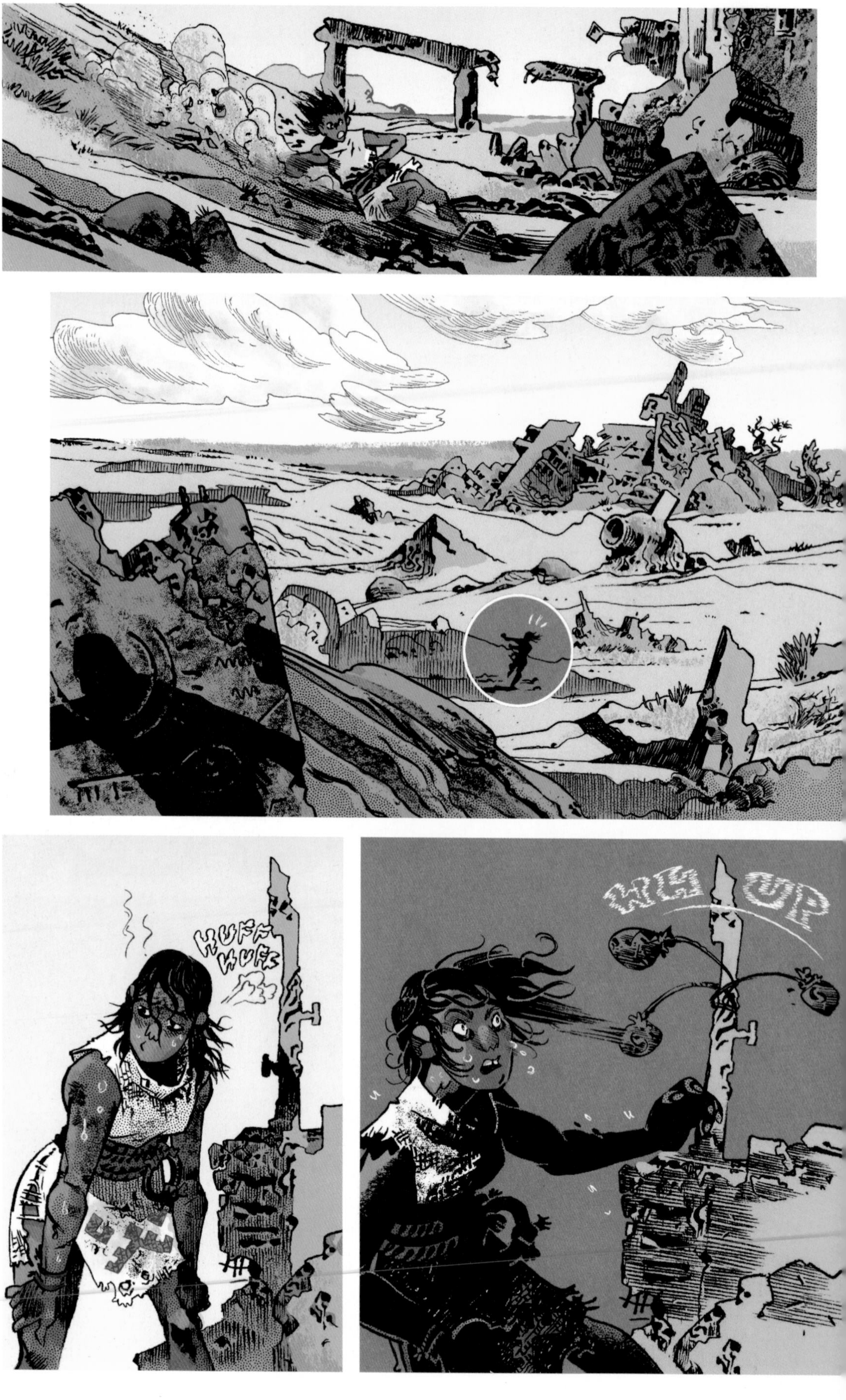
HUFF
HUFF
WHUP

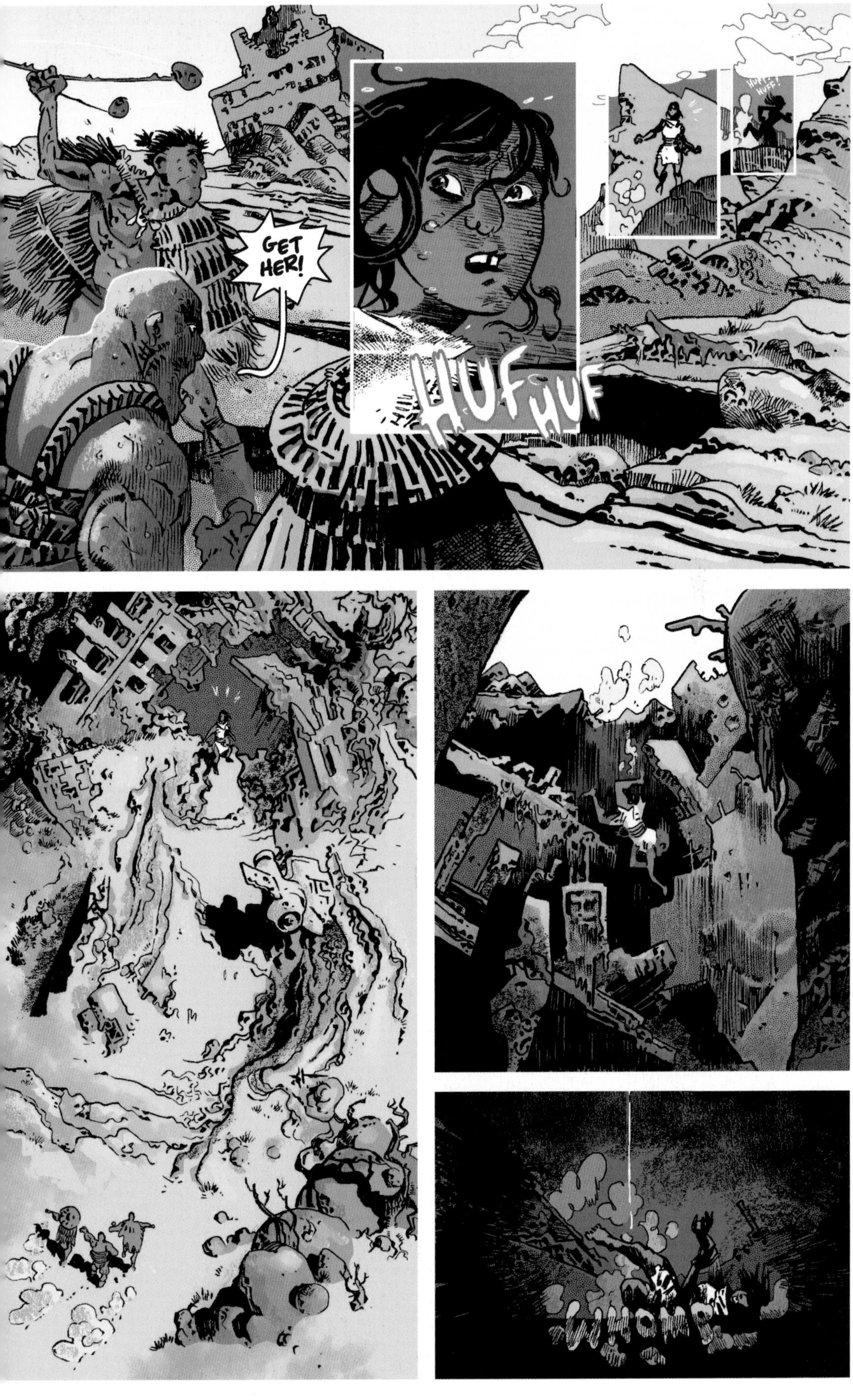
GET HER!
HUF HUF
HUFF! HUFF!

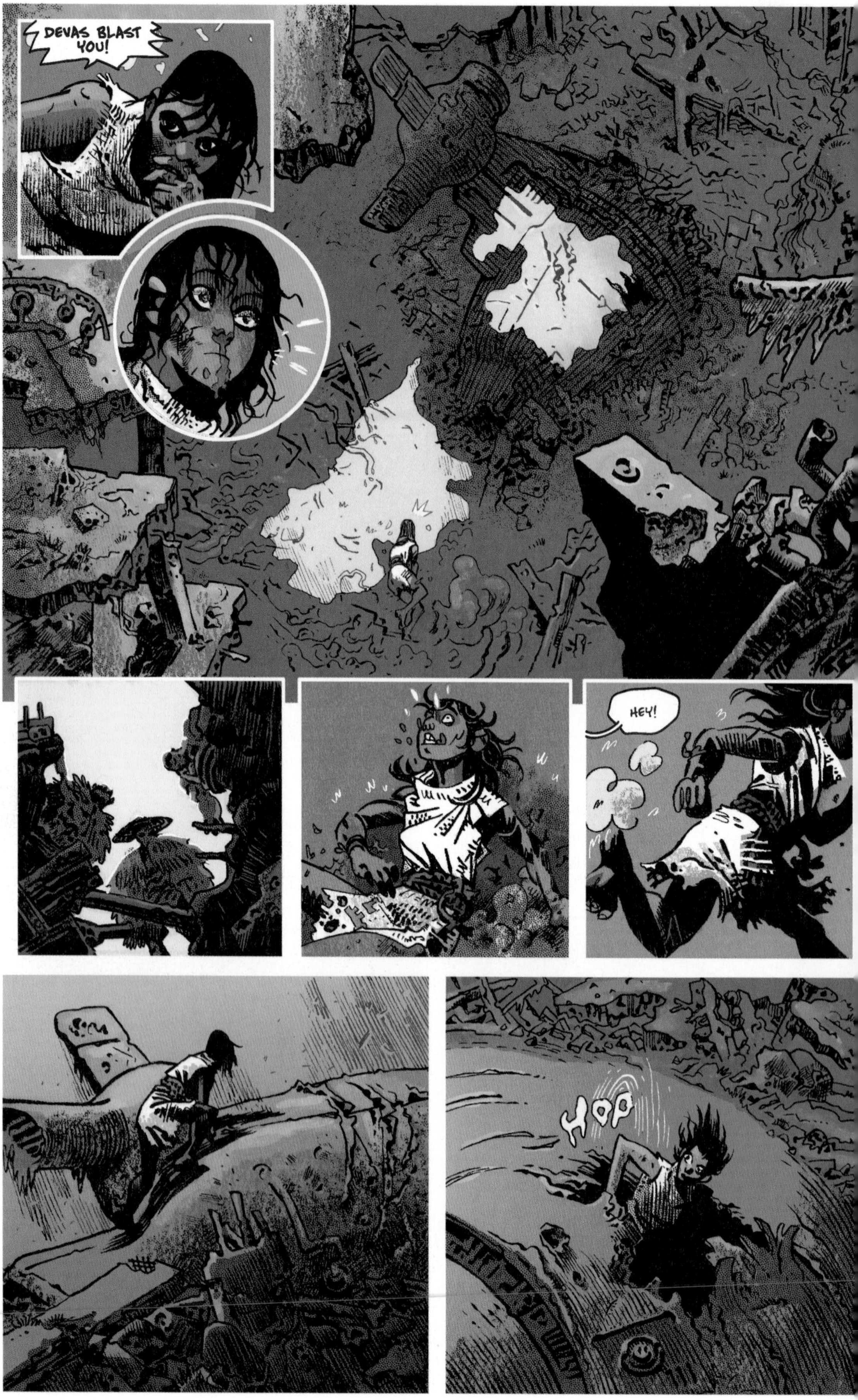
DEVAS BLAST YOU!
HEY!
HOP

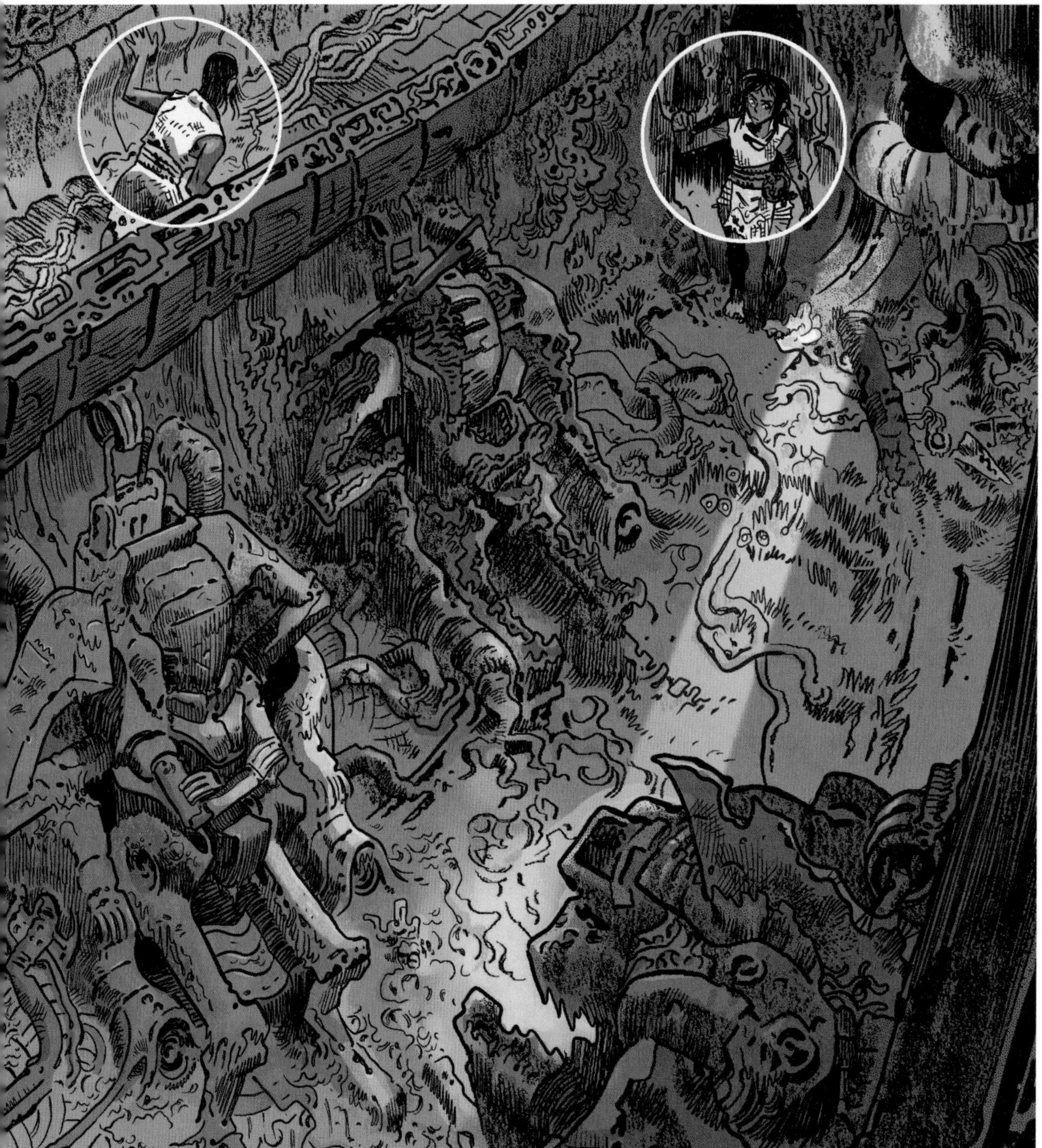

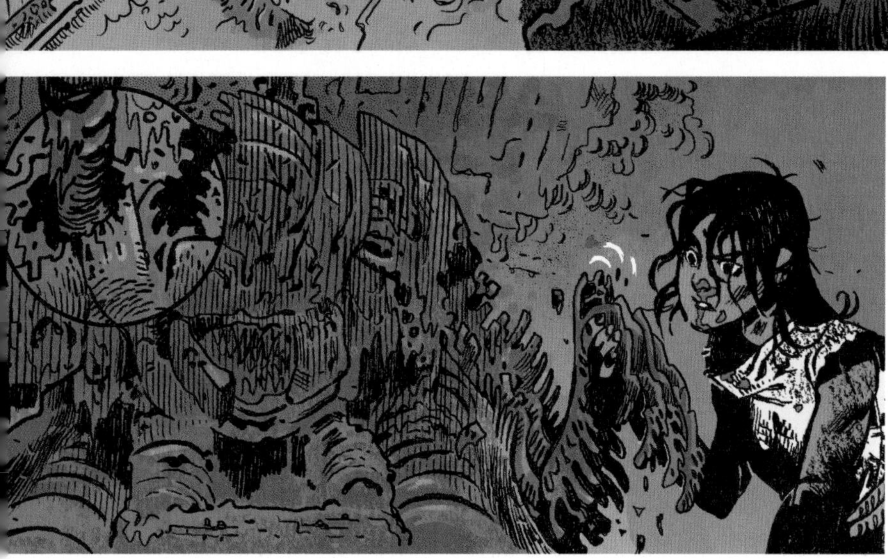

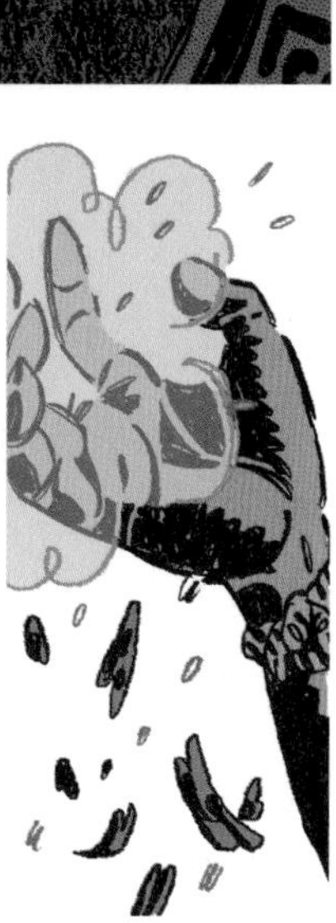

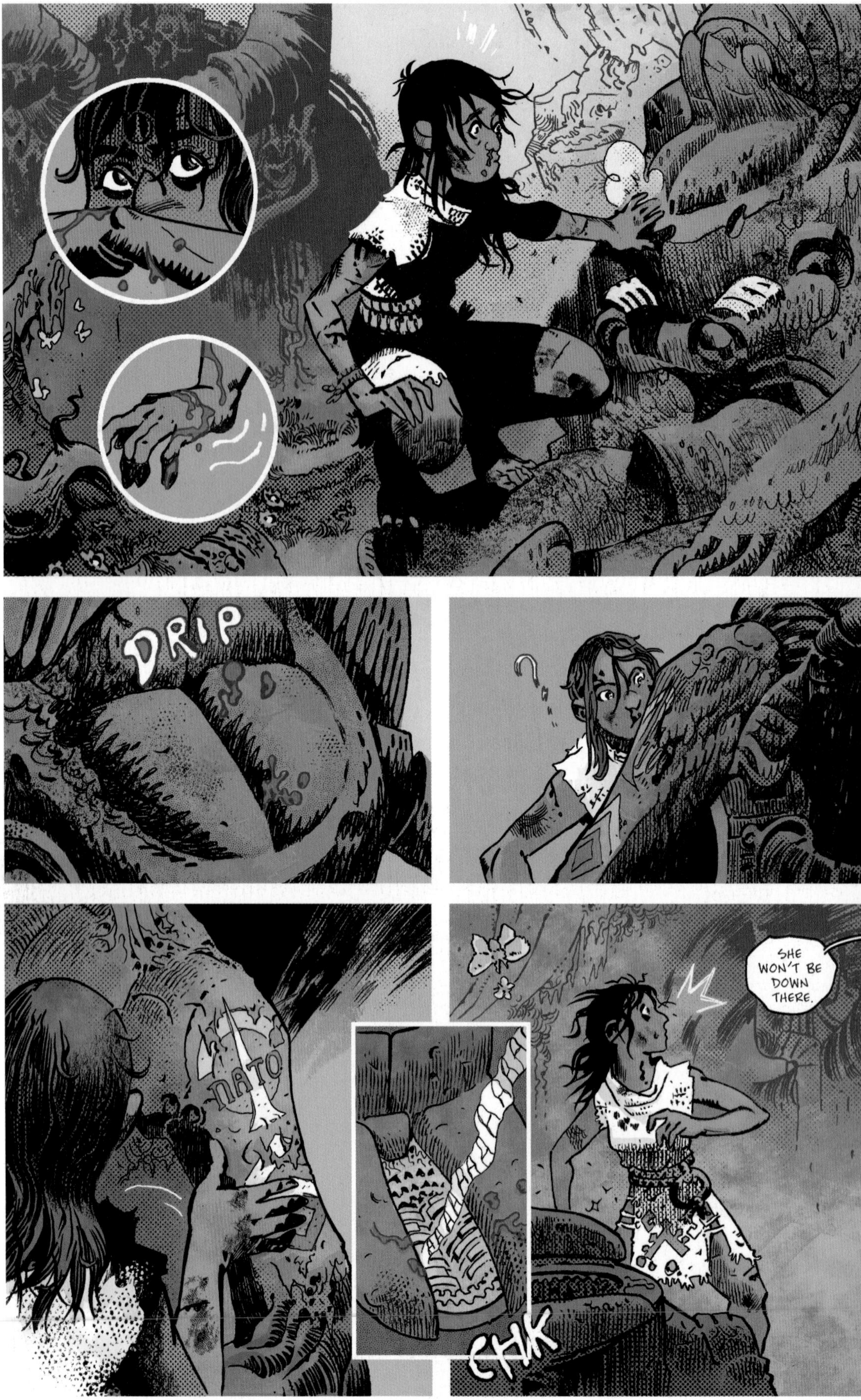
DRIP
NATO
SHE WON'T BE DOWN THERE.
CHK

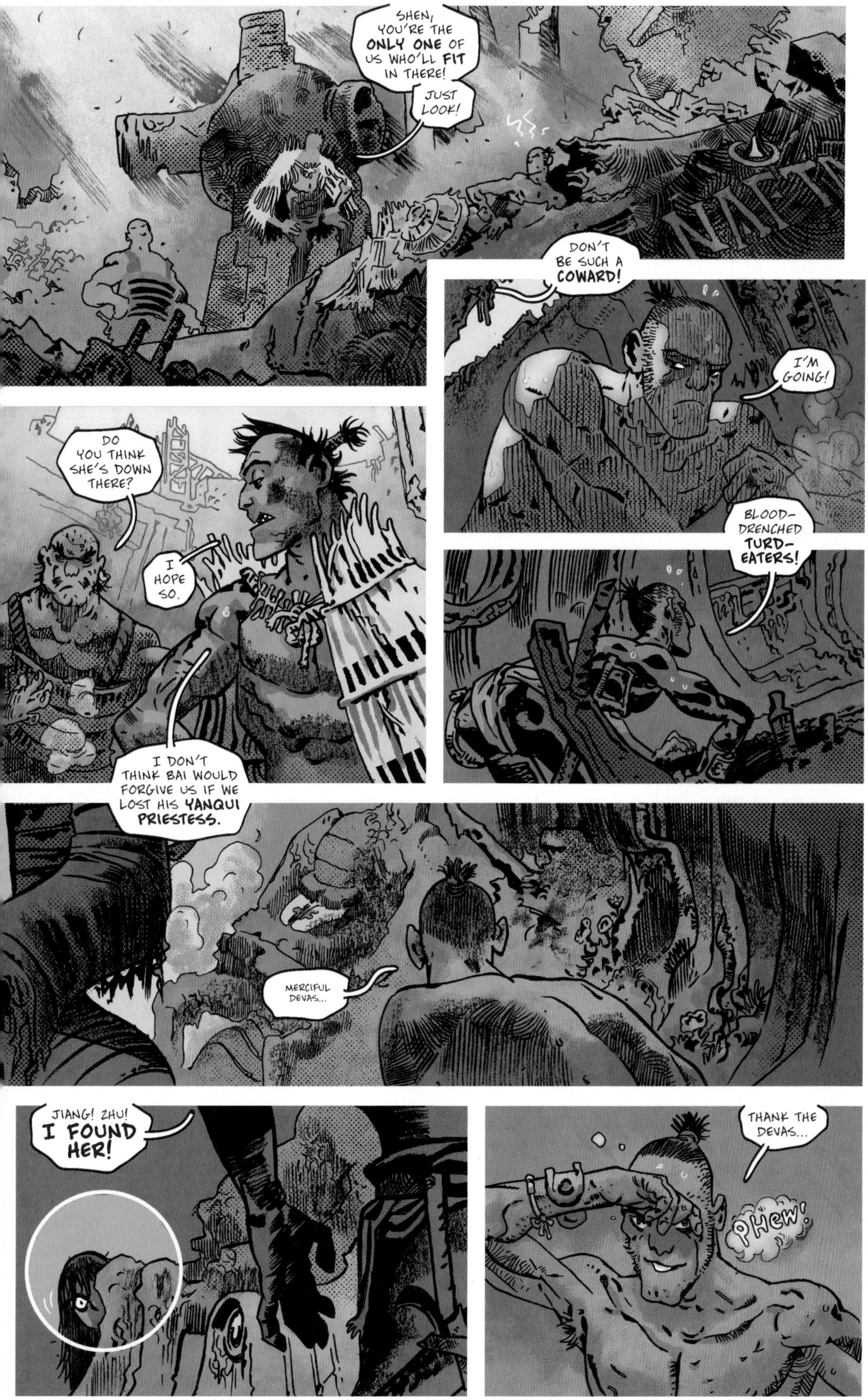

SHEN, YOU'RE THE **ONLY ONE** OF US WHO'LL **FIT** IN THERE!
JUST LOOK!
DON'T BE SUCH A **COWARD!**
I'M GOING!
DO YOU THINK SHE'S DOWN THERE?
I HOPE SO.
I DON'T THINK BAI WOULD FORGIVE US IF WE LOST HIS **YANQUI PRIESTESS.**
BLOOD-DRENCHED **TURD-EATERS!**
MERCIFUL DEVAS...
JIANG! ZHU! **I FOUND HER!**
THANK THE DEVAS...
PHEW!

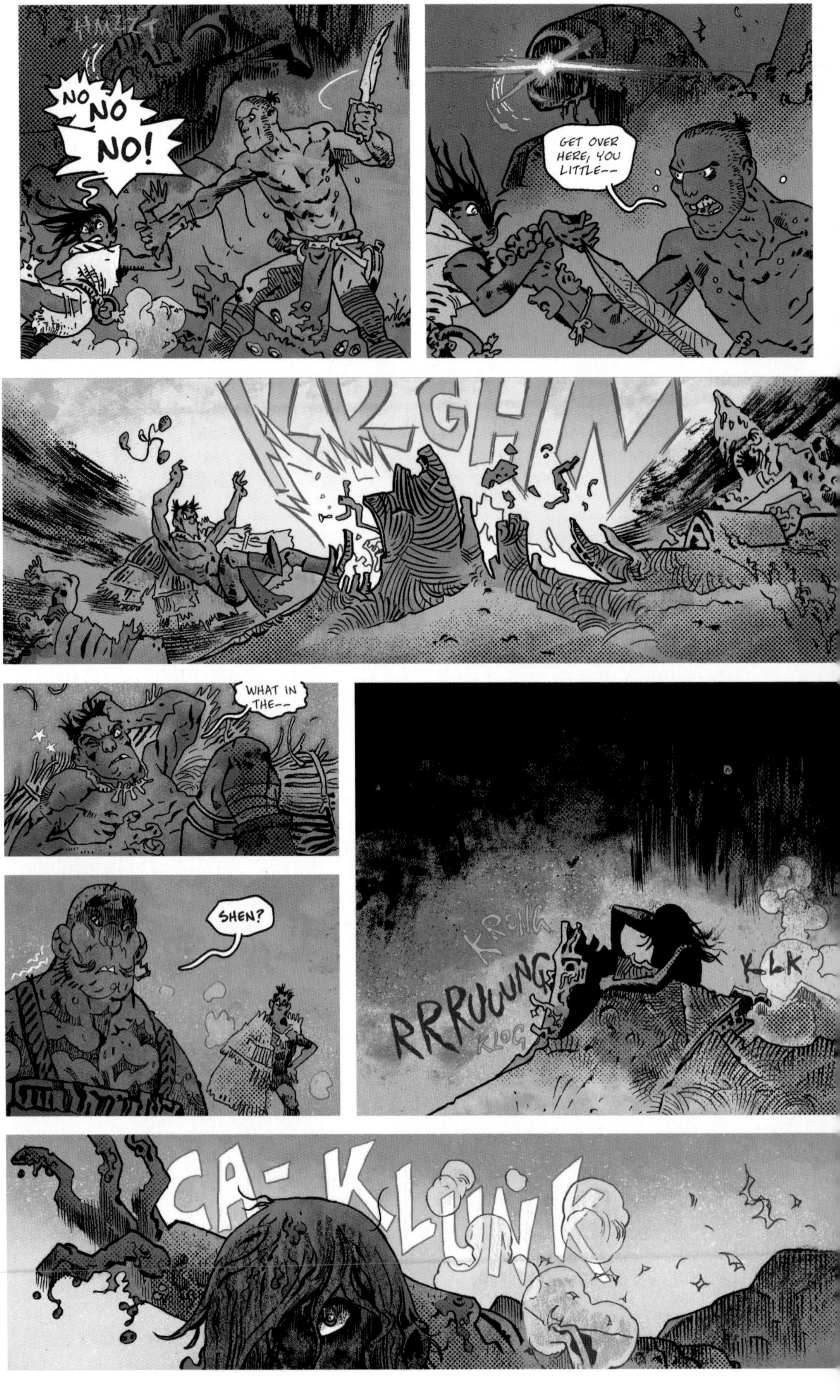
HMZZT
NO NO NO!
GET OVER HERE, YOU LITTLE--
KLRGHM
WHAT IN THE--
SHEN?
KRONG
RRRUUUNG
KLOG
KLK
CA-KLUNK

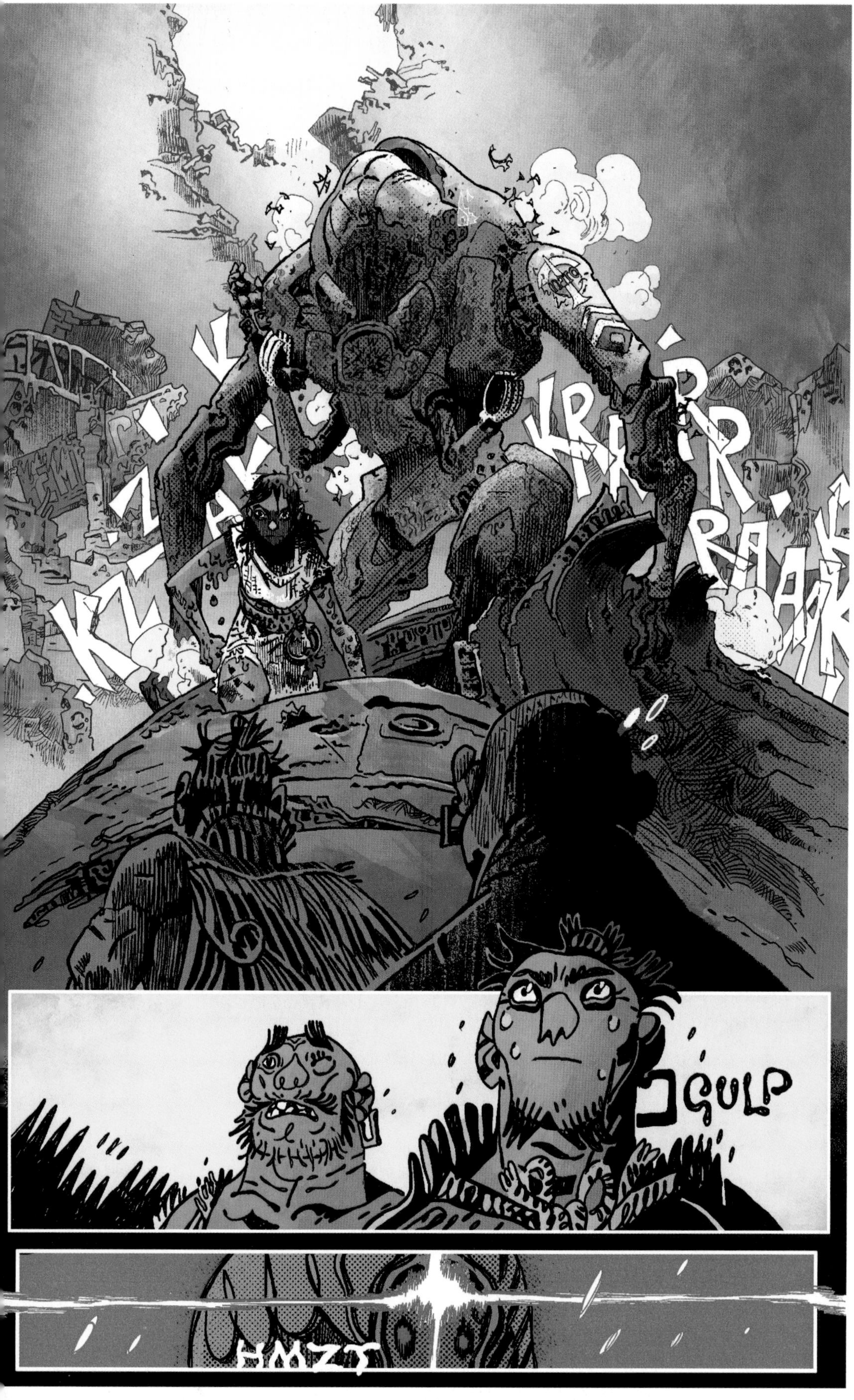
GULP
HMZT

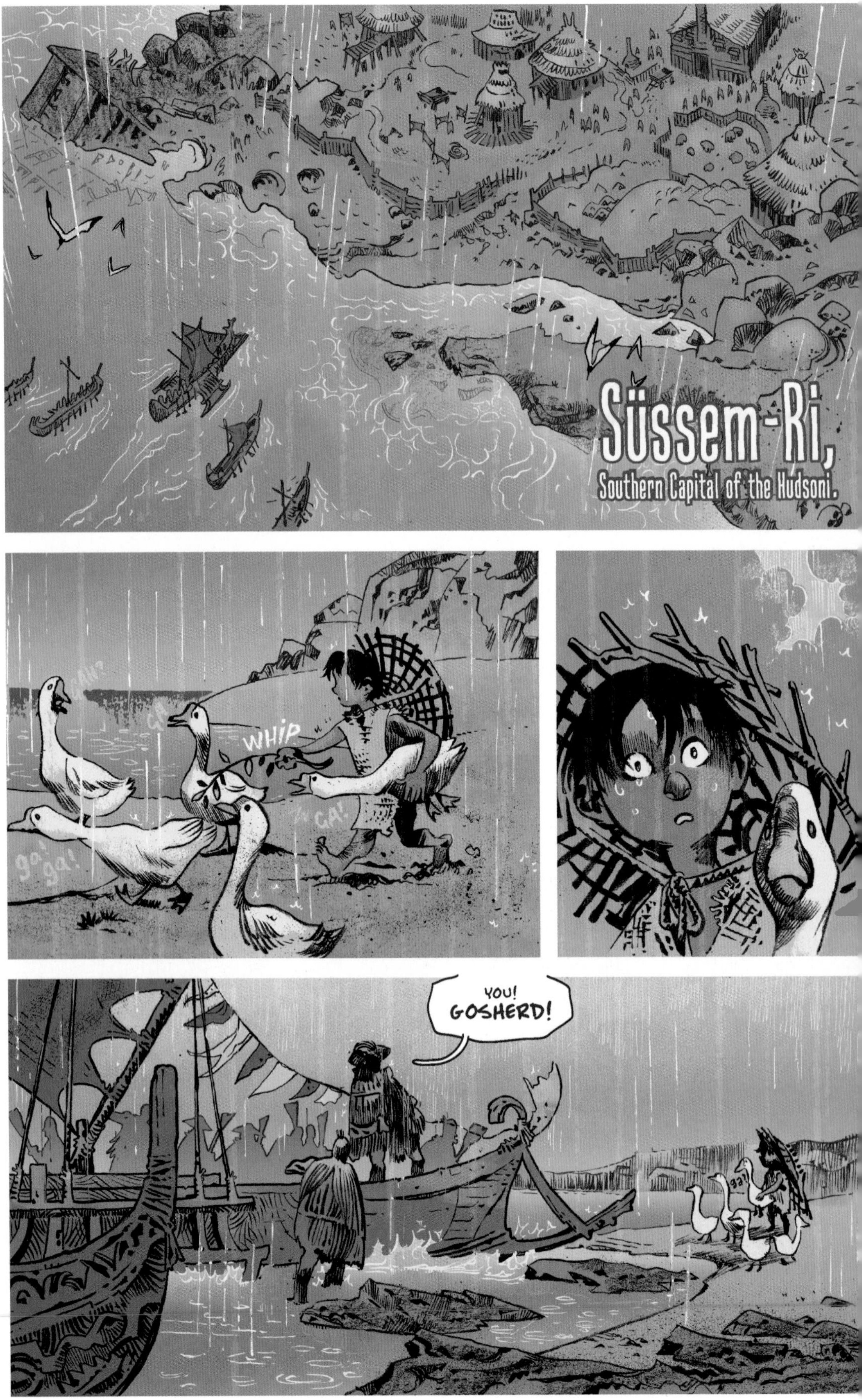
Süssem-Ri,
Southern Capital of the Hudsoni.
WHIP
GA!
ga! ga!
YOU! GOSHERD!
ga!

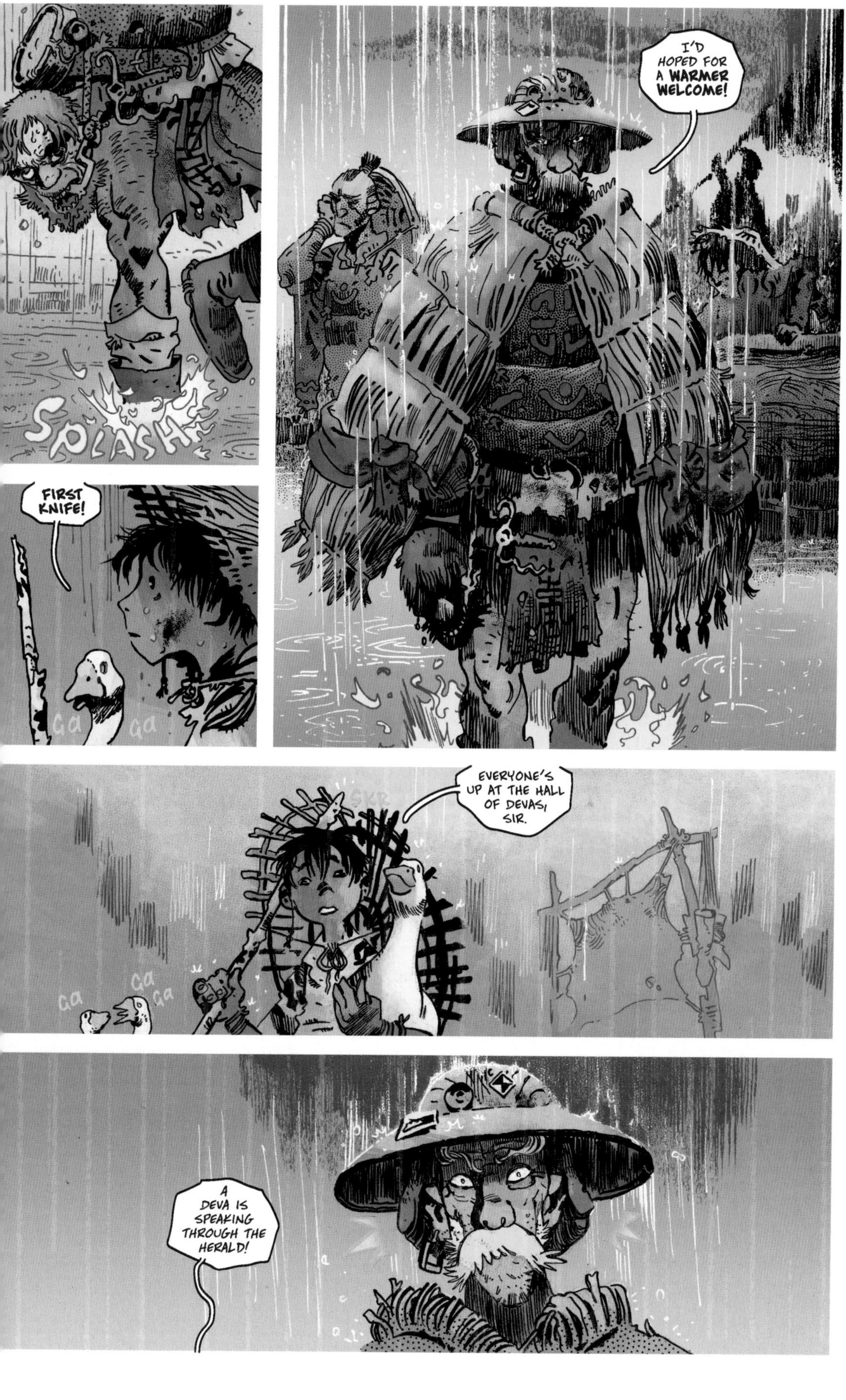
SPLASH
I'D HOPED FOR A WARMER WELCOME!
FIRST KNIFE!
GA GA
EVERYONE'S UP AT THE HALL OF DEVAS, SIR.
SKR
GA GA GA
A DEVA IS SPEAKING THROUGH THE HERALD!

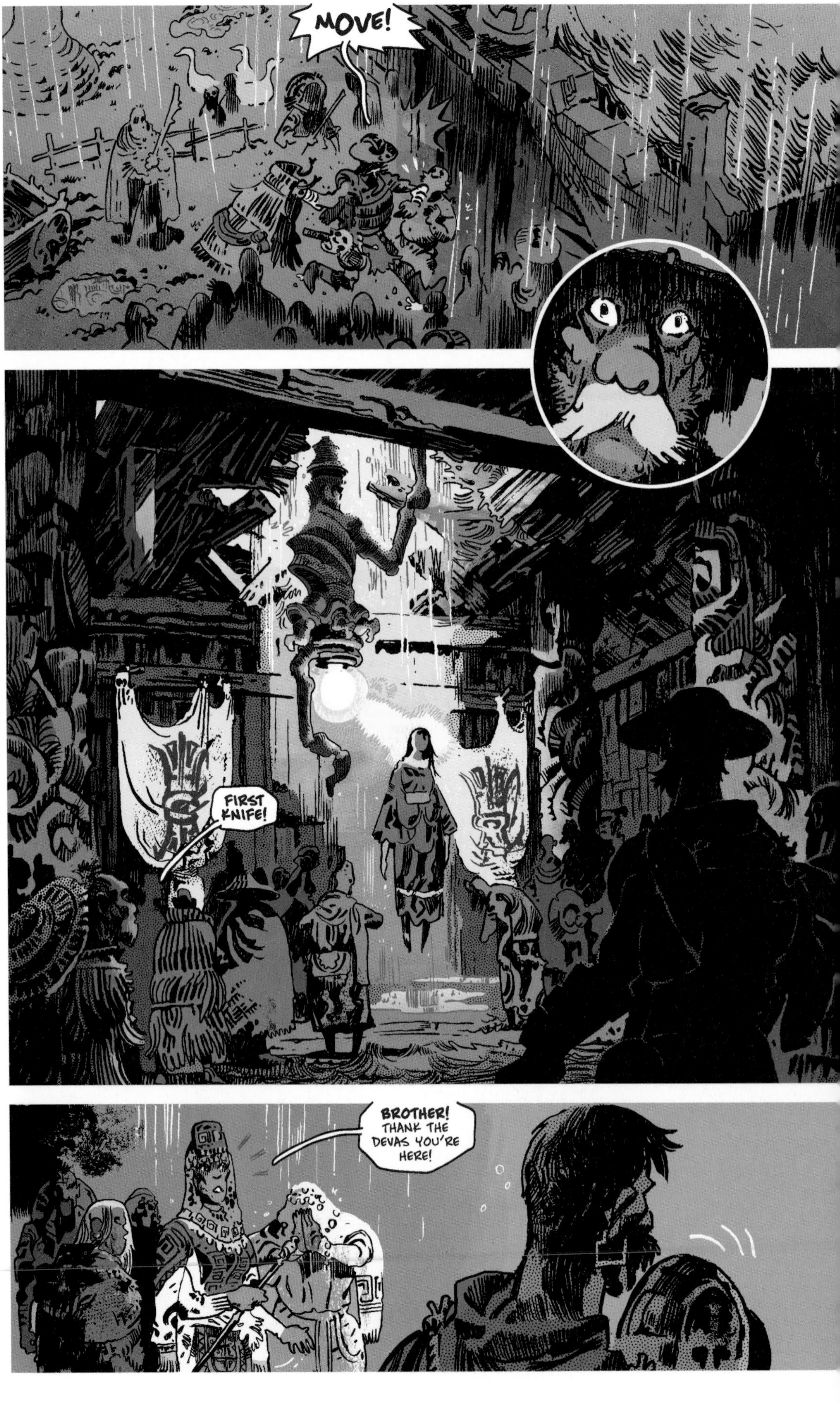
MOVE!
FIRST KNIFE!
BROTHER! THANK THE DEVAS YOU'RE HERE!

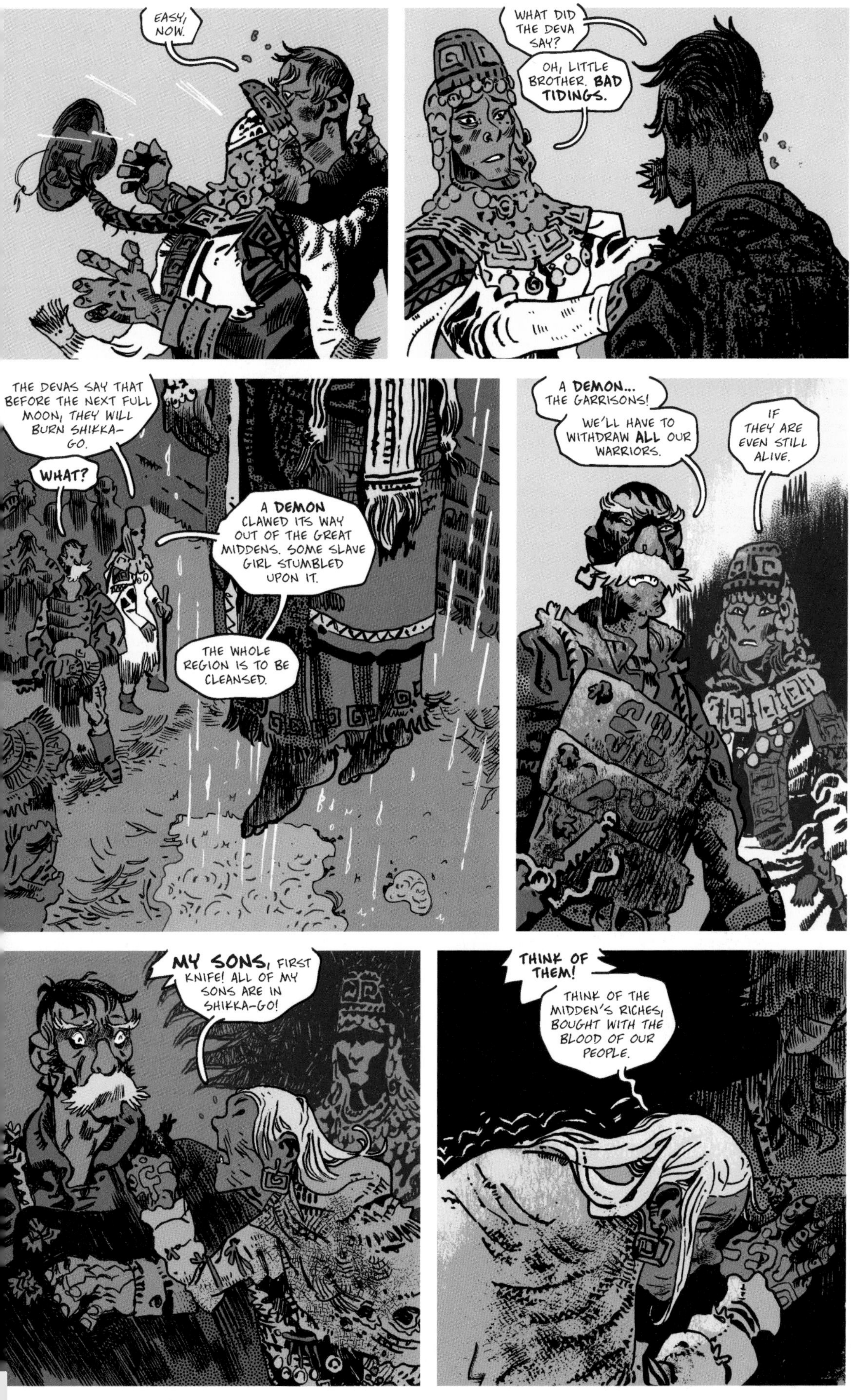

EASY, NOW.
WHAT DID THE DEVA SAY?
OH, LITTLE BROTHER. **BAD TIDINGS.**
THE DEVAS SAY THAT BEFORE THE NEXT FULL MOON, THEY WILL BURN SHIKKA-GO.
WHAT?
A **DEMON** CLAWED ITS WAY OUT OF THE GREAT MIDDENS. SOME SLAVE GIRL STUMBLED UPON IT.
THE WHOLE REGION IS TO BE CLEANSED.
A **DEMON**... THE GARRISONS!
WE'LL HAVE TO WITHDRAW **ALL** OUR WARRIORS.
IF THEY ARE EVEN STILL ALIVE.
MY SONS, FIRST KNIFE! ALL OF MY SONS ARE IN SHIKKA-GO!
THINK OF THEM!
THINK OF THE MIDDEN'S RICHES, BOUGHT WITH THE BLOOD OF OUR PEOPLE.

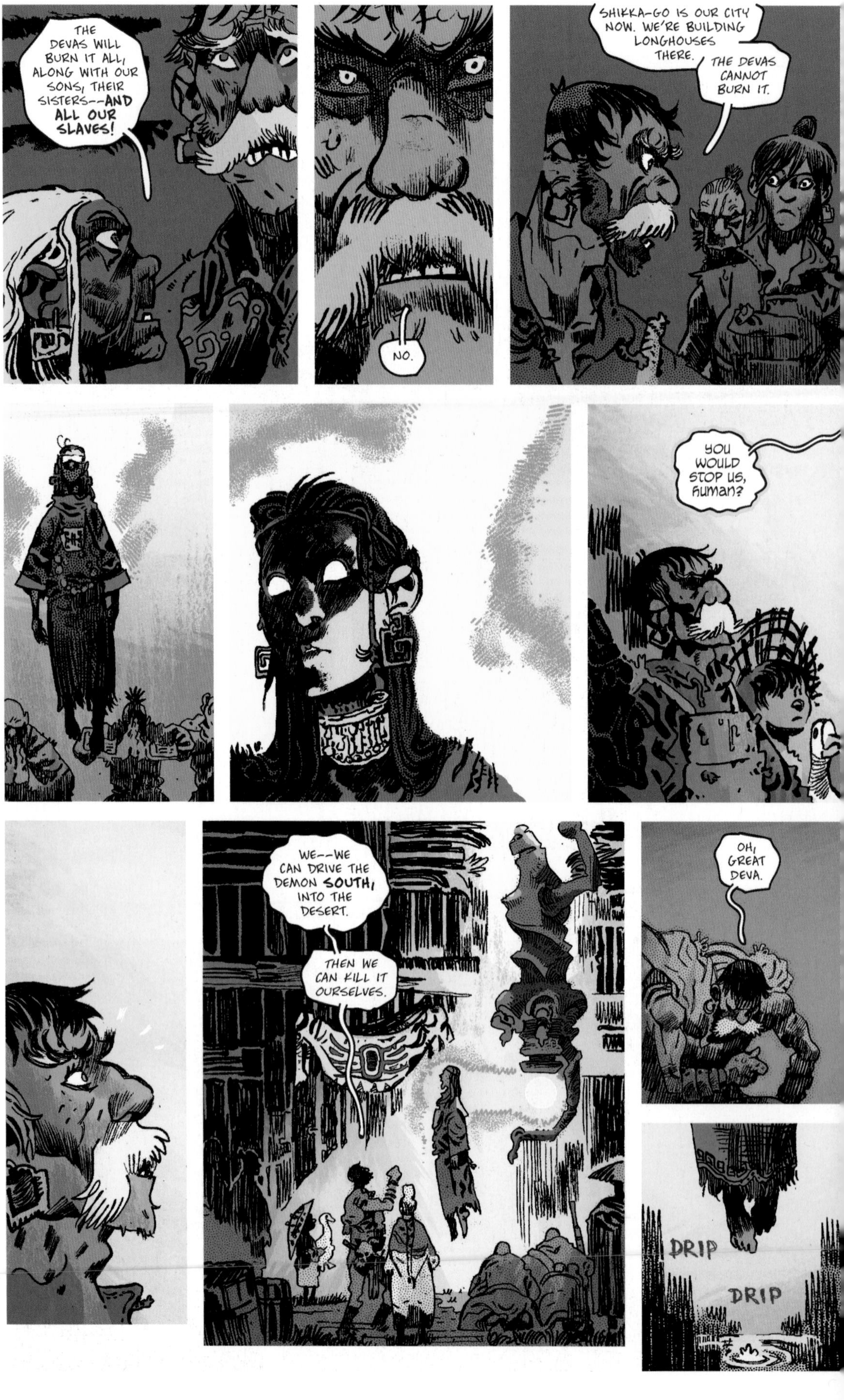
THE DEVAS WILL BURN IT ALL, ALONG WITH OUR SONS, THEIR SISTERS--AND ALL OUR SLAVES!
NO.
SHIKKA-GO IS OUR CITY NOW. WE'RE BUILDING LONGHOUSES THERE.
THE DEVAS CANNOT BURN IT.
YOU WOULD STOP US, HUMAN?
WE--WE CAN DRIVE THE DEMON SOUTH, INTO THE DESERT.
THEN WE CAN KILL IT OURSELVES.
OH, GREAT DEVA.
DRIP
DRIP

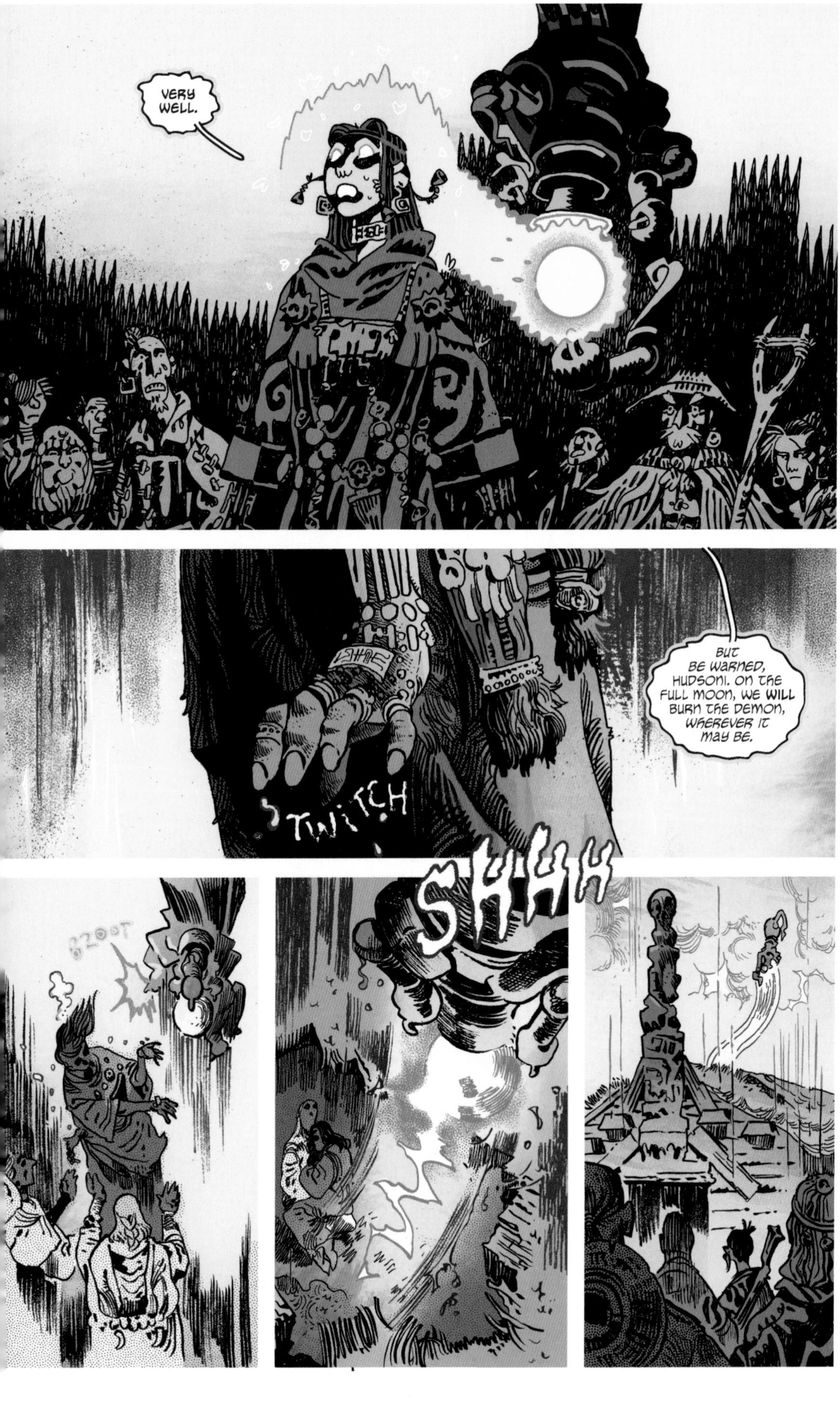
VERY WELL.
BUT BE WARNED, HUDSONI. ON THE FULL MOON, WE WILL BURN THE DEMON, WHEREVER IT MAY BE.
TWITCH
BZOOT
SHHH

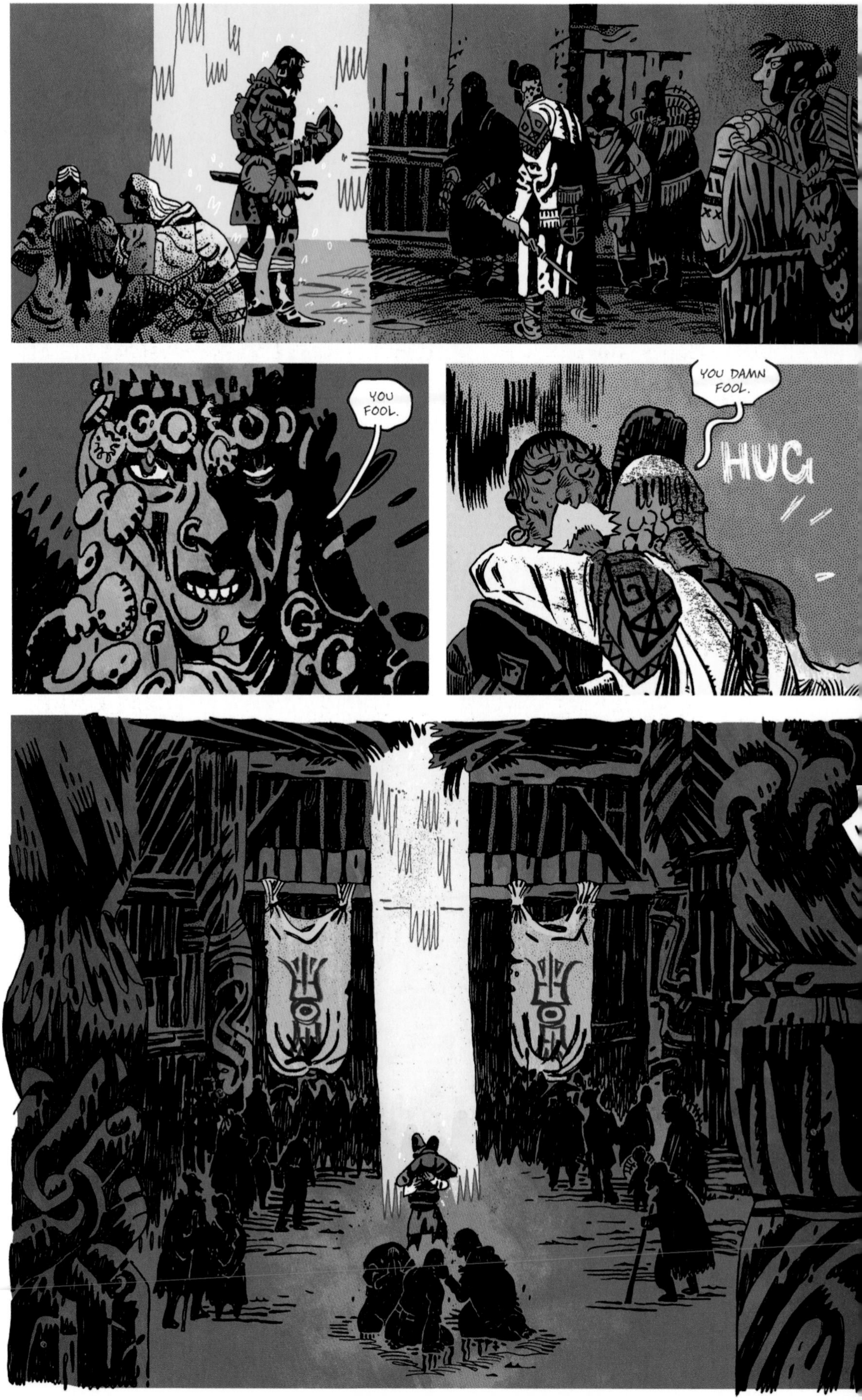
YOU FOOL.
YOU DAMN FOOL.
HUG

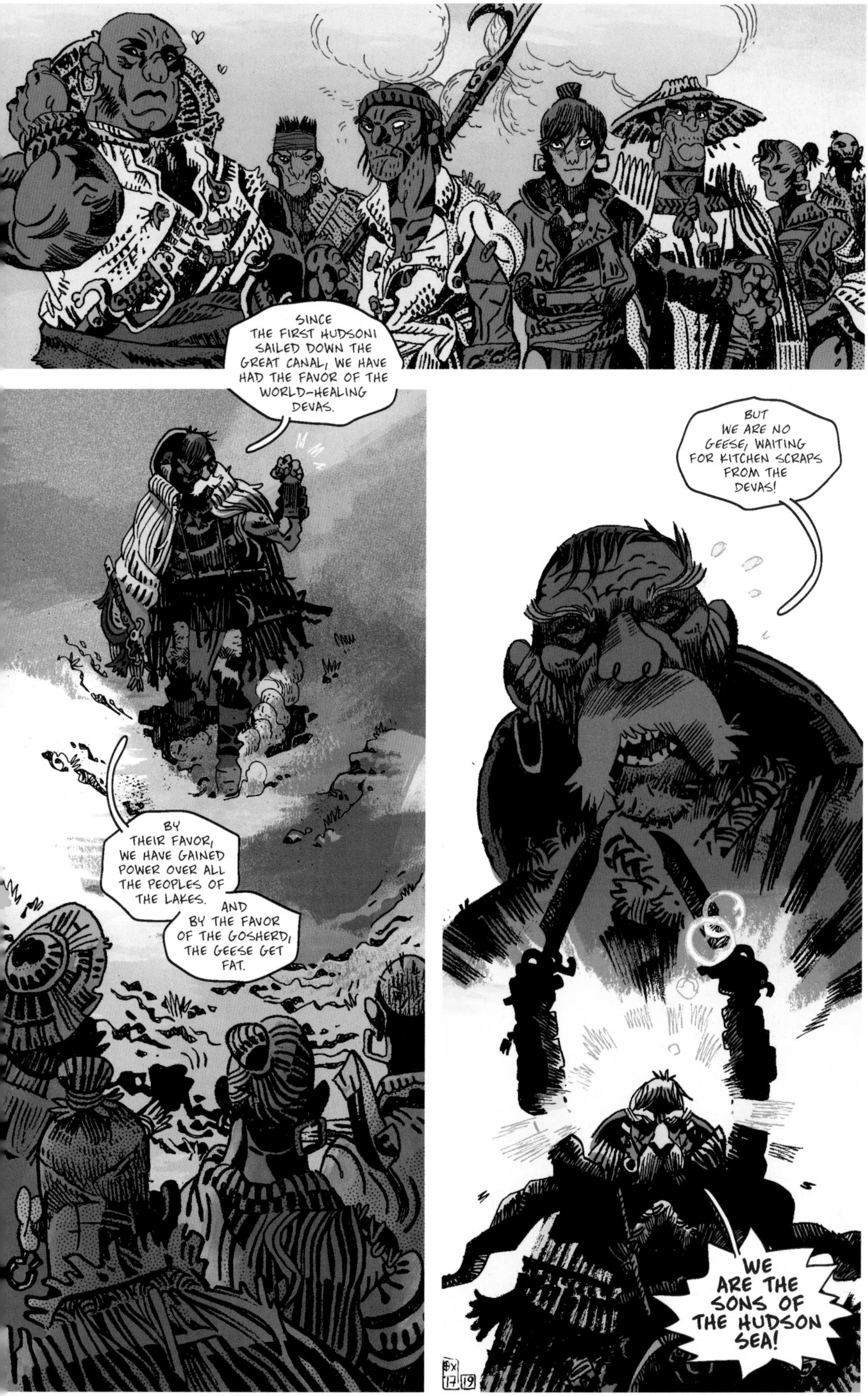
SINCE THE FIRST HUDSONI SAILED DOWN THE GREAT CANAL, WE HAVE HAD THE FAVOR OF THE WORLD-HEALING DEVAS.
BY THEIR FAVOR, WE HAVE GAINED POWER OVER ALL THE PEOPLES OF THE LAKES.
AND BY THE FAVOR OF THE GOSHERD, THE GEESE GET FAT.
BUT WE ARE NO GEESE, WAITING FOR KITCHEN SCRAPS FROM THE DEVAS!
WE ARE THE SONS OF THE HUDSON SEA!

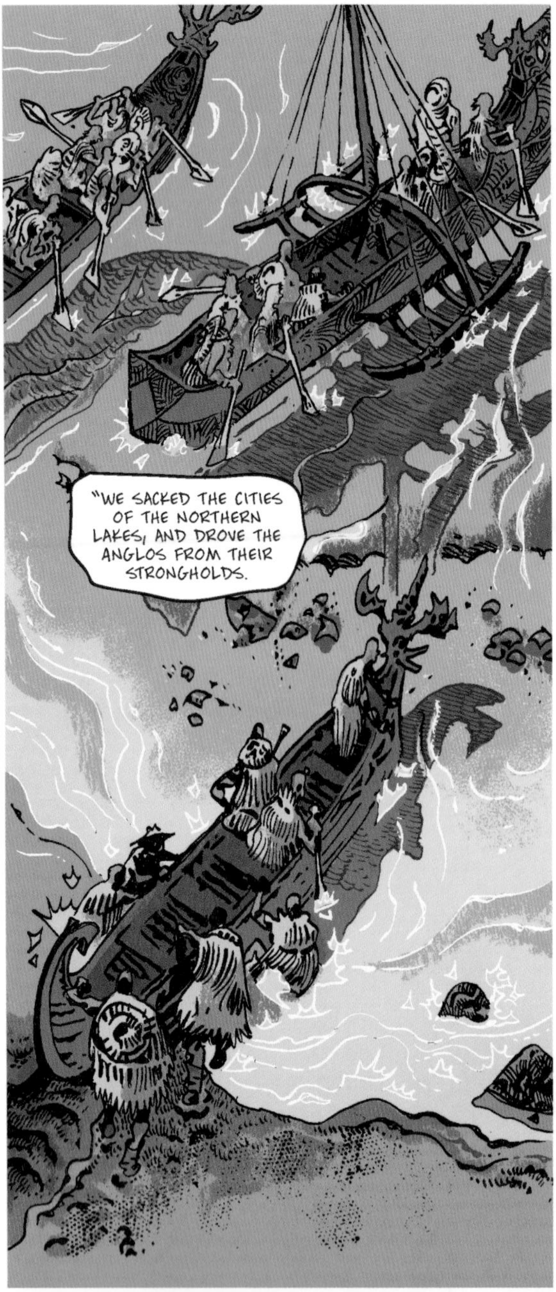
"WE SACKED THE CITIES OF THE NORTHERN LAKES, AND DROVE THE ANGLOS FROM THEIR STRONGHOLDS.

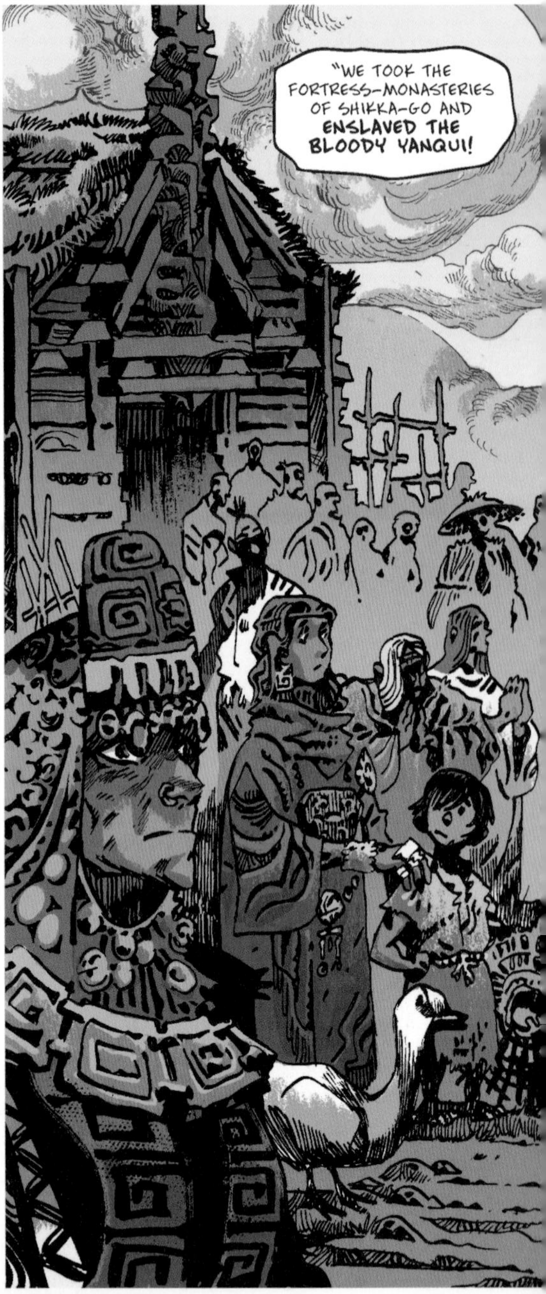
"WE TOOK THE FORTRESS-MONASTERIES OF SHIKKA-GO AND **ENSLAVED THE BLOODY YANQUI!**

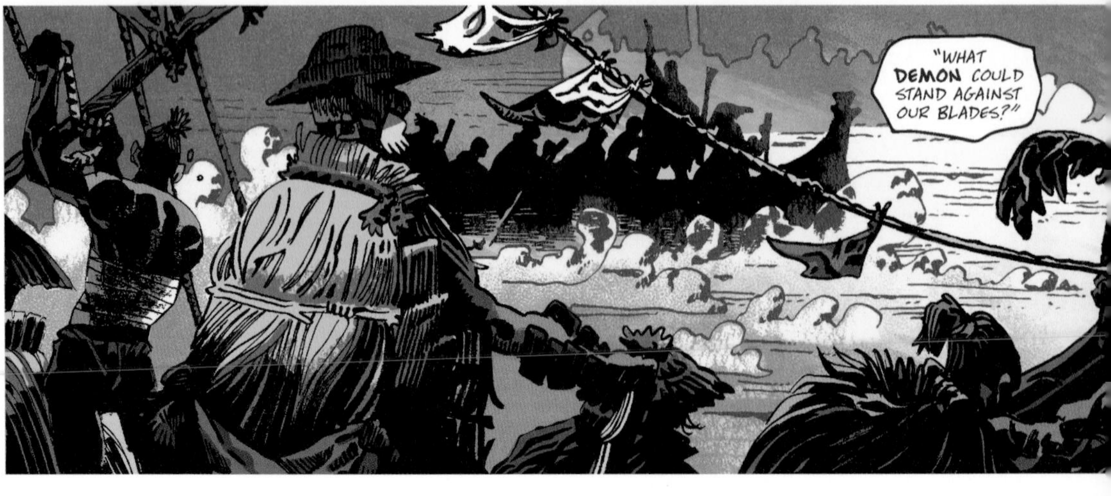
"WHAT **DEMON** COULD STAND AGAINST OUR BLADES?"

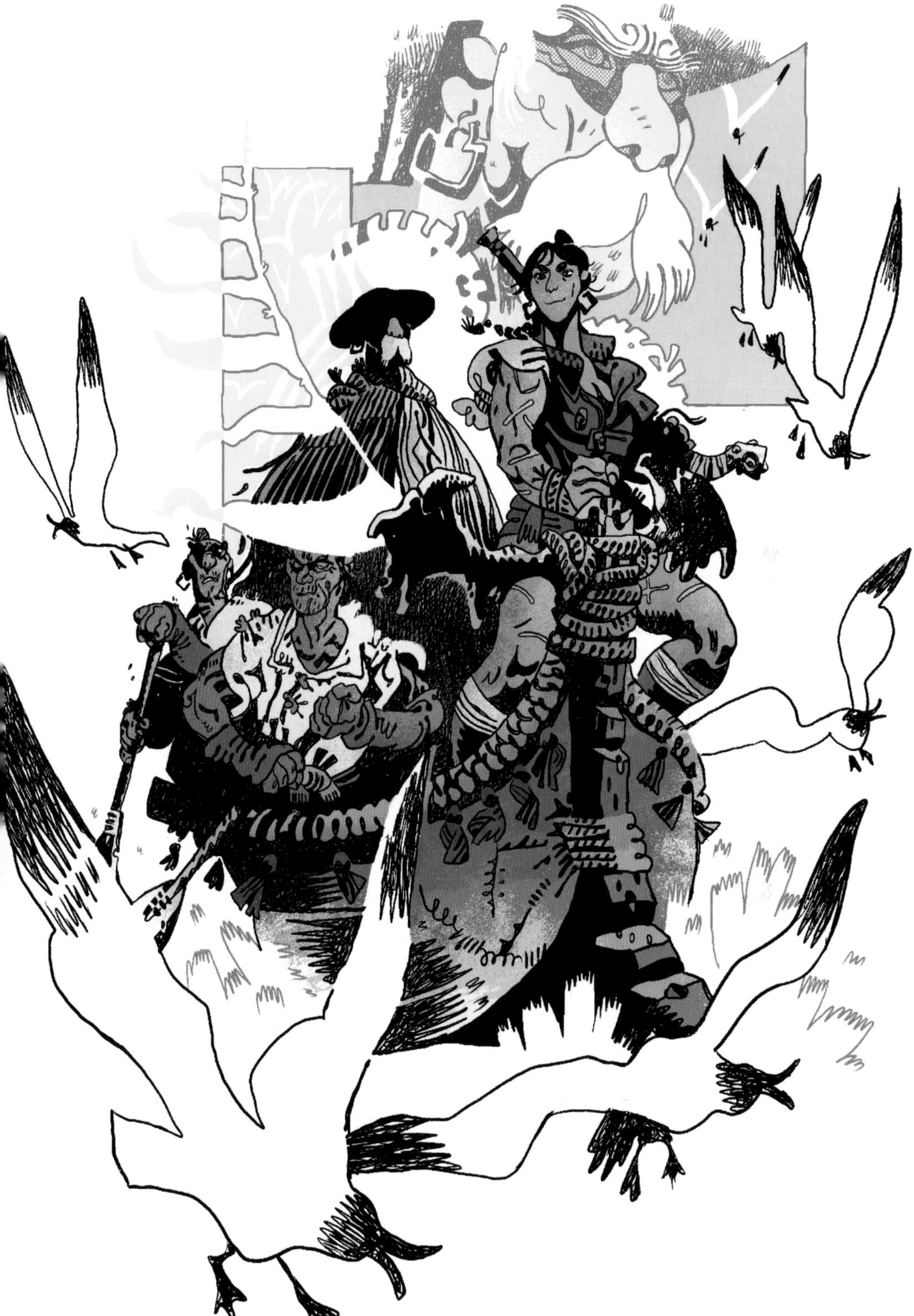

TRIBES OF THE CANADIAN SHIELD

The diverse ancestors of the Hudsoni began to migrate out of East Asia and Siberia during the height of the Anthropocene Thermal Maximum, settling among the islands of the Canadian Arctic Archipelago. Centered around Ellesmere island, these bedraggled climate refugees coalesced into one of the more influential ethno-cultural groups of Arctic and Subarctic North America. The Ellesmiri became accomplished fishermen, traders, and raiders, spreading wealth and warfare throughout the Archipelago. But, at the end of the third millennium, a war of succession forced a large cadre of Ellesmiri noble clans to flee south, into the Hudson Sea. It was these clans that would settle along the shores of the Hudson and become the Hudsoni.

Much like their Ellesmiri predecessors, life among the Hudsoni revolves around the sea. An estimated 90% of the Hudsoni diet comes from marine sources, with algae, jellyfish, and cephalopods serving as staple foods.

THE HUDSONI

They pride themselves on their sailing skills, and are much feared throughout the Canadian Shield as raiders, warriors, and slavers.

Hudsoni social structure is marked by a practice of divided leadership, where a hereditary village chieftain will lead the farmers, fishers, and herdsfolk, with a separate war chief to lead the village's warriors on long-distance raids. Unlike their Ellesmiri relatives, the Hudsoni are more egalitarian between the genders, with both men and women known to hold positions of power. Descent is determined matrilineally, which means that often a father will play a lesser role in his offspring's life then their maternal uncle will.

Since the late 3100s, the Hudsoni have followed the Deva-built canals from the James Bay megadam south into the Great Lakes, where they have established numerous colonies.

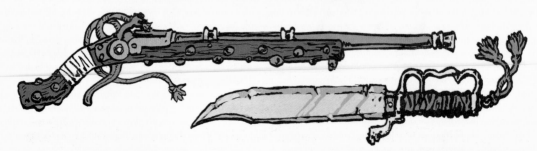

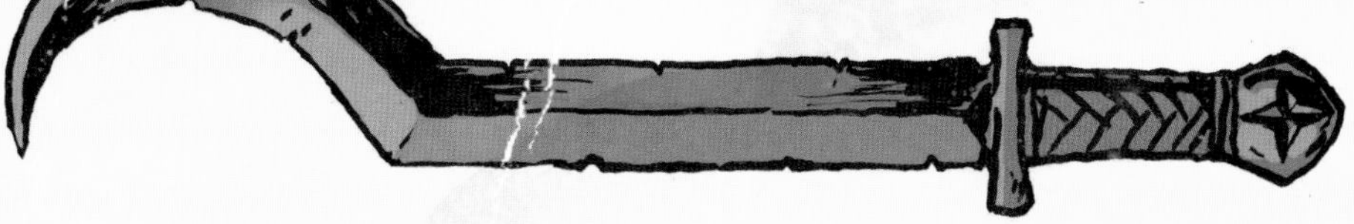

THE YANQUI

Until the Hudsoni invasion of the late 3100s, the Great Lakes region was ruled by the Yanqui Monastic Coalition. This loose polity claimed continuity with the ancient American post-Catholic Foundation, although in reality its cultural background owes at least as much to Anglo traders and Prairier nomads as it does to Hesukristian monks. The language of the Yanqui reflects this mixed history; its wealth of Hispanic-derived vocabulary and grammar sets Yanqui apart from the Anglic Dialect Continuum of northern North America.

Coming to power after the Prairier Invasions, the Yanqui ended the inter-ethnic warfare and tribal warlordism that had long defined the region. The key to their success was the post-Catholic Hesukristian religion, and its literate bureaucracy. The Yanqui priesthood was open to all, and offered an ordered worldview, where revealed truth granted salvation to believers, in contrast to the demon-haunted world that sought to destroy them. Fortress-monasteries were built along lakes and water-courses, directing everything from marriage to irrigation to warfare.

Originally, each fortress-monastery was responsible for the recruitment, training, and maintenance of its own professional army. Increasingly, however, this practice was phased out in favor of hereditary soldier clans based in the capital city of Shikka-Go. These musketeers and cannoneers would command peasants levied at need from other communities. This practice sufficed for the highly formalized "intermural warfare" within the Coalition, but failed to withstand the Hudsoni invasion. The Yanqui's animosity toward the Devas would also prove disastrous.

Despite the Hudsoni invasion, Shikka-Go remains a center of culture. It is home to Great Middens, the Pyramid of the Bride of Hesukristos, the Sanguine Field, and many other important pilgrimage sites. The Shikka-Go dialect of the Yanqui language remains the lingua franca of central North America, and even the Hudsoni speak it among themselves.

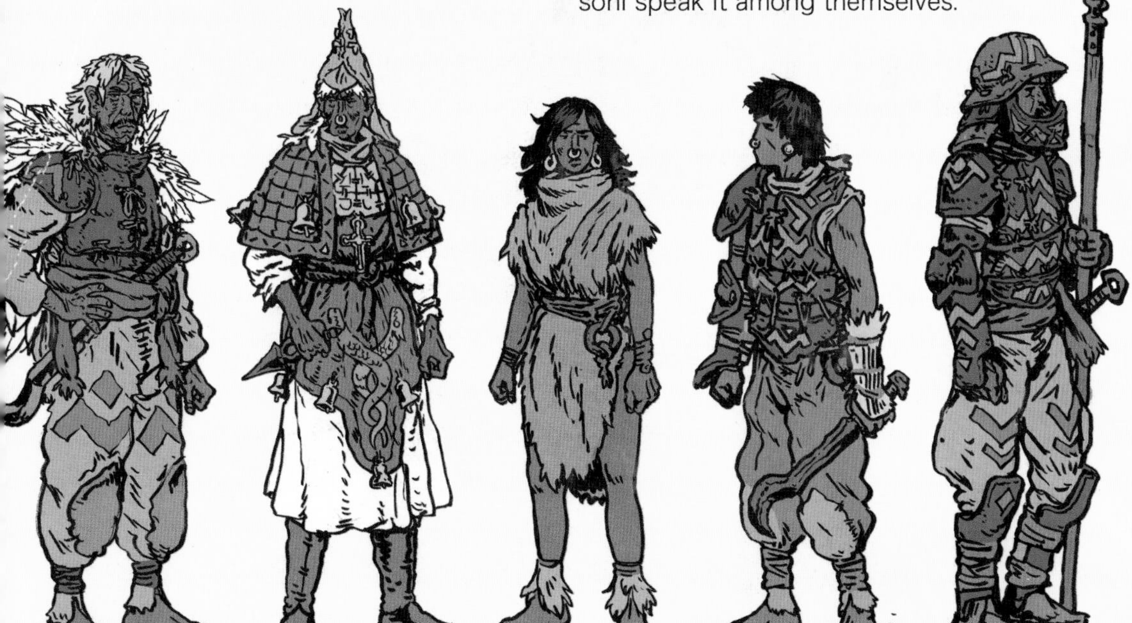

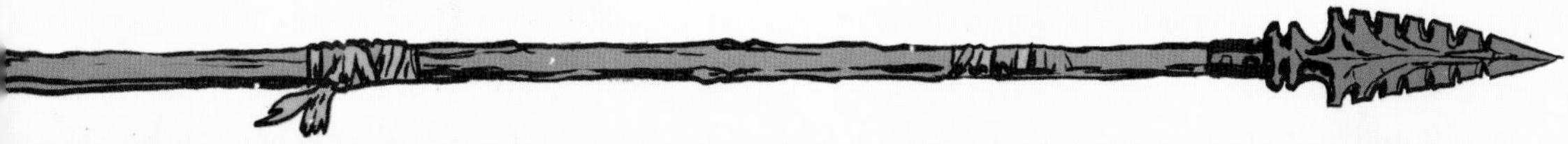

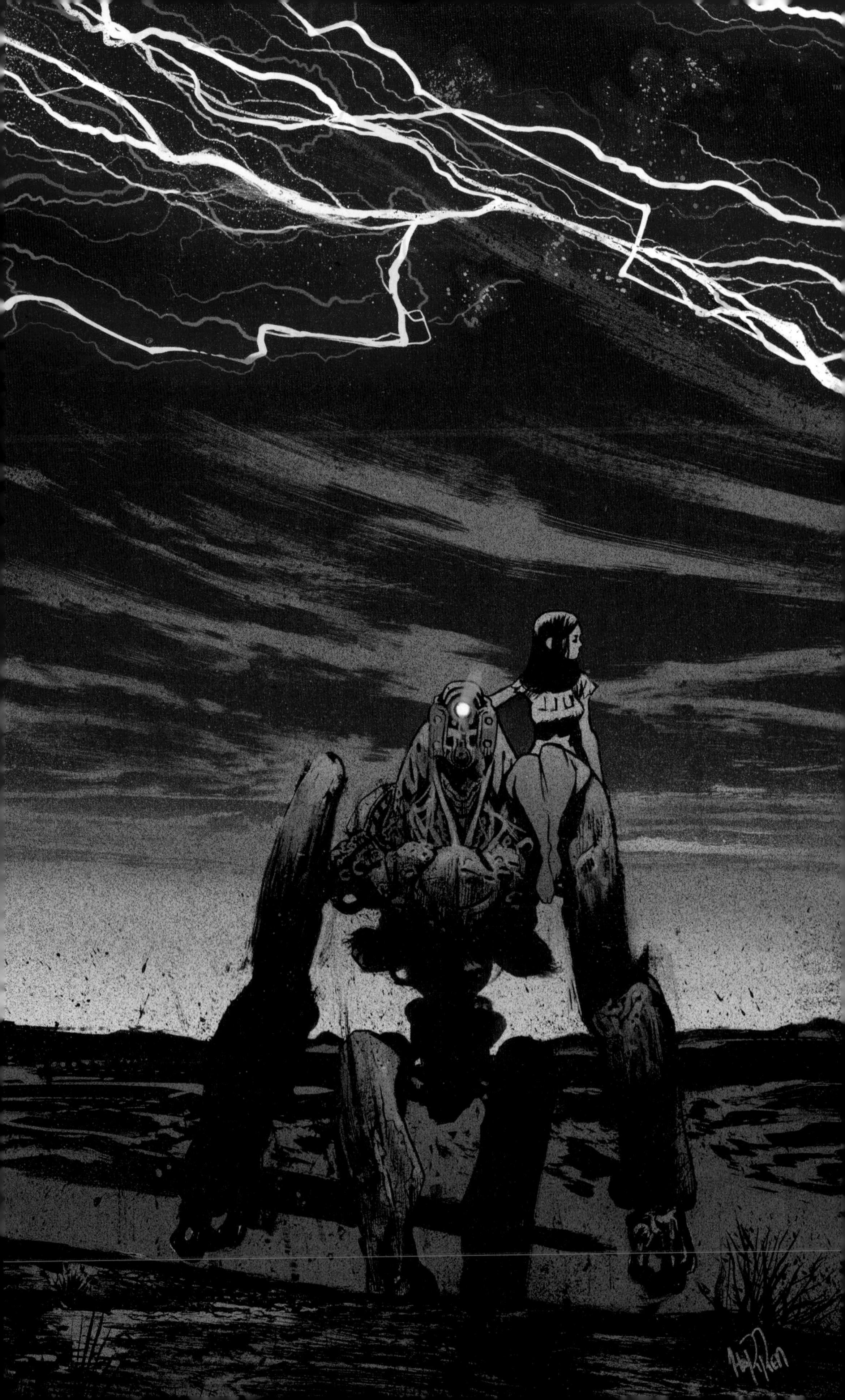

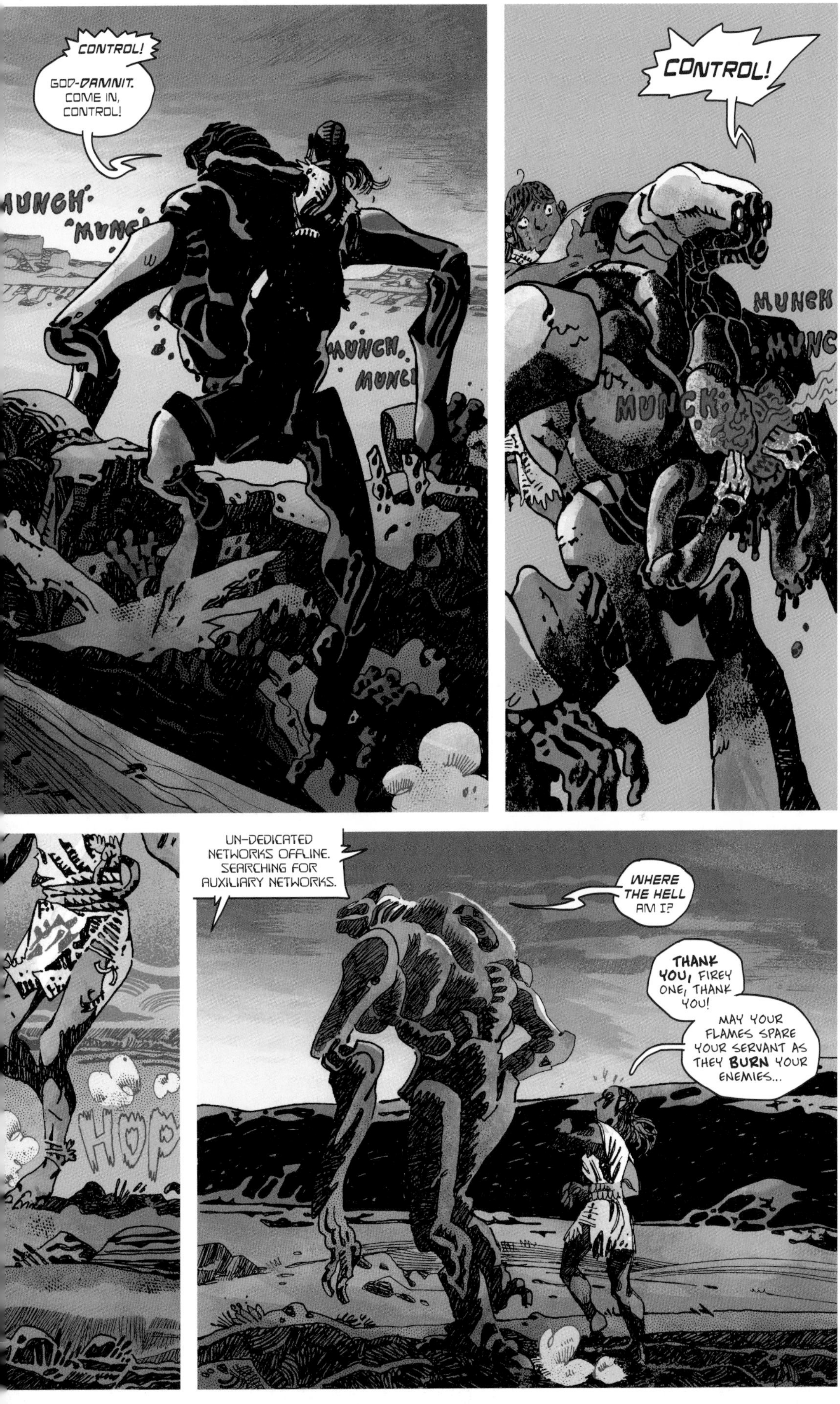
CONTROL!
GOD-DAMNIT. COME IN, CONTROL!
MUNCH
MUNCH
MUNCH
CONTROL!
MUNCH
MUNCH
UN-DEDICATED NETWORKS OFFLINE. SEARCHING FOR AUXILIARY NETWORKS.
WHERE THE HELL AM I?
THANK YOU, FIREY ONE, THANK YOU!
MAY YOUR FLAMES SPARE YOUR SERVANT AS THEY BURN YOUR ENEMIES...

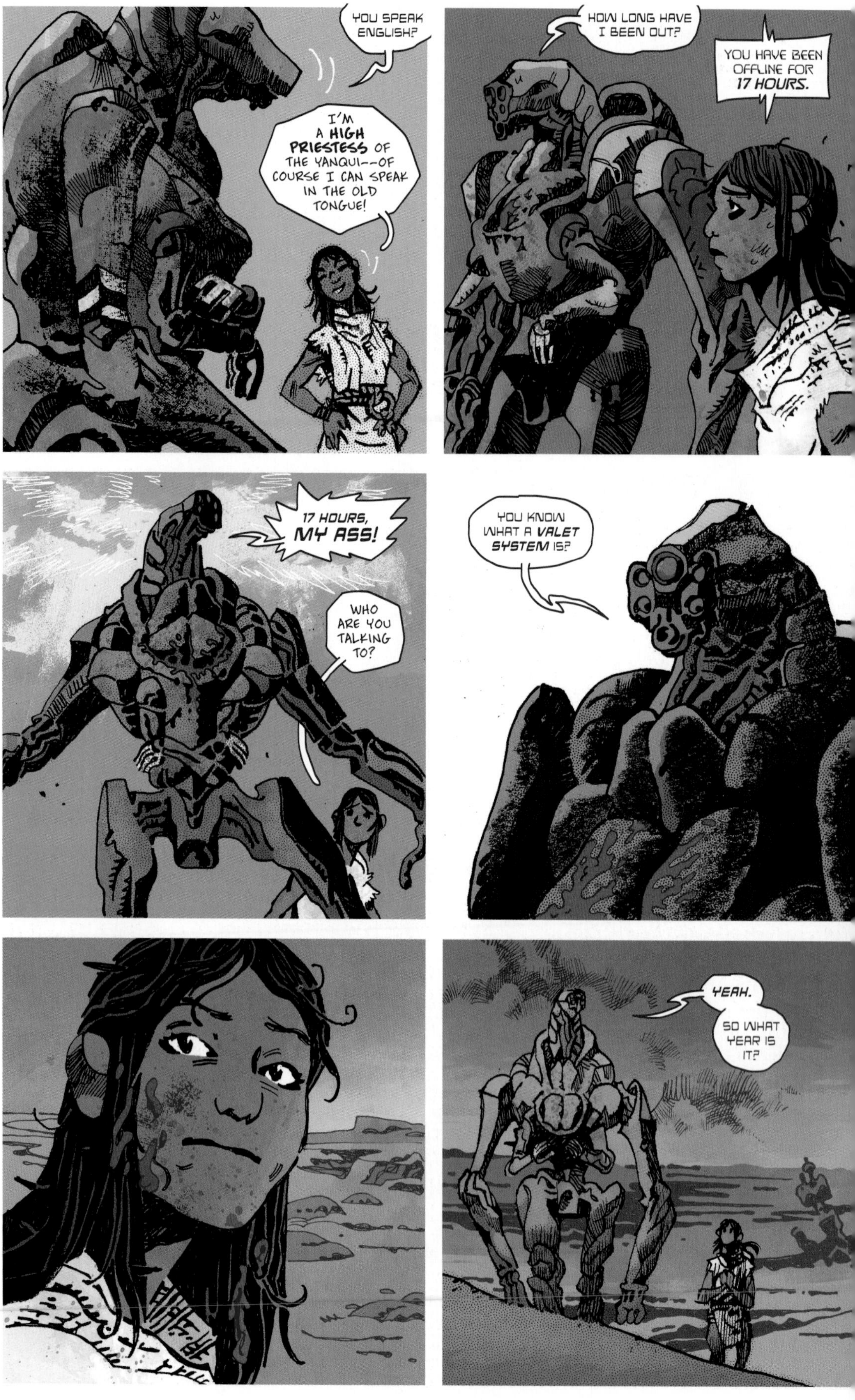
YOU SPEAK ENGLISH?
I'M A **HIGH PRIESTESS** OF THE YANQUI--OF COURSE I CAN SPEAK IN THE OLD TONGUE!
HOW LONG HAVE I BEEN OUT?
YOU HAVE BEEN OFFLINE FOR **17 HOURS.**
17 HOURS, **MY ASS!**
WHO ARE YOU TALKING TO?
YOU KNOW WHAT A ***VALET SYSTEM*** IS?
YEAH.
SO WHAT YEAR IS IT?

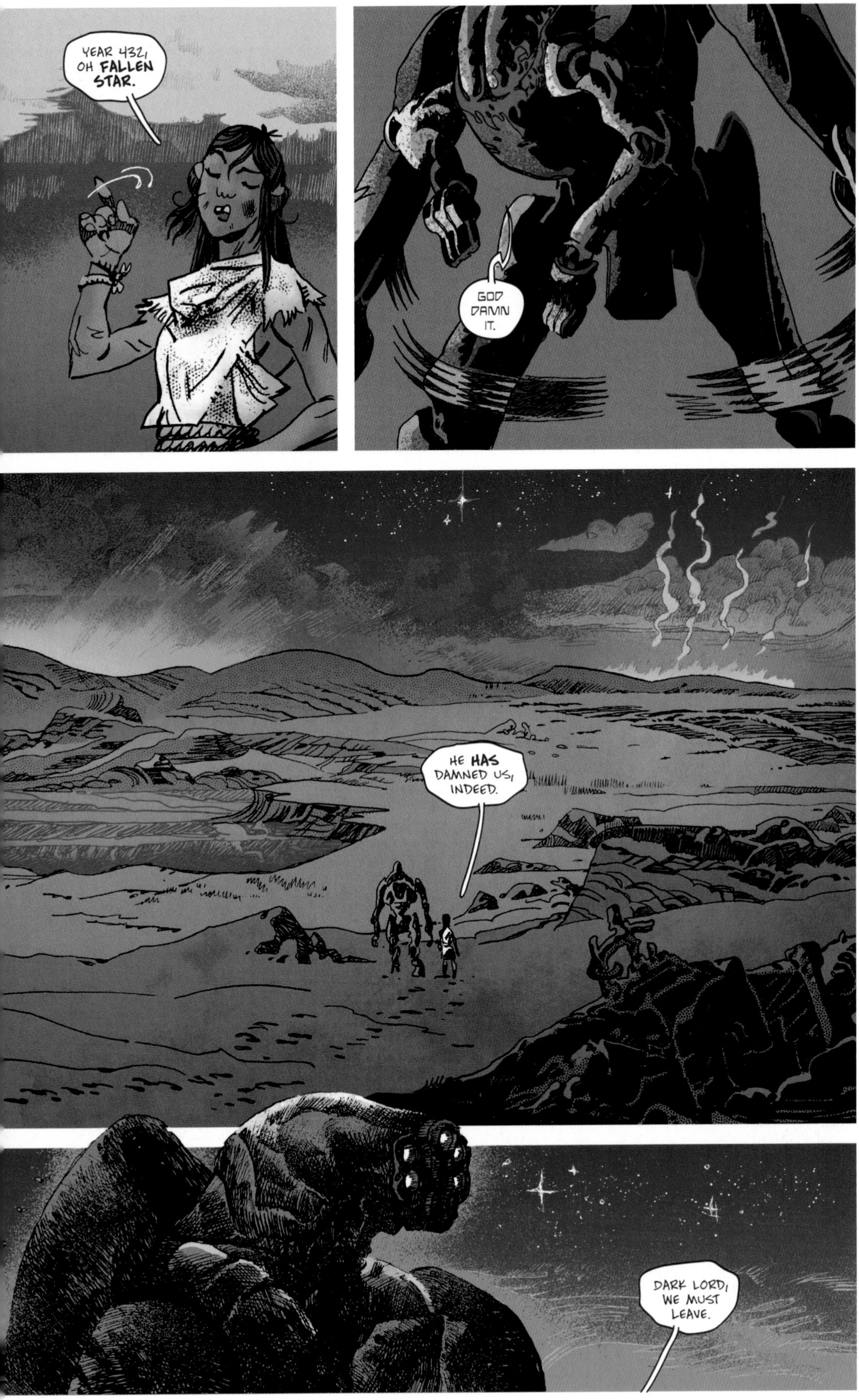
YEAR 432, OH **FALLEN STAR.**
GOD DAMN IT.
HE **HAS** DAMNED US, INDEED.
DARK LORD, WE MUST LEAVE.

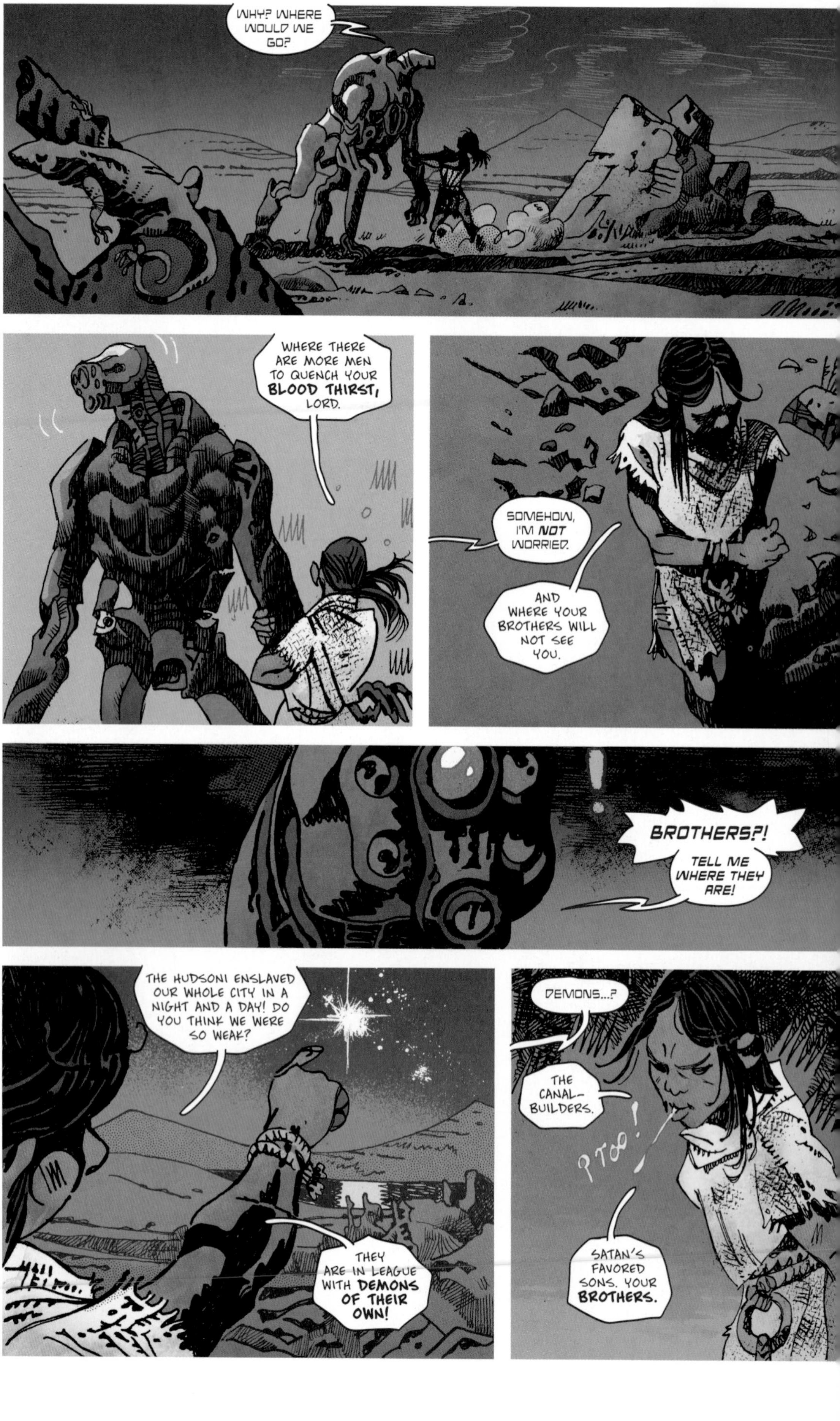
WHY? WHERE WOULD WE GO?
WHERE THERE ARE MORE MEN TO QUENCH YOUR BLOOD THIRST, LORD.
SOMEHOW, I'M NOT WORRIED.
AND WHERE YOUR BROTHERS WILL NOT SEE YOU.
BROTHERS?!
TELL ME WHERE THEY ARE!
THE HUDSONI ENSLAVED OUR WHOLE CITY IN A NIGHT AND A DAY! DO YOU THINK WE WERE SO WEAK?
THEY ARE IN LEAGUE WITH DEMONS OF THEIR OWN!
DEMONS...?
THE CANAL-BUILDERS.
PTOO!
SATAN'S FAVORED SONS. YOUR BROTHERS.

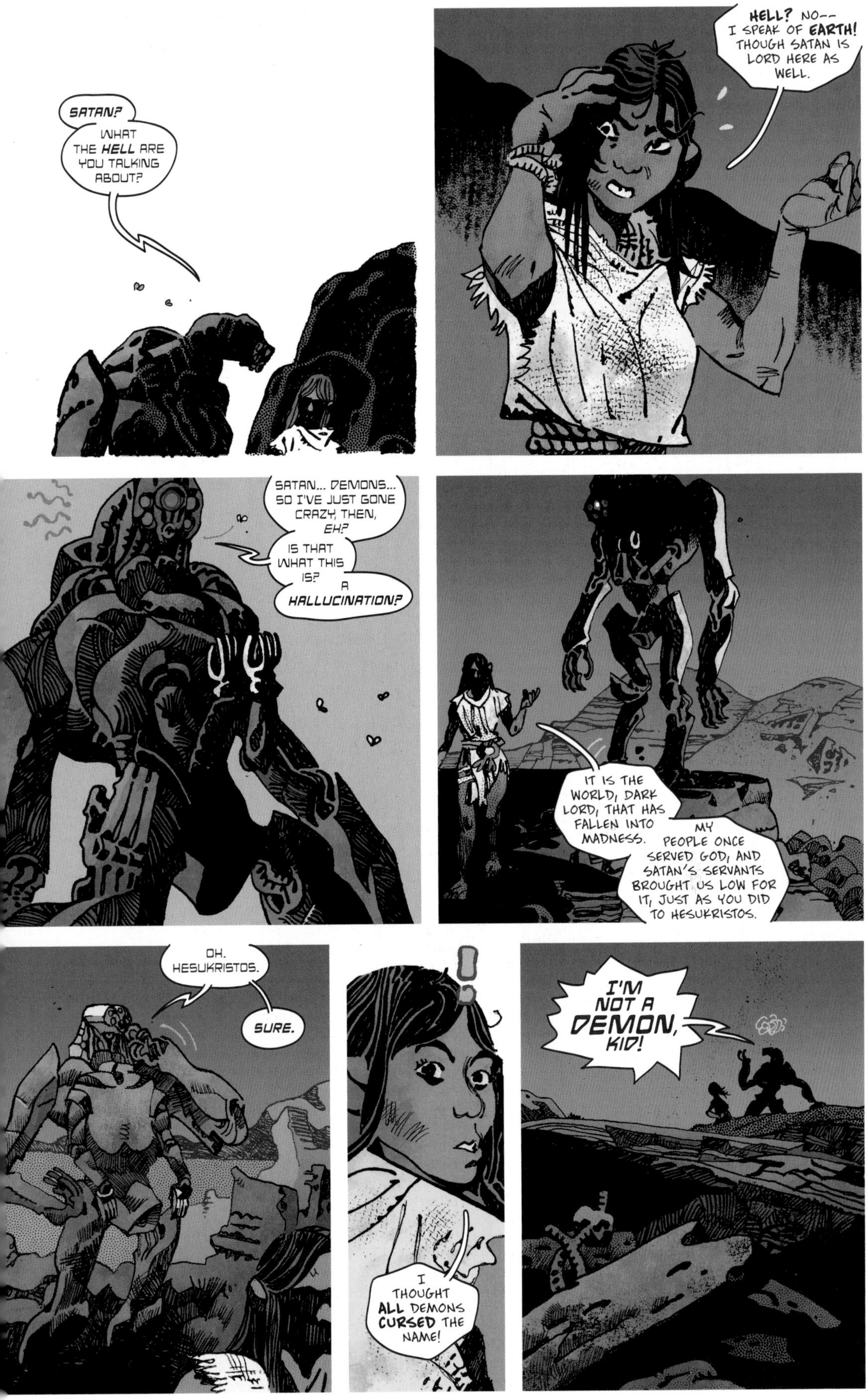
SATAN? WHAT THE HELL ARE YOU TALKING ABOUT?
HELL? NO-- I SPEAK OF EARTH! THOUGH SATAN IS LORD HERE AS WELL.
SATAN... DEMONS... SO I'VE JUST GONE CRAZY, THEN, EH?
IS THAT WHAT THIS IS?
A HALLUCINATION?
IT IS THE WORLD, DARK LORD, THAT HAS FALLEN INTO MADNESS.
MY PEOPLE ONCE SERVED GOD, AND SATAN'S SERVANTS BROUGHT US LOW FOR IT, JUST AS YOU DID TO HESUKRISTOS.
OH. HESUKRISTOS.
SURE.
I THOUGHT ALL DEMONS CURSED THE NAME!
I'M NOT A DEMON, KID!

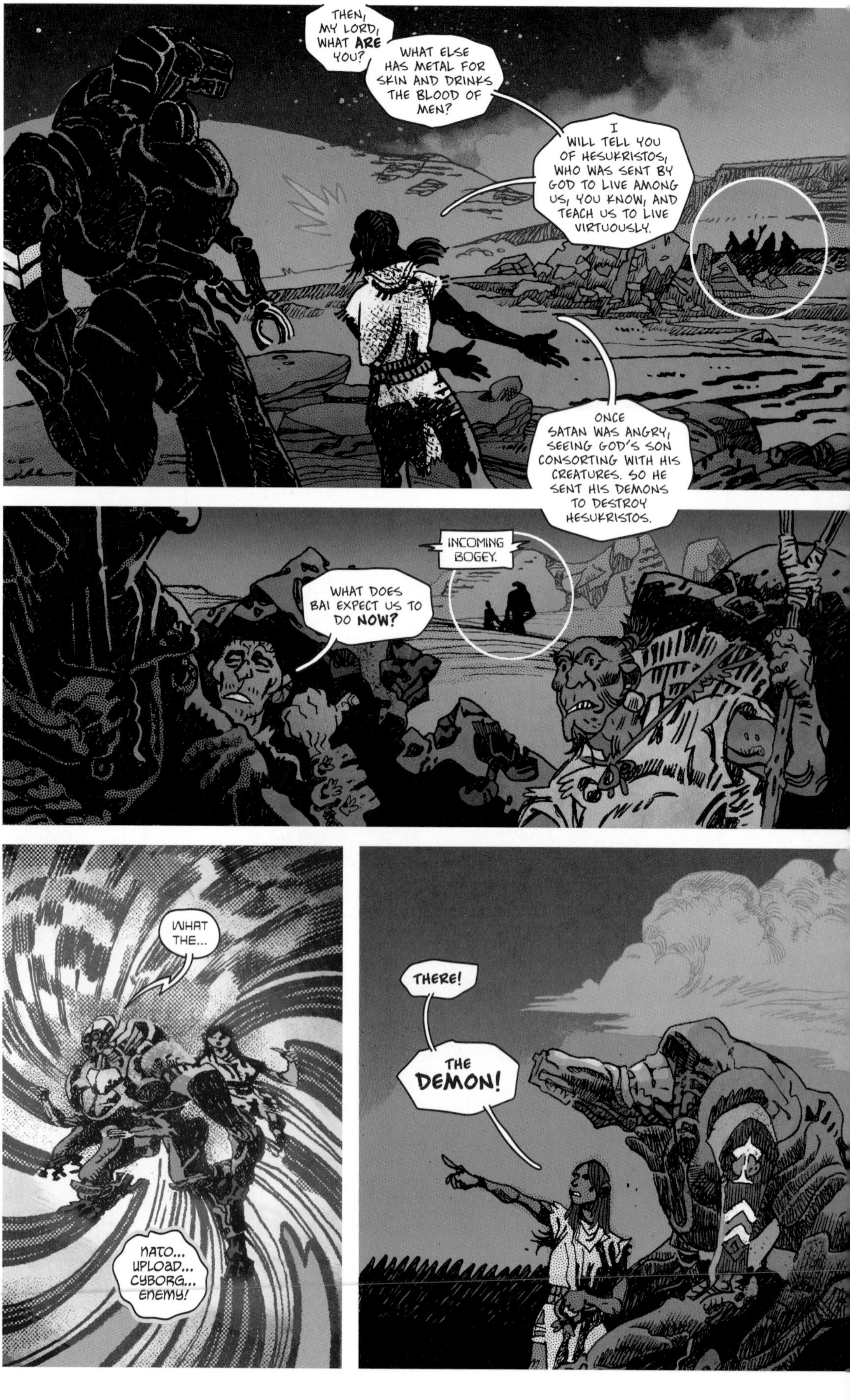
THEN, MY LORD, WHAT ARE YOU?
WHAT ELSE HAS METAL FOR SKIN AND DRINKS THE BLOOD OF MEN?
I WILL TELL YOU OF HESUKRISTOS, WHO WAS SENT BY GOD TO LIVE AMONG US, YOU KNOW, AND TEACH US TO LIVE VIRTUOUSLY.
ONCE SATAN WAS ANGRY, SEEING GOD'S SON CONSORTING WITH HIS CREATURES. SO HE SENT HIS DEMONS TO DESTROY HESUKRISTOS.
INCOMING BOGEY.
WHAT DOES BAI EXPECT US TO DO NOW?
WHAT THE...
NATO... UPLOAD... CYBORG... ENEMY!
THERE!
THE DEMON!

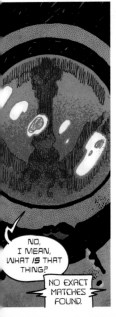

NO, I MEAN, WHAT *IS* THAT THING?

NO EXACT MATCHES FOUND.

SO GIVE ME AN *INEXACT* FUCKING MATCH.

MY LORD, LISTEN. THE DEMONS KILLED HESUKRISTOS, AND CAST HIS BLOODY PIECES ACROSS THE EARTH.

DO YOU NOT REMEMBER IT?

33% CONFIDENCE MATCH WITH GLEISNER-CLASS MARTIAN TERRAFORMER.

BUT SATAN HAD ALREADY LOST!

WEAPONS?

YES.

EVERYWHERE HESUKRISTOS' BLOOD FELL, THERE GREW THE CROPS OF THE WORLD.

PREPARE DEFENSES. TARGET MAIN LASER.

E OF MAIN SER WILL 'ESULT IN GNIFICANT WER LOSS.

HIS WIFE, MARI, BURIED HIS HEART IN A PLACE SO SECRET EVEN SATAN COULDN'T FIND IT.

SHE WATERED HIS HEART WITH HER OWN BLOOD.

SHUT UP AND *DO* IT.

AND, LIKE THE CROPS, HESUKRISTOS ROSE AGAIN, TO SET THE WORLD RIGHT.

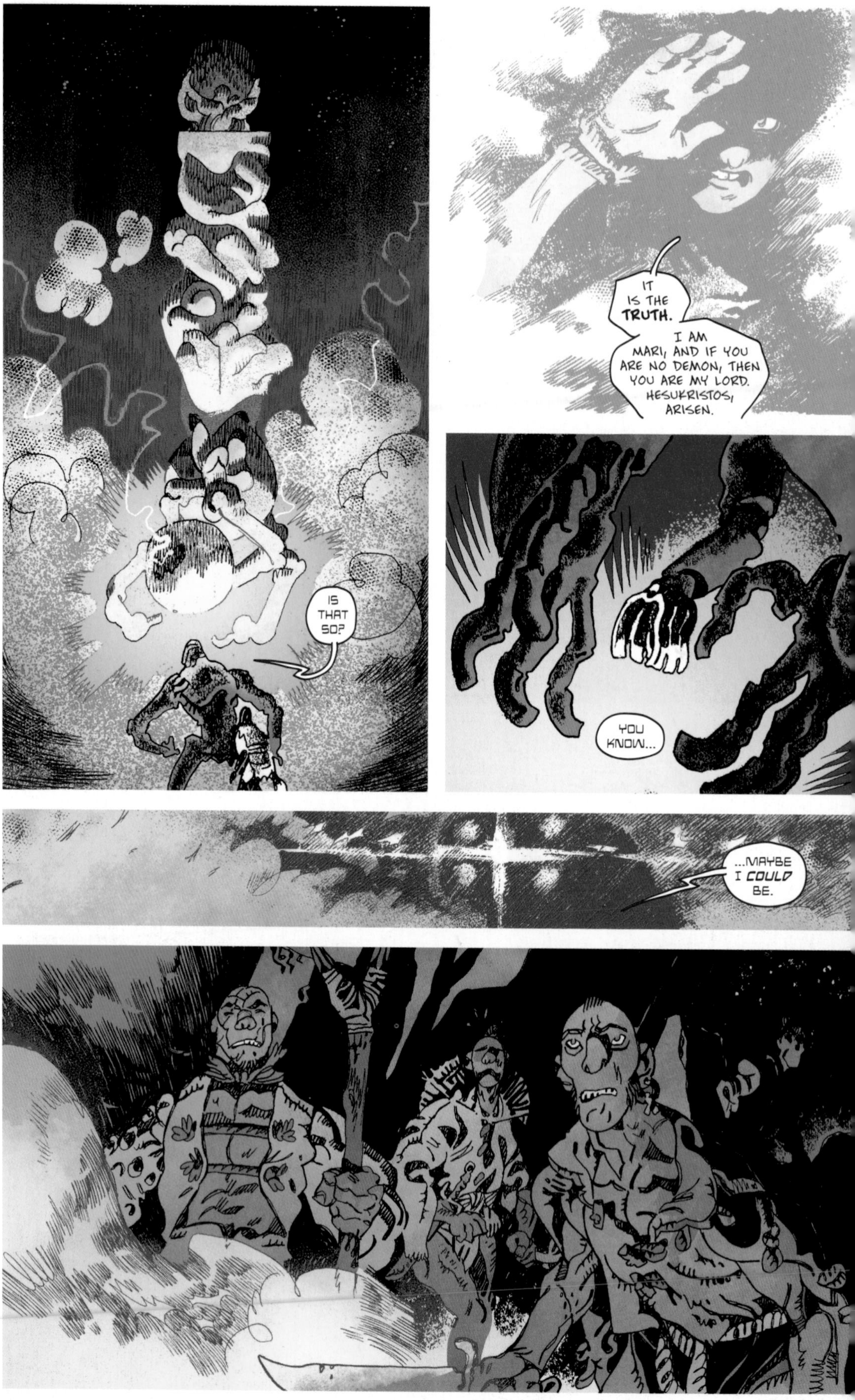
IS THAT SO?
IT IS THE TRUTH.
I AM MARI, AND IF YOU ARE NO DEMON, THEN YOU ARE MY LORD. HESUKRISTOS, ARISEN.
YOU KNOW...
...MAYBE I COULD BE.

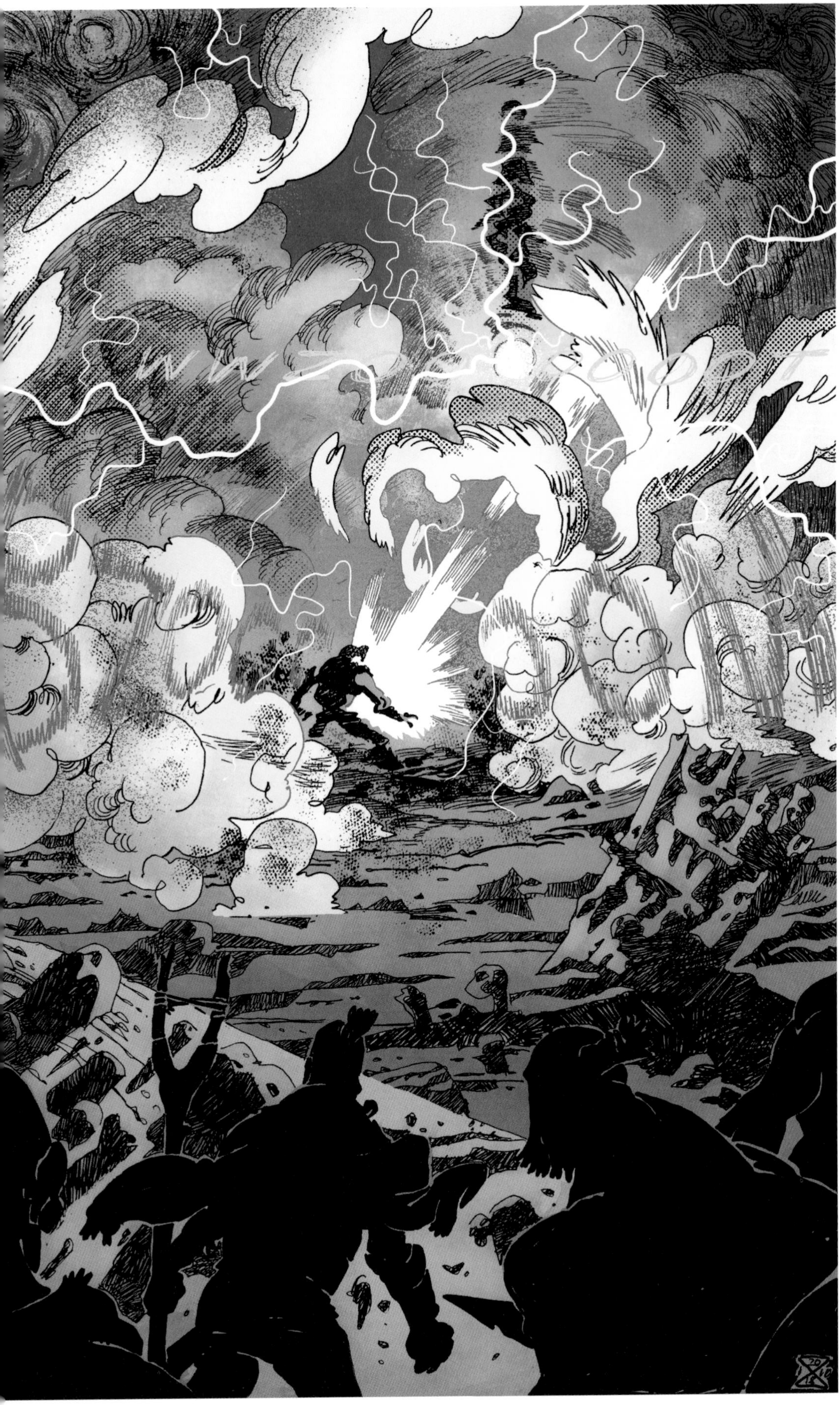

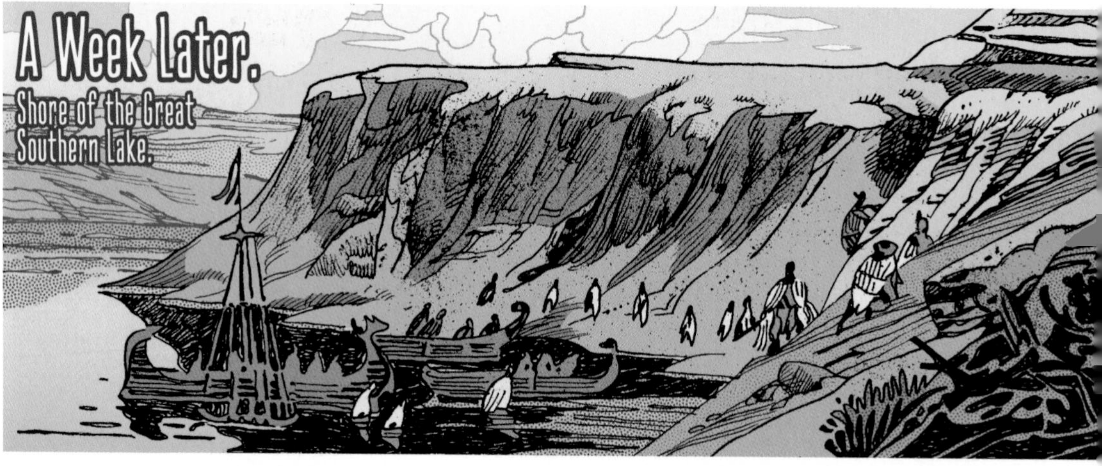
A Week Later.
Shore of the Great Southern Lake.

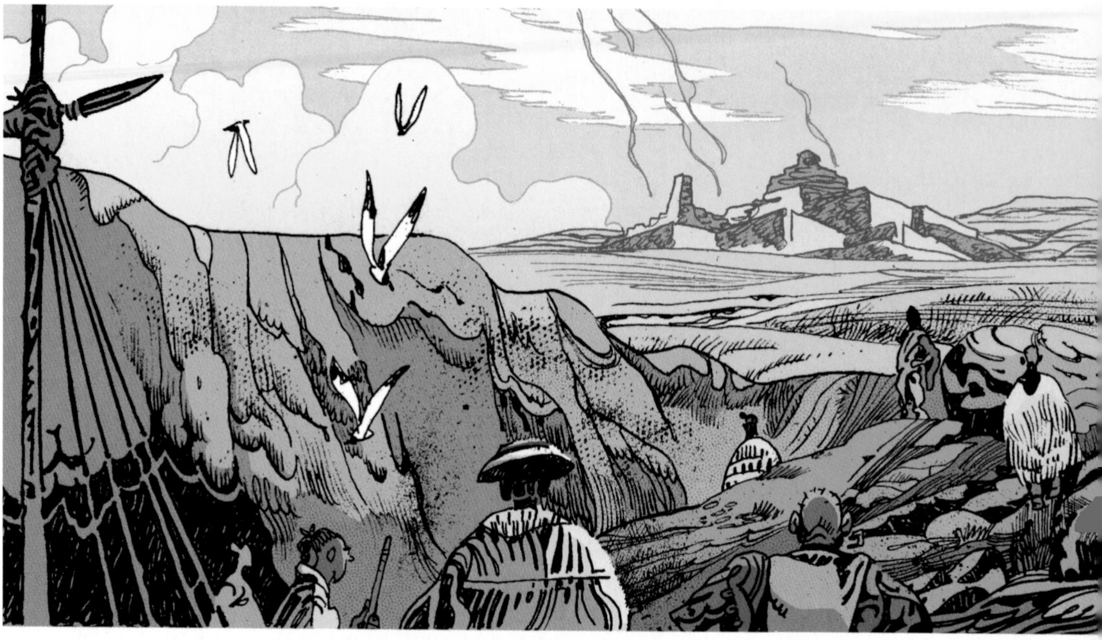

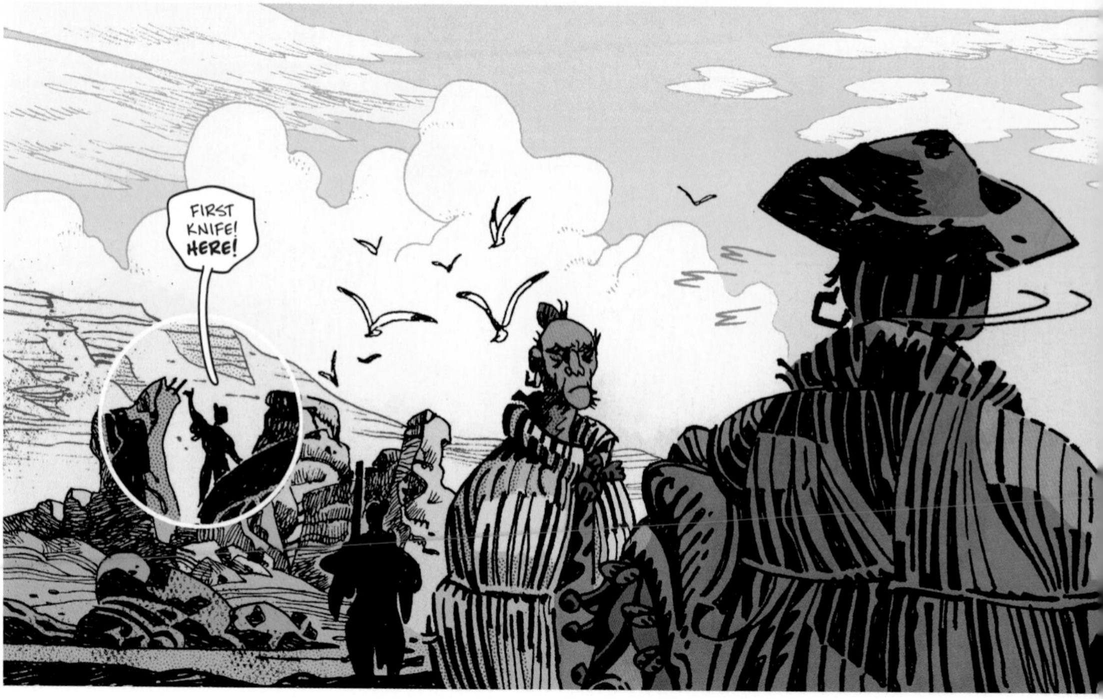
FIRST KNIFE! HERE!

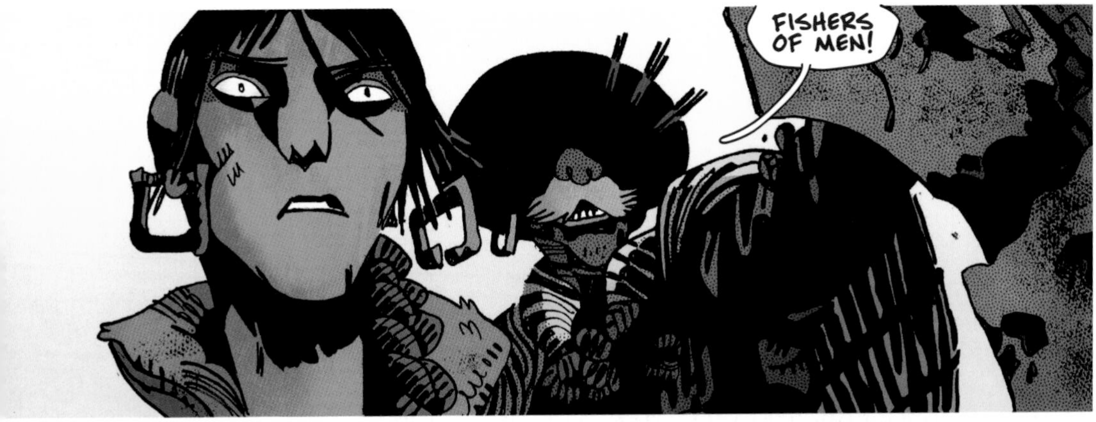
FISHERS OF MEN!

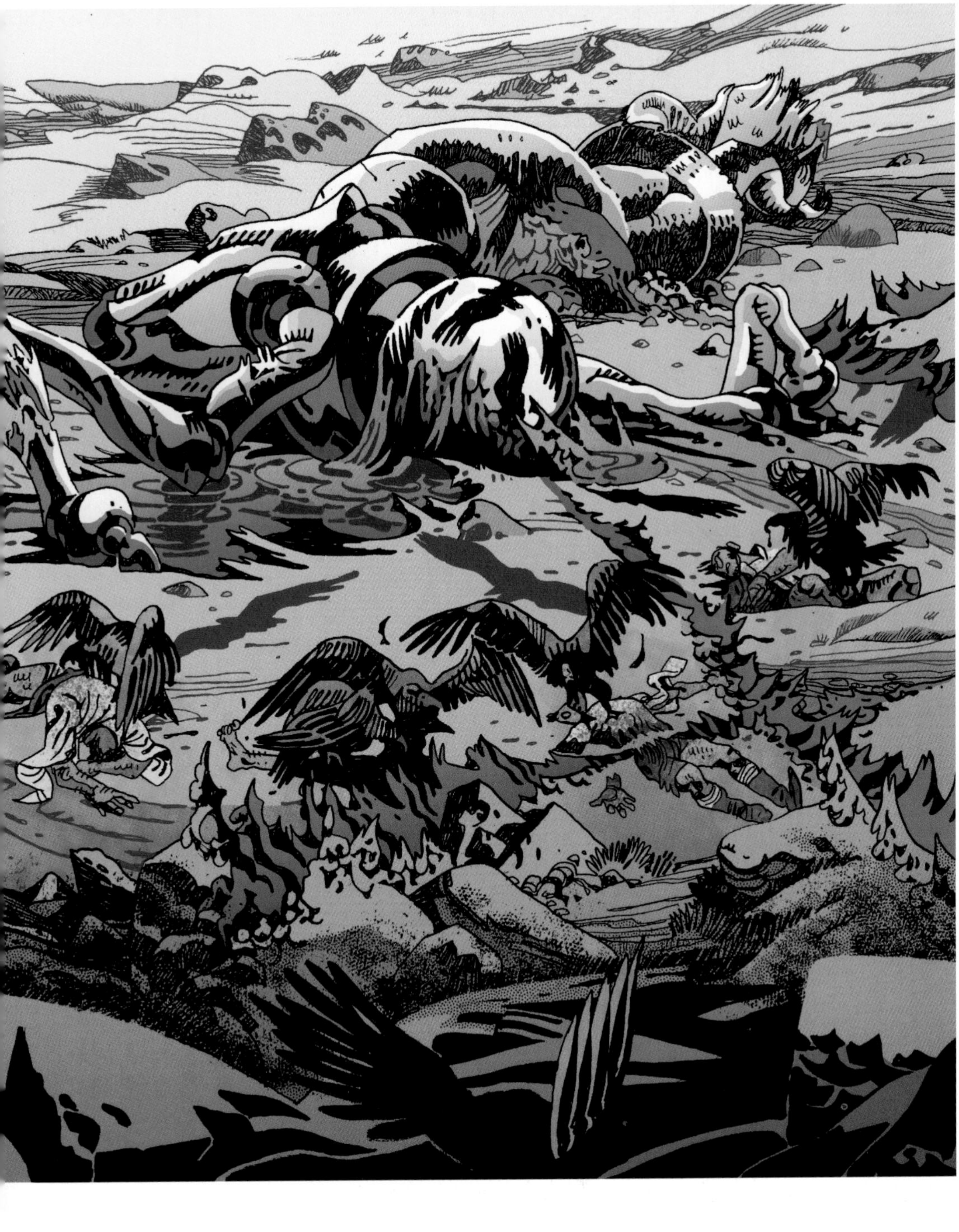

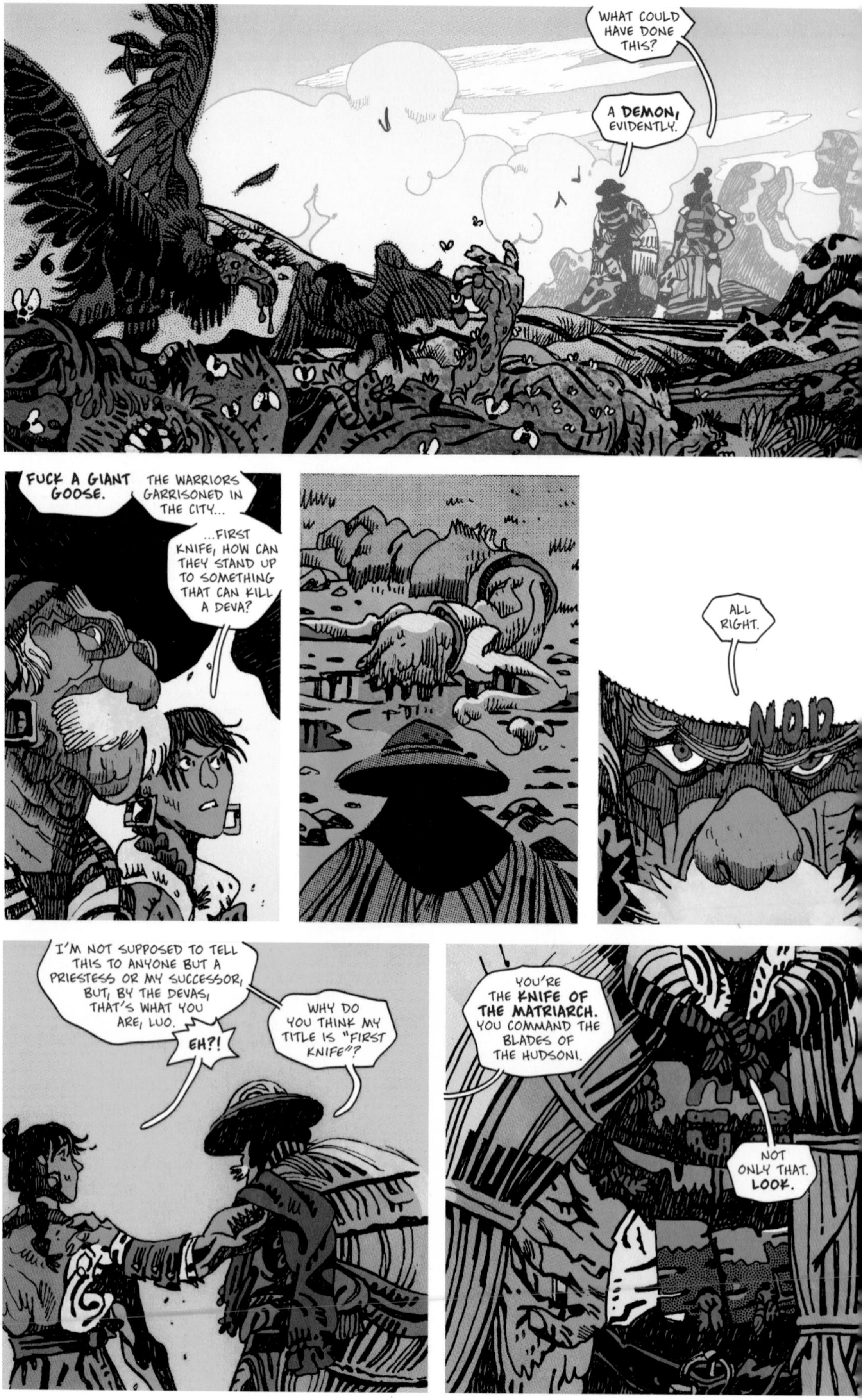
WHAT COULD HAVE DONE THIS?
A **DEMON**, EVIDENTLY.
FUCK A GIANT GOOSE.
THE WARRIORS GARRISONED IN THE CITY...
...FIRST KNIFE, HOW CAN THEY STAND UP TO SOMETHING THAT CAN KILL A DEVA?
ALL RIGHT.
NOD
I'M NOT SUPPOSED TO TELL THIS TO ANYONE BUT A PRIESTESS OR MY SUCCESSOR, BUT, BY THE DEVAS, THAT'S WHAT YOU ARE, LUO.
EH?!
WHY DO YOU THINK MY TITLE IS "FIRST KNIFE"?
YOU'RE THE **KNIFE OF THE MATRIARCH.** YOU COMMAND THE BLADES OF THE HUDSONI.
NOT ONLY THAT. **LOOK.**

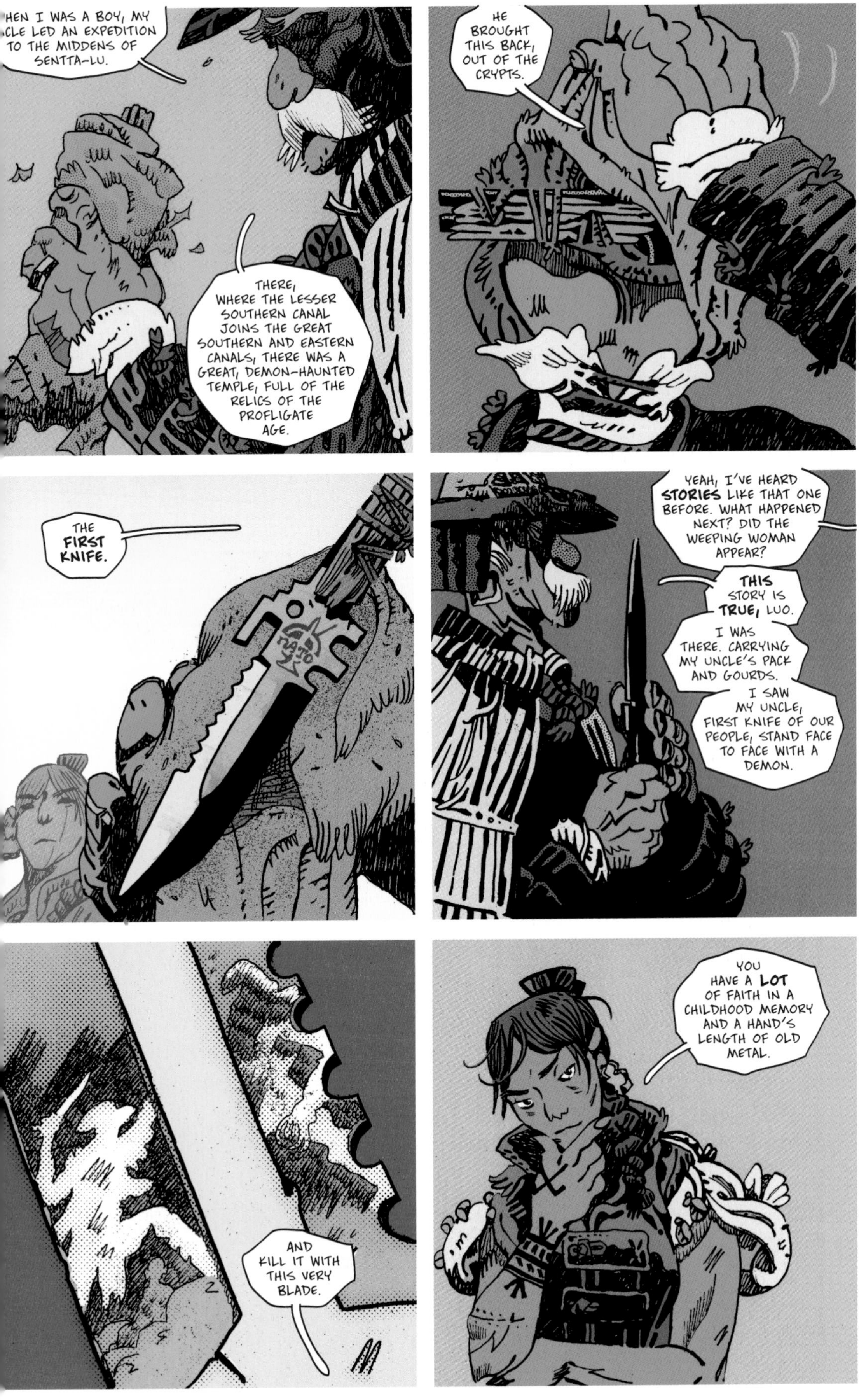
HEN I WAS A BOY, MY
CLE LED AN EXPEDITION TO THE MIDDENS OF SENTTA-LU.
THERE, WHERE THE LESSER SOUTHERN CANAL JOINS THE GREAT SOUTHERN AND EASTERN CANALS, THERE WAS A GREAT, DEMON-HAUNTED TEMPLE, FULL OF THE RELICS OF THE PROFLIGATE AGE.
HE BROUGHT THIS BACK, OUT OF THE CRYPTS.
THE FIRST KNIFE.
YEAH, I'VE HEARD STORIES LIKE THAT ONE BEFORE. WHAT HAPPENED NEXT? DID THE WEEPING WOMAN APPEAR?
THIS STORY IS TRUE, LUO.
I WAS THERE. CARRYING MY UNCLE'S PACK AND GOURDS.
I SAW MY UNCLE, FIRST KNIFE OF OUR PEOPLE, STAND FACE TO FACE WITH A DEMON.
AND KILL IT WITH THIS VERY BLADE.
YOU HAVE A LOT OF FAITH IN A CHILDHOOD MEMORY AND A HAND'S LENGTH OF OLD METAL.

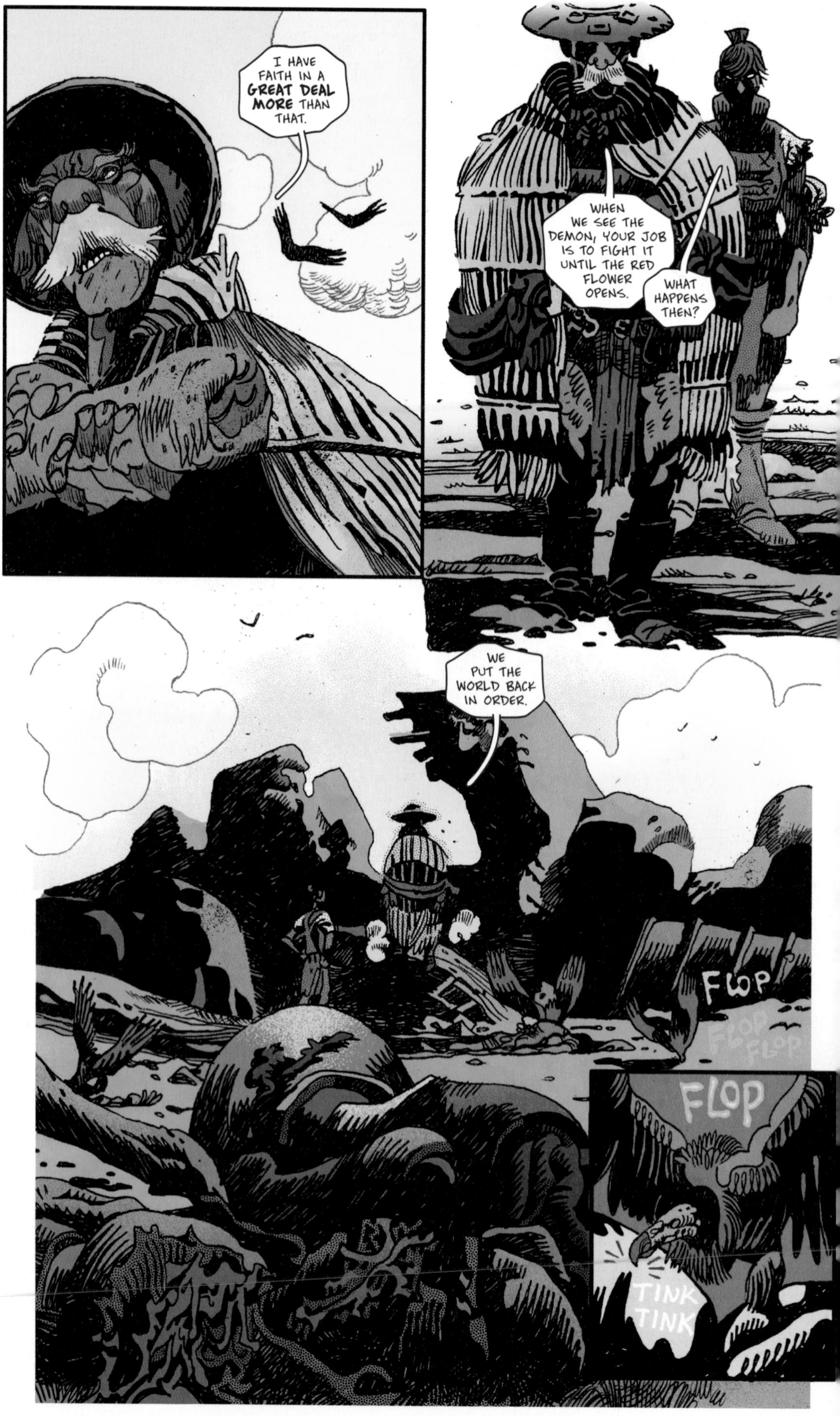
I HAVE FAITH IN A **GREAT DEAL MORE** THAN THAT.
WHEN WE SEE THE DEMON, YOUR JOB IS TO FIGHT IT UNTIL THE RED FLOWER OPENS.
WHAT HAPPENS THEN?
WE PUT THE WORLD BACK IN ORDER.
FLOP
FLOP FLOP
FLOP
TINK TINK

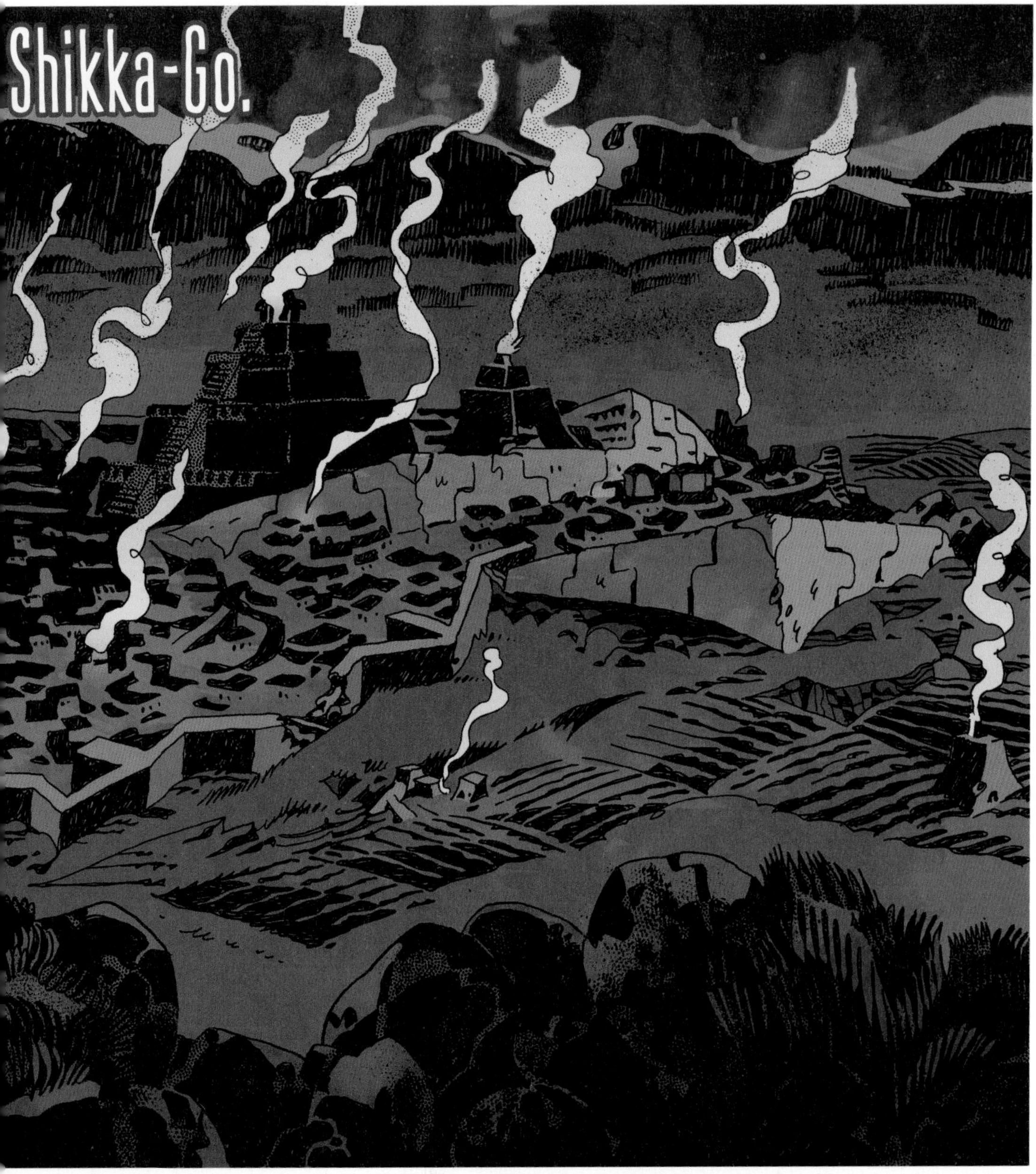
Shikka-Go.

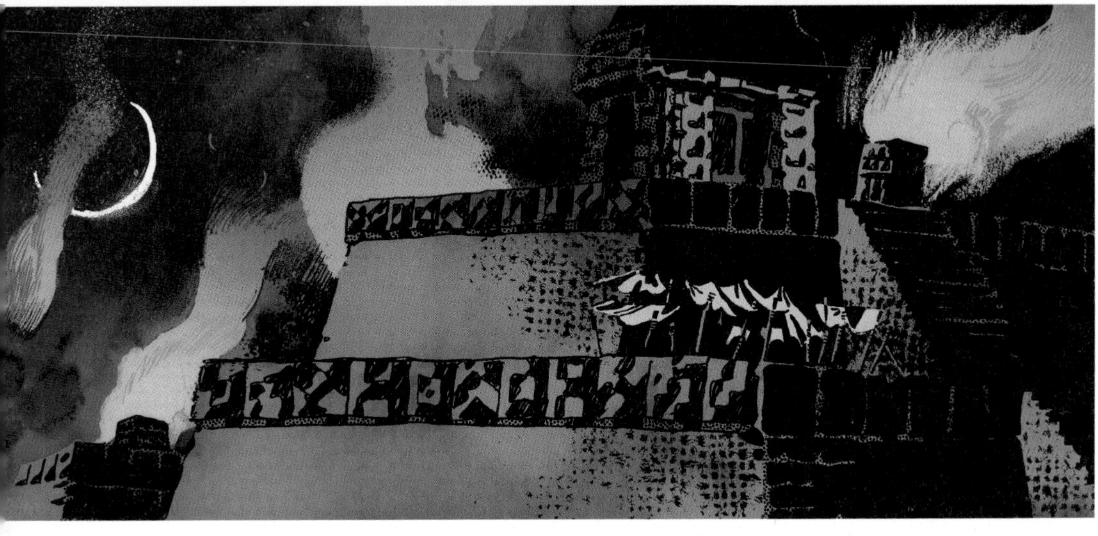

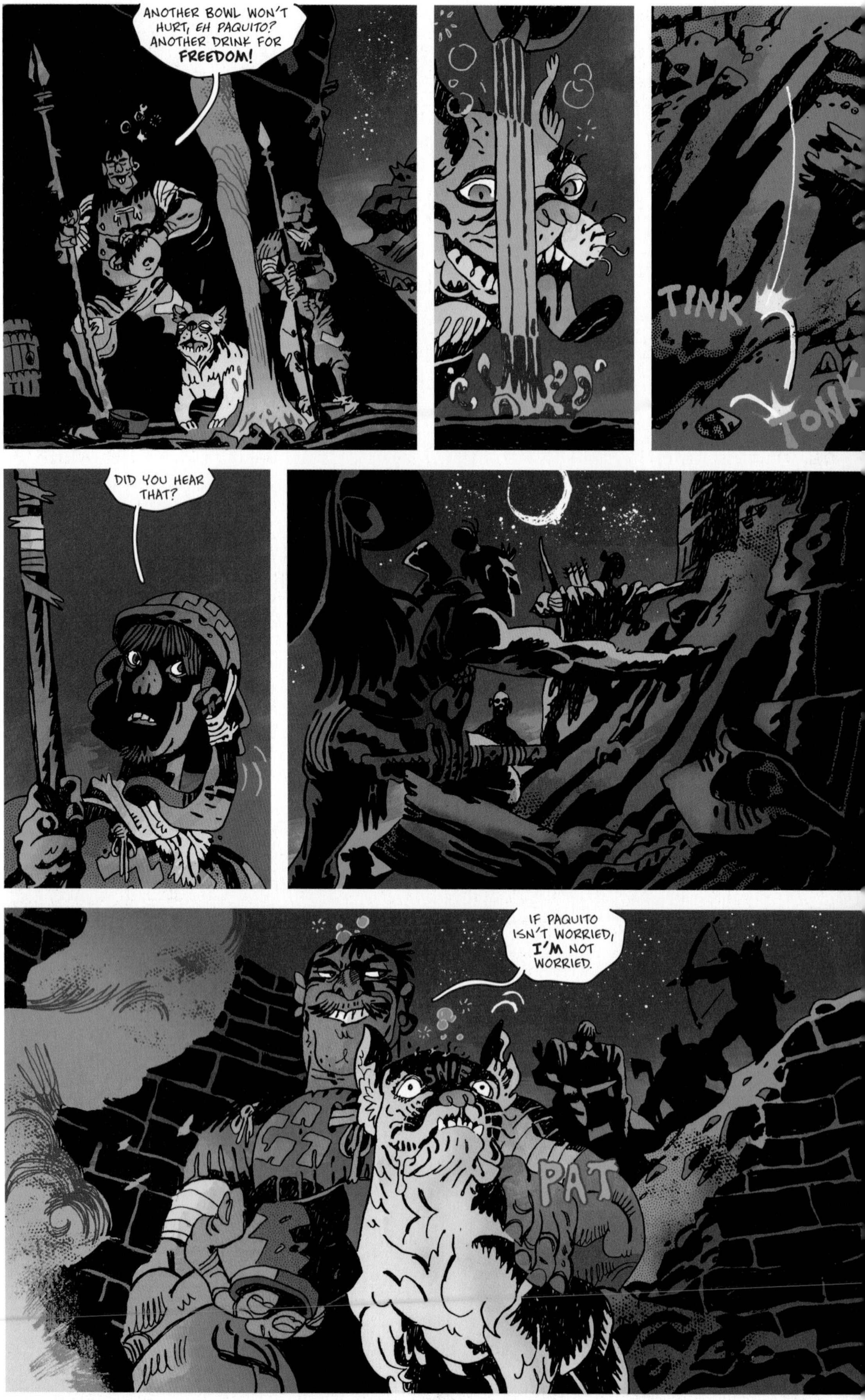
ANOTHER BOWL WON'T HURT, EH PAQUITO? ANOTHER DRINK FOR **FREEDOM!**
TINK
TONK
DID YOU HEAR THAT?
IF PAQUITO ISN'T WORRIED, **I'M** NOT WORRIED.
PAT

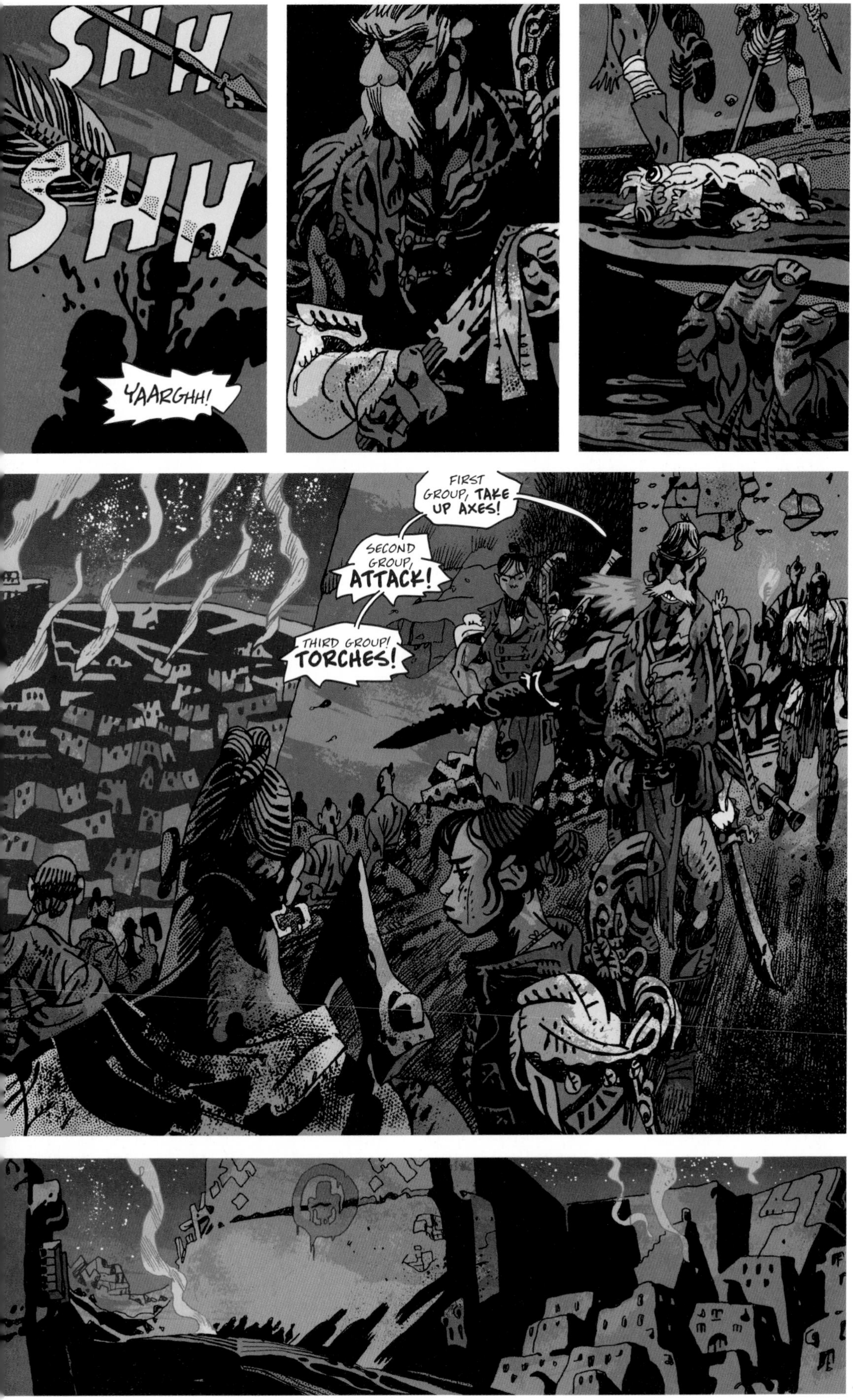
SHH
SHH
YAARGHH!
FIRST GROUP, TAKE UP AXES!
SECOND GROUP, ATTACK!
THIRD GROUP! TORCHES!

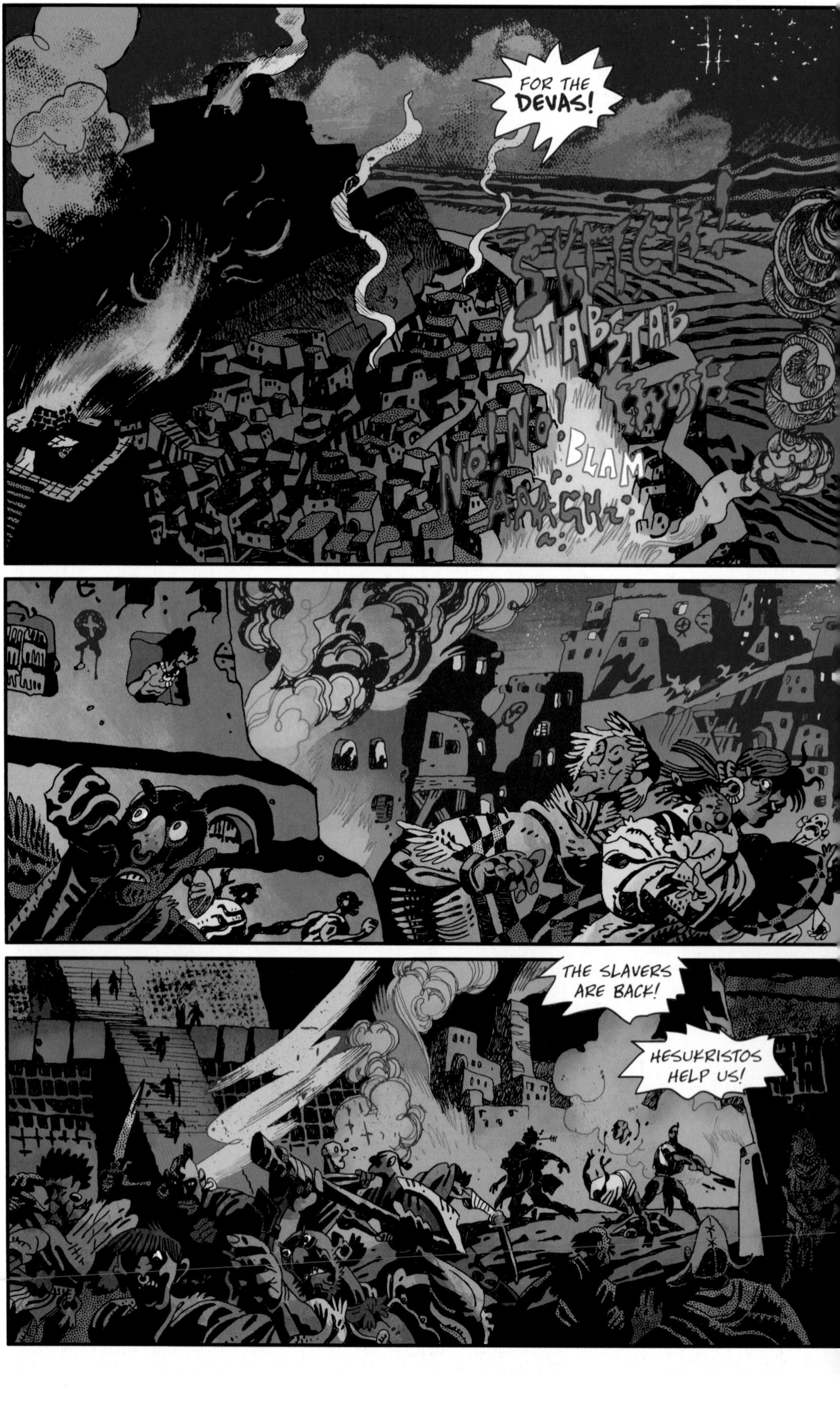
FOR THE DEVAS!
STABSTAB
NO! NO!
BLAM
AAAGH
THE SLAVERS ARE BACK!
HESUKRISTOS HELP US!

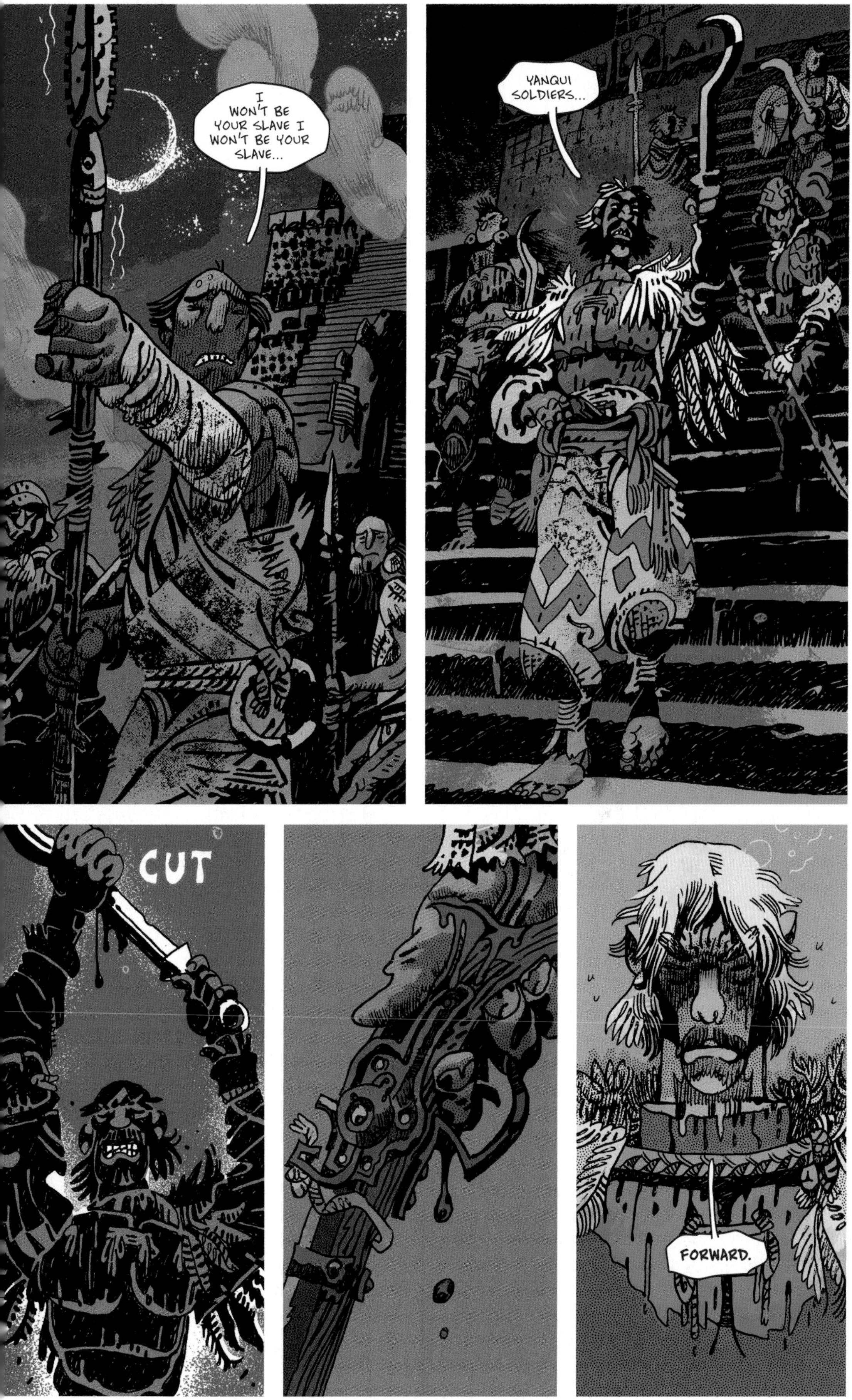
I WON'T BE YOUR SLAVE I WON'T BE YOUR SLAVE...
YANQUI SOLDIERS...
CUT
FORWARD.

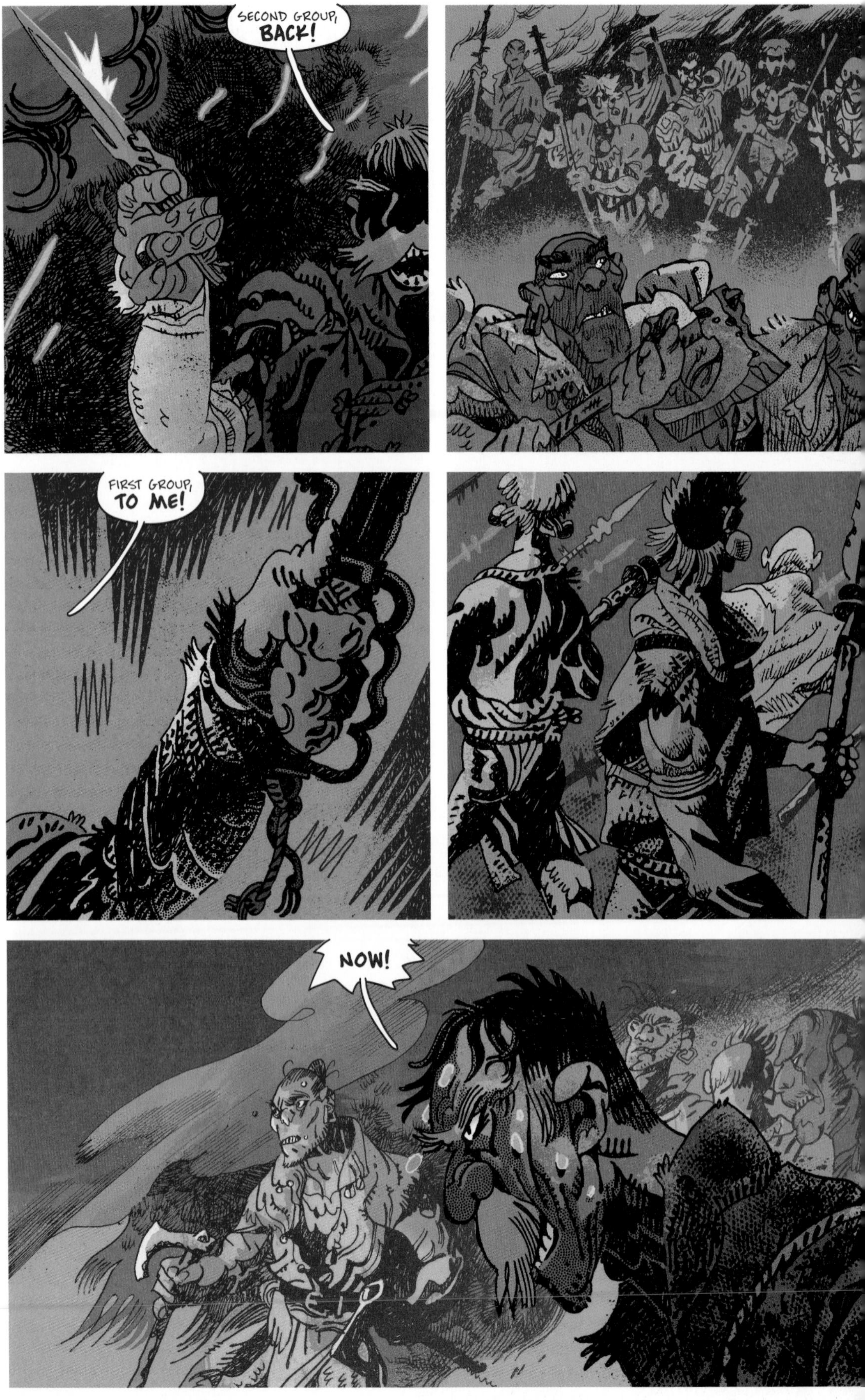
SECOND GROUP, BACK!
FIRST GROUP, TO ME!
NOW!

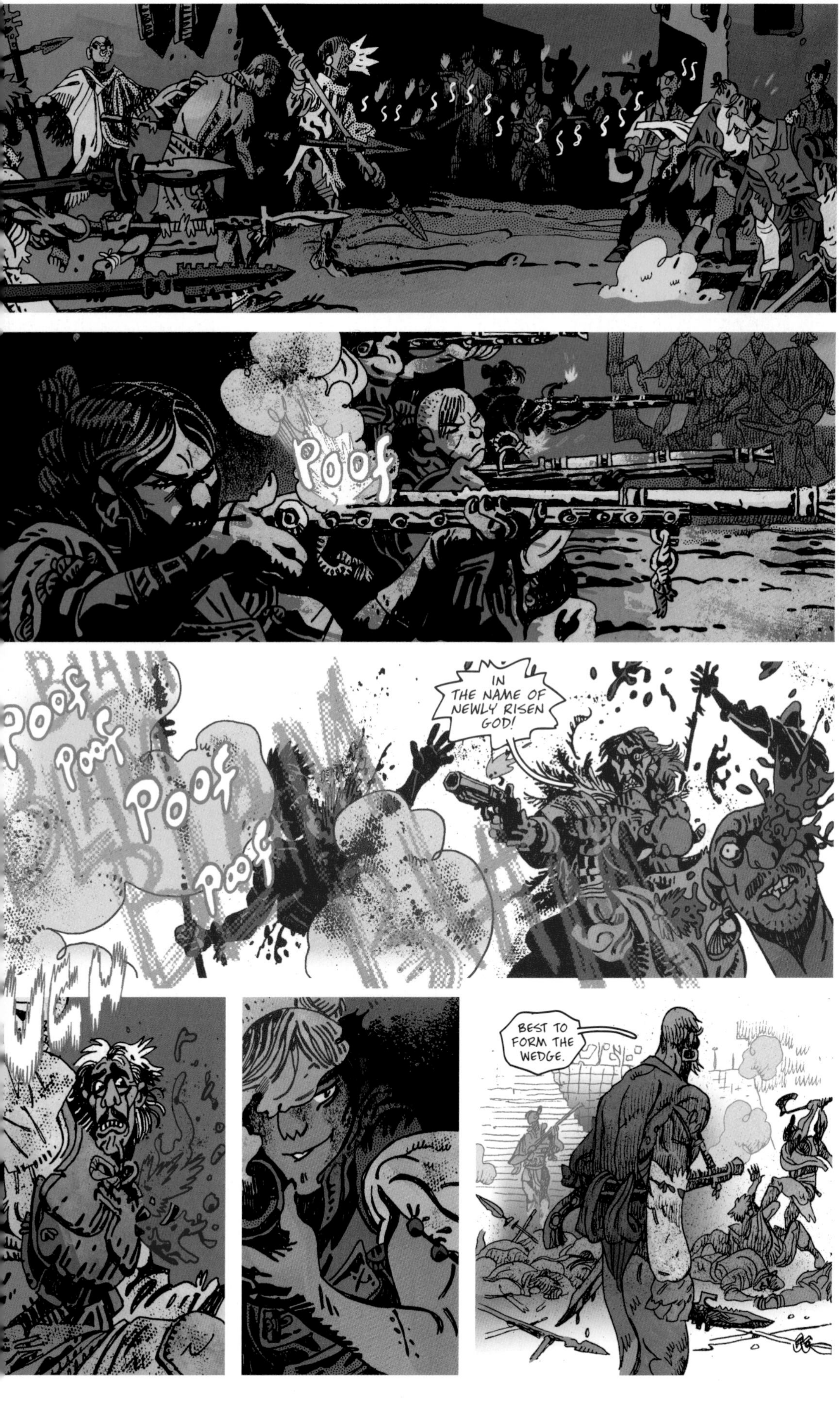
POOF
POOF
POOF
POOF
POOF
IN THE NAME OF NEWLY RISEN GOD!
BEST TO FORM THE WEDGE.

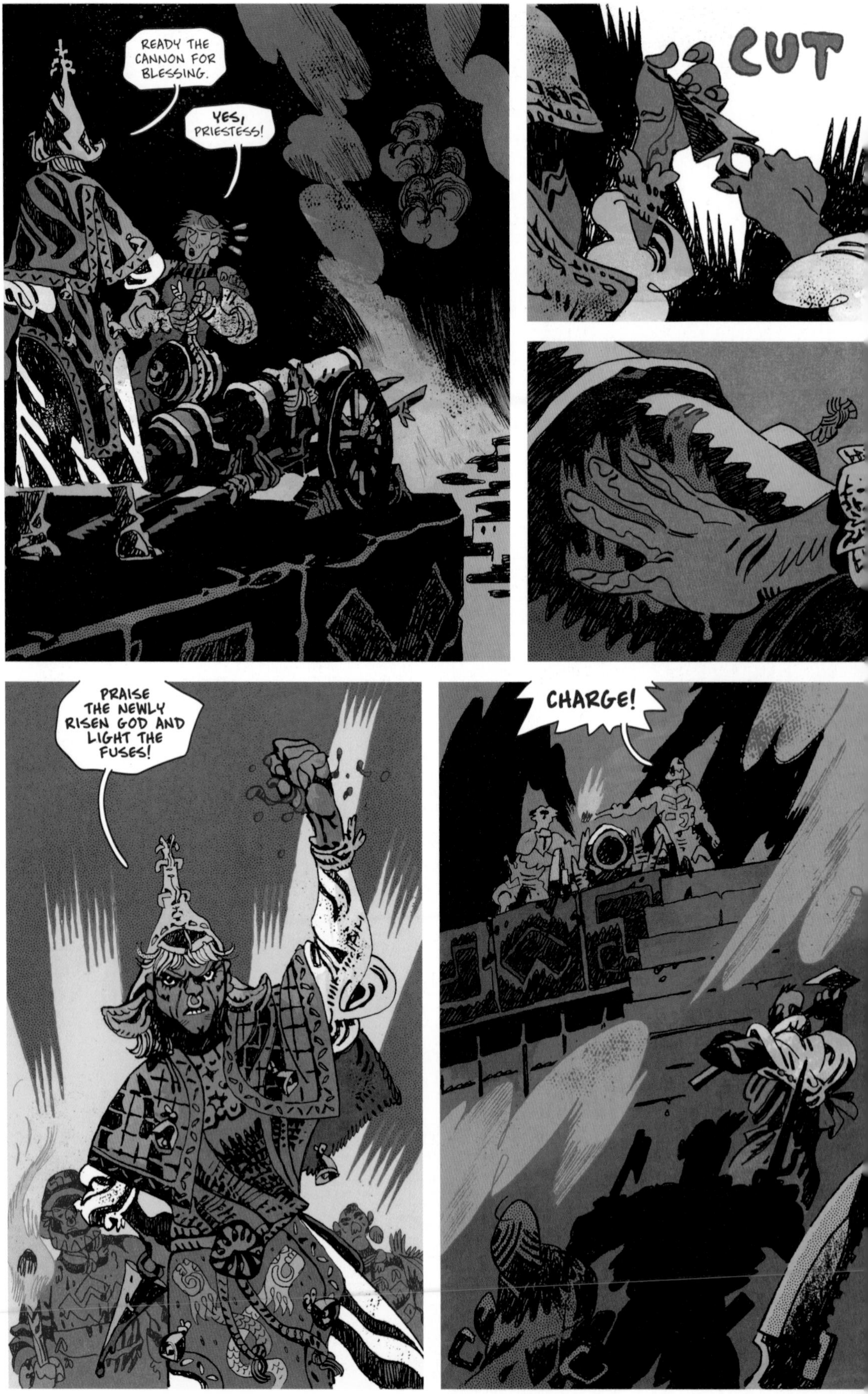
READY THE CANNON FOR BLESSING.
YES, PRIESTESS!
CUT
PRAISE THE NEWLY RISEN GOD AND LIGHT THE FUSES!
CHARGE!

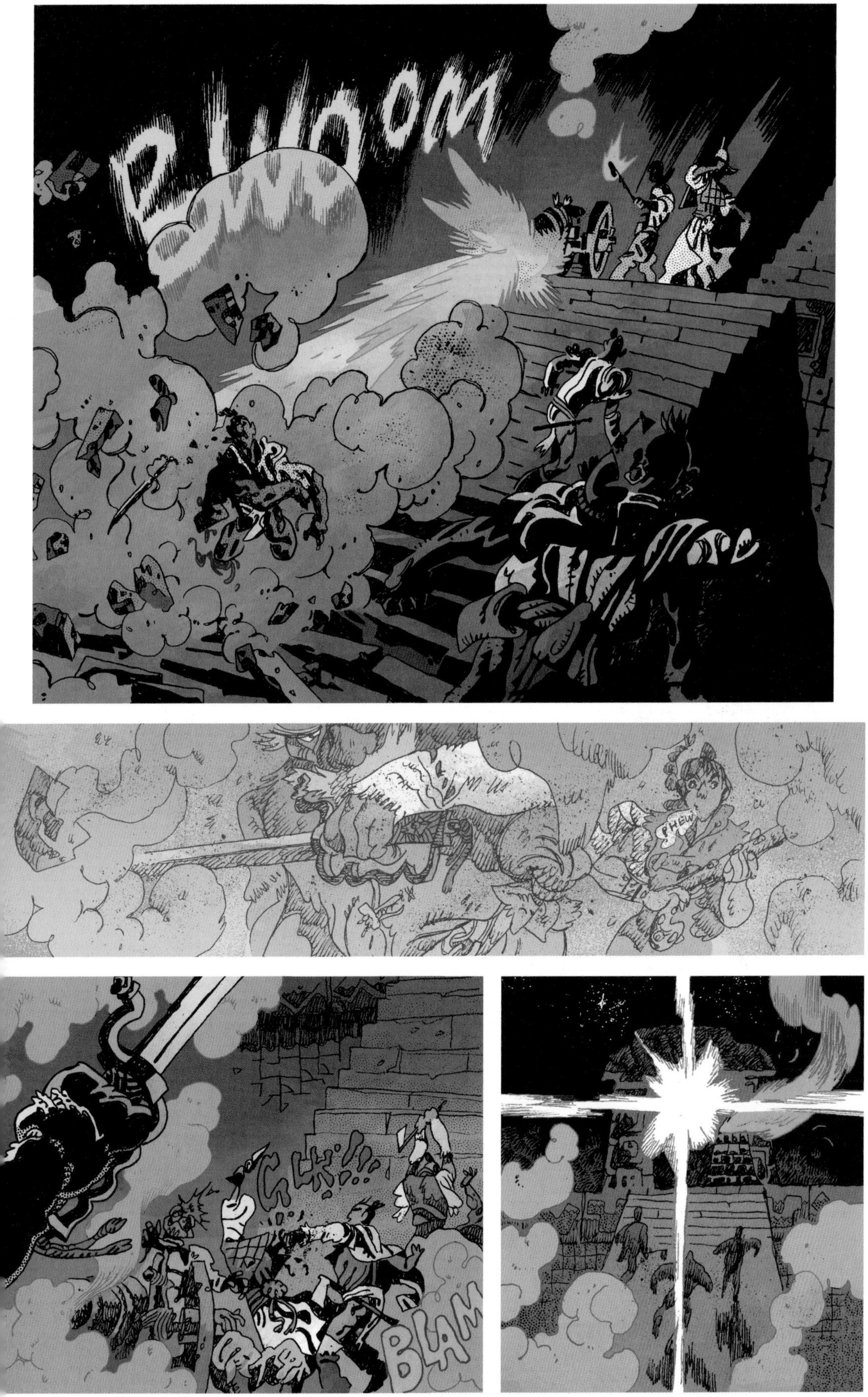
BWOOM
PHEW
GLK!!!
BLAM

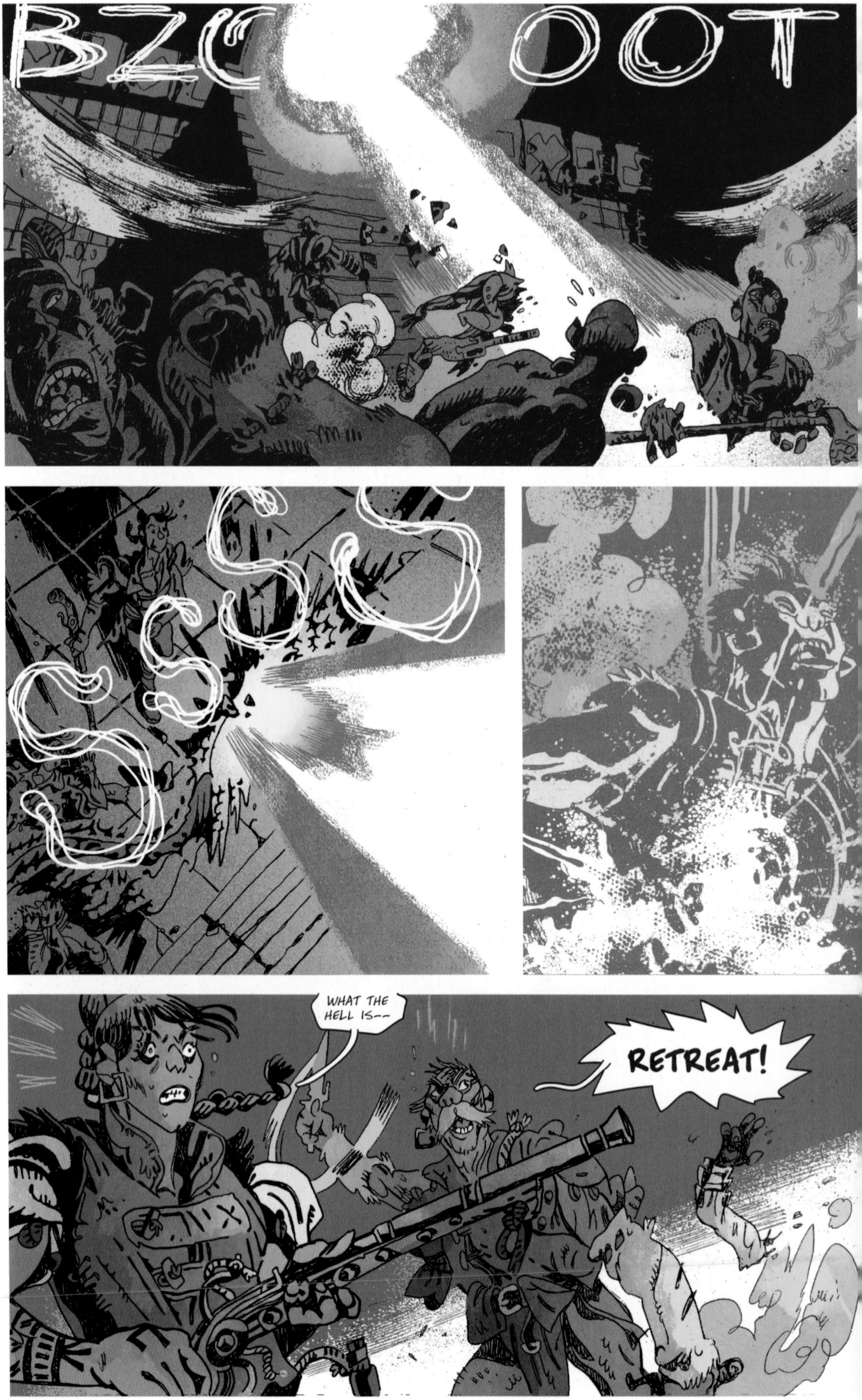
BZZOOT
SSSS
WHAT THE HELL IS--
RETREAT!

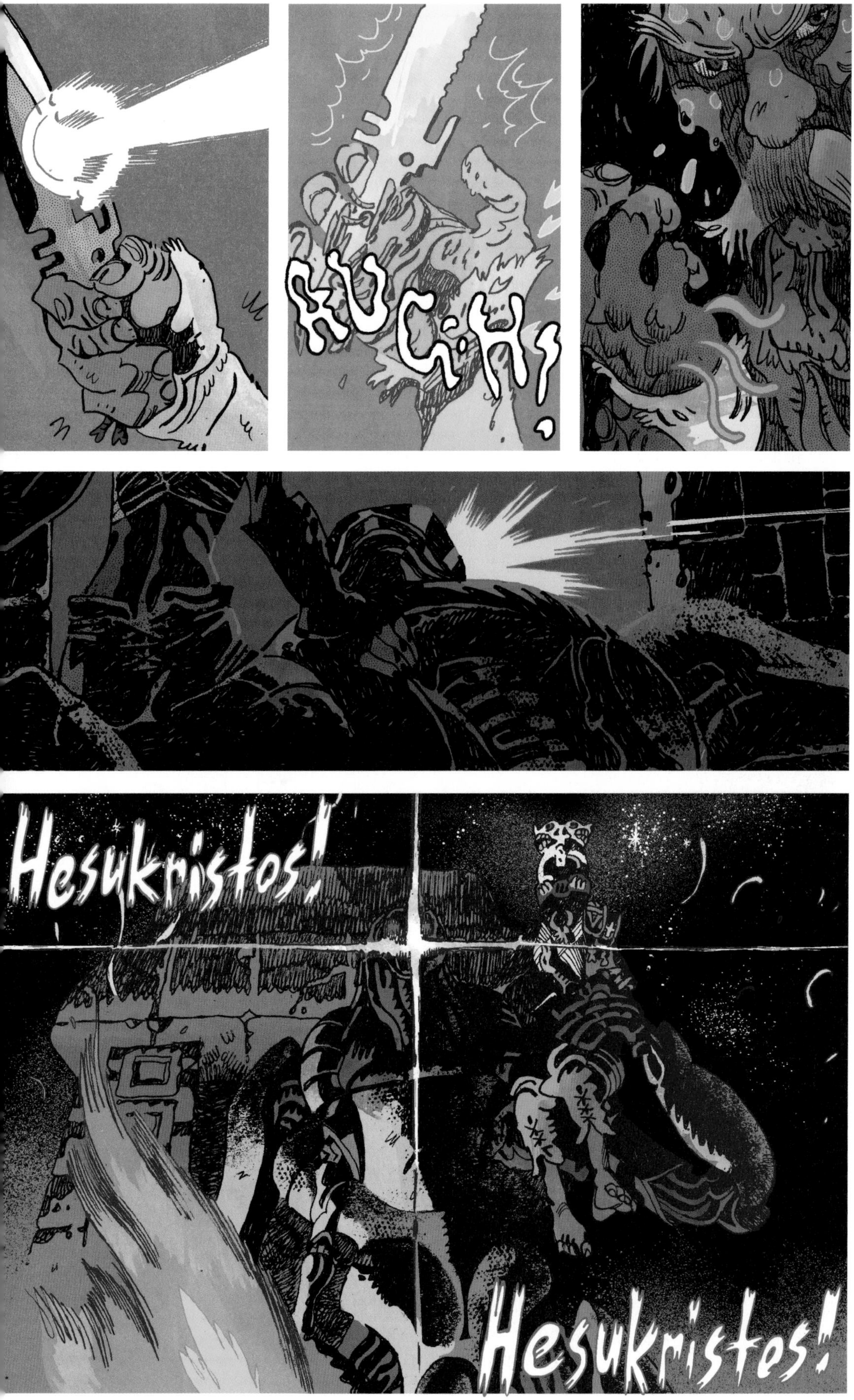
KUCHH!
Hesukristos!
Hesukristos!

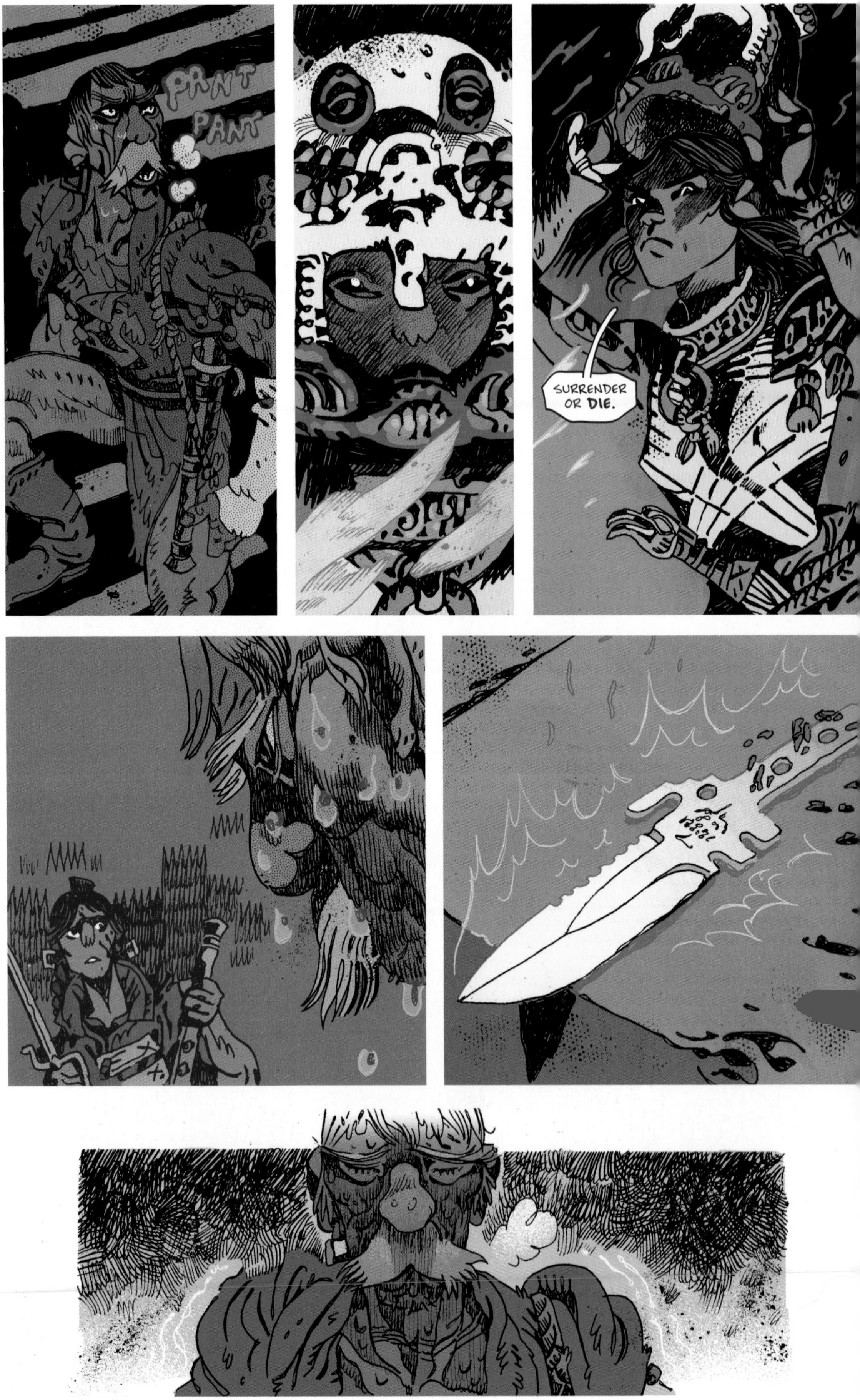
PANT
PANT
SURRENDER OR DIE.

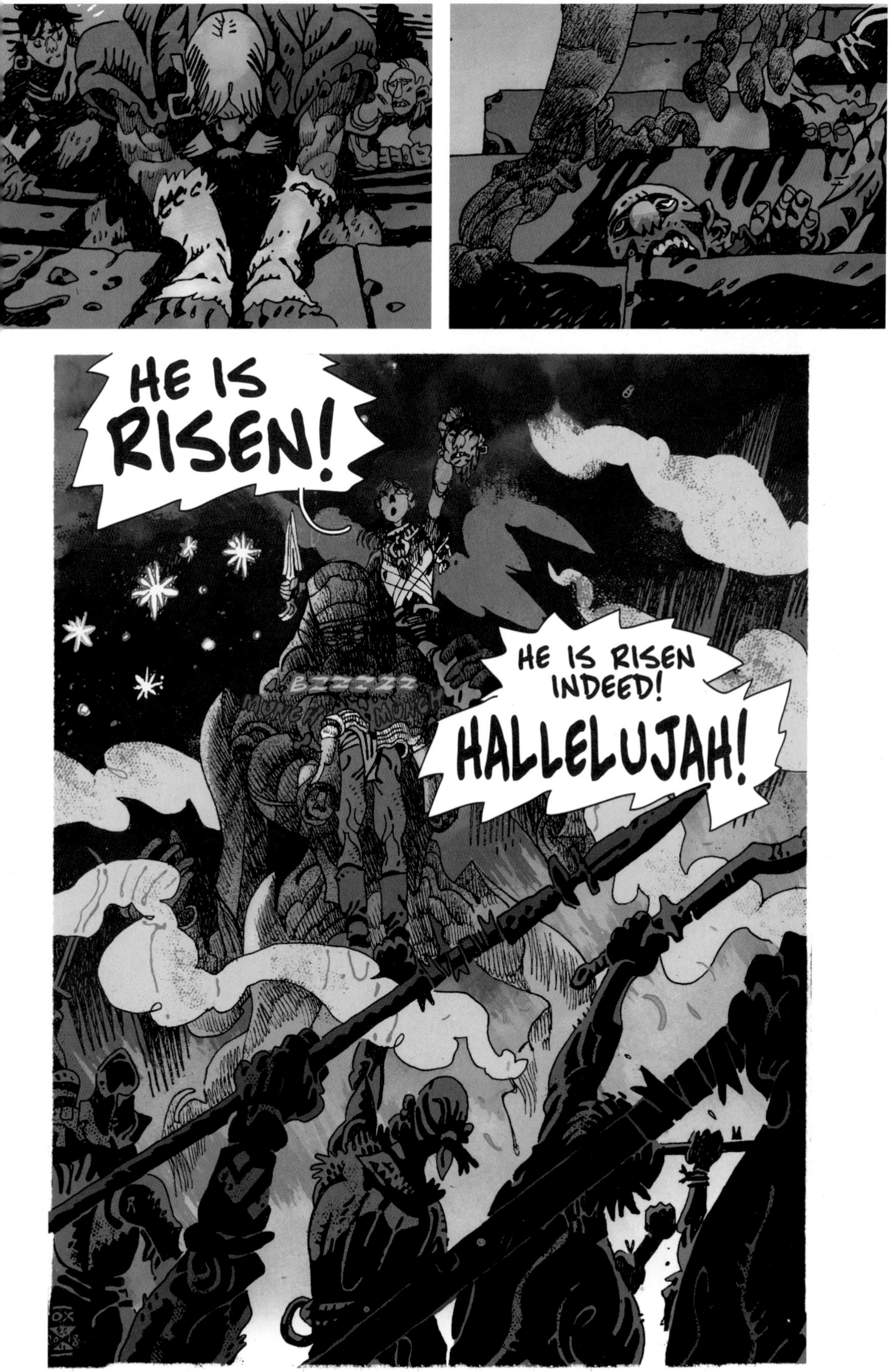
HE IS RISEN!
BZZZZZ
MUNCH MUNCH
HE IS RISEN INDEED!
HALLELUJAH!

The Onions of Old Chicago

Oh, I knew me a girl from the North!
She thinks she's of such great import!
But they know, the priestesses,
to clear the premises
of the maidens of old Shikka-go!
Oh! Oh, the maidens of old Shikka-go!

Oh, I know me a girl from the South!
Any soldier's a pawn in her...hands! Oh!
But they know, the brave soldiers,
to defend all the borders
from the maidens of old Shikka-go!
Oh! Oh, the maidens of old Shikka-go!

Oh, I knew me a girl from the East!
The rent was a dollar at least! Hey!
But they know, all the monks
That your money's all sunk
in the maidens of old Shikka-go!
Oh! Oh, the maidens of old Shikka-go!

Oh, I knew me a girl from the West!
In total, that's all sins confessed! Yes!
Every pot-mender knows...
That the best women grow...
With the onions of old Shikka-go!
Oh! Oh the onions of old Shikka-go!

Traditional Yanqui Drinking Song,
Collected near the Southern Shores of
Lake Michigan in 3515 AD
by Dr. D. M. Benson, Folklorist

The Gosherd's Song

As a youngster I was well known for a life lived fast and loose
Slept with a war chief's daughter underneath the spreading spruce
Found the Herald's secret still and drank up all that it produced
Which is why today I'm living with a goose.

(chorus)
Oh, a honka-dilly honka-dilly hoo!
Cleaning goose-shit's all I ever get to do!
How I wish that instead of me I could be you.
Oh, A honka-dilly honka-dilly hoo.

Oh, they chased me and they caught me, kicked me right in the caboose
They said that I was destined to be hanging from a noose
But before I could escape or bribe or try some other ruse,
They sent me here to live with the goose.

(chorus)

Now let me make my story clear, so I am not abstruse
That's why I'm sitting in the guano with my face chartreuse
For my current state I offer only this honest excuse...
Never wanted to be keeper of the goose.

(chorus) (minor key)

Traditional Hudsoni Drinking Song,
Collected near the Northern Shores of
Lake Huron in 3512 AD
by Dr. D. M. Benson, Folklorist

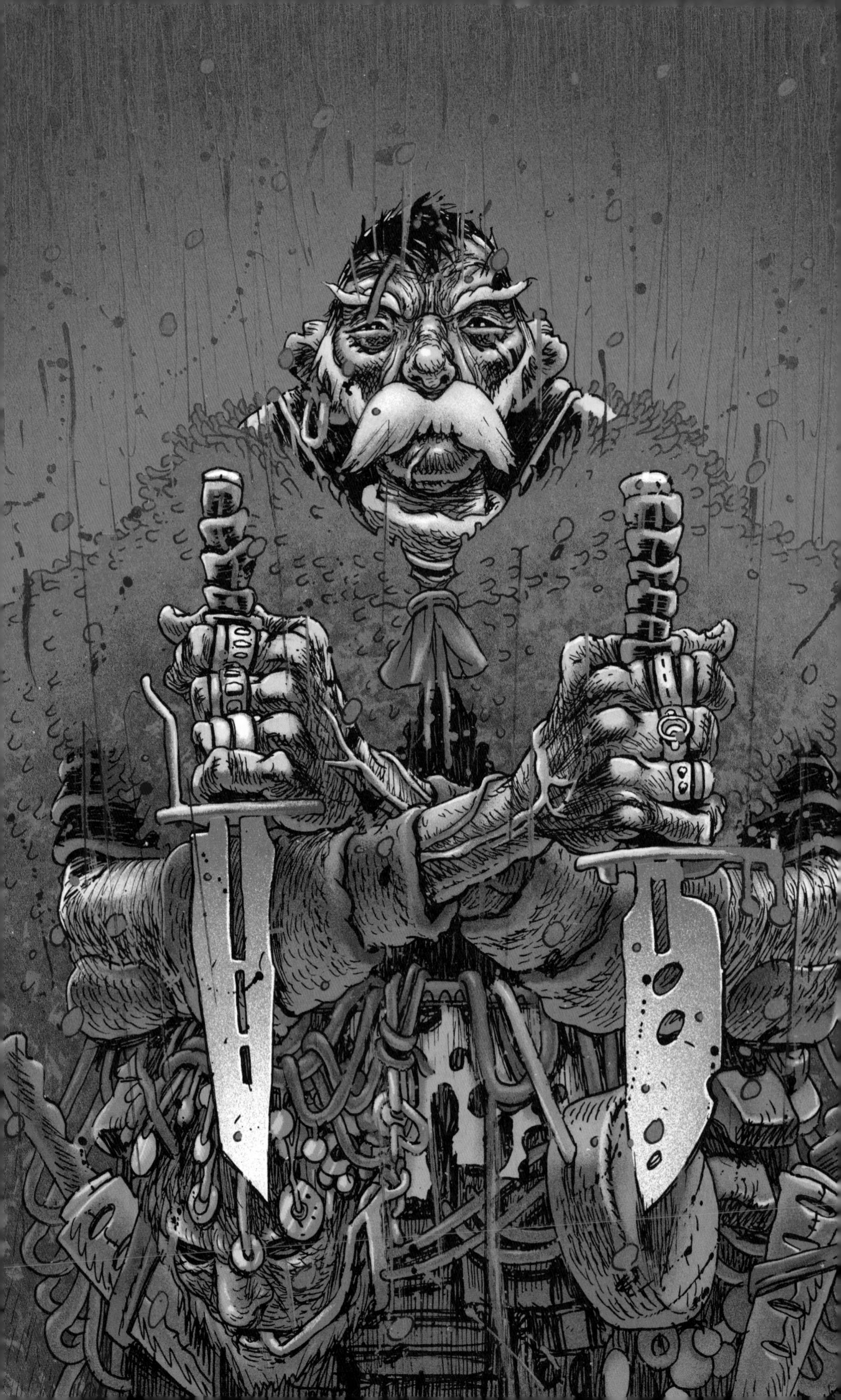

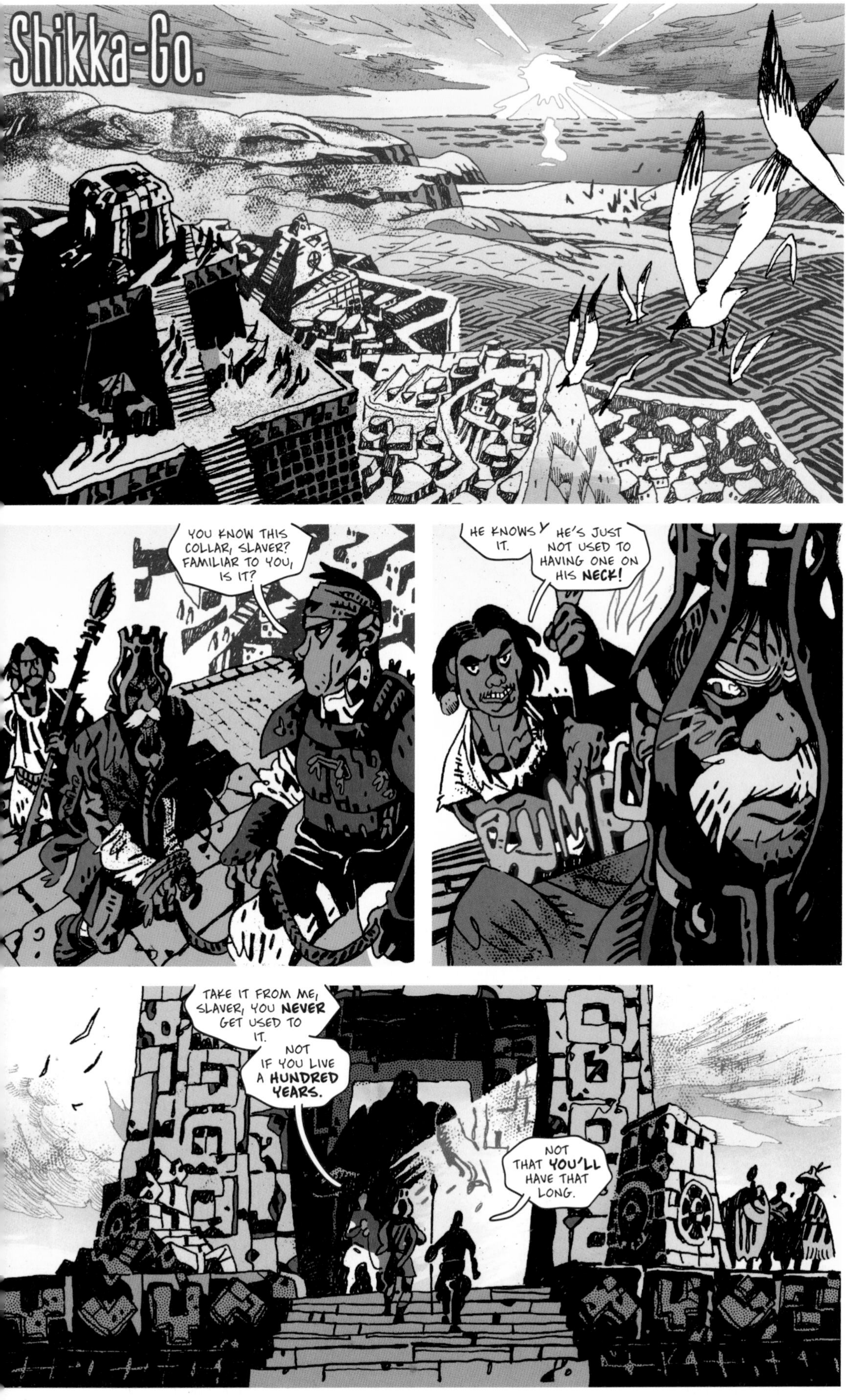

Shikka-Go.
YOU KNOW THIS COLLAR, SLAVER? FAMILIAR TO YOU, IS IT?
HE KNOWS IT.
HE'S JUST NOT USED TO HAVING ONE ON HIS NECK!
TAKE IT FROM ME, SLAVER, YOU NEVER GET USED TO IT.
NOT IF YOU LIVE A HUNDRED YEARS.
NOT THAT YOU'LL HAVE THAT LONG.

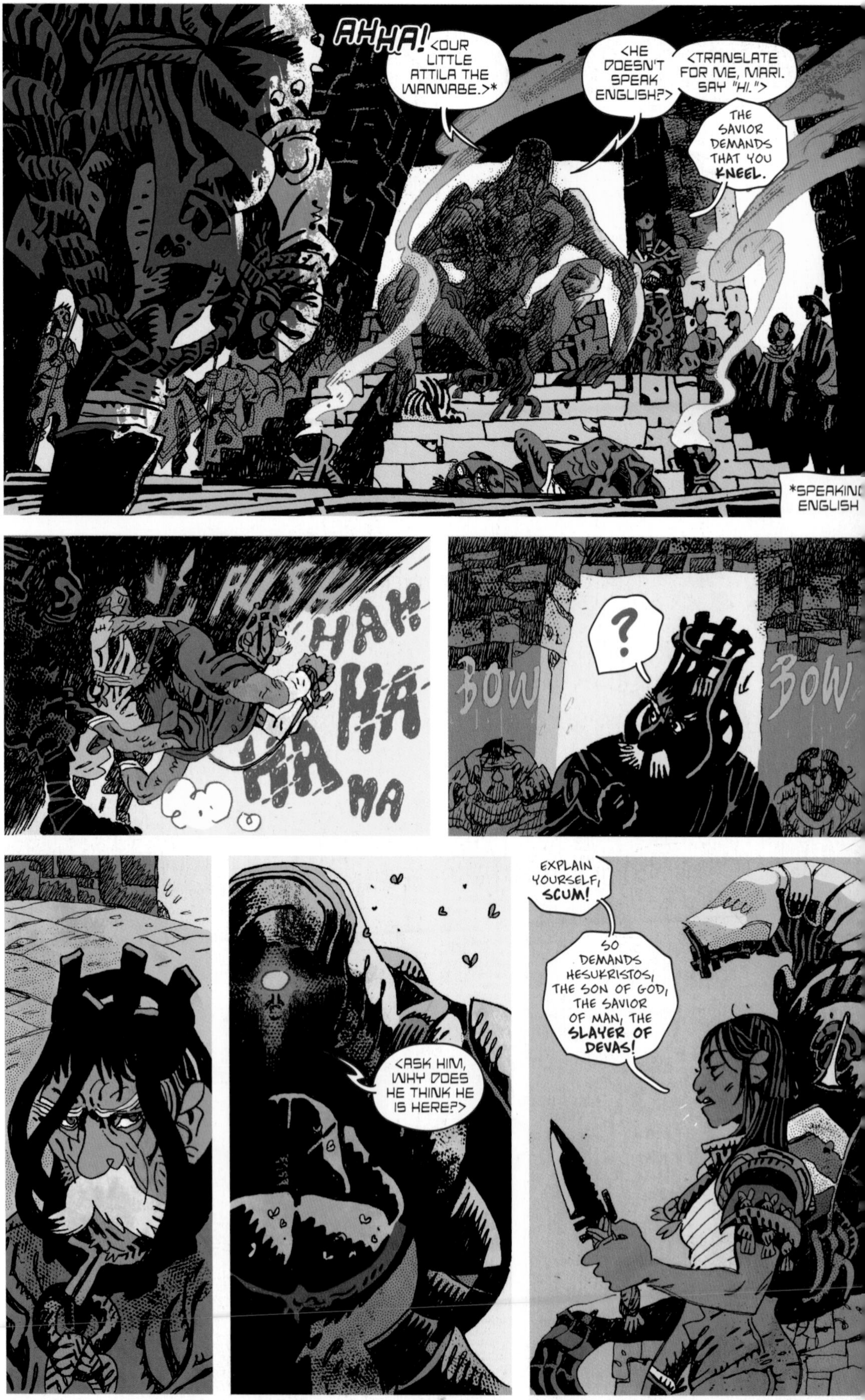
AHHA!
<OUR LITTLE ATTILA THE WANNABE.>*
<HE DOESN'T SPEAK ENGLISH?>
<TRANSLATE FOR ME, MARI. SAY "HI.">
THE SAVIOR DEMANDS THAT YOU **KNEEL.**
*SPEAKING ENGLISH
PUSH
HAH HA HA HA
?
BOW
BOW
<ASK HIM, WHY DOES HE THINK HE IS HERE?>
EXPLAIN YOURSELF, **SCUM!**
SO DEMANDS HESUKRISTOS, THE SON OF GOD, THE SAVIOR OF MAN, THE **SLAYER OF DEVAS!**

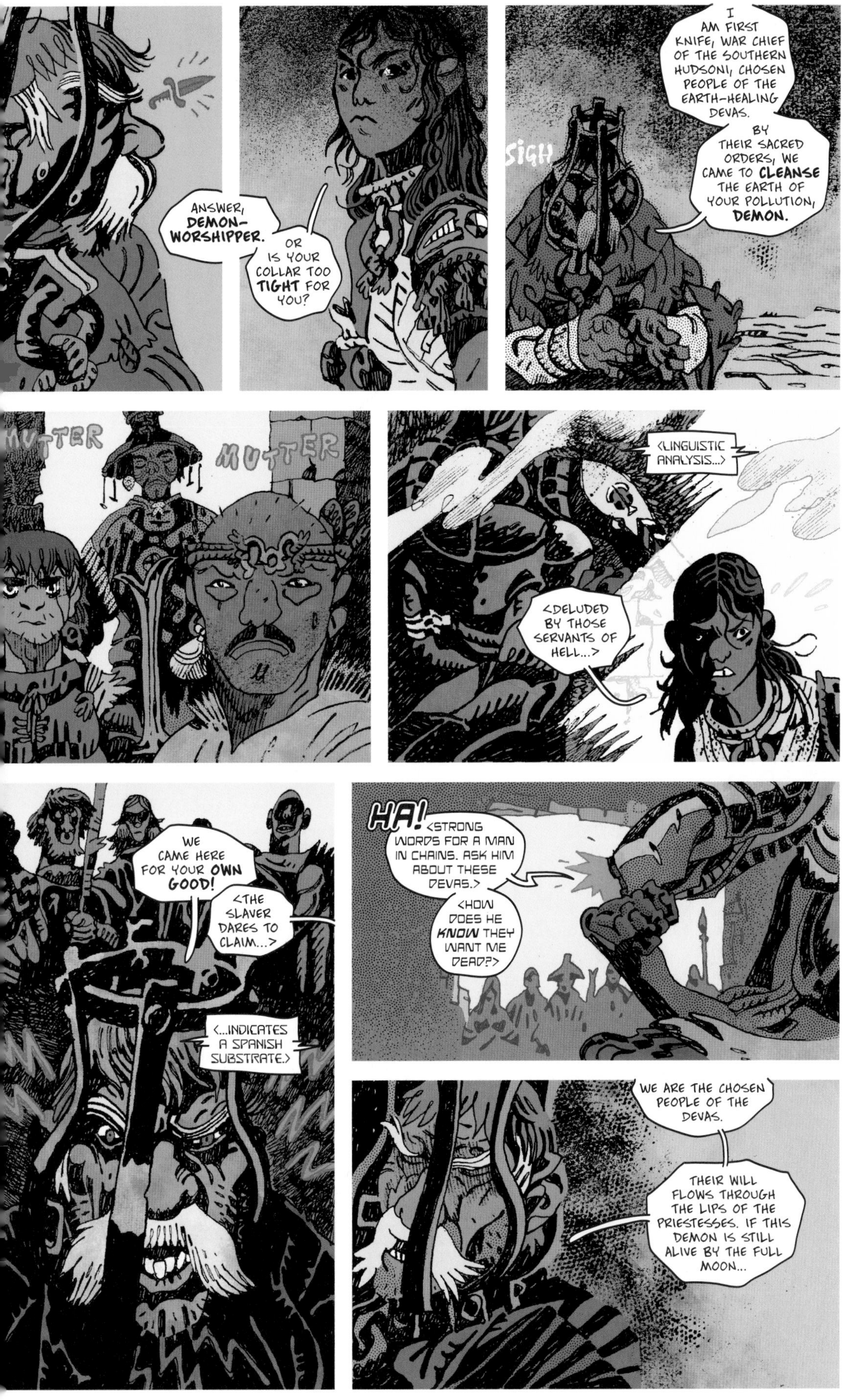

ANSWER, DEMON-WORSHIPPER.
OR IS YOUR COLLAR TOO TIGHT FOR YOU?
SIGH
I AM FIRST KNIFE, WAR CHIEF OF THE SOUTHERN HUDSONI, CHOSEN PEOPLE OF THE EARTH-HEALING DEVAS.
BY THEIR SACRED ORDERS, WE CAME TO CLEANSE THE EARTH OF YOUR POLLUTION, DEMON.
MUTTER
MUTTER
<LINGUISTIC ANALYSIS...>
<DELUDED BY THOSE SERVANTS OF HELL...>
WE CAME HERE FOR YOUR OWN GOOD!
<THE SLAVER DARES TO CLAIM...>
<...INDICATES A SPANISH SUBSTRATE.>
HA!
<STRONG WORDS FOR A MAN IN CHAINS. ASK HIM ABOUT THESE DEVAS.>
<HOW DOES HE KNOW THEY WANT ME DEAD?>
WE ARE THE CHOSEN PEOPLE OF THE DEVAS.
THEIR WILL FLOWS THROUGH THE LIPS OF THE PRIESTESSES. IF THIS DEMON IS STILL ALIVE BY THE FULL MOON...

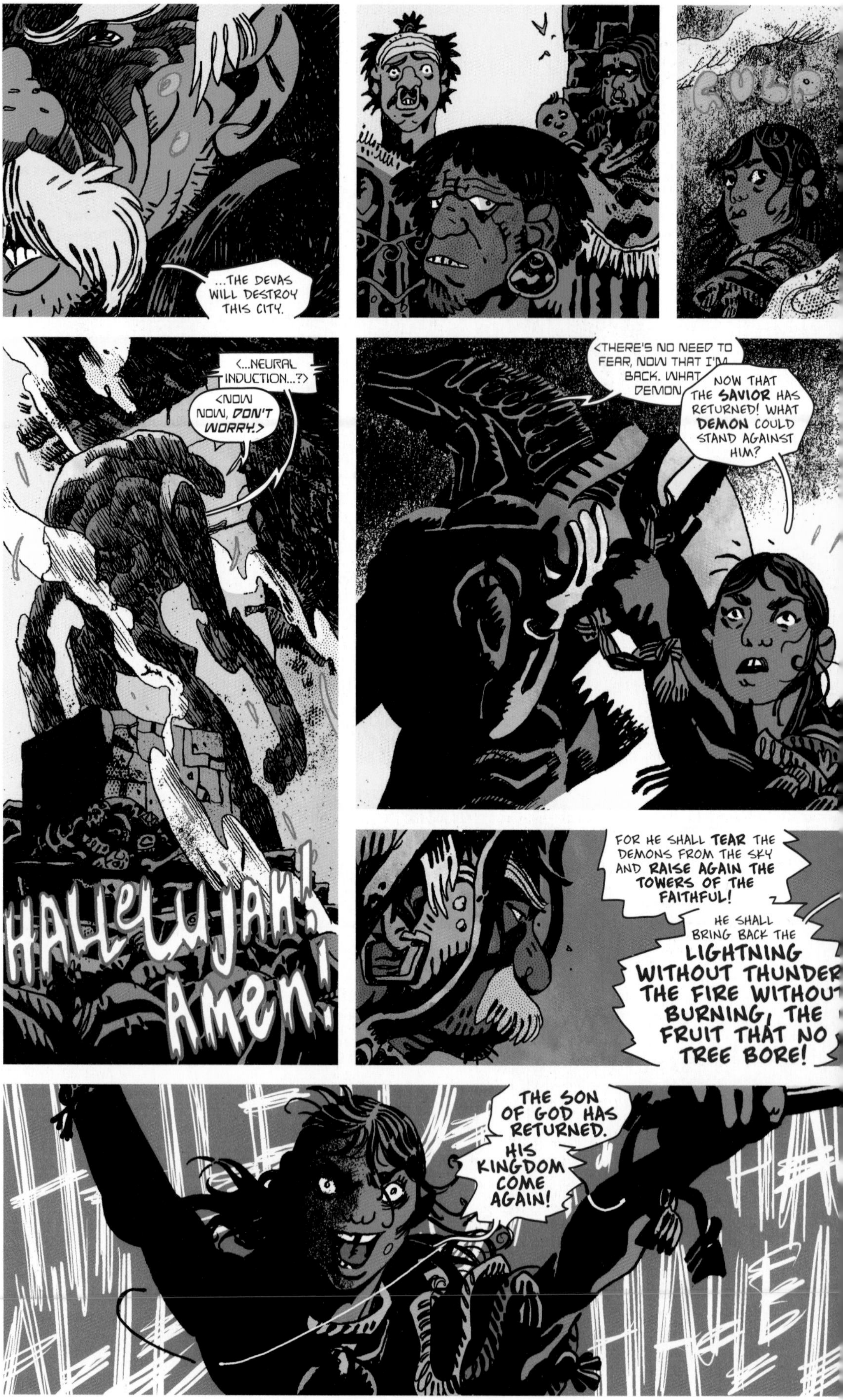
...THE DEVAS WILL DESTROY THIS CITY.
GULP
<...NEURAL INDUCTION...?>
<NOW NOW, DON'T WORRY.>
HALLELUJAH! AMEN!
<THERE'S NO NEED TO FEAR, NOW THAT I'M BACK. WHAT DEMON
NOW THAT THE SAVIOR HAS RETURNED! WHAT DEMON COULD STAND AGAINST HIM?
FOR HE SHALL TEAR THE DEMONS FROM THE SKY AND RAISE AGAIN THE TOWERS OF THE FAITHFUL!
HE SHALL BRING BACK THE LIGHTNING WITHOUT THUNDER, THE FIRE WITHOUT BURNING, THE FRUIT THAT NO TREE BORE!
THE SON OF GOD HAS RETURNED.
HIS KINGDOM COME AGAIN!

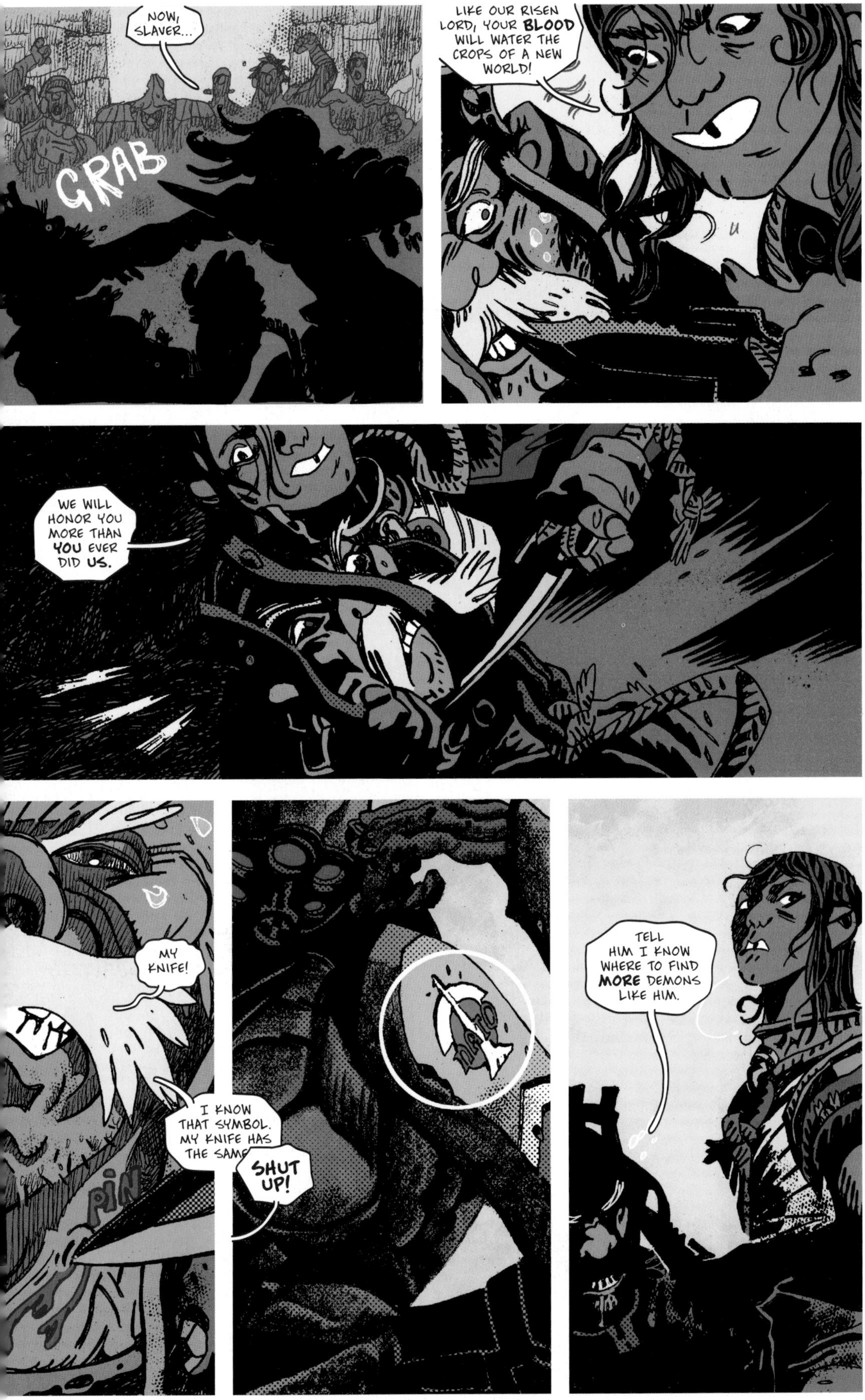
NOW, SLAVER...
GRAB
LIKE OUR RISEN LORD, YOUR BLOOD WILL WATER THE CROPS OF A NEW WORLD!
WE WILL HONOR YOU MORE THAN YOU EVER DID US.
MY KNIFE!
I KNOW THAT SYMBOL. MY KNIFE HAS THE SAME
SHUT UP!
TELL HIM I KNOW WHERE TO FIND MORE DEMONS LIKE HIM.

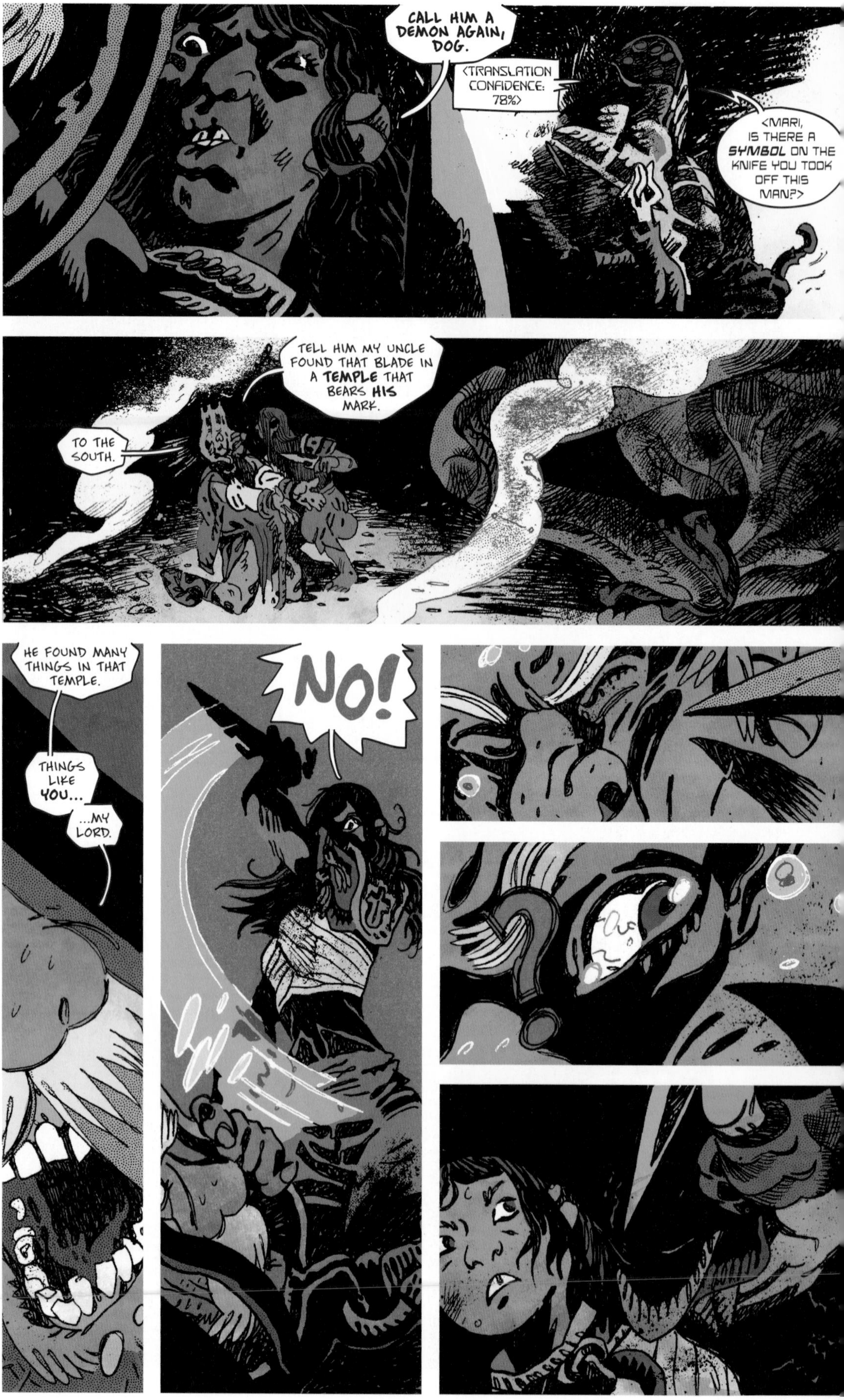

CALL HIM A DEMON AGAIN, DOG.
<TRANSLATION CONFIDENCE: 78%>
<MARI, IS THERE A SYMBOL ON THE KNIFE YOU TOOK OFF THIS MAN?>
TELL HIM MY UNCLE FOUND THAT BLADE IN A TEMPLE THAT BEARS HIS MARK.
TO THE SOUTH.
HE FOUND MANY THINGS IN THAT TEMPLE.
THINGS LIKE YOU...
...MY LORD.
NO!

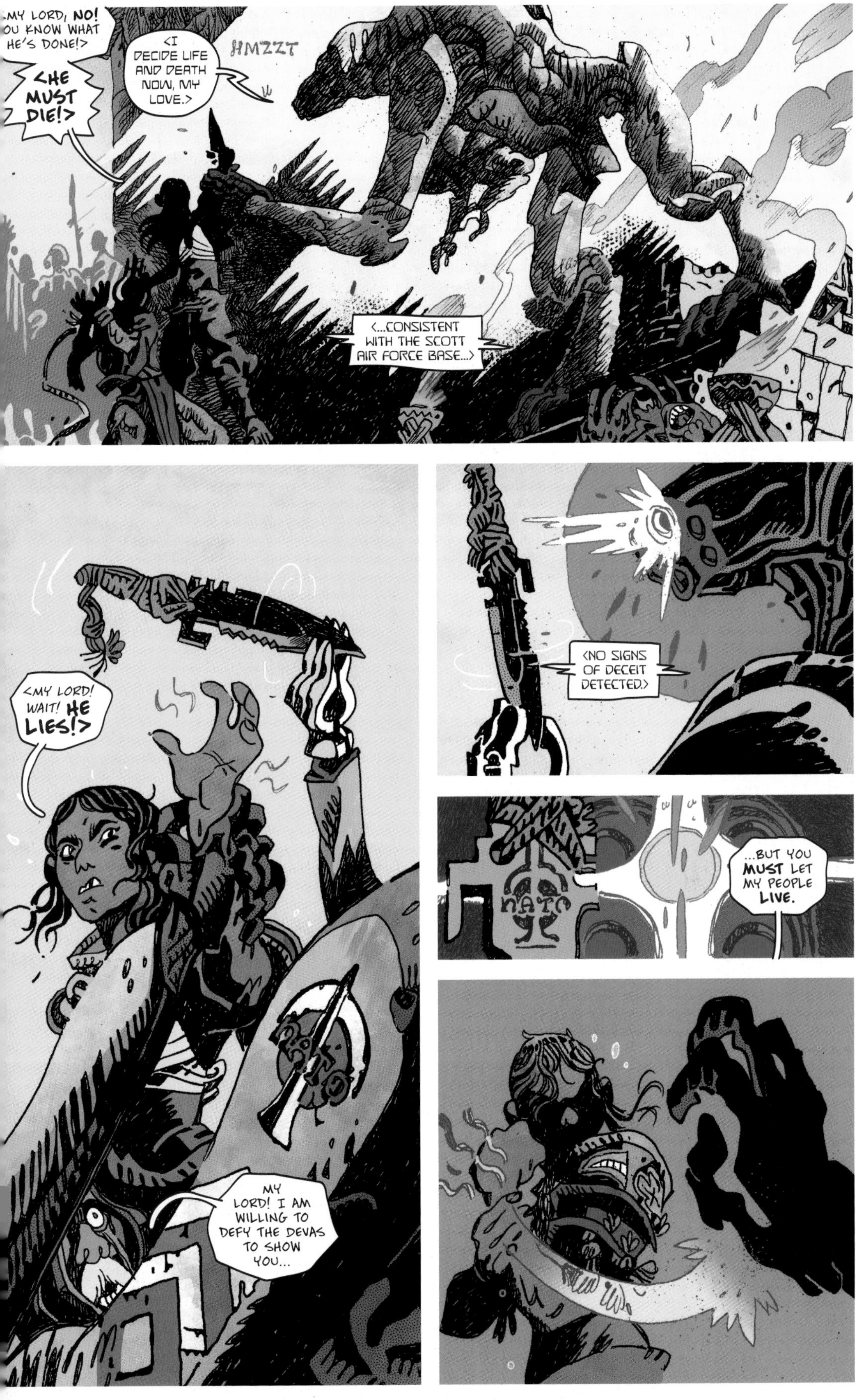
<MY LORD, NO! YOU KNOW WHAT HE'S DONE!>
<HE MUST DIE!>
<I DECIDE LIFE AND DEATH NOW, MY LOVE.>
HMZZT
<...CONSISTENT WITH THE SCOTT AIR FORCE BASE...>
<MY LORD! WAIT! HE LIES!>
MY LORD! I AM WILLING TO DEFY THE DEVAS TO SHOW YOU...
<NO SIGNS OF DECEIT DETECTED.>
...BUT YOU MUST LET MY PEOPLE LIVE.

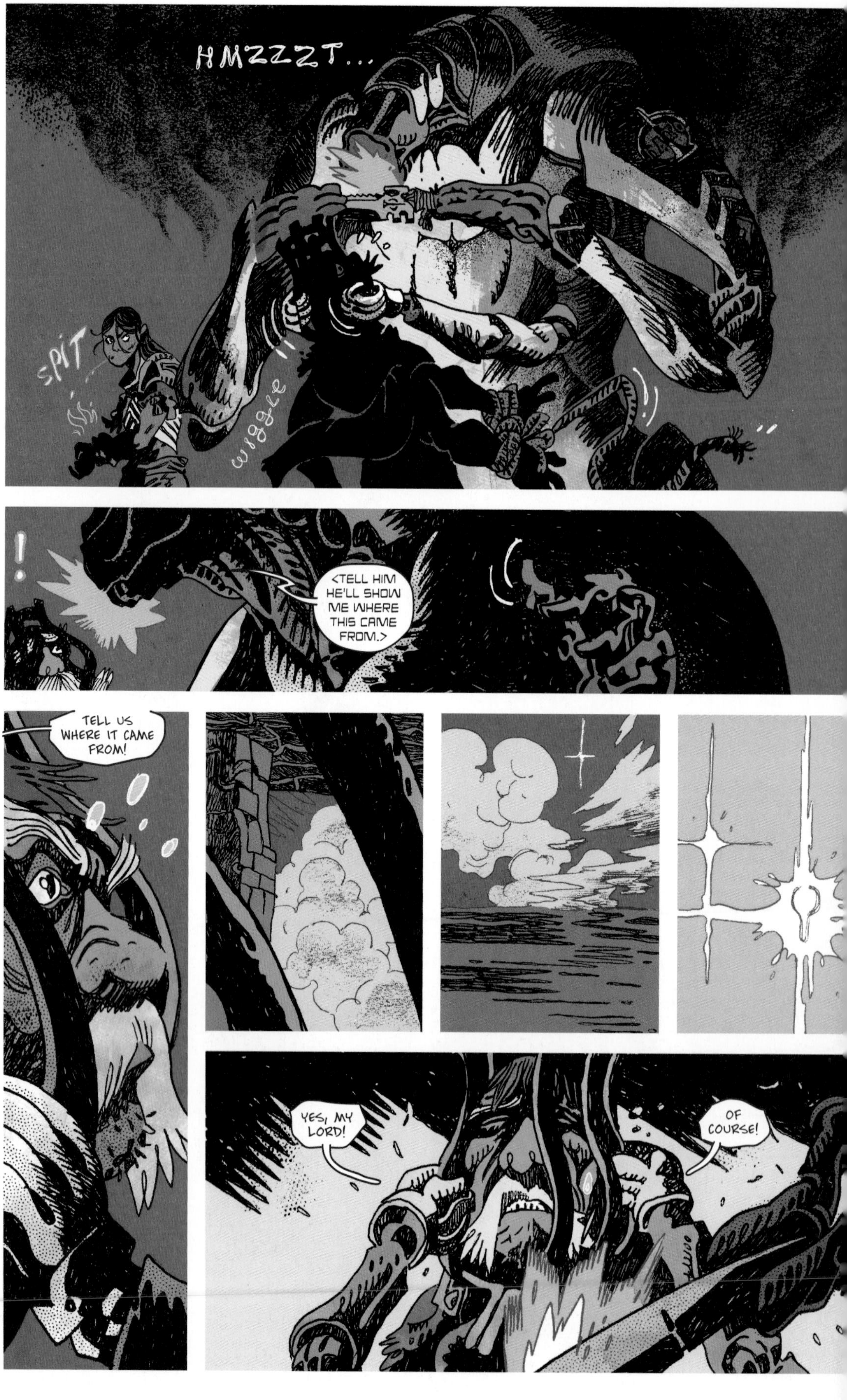
HMZZZT...
SPIT
WIGGLE
!
<TELL HIM HE'LL SHOW ME WHERE THIS CAME FROM.>
TELL US WHERE IT CAME FROM!
YES, MY LORD!
OF COURSE!

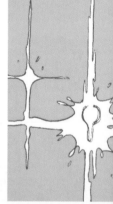

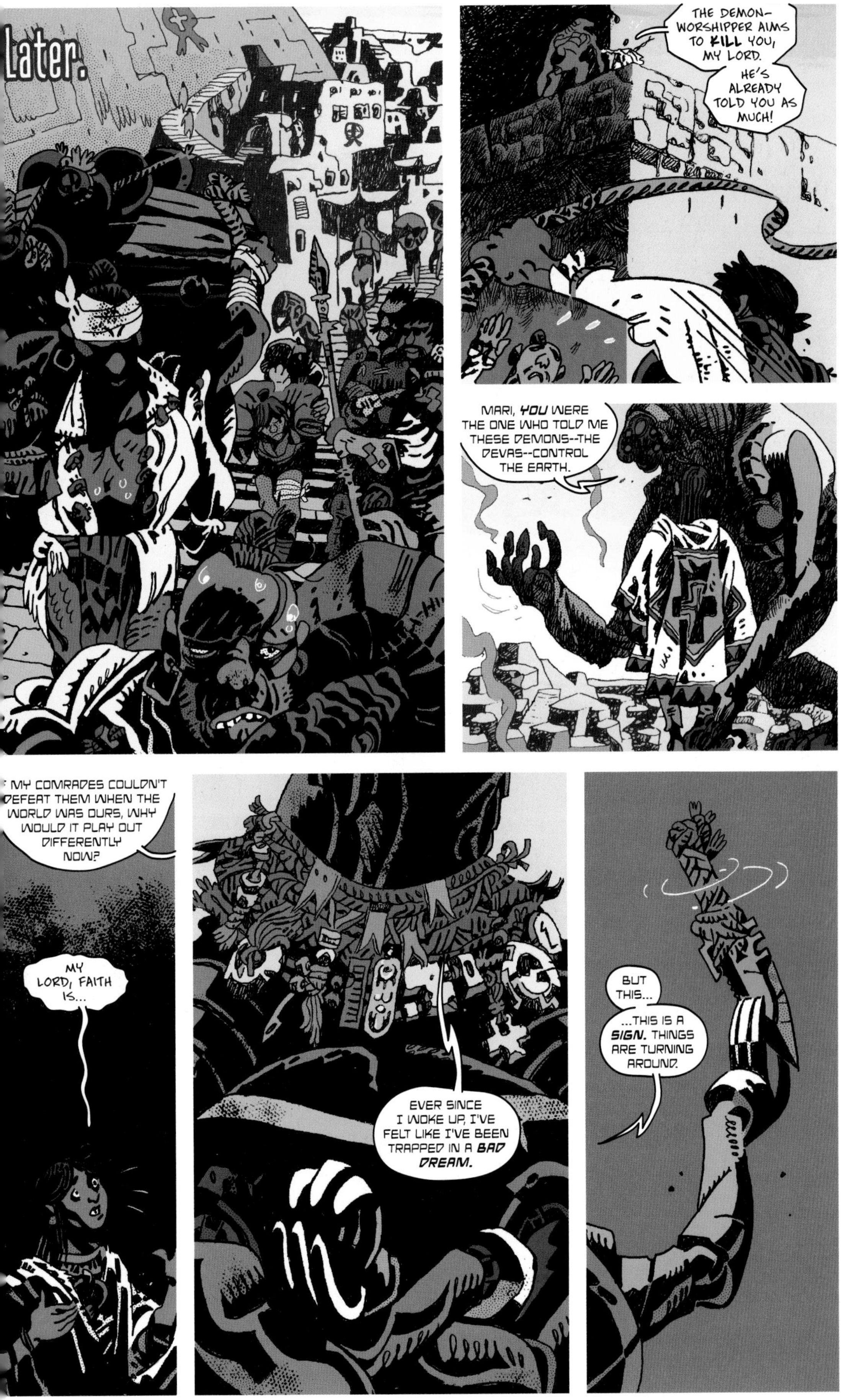
Later.
THE DEMON-WORSHIPPER AIMS TO KILL YOU, MY LORD.
HE'S ALREADY TOLD YOU AS MUCH!
MARI, YOU WERE THE ONE WHO TOLD ME THESE DEMONS--THE DEVAS--CONTROL THE EARTH.
IF MY COMRADES COULDN'T DEFEAT THEM WHEN THE WORLD WAS OURS, WHY WOULD IT PLAY OUT DIFFERENTLY NOW?
MY LORD, FAITH IS...
EVER SINCE I WOKE UP, I'VE FELT LIKE I'VE BEEN TRAPPED IN A BAD DREAM.
BUT THIS...
...THIS IS A SIGN. THINGS ARE TURNING AROUND.

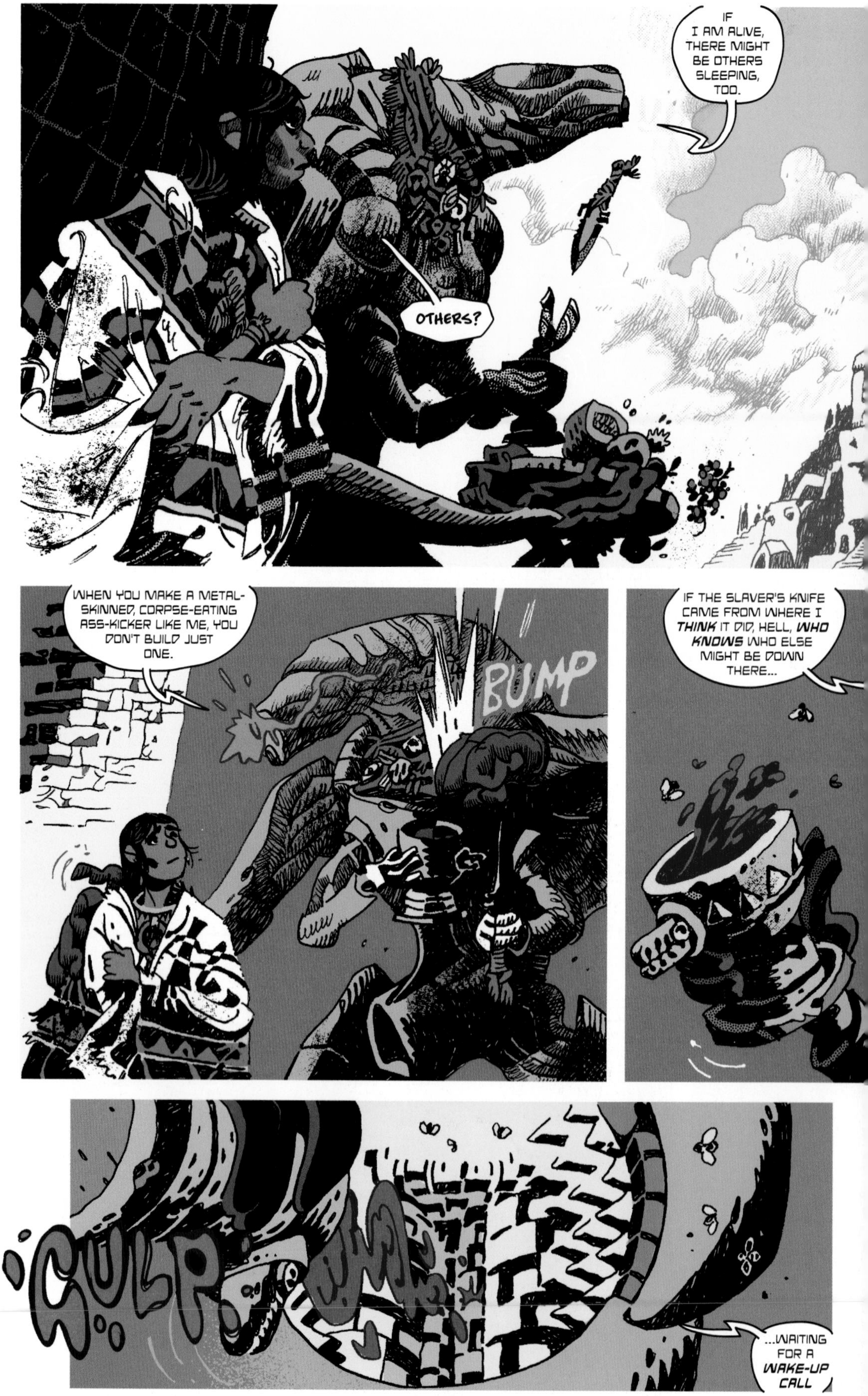
IF I AM ALIVE, THERE MIGHT BE OTHERS SLEEPING, TOO.
OTHERS?
WHEN YOU MAKE A METAL-SKINNED, CORPSE-EATING ASS-KICKER LIKE ME, YOU DON'T BUILD JUST ONE.
BUMP
IF THE SLAVER'S KNIFE CAME FROM WHERE I THINK IT DID, HELL, WHO KNOWS WHO ELSE MIGHT BE DOWN THERE...
GULP
...WAITING FOR A WAKE-UP CALL

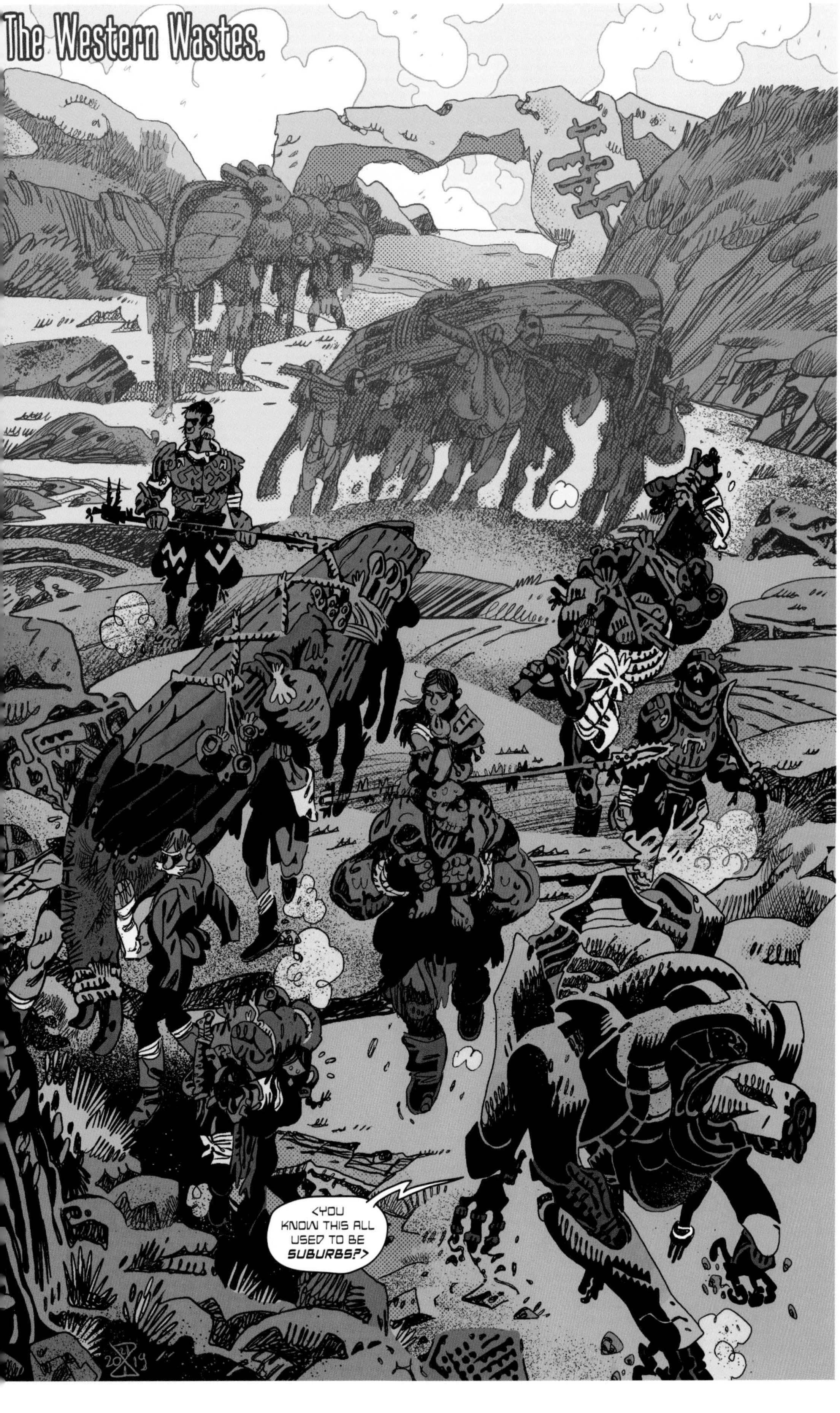
The Western Wastes.
<YOU KNOW THIS ALL USED TO BE SUBURBS?>

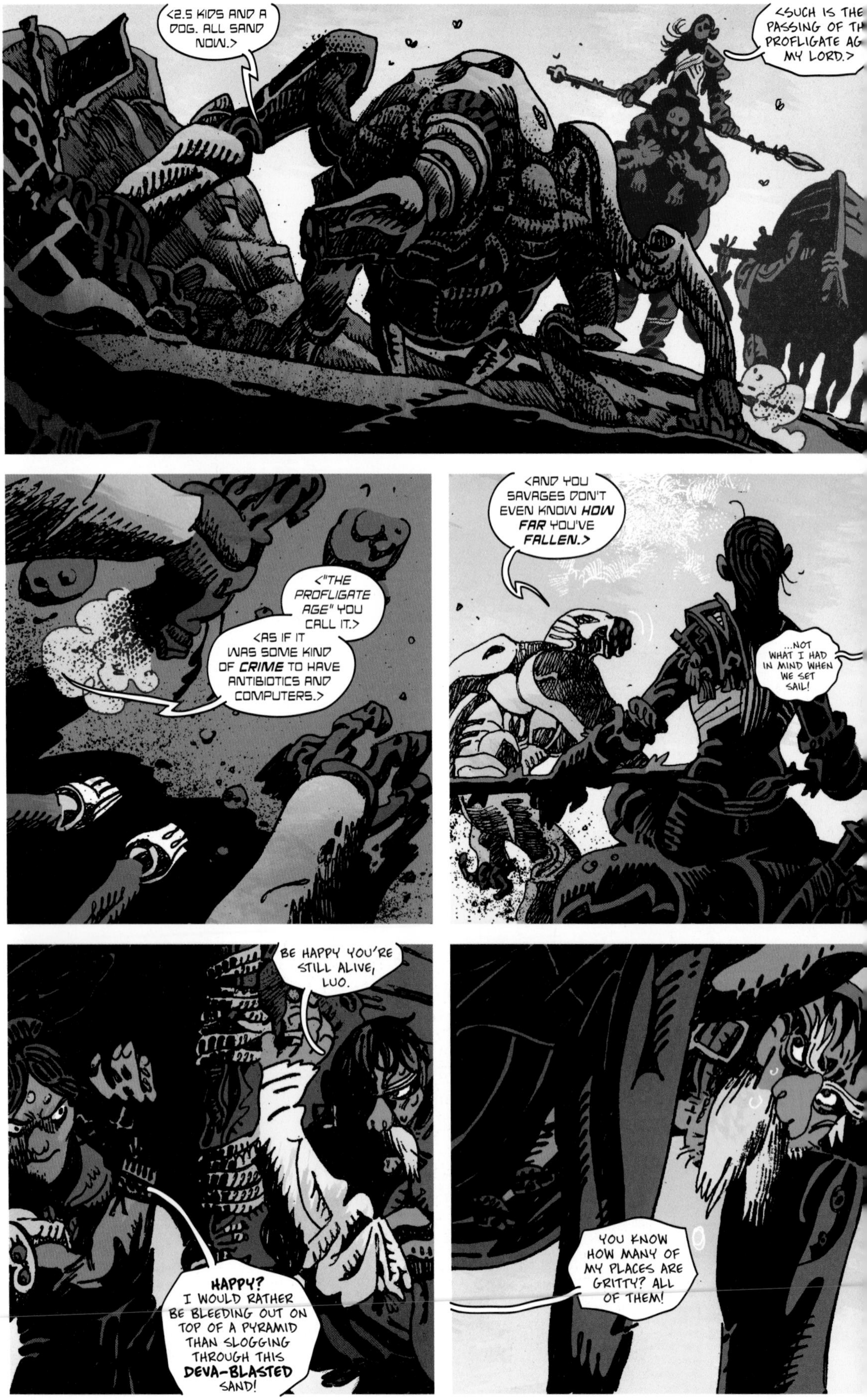

<2.5 KIDS AND A DOG. ALL SAND NOW.>
<SUCH IS THE PASSING OF TH PROFLIGATE AG MY LORD.>
<"THE PROFLIGATE AGE" YOU CALL IT.>
<AS IF IT WAS SOME KIND OF CRIME TO HAVE ANTIBIOTICS AND COMPUTERS.>
<AND YOU SAVAGES DON'T EVEN KNOW HOW FAR YOU'VE FALLEN.>
...NOT WHAT I HAD IN MIND WHEN WE SET SAIL!
BE HAPPY YOU'RE STILL ALIVE, LUO.
HAPPY? I WOULD RATHER BE BLEEDING OUT ON TOP OF A PYRAMID THAN SLOGGING THROUGH THIS DEVA-BLASTED SAND!
YOU KNOW HOW MANY OF MY PLACES ARE GRITTY? ALL OF THEM!

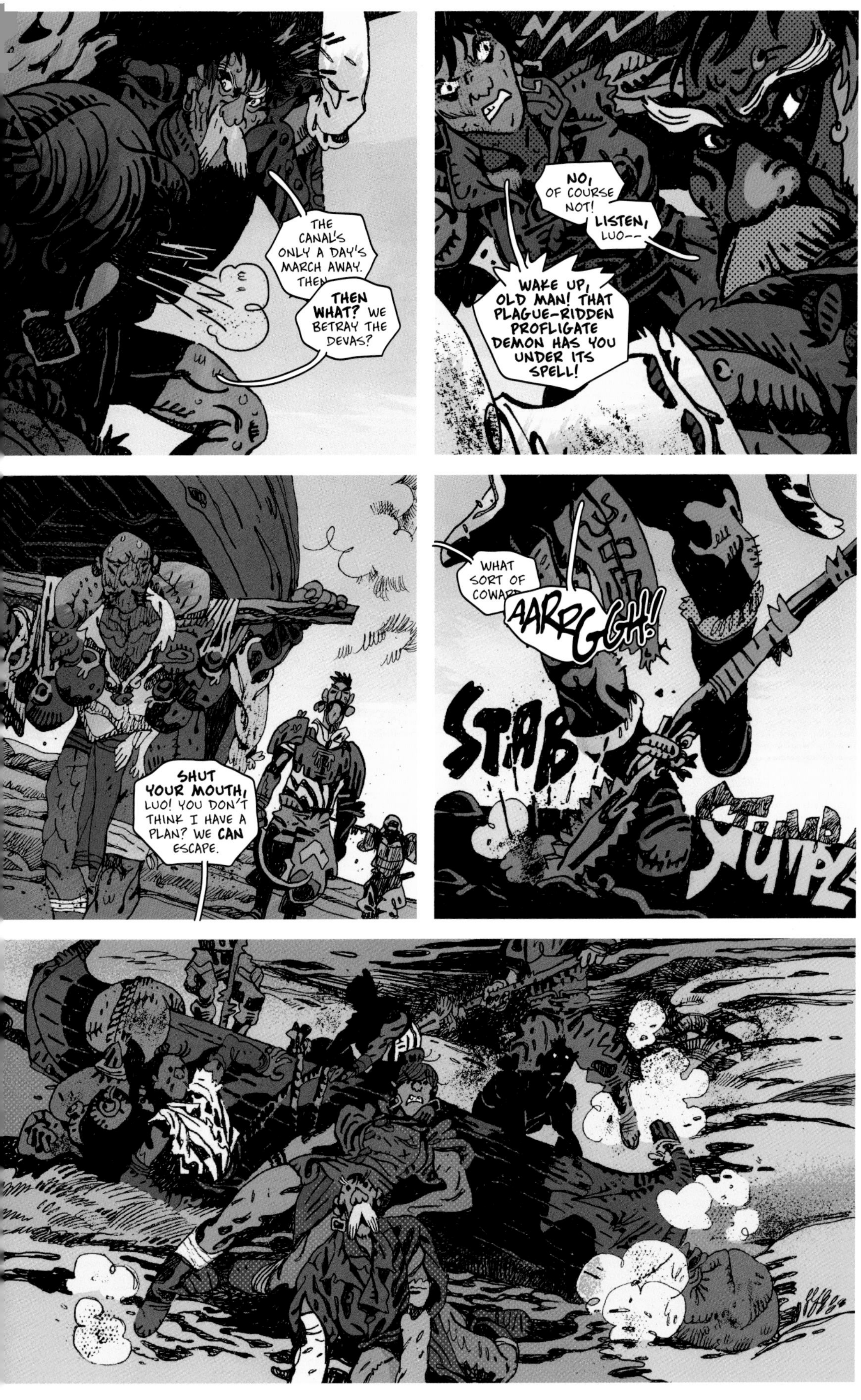

THE CANAL'S ONLY A DAY'S MARCH AWAY. THEN
THEN WHAT? WE BETRAY THE DEVAS?
NO, OF COURSE NOT!
LISTEN, LUO--
WAKE UP, OLD MAN! THAT PLAGUE-RIDDEN PROFLIGATE DEMON HAS YOU UNDER ITS SPELL!
SHUT YOUR MOUTH, LUO! YOU DON'T THINK I HAVE A PLAN? WE CAN ESCAPE.
WHAT SORT OF COWARD
AARRGGH!
STAB
STUMBLE

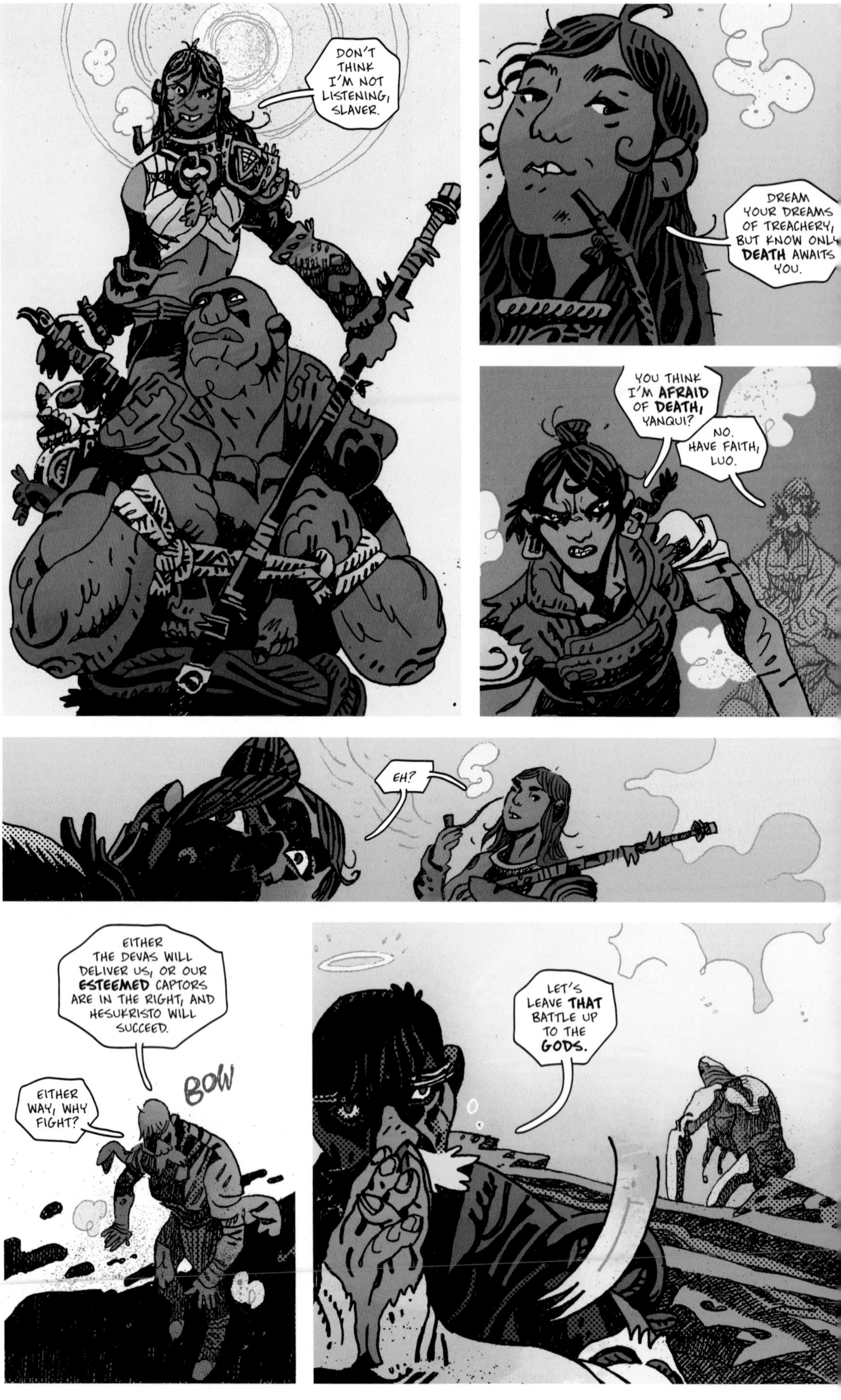
DON'T THINK I'M NOT LISTENING, SLAVER.
DREAM YOUR DREAMS OF TREACHERY, BUT KNOW ONLY DEATH AWAITS YOU.
YOU THINK I'M AFRAID OF DEATH, YANQUI?
NO. HAVE FAITH, LUO.
EH?
EITHER THE DEVAS WILL DELIVER US, OR OUR ESTEEMED CAPTORS ARE IN THE RIGHT, AND HESUKRISTO WILL SUCCEED.
EITHER WAY, WHY FIGHT?
BOW
LET'S LEAVE THAT BATTLE UP TO THE GODS.

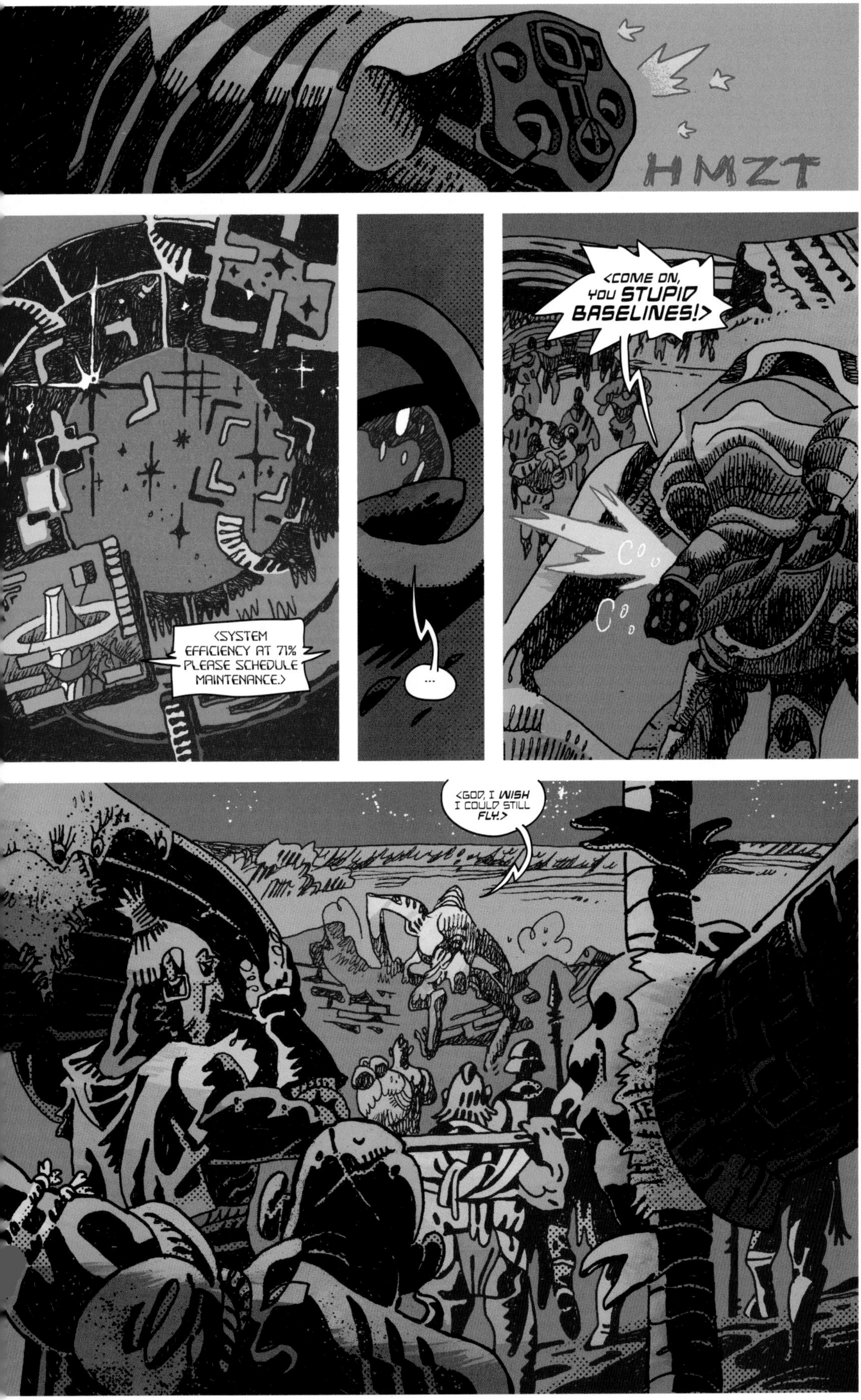
HMZT
<SYSTEM EFFICIENCY AT 71% PLEASE SCHEDULE MAINTENANCE.>
...
<COME ON, YOU STUPID BASELINES!>
<GOD, I WISH I COULD STILL FLY.>

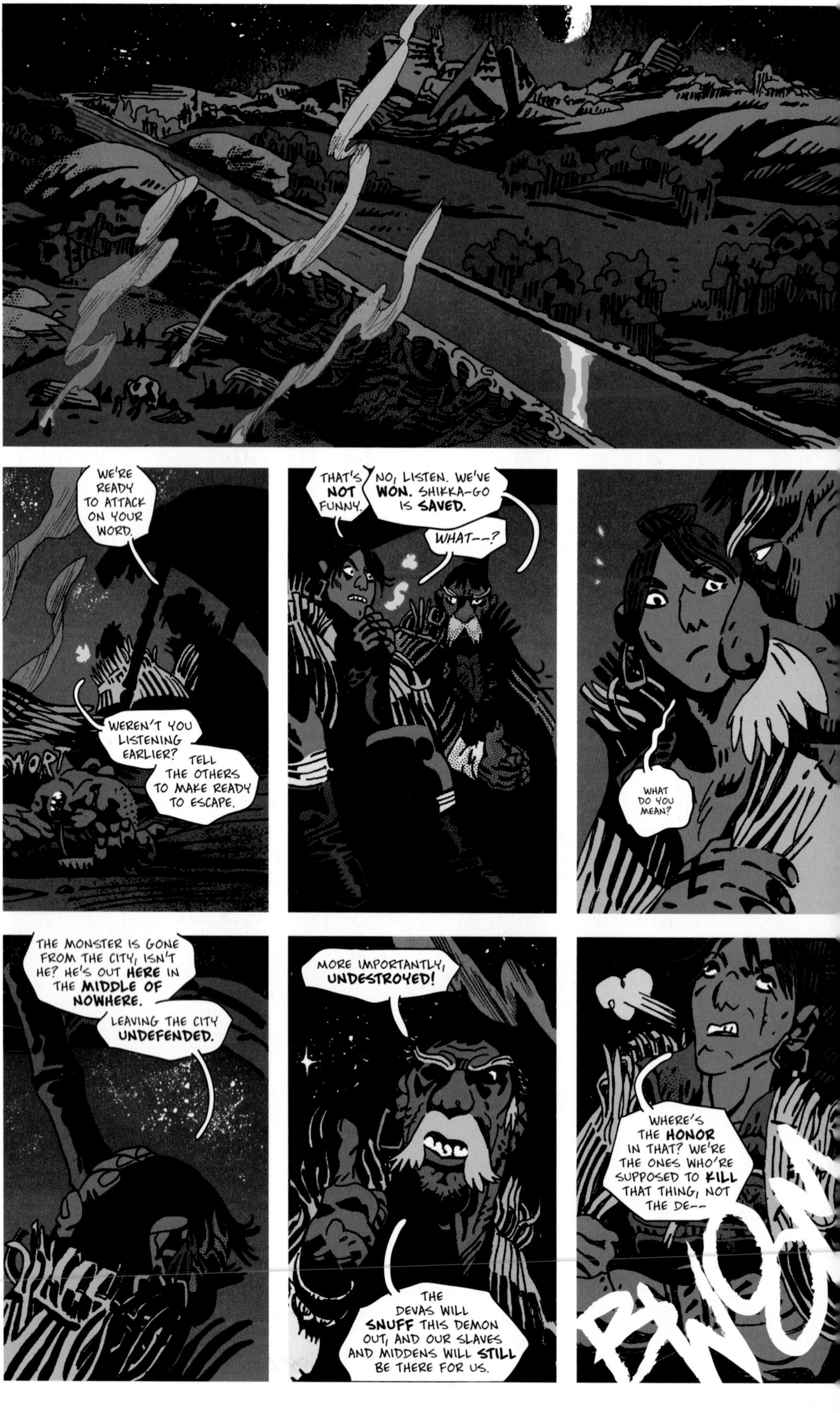

WE'RE READY TO ATTACK ON YOUR WORD.
WEREN'T YOU LISTENING EARLIER?
TELL THE OTHERS TO MAKE READY TO ESCAPE.
WORT
THAT'S **NOT** FUNNY.
NO, LISTEN. WE'VE **WON.** SHIKKA-GO IS **SAVED.**
WHAT--?
WHAT DO YOU MEAN?
THE MONSTER IS GONE FROM THE CITY, ISN'T HE? HE'S OUT **HERE** IN THE **MIDDLE OF NOWHERE.**
LEAVING THE CITY **UNDEFENDED.**
MORE IMPORTANTLY, **UNDESTROYED!**
THE DEVAS WILL **SNUFF** THIS DEMON OUT, AND OUR SLAVES AND MIDDENS WILL **STILL** BE THERE FOR US.
WHERE'S THE **HONOR** IN THAT? WE'RE THE ONES WHO'RE SUPPOSED TO **KILL** THAT THING, NOT THE DE--

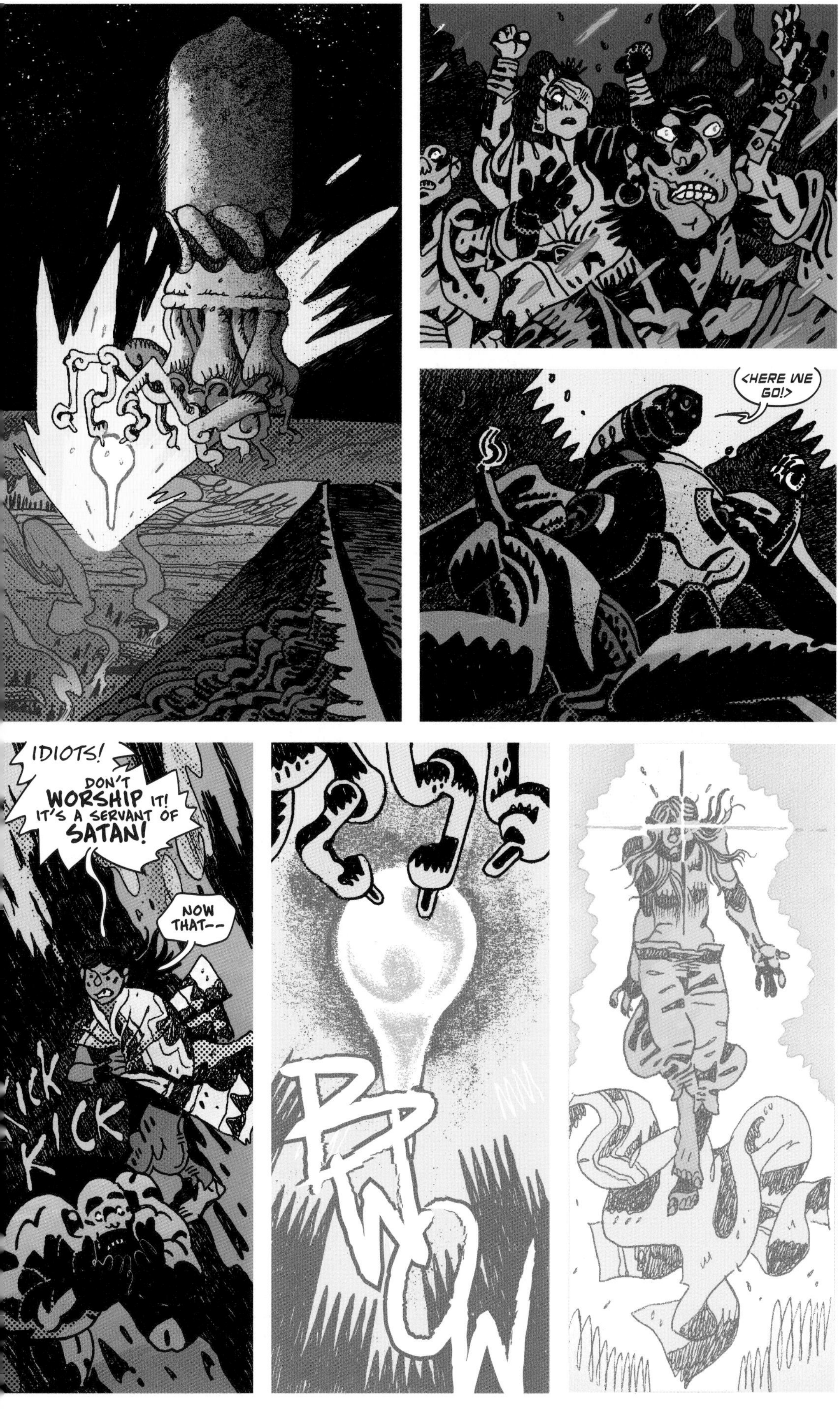
<HERE WE GO!>
IDIOTS!
DON'T WORSHIP IT! IT'S A SERVANT OF SATAN!
NOW THAT--
KICK KICK
BRWOM

HUMANS! A CLEANSING IS UPON YOU! CLEAR THE AREA AROUND THIS DEMON.

THE DEVA CHOSE...

...MARI?

RELOCATE IMMEDIATELY TO A DISTANCE OF...

<WARNING, DESTRUCTION OF DEVA ROBOT DURING NEURAL INDUCTION RISKS BRAIN DAMAGE TO INDUCTEE.>

<SHIT.>

BOW, LUO, SHOW YOUR RESPECT.

...OR YOU WILL ALL BURN ALONGSIDE IT.

LUO!

NEVER! SHE'S NO HUDSONI!

I WILL NEVER BOW DOWN TO HER.

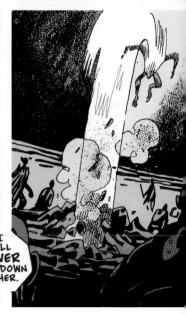

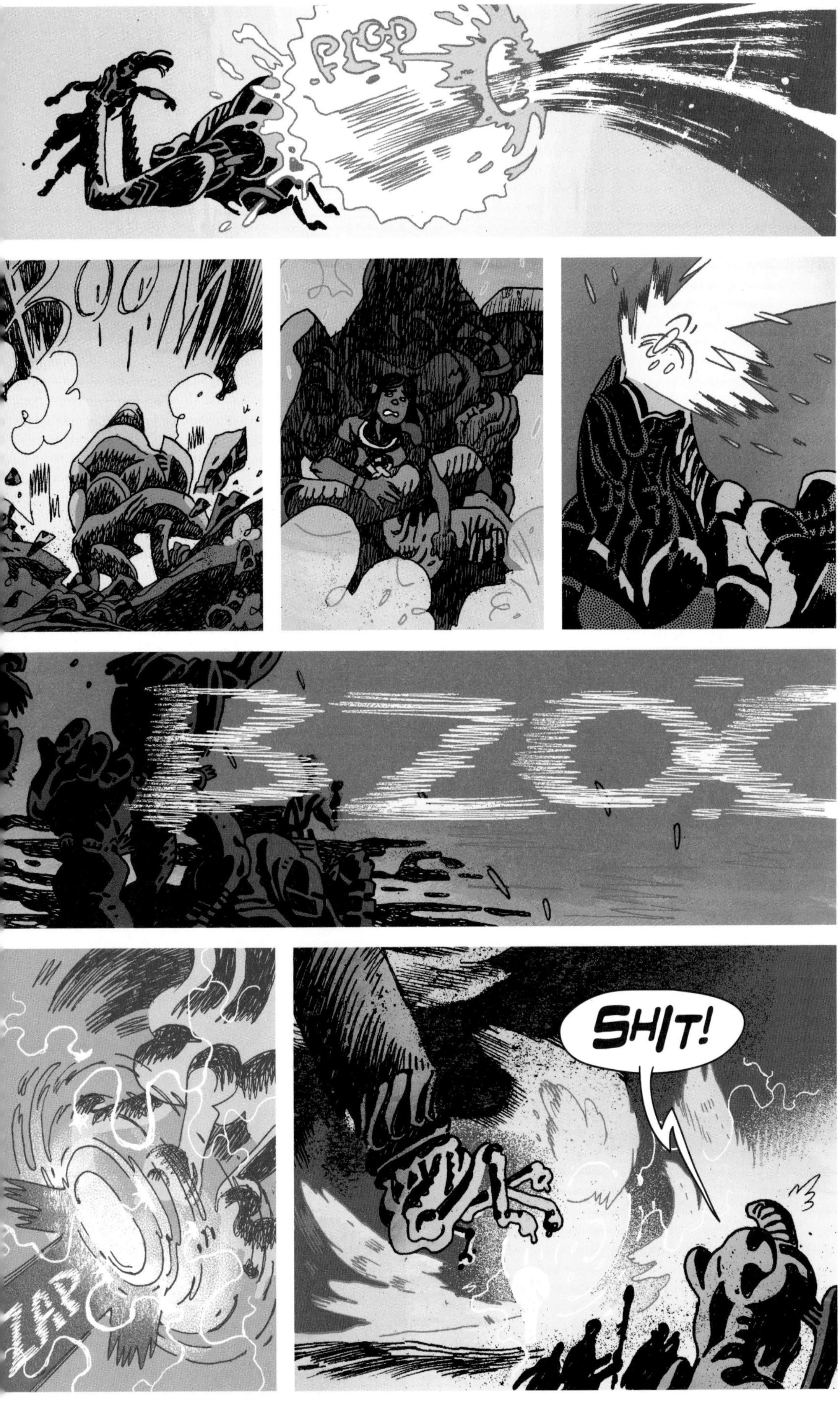
FLOP
BOOM
BZOX
ZAP
SHIT!

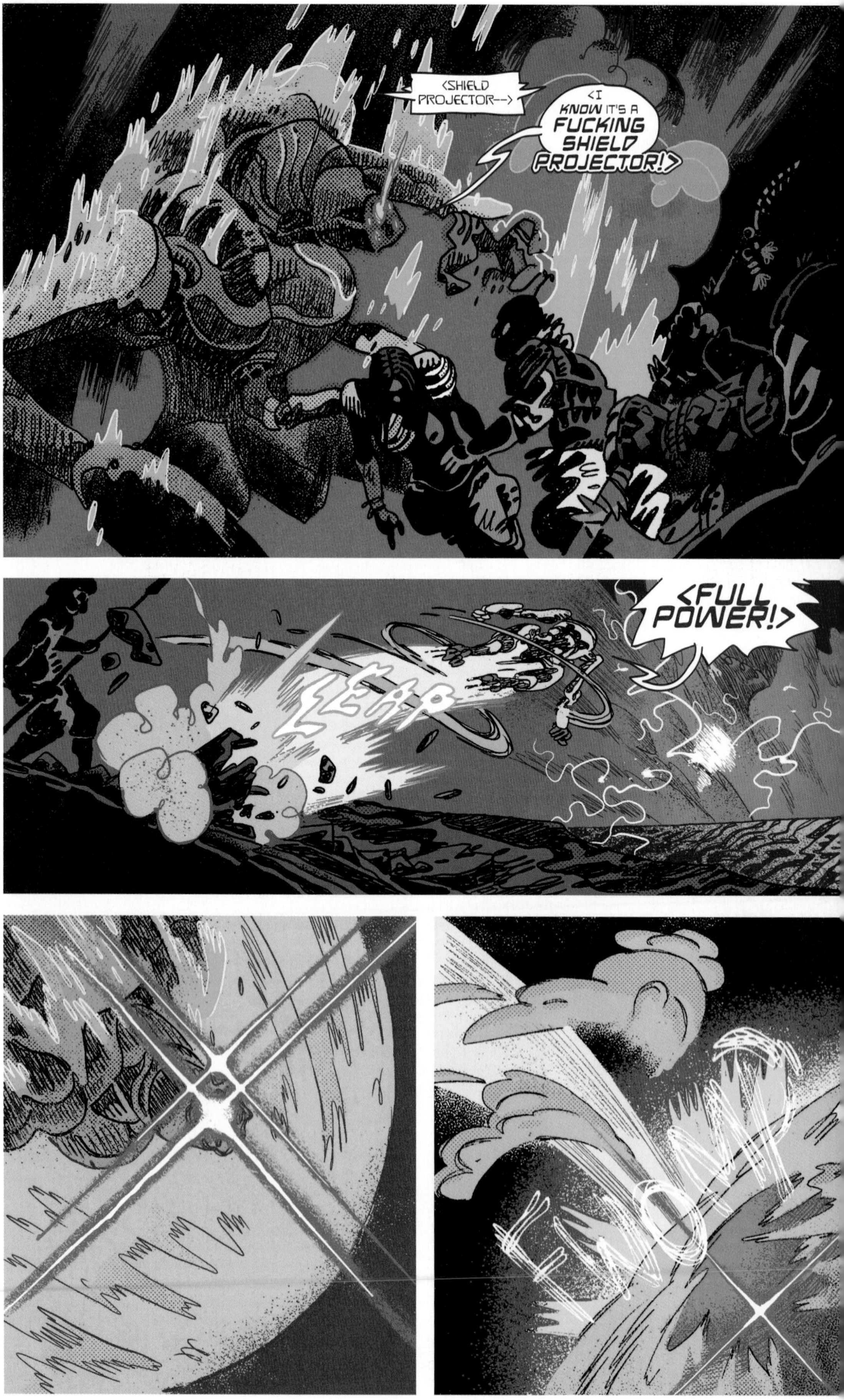
<SHIELD PROJECTOR-->
<I KNOW IT'S A FUCKING SHIELD PROJECTOR!>
<FULL POWER!>
LEAP
FWOOMP

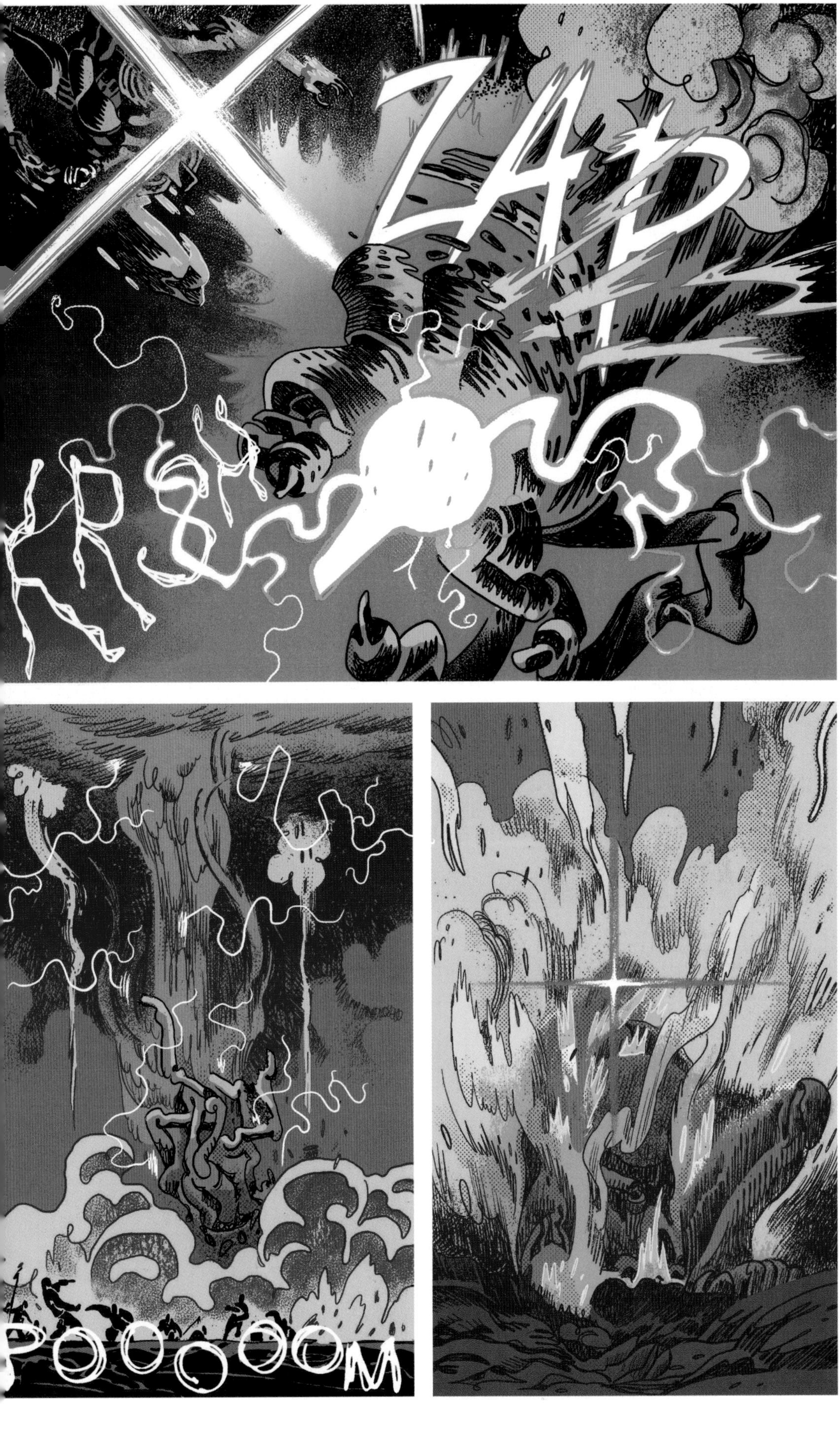
ZAP
KRSSH
POOOOOM

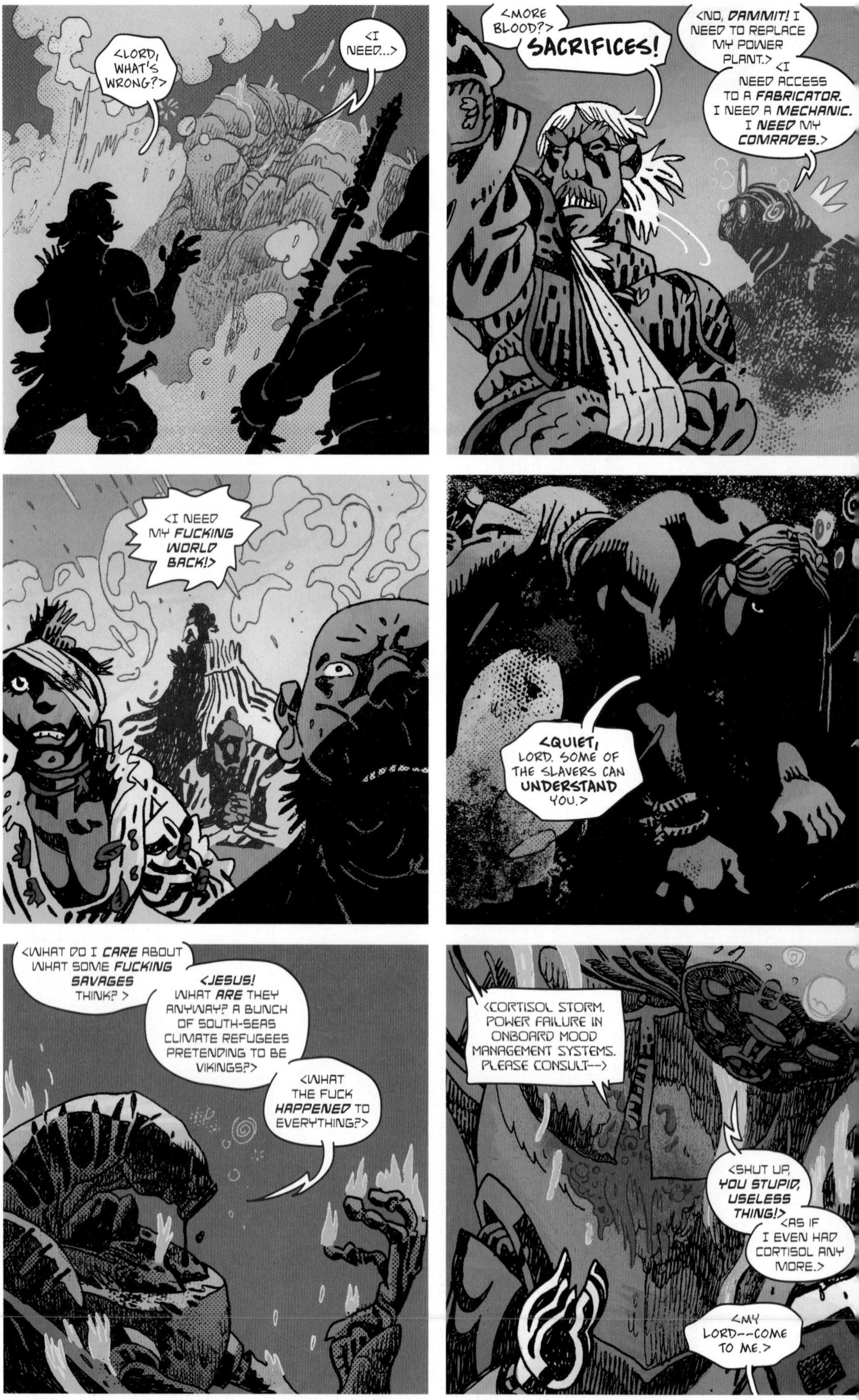
<LORD, WHAT'S WRONG?>
<I NEED...>
<MORE BLOOD?> SACRIFICES!
<NO, DAMMIT! I NEED TO REPLACE MY POWER PLANT.>
<I NEED ACCESS TO A FABRICATOR. I NEED A MECHANIC. I NEED MY COMRADES.>
<I NEED MY FUCKING WORLD BACK!>
<QUIET, LORD. SOME OF THE SLAVERS CAN UNDERSTAND YOU.>
<WHAT DO I CARE ABOUT WHAT SOME FUCKING SAVAGES THINK? >
<JESUS! WHAT ARE THEY ANYWAY? A BUNCH OF SOUTH-SEAS CLIMATE REFUGEES PRETENDING TO BE VIKINGS?>
<WHAT THE FUCK HAPPENED TO EVERYTHING?>
<CORTISOL STORM. POWER FAILURE IN ONBOARD MOOD MANAGEMENT SYSTEMS. PLEASE CONSULT-->
<SHUT UP, YOU STUPID, USELESS THING!>
<AS IF I EVEN HAD CORTISOL ANY MORE.>
<MY LORD--COME TO ME.>

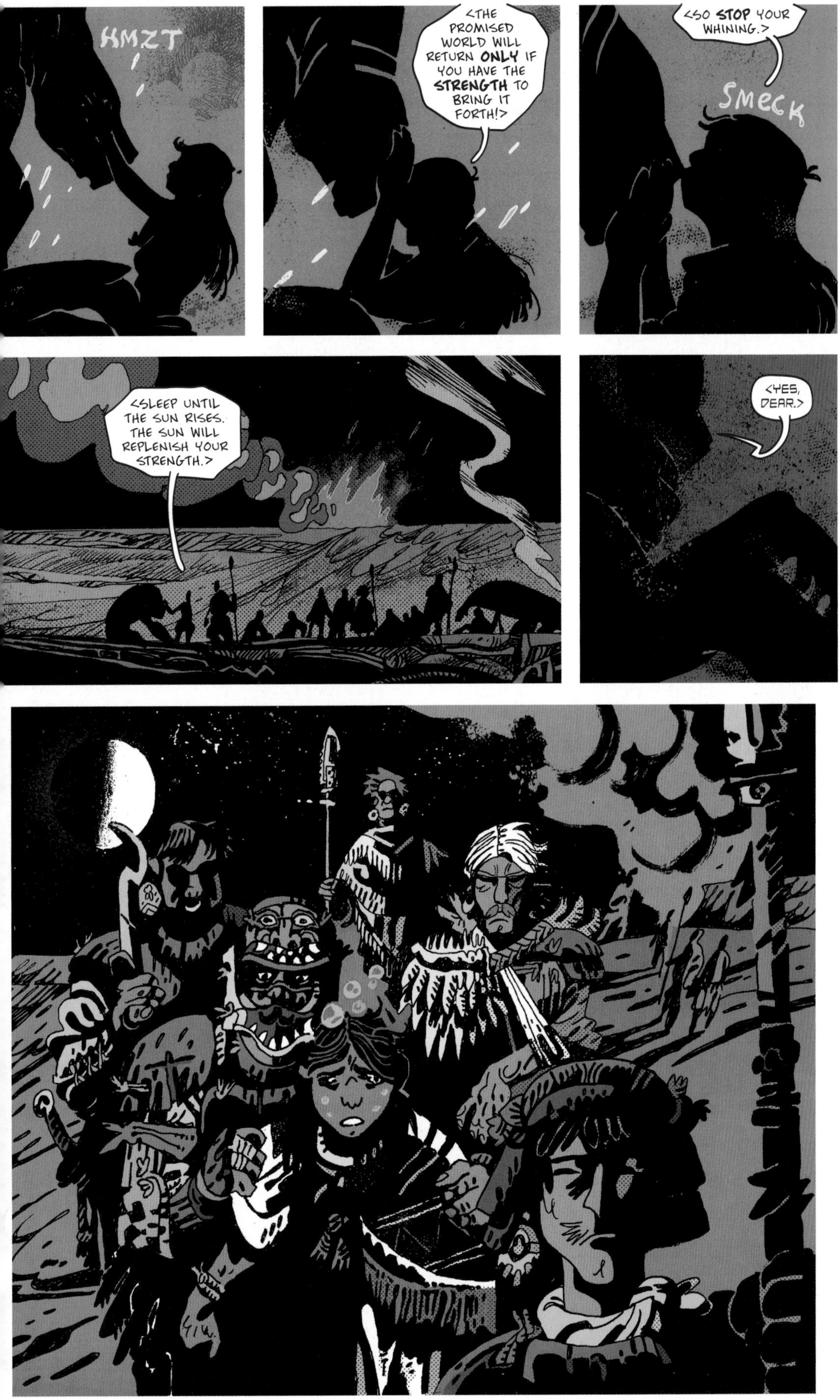
HMZT
<THE PROMISED WORLD WILL RETURN ONLY IF YOU HAVE THE STRENGTH TO BRING IT FORTH!>
<SO STOP YOUR WHINING.>
SMECK
<SLEEP UNTIL THE SUN RISES. THE SUN WILL REPLENISH YOUR STRENGTH.>
<YES, DEAR.>

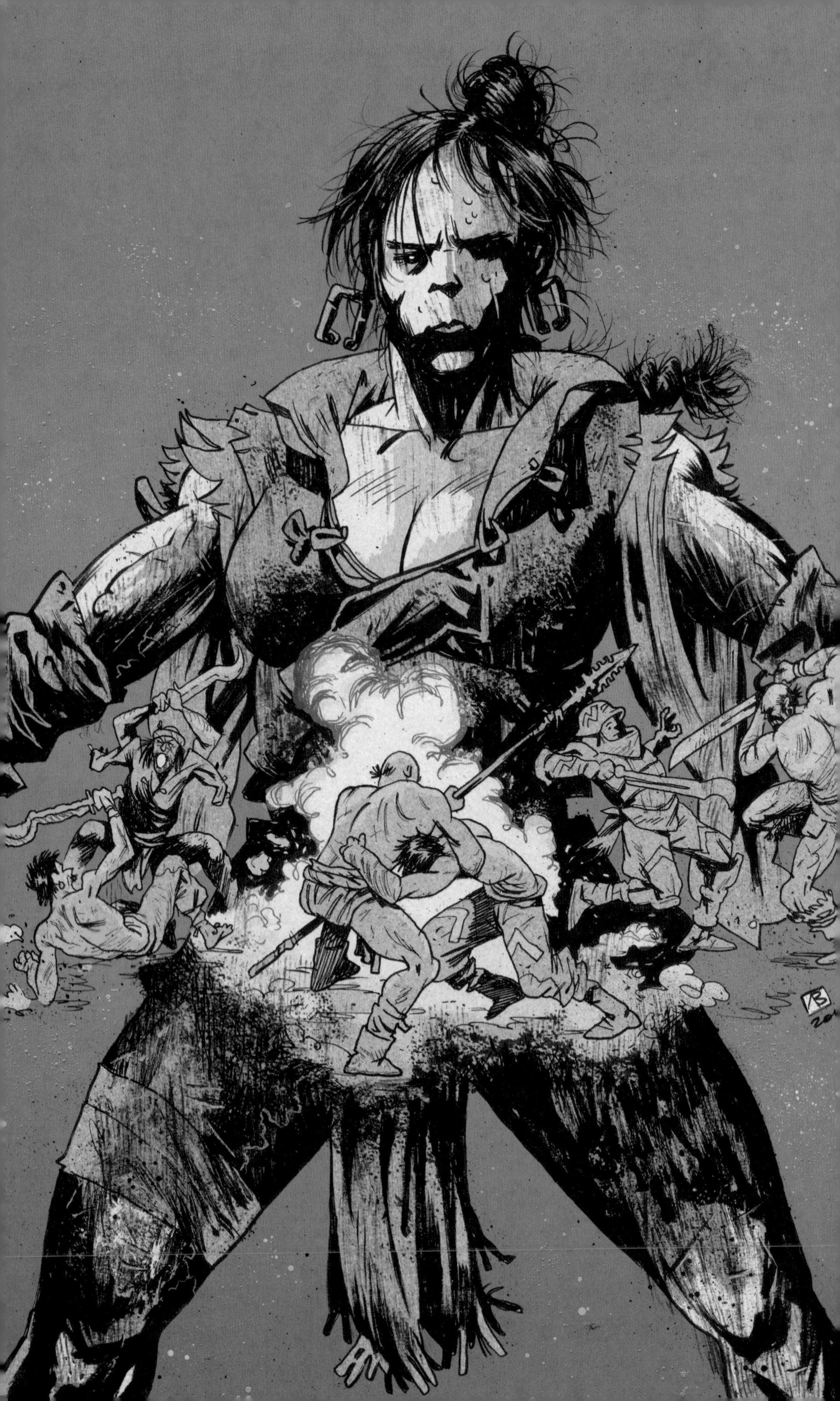

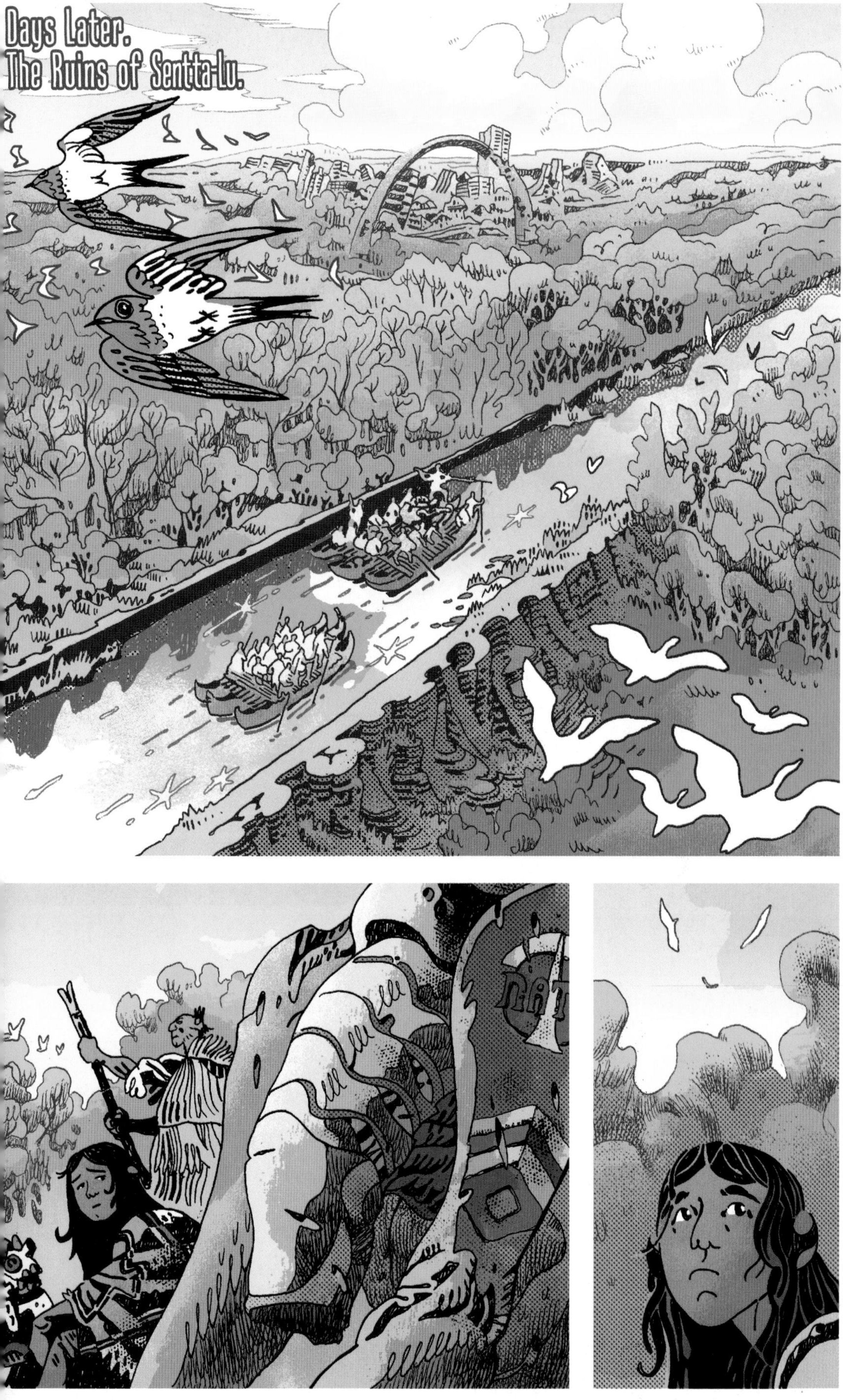
Days Later.
The Ruins of Sentta-Lu.

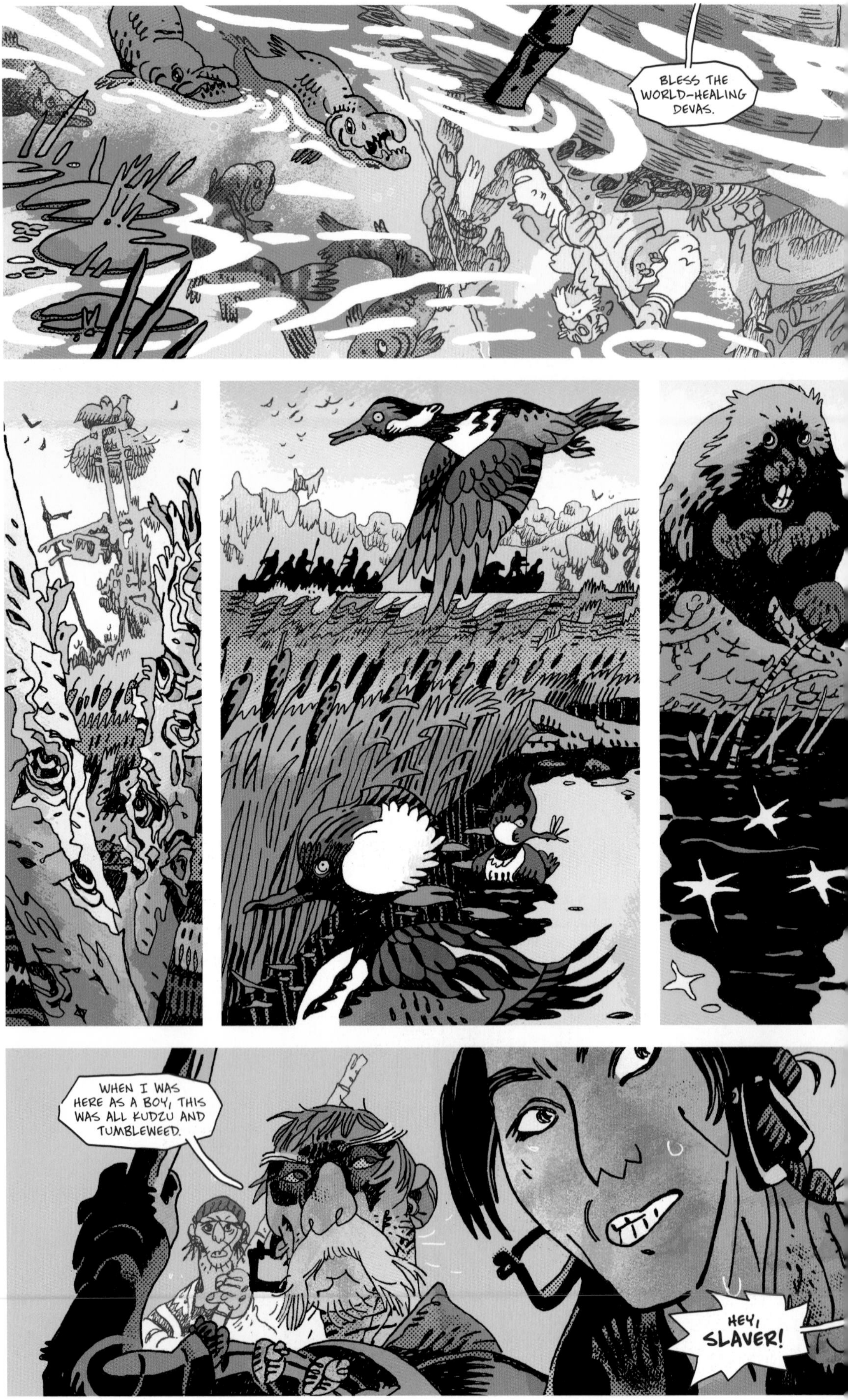
BLESS THE WORLD-HEALING DEVAS.
WHEN I WAS HERE AS A BOY, THIS WAS ALL KUDZU AND TUMBLEWEED.
HEY, SLAVER!

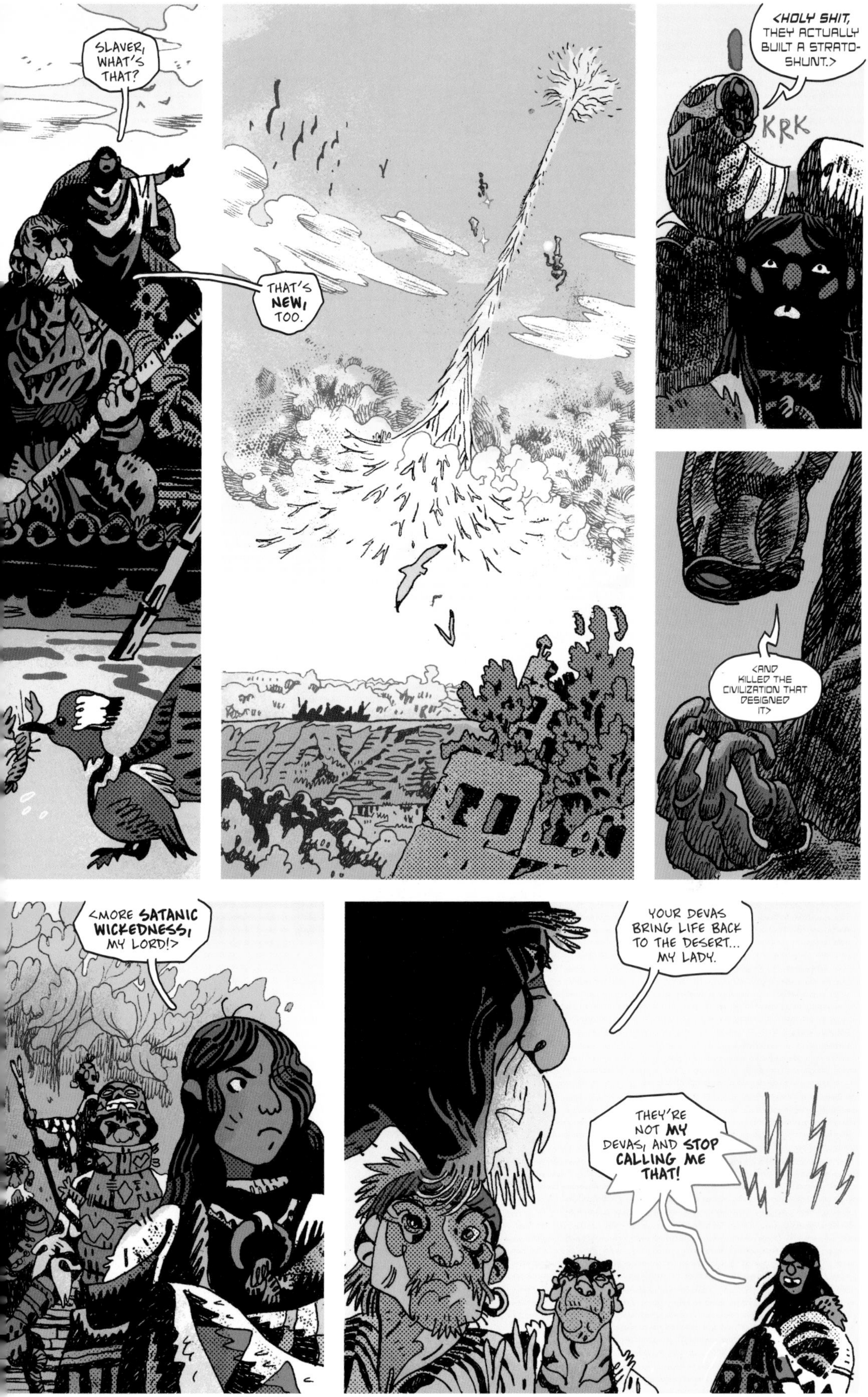
SLAVER, WHAT'S THAT?
THAT'S NEW, TOO.
<HOLY SHIT, THEY ACTUALLY BUILT A STRATO-SHUNT.>
KRK
<AND KILLED THE CIVILIZATION THAT DESIGNED IT>
<MORE SATANIC WICKEDNESS, MY LORD!>
YOUR DEVAS BRING LIFE BACK TO THE DESERT... MY LADY.
THEY'RE NOT MY DEVAS, AND STOP CALLING ME THAT!

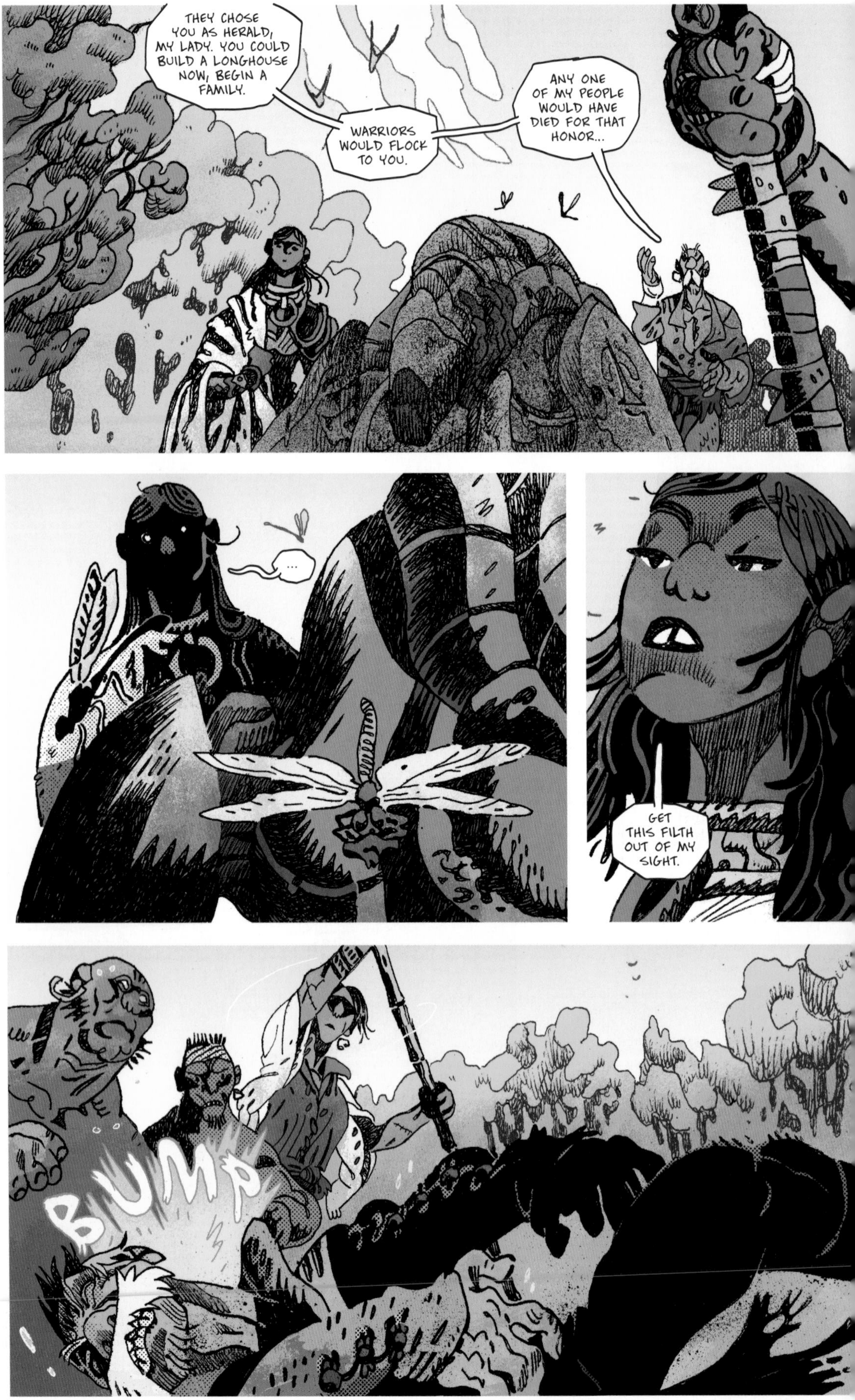
THEY CHOSE YOU AS HERALD, MY LADY. YOU COULD BUILD A LONGHOUSE NOW, BEGIN A FAMILY.
WARRIORS WOULD FLOCK TO YOU.
ANY ONE OF MY PEOPLE WOULD HAVE DIED FOR THAT HONOR...
...
GET THIS FILTH OUT OF MY SIGHT.
BUMP

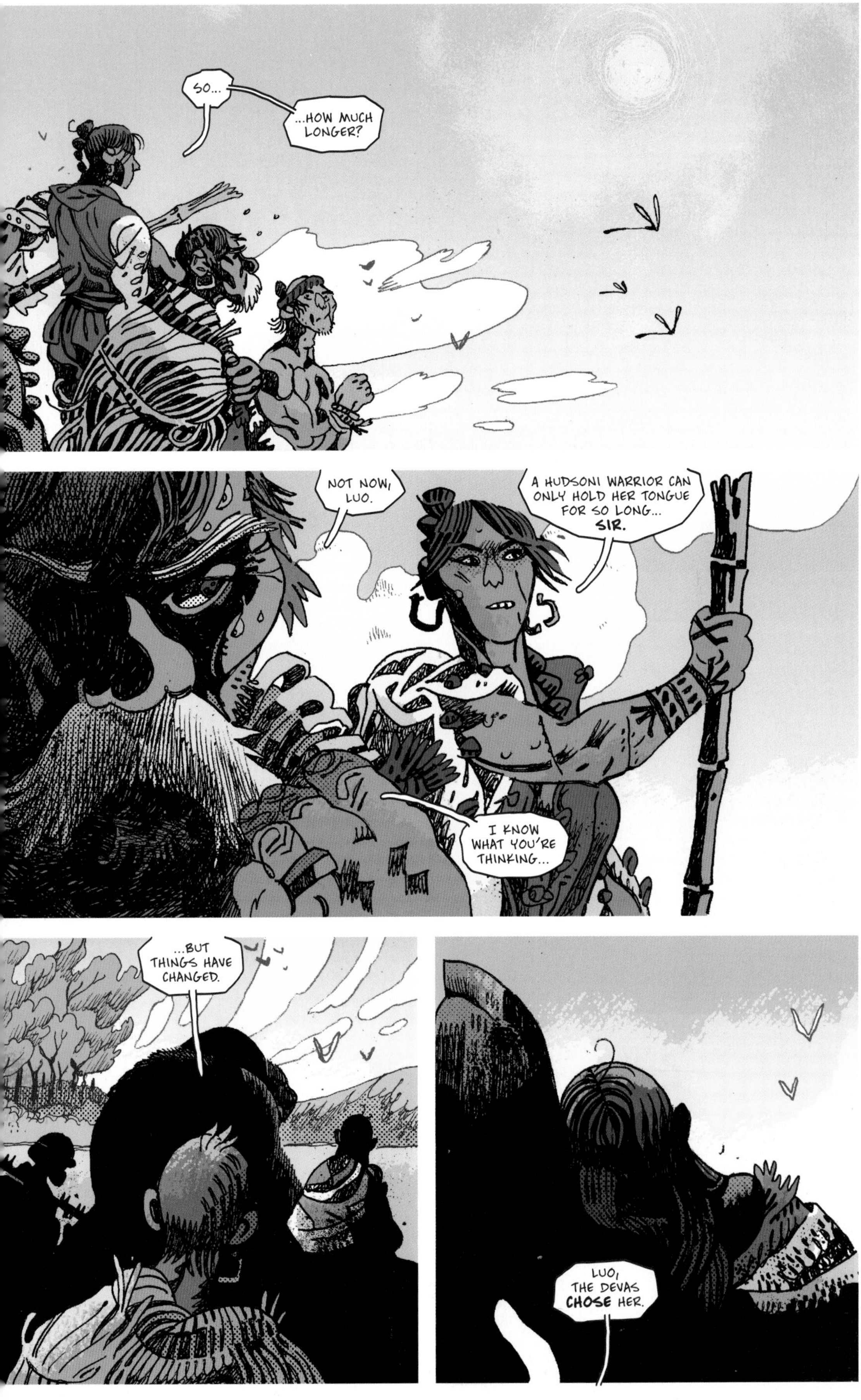
SO...
...HOW MUCH LONGER?
NOT NOW, LUO.
A HUDSONI WARRIOR CAN ONLY HOLD HER TONGUE FOR SO LONG... SIR.
I KNOW WHAT YOU'RE THINKING...
...BUT THINGS HAVE CHANGED.
LUO, THE DEVAS CHOSE HER.

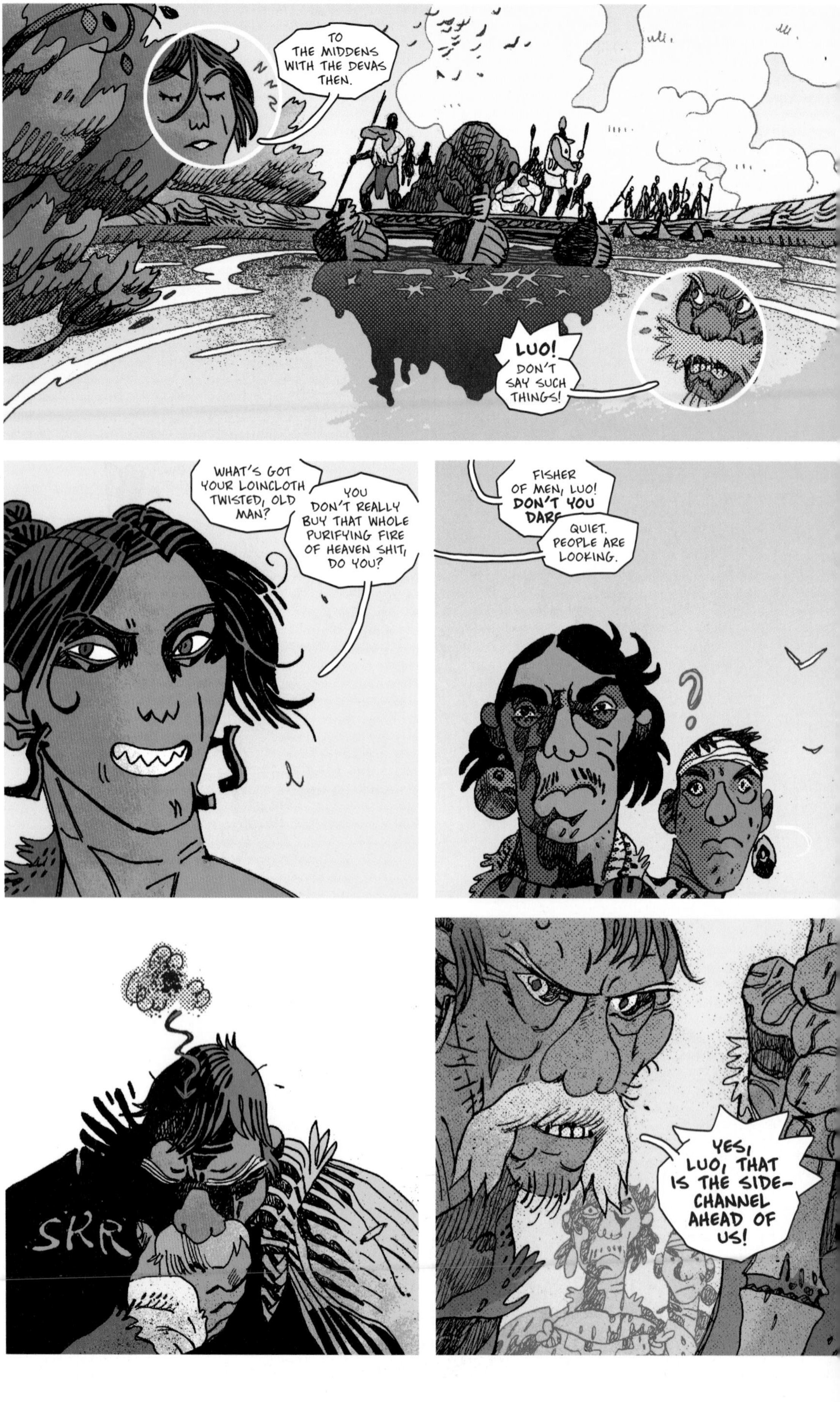
TO THE MIDDENS WITH THE DEVAS THEN.
LUO! DON'T SAY SUCH THINGS!
WHAT'S GOT YOUR LOINCLOTH TWISTED, OLD MAN?
YOU DON'T REALLY BUY THAT WHOLE PURIFYING FIRE OF HEAVEN SHIT, DO YOU?
FISHER OF MEN, LUO! DON'T YOU DAR
QUIET. PEOPLE ARE LOOKING.
SKR
YES, LUO, THAT IS THE SIDE-CHANNEL AHEAD OF US!

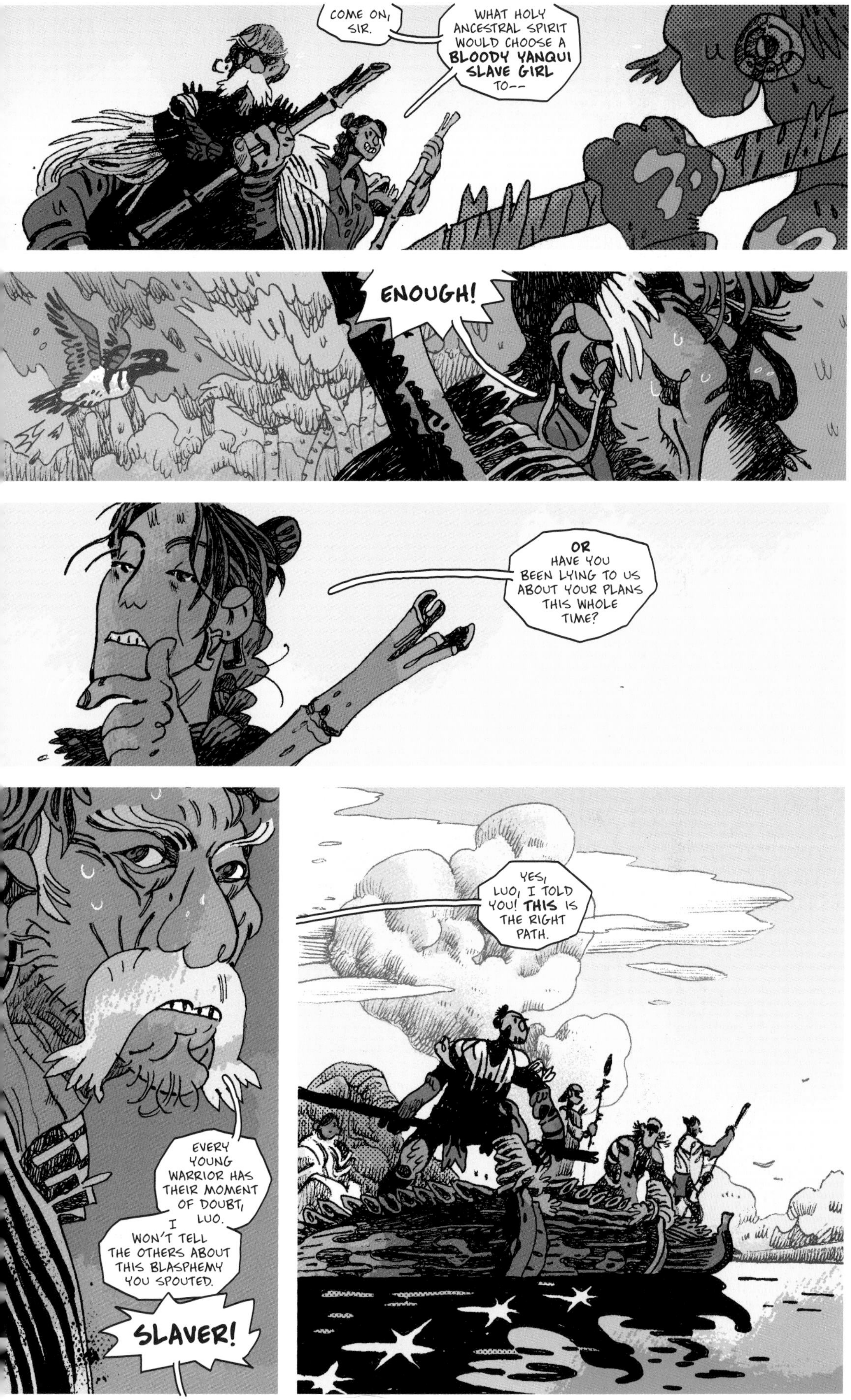
COME ON, SIR.
WHAT HOLY ANCESTRAL SPIRIT WOULD CHOOSE A BLOODY YANQUI SLAVE GIRL TO--
ENOUGH!
OR HAVE YOU BEEN LYING TO US ABOUT YOUR PLANS THIS WHOLE TIME?
EVERY YOUNG WARRIOR HAS THEIR MOMENT OF DOUBT, LUO.
I WON'T TELL THE OTHERS ABOUT THIS BLASPHEMY YOU SPOUTED.
SLAVER!
YES, LUO, I TOLD YOU! THIS IS THE RIGHT PATH.

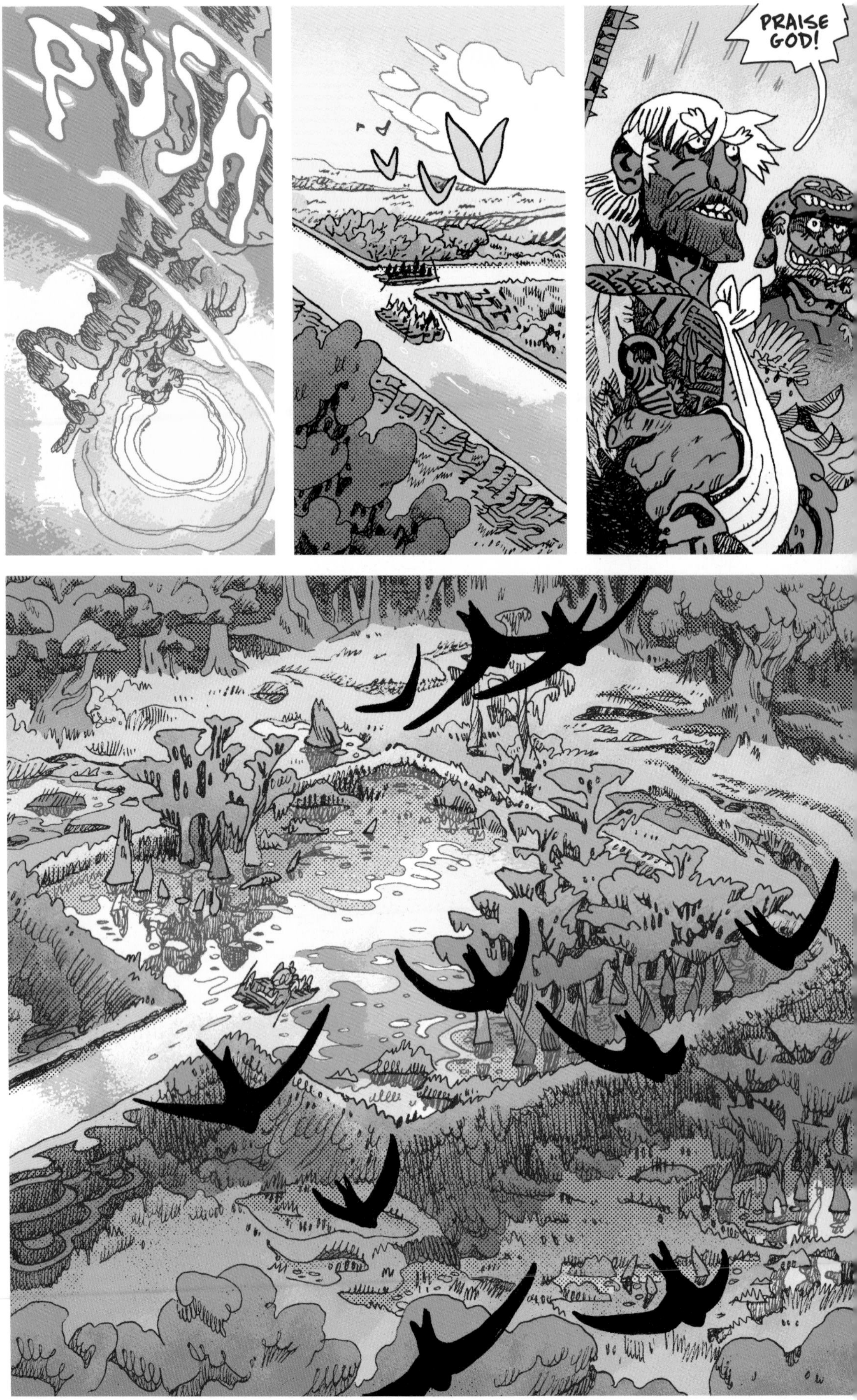
PUSH
PRAISE GOD!

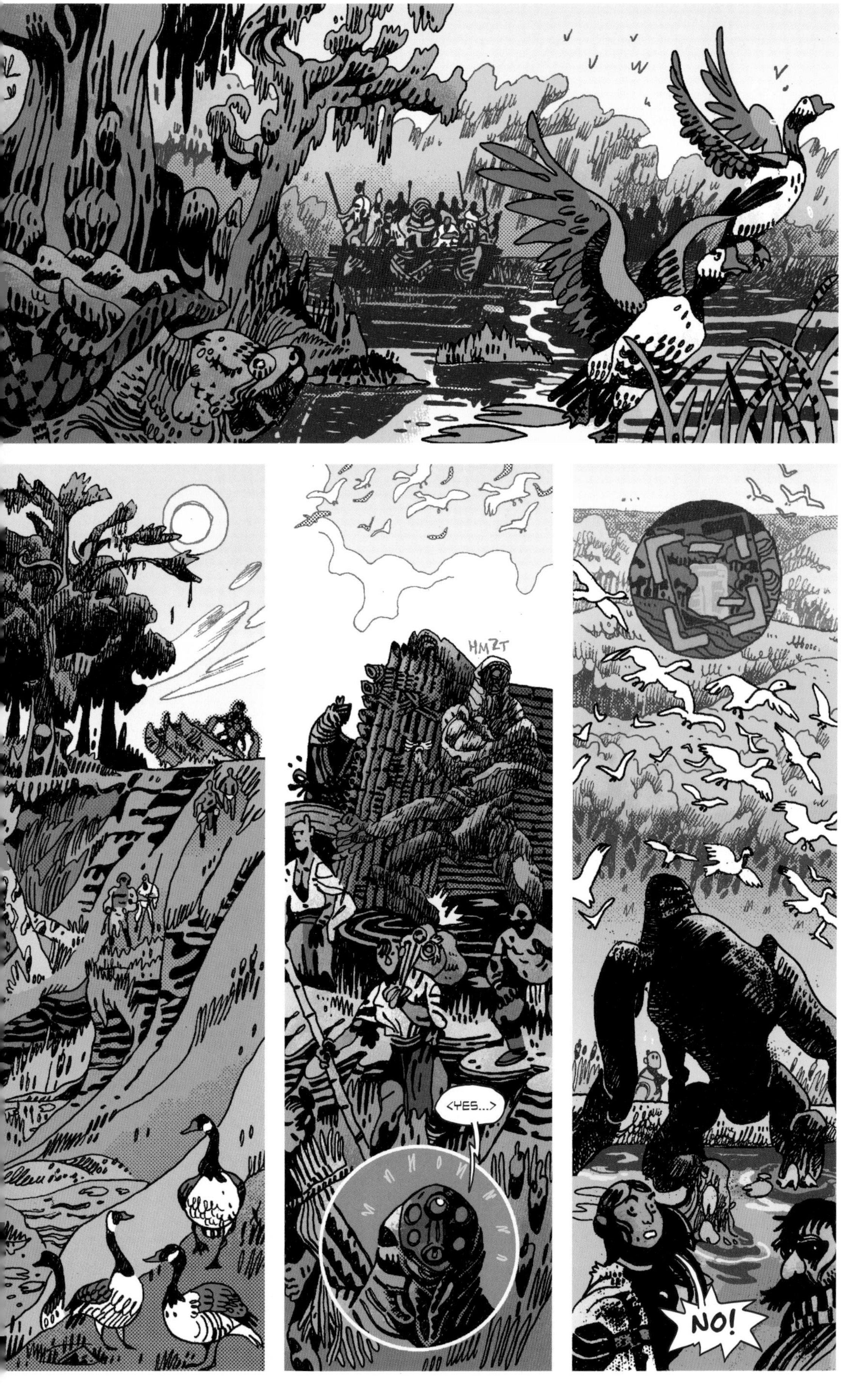
HMZT
<YES...>
NO!

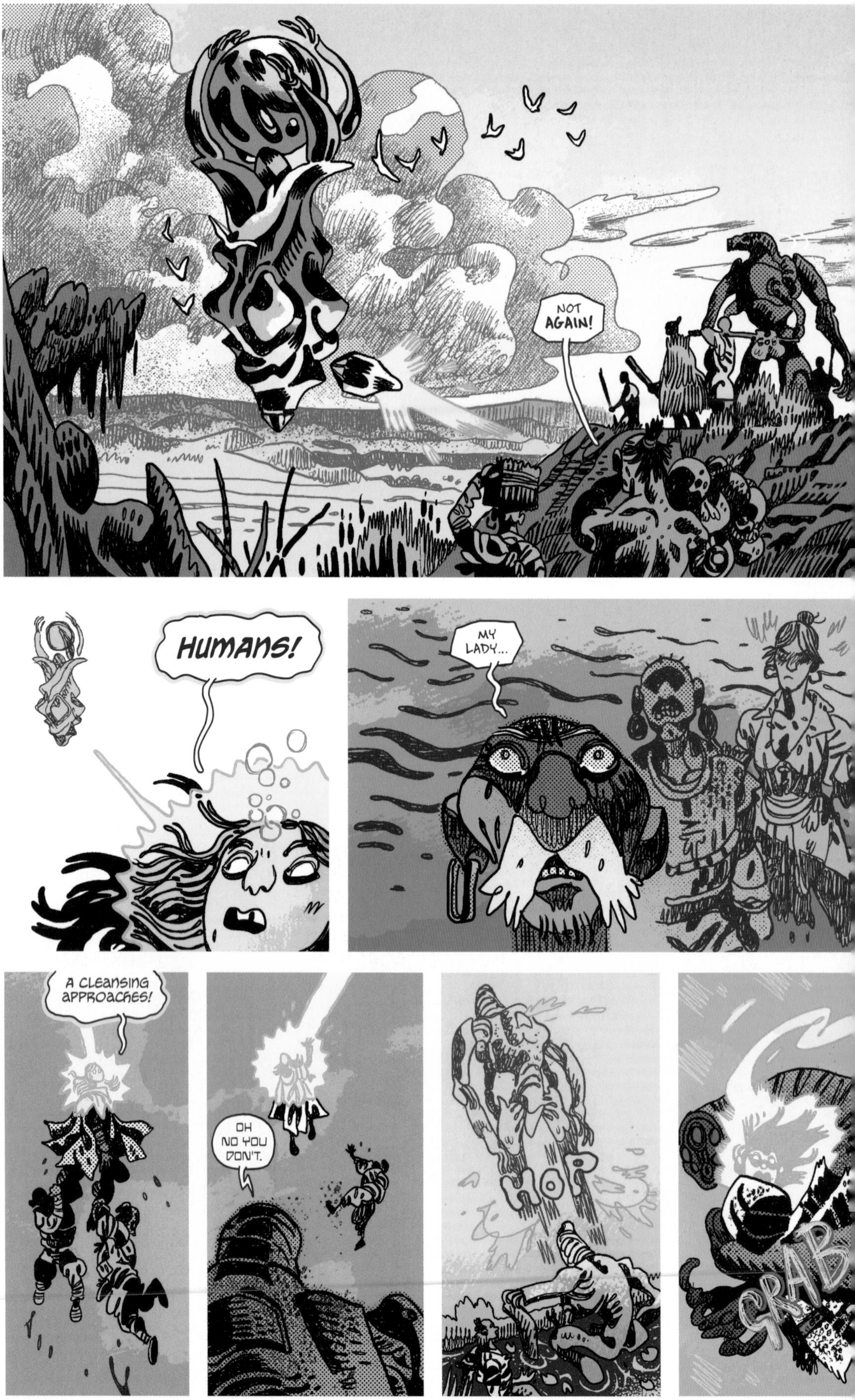
NOT AGAIN!
HUMANS!
MY LADY...
A CLEANSING APPROACHES!
OH NO YOU DON'T.
HOP
GRAB

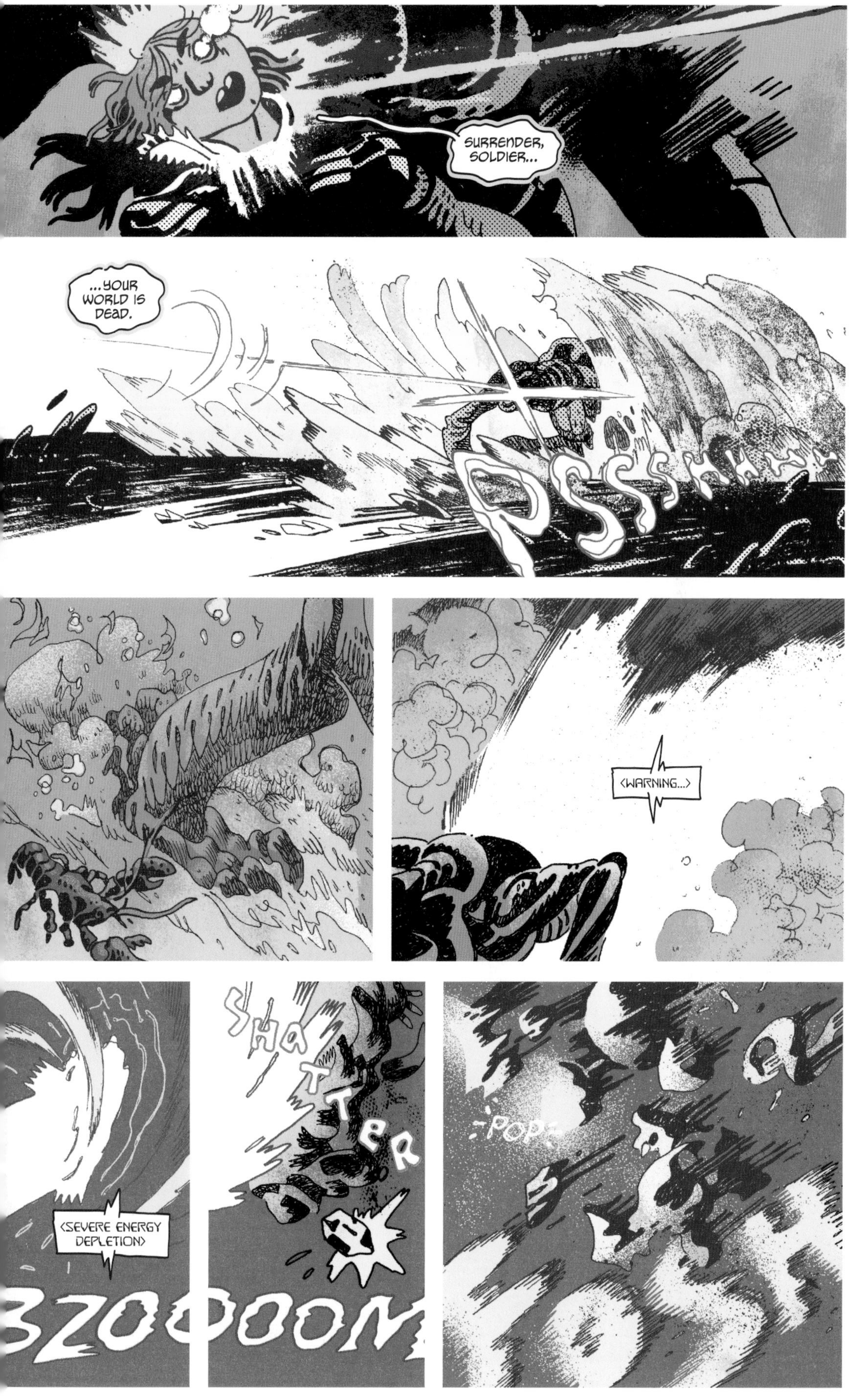
SURRENDER, SOLDIER...
...YOUR WORLD IS DEAD.
PSSSHHH
<WARNING...>
<SEVERE ENERGY DEPLETION>
BZOOOOOM
SHATTER
POP

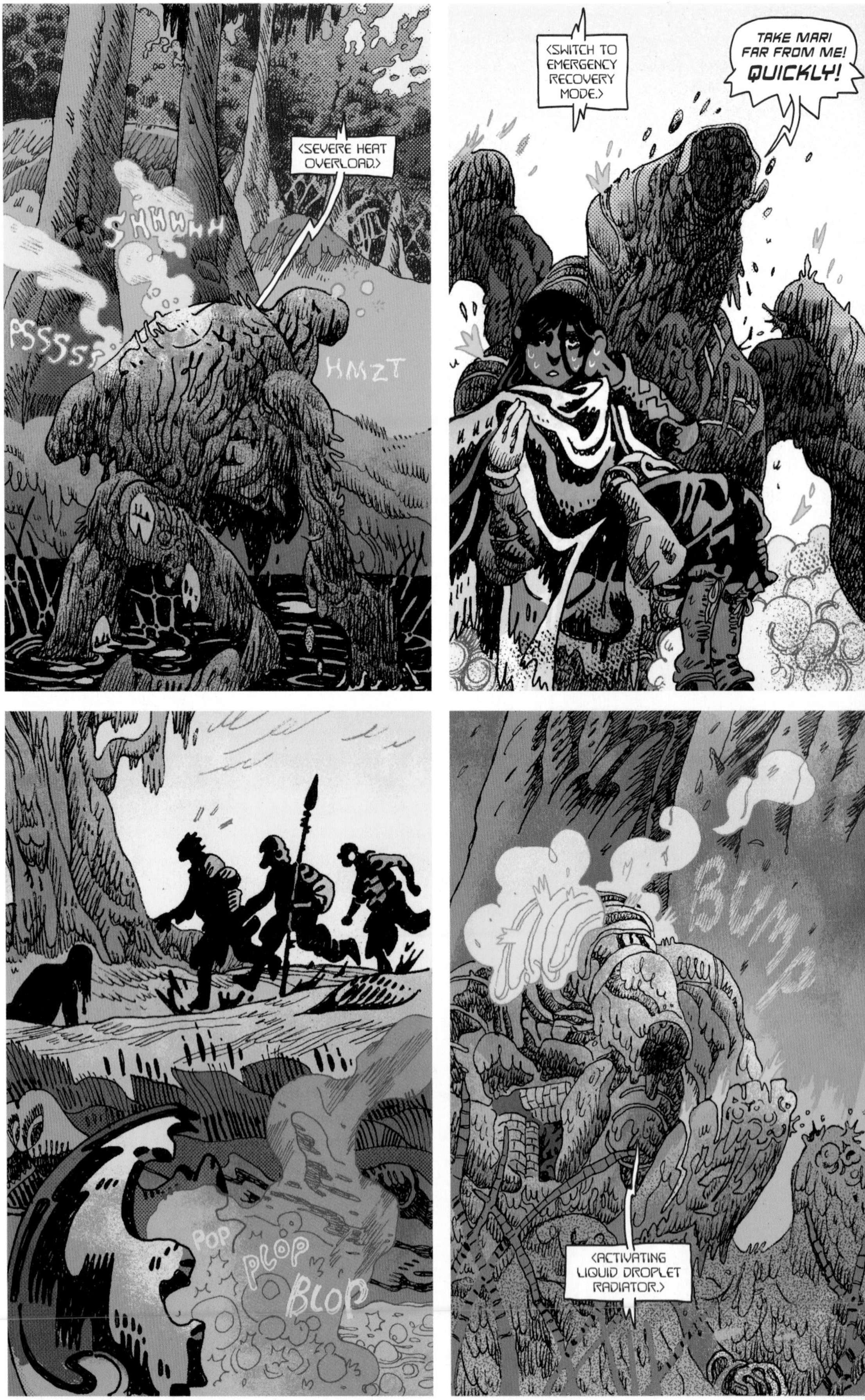
<SEVERE HEAT OVERLOAD.>
SHHHHH
PSSSSS
HMZT
<SWITCH TO EMERGENCY RECOVERY MODE.>
TAKE MARI FAR FROM ME! QUICKLY!
POP
PLOP
BLOP
BUMP
<ACTIVATING LIQUID DROPLET RADIATOR.>

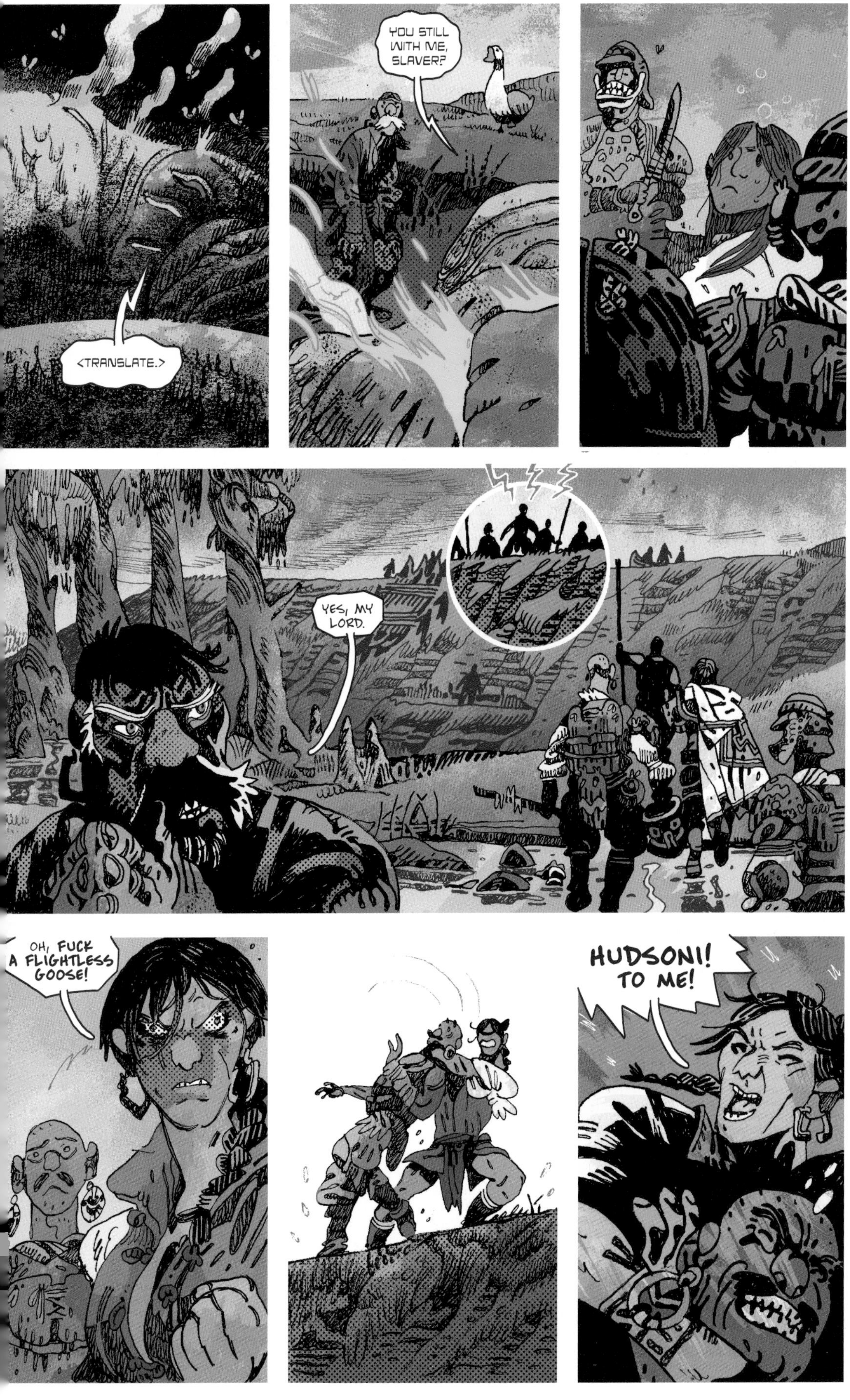
<TRANSLATE.>
YOU STILL WITH ME, SLAVER?
YES, MY LORD.
OH, FUCK A FLIGHTLESS GOOSE!
HUDSONI! TO ME!

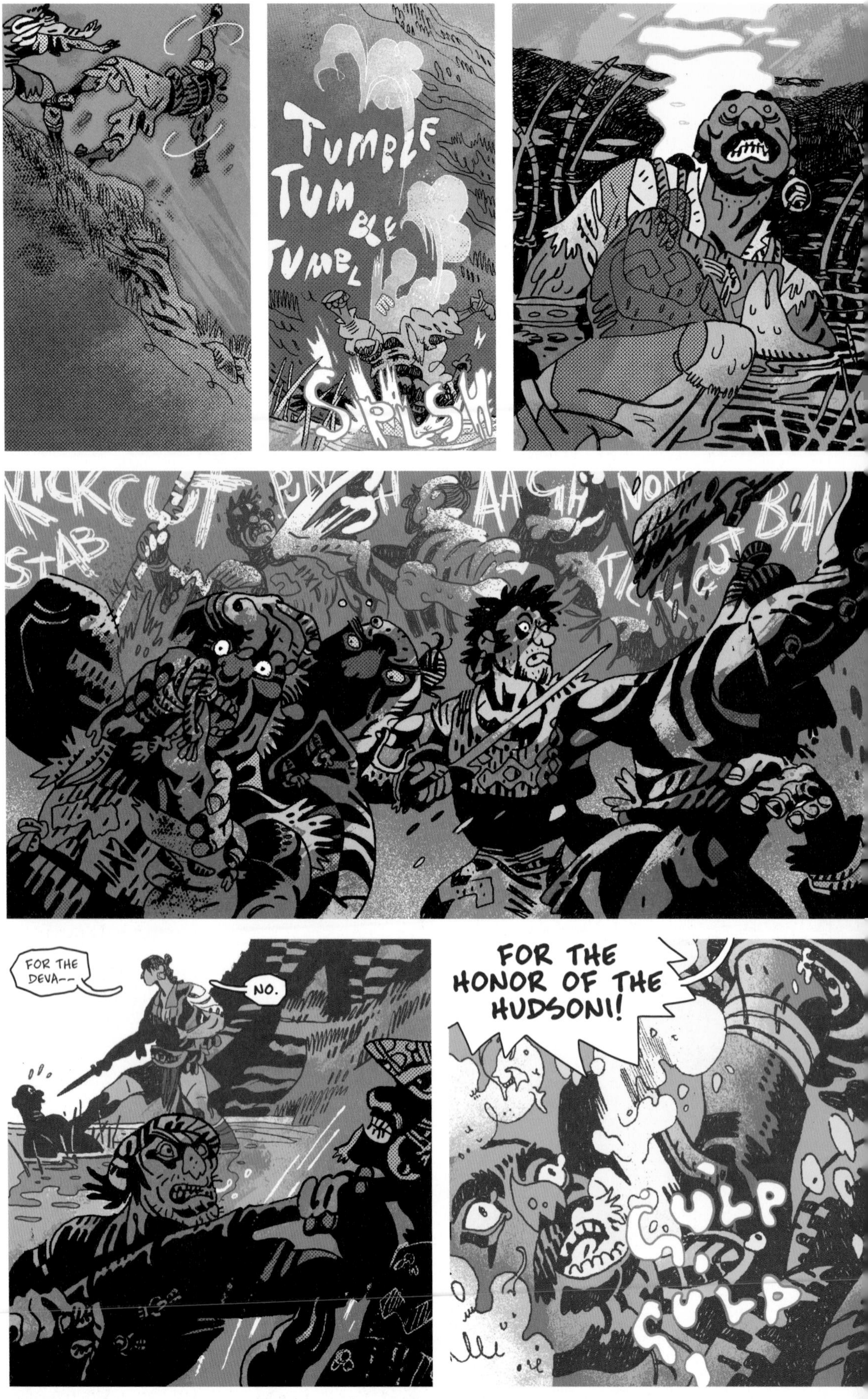
TUMBLE
TUMBLE
TUMBL
SPLSH
KICKCUT
STAB
AAGH
FOR THE DEVA--
NO.
FOR THE HONOR OF THE HUDSONI!
GULP
GULP

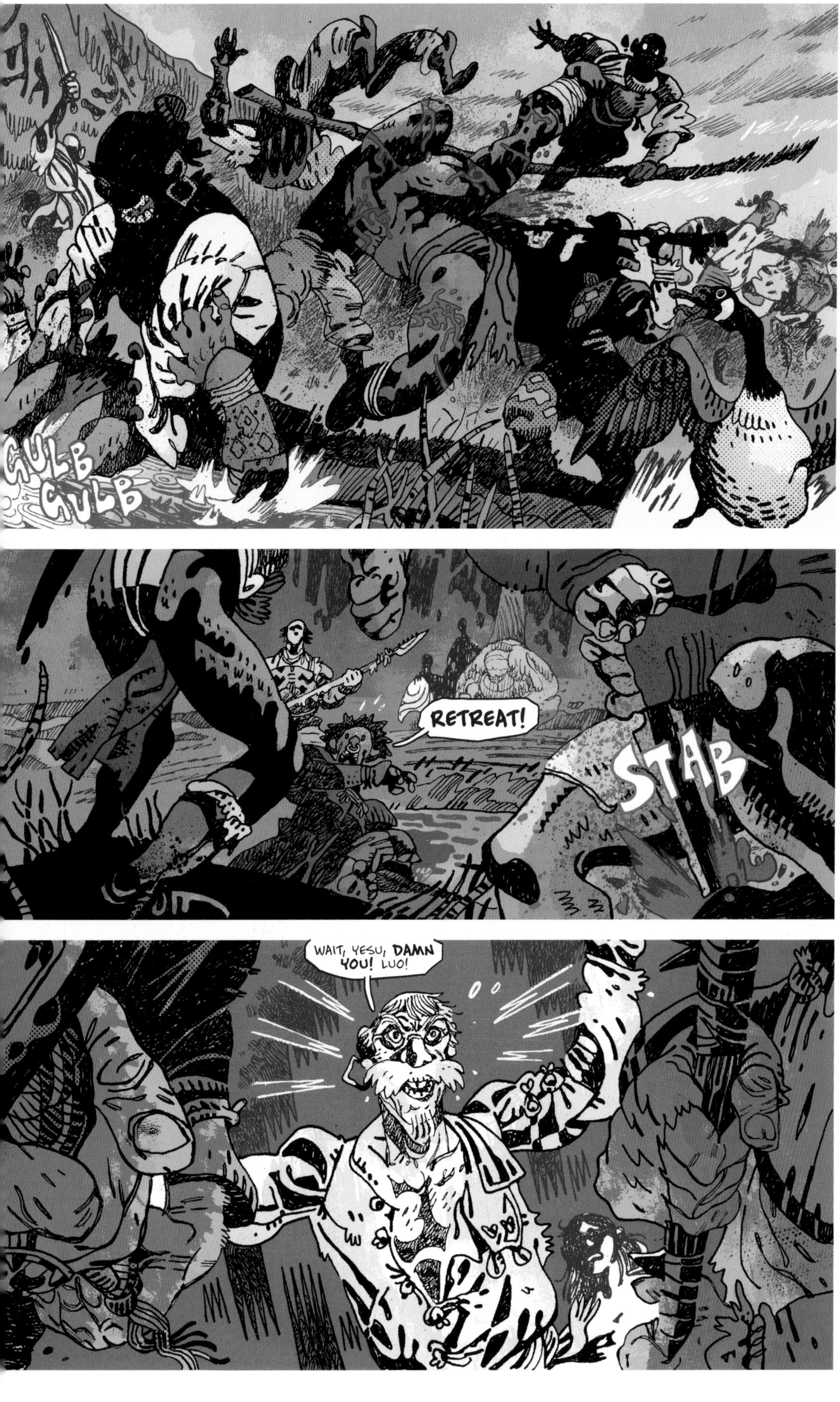
GULB
GULB
RETREAT!
STAB
WAIT, YESU, DAMN YOU! LUO!

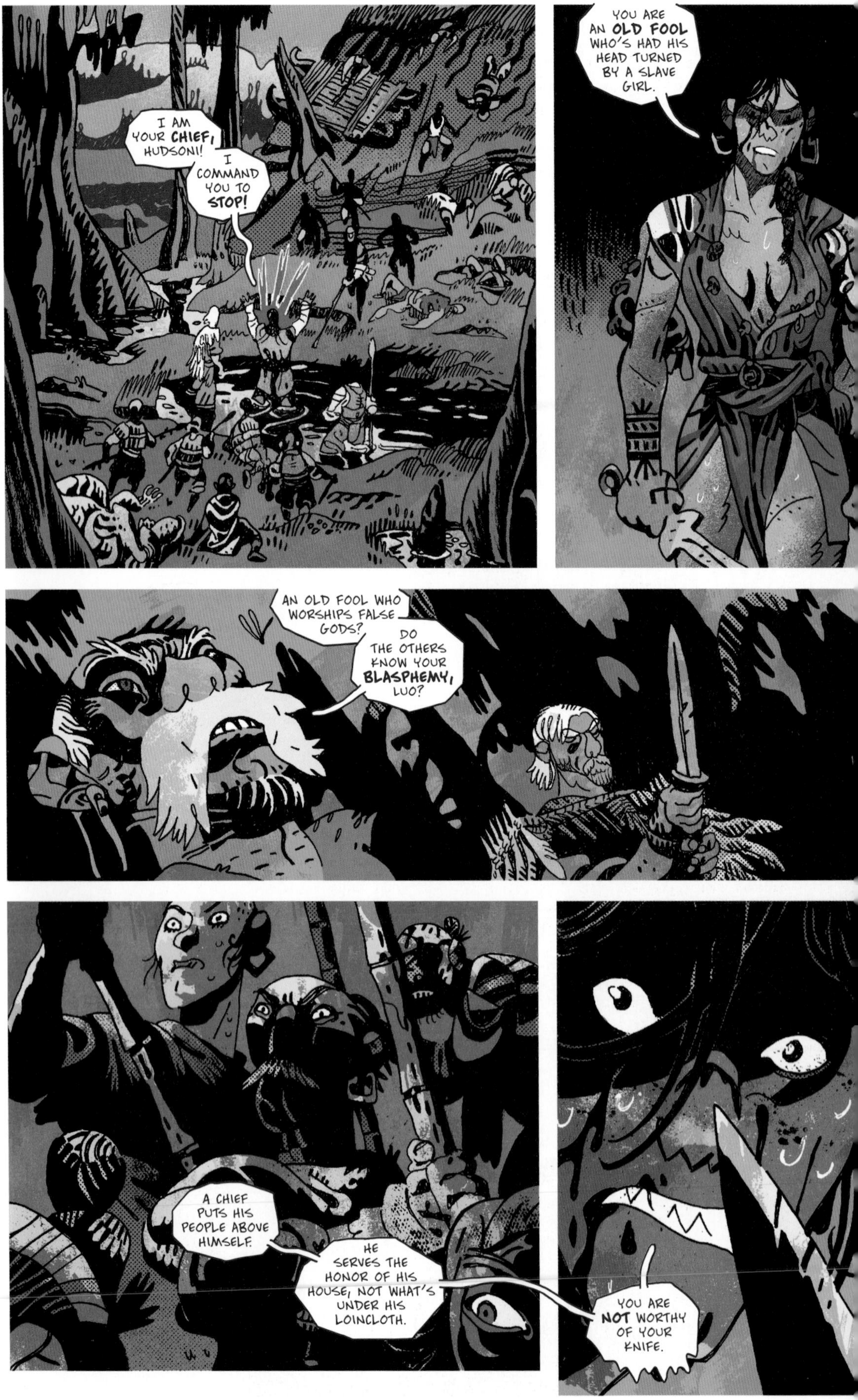
I AM YOUR **CHIEF**, HUDSONI!
I COMMAND YOU TO **STOP!**
YOU ARE AN **OLD FOOL** WHO'S HAD HIS HEAD TURNED BY A SLAVE GIRL.
AN OLD FOOL WHO WORSHIPS FALSE GODS?
DO THE OTHERS KNOW YOUR **BLASPHEMY**, LUO?
A CHIEF PUTS HIS PEOPLE ABOVE HIMSELF.
HE SERVES THE HONOR OF HIS HOUSE, NOT WHAT'S UNDER HIS LOINCLOTH.
YOU ARE **NOT** WORTHY OF YOUR KNIFE.

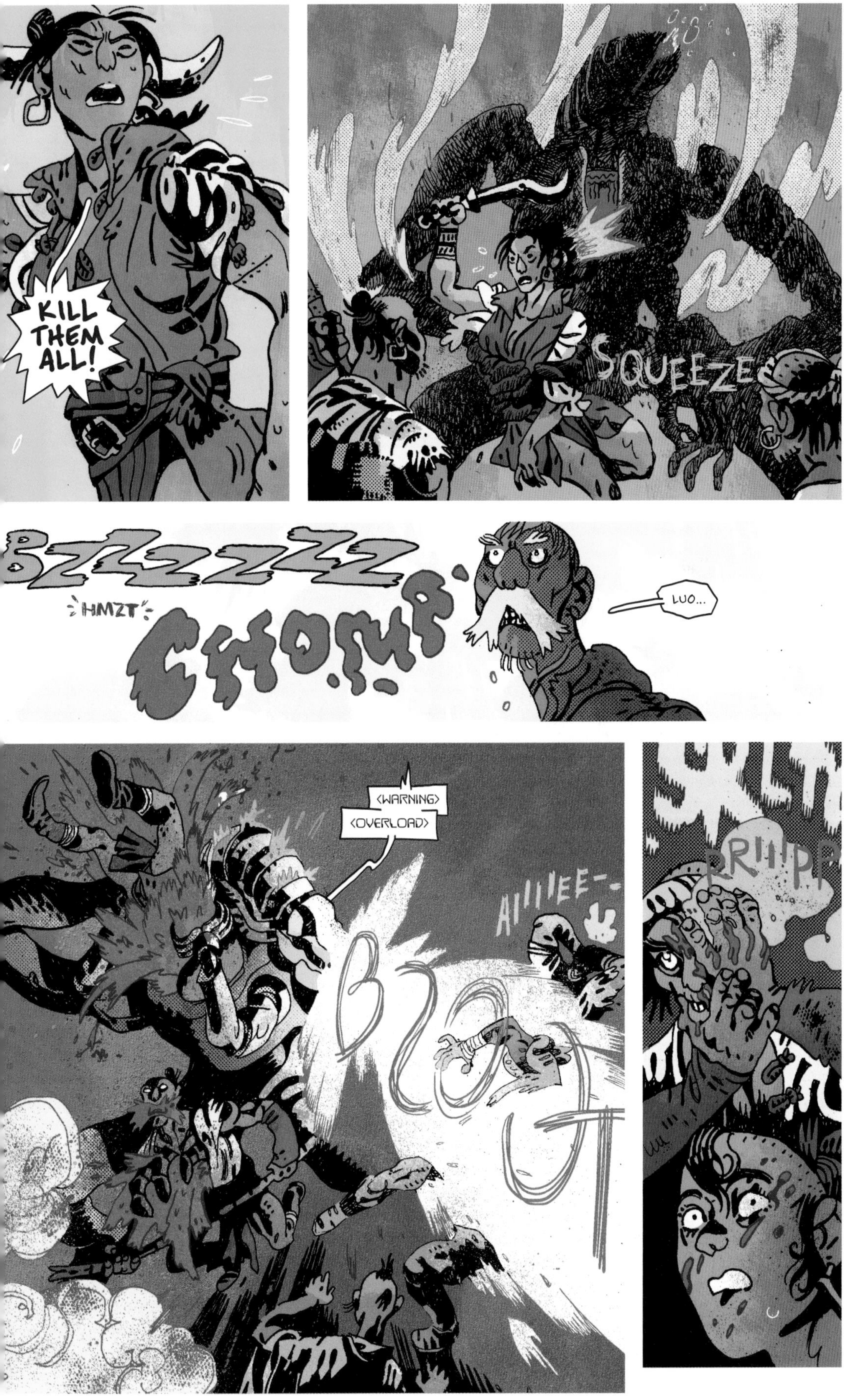
KILL THEM ALL!
SQUEEZE
BZZZZZZZ
HMZT
CHOMP
LUO...
<WARNING>
<OVERLOAD>
AIIIEE-
BLOOT
RRIIPP

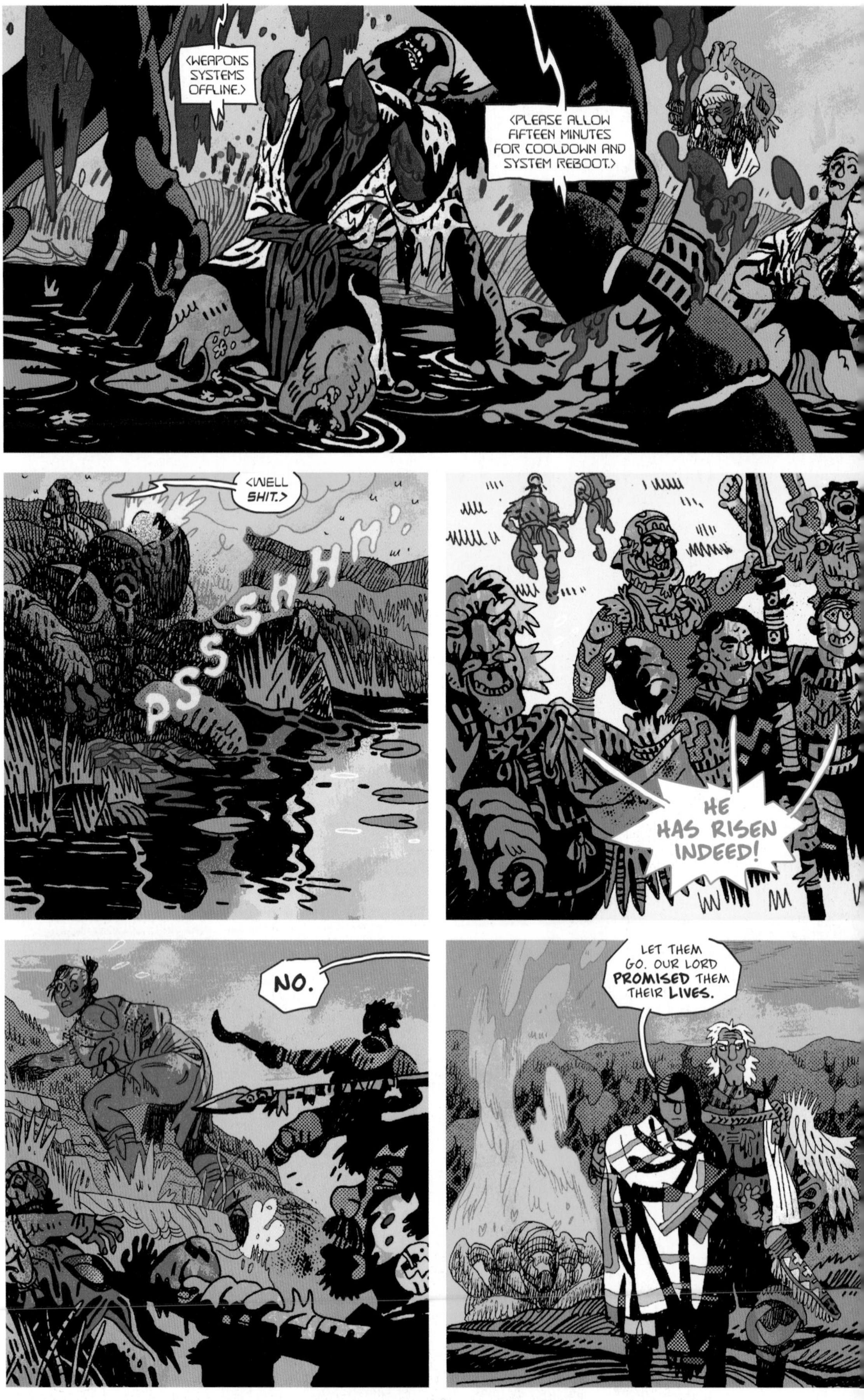
<WEAPONS SYSTEMS OFFLINE.>
<PLEASE ALLOW FIFTEEN MINUTES FOR COOLDOWN AND SYSTEM REBOOT.>
<WELL SHIT.>
PSSSHHH
HE HAS RISEN INDEED!
NO.
LET THEM GO. OUR LORD PROMISED THEM THEIR LIVES.

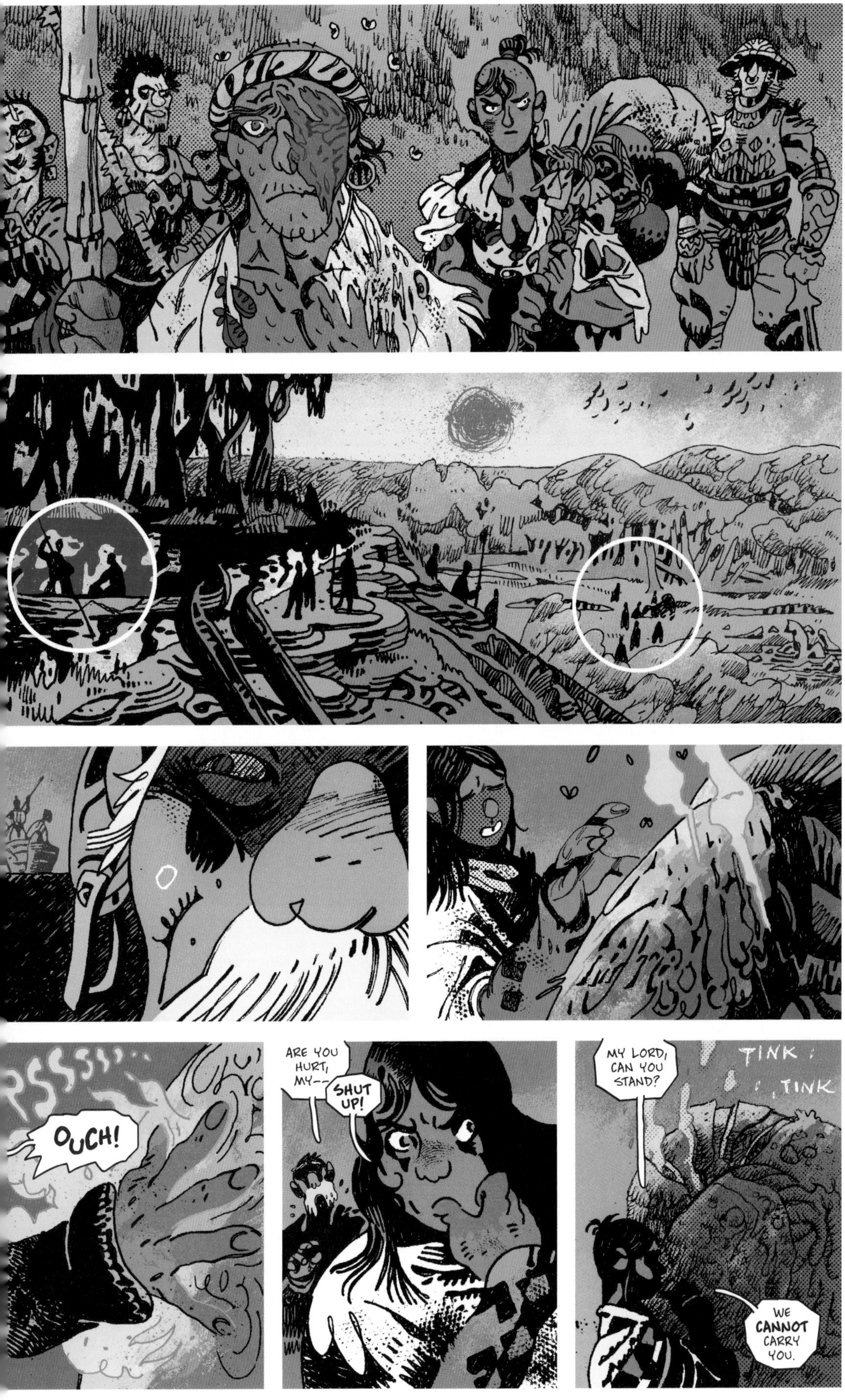
PSSSSS...
OUCH!
ARE YOU HURT, MY--
SHUT UP!
MY LORD, CAN YOU STAND?
TINK
TINK
WE CANNOT CARRY YOU.

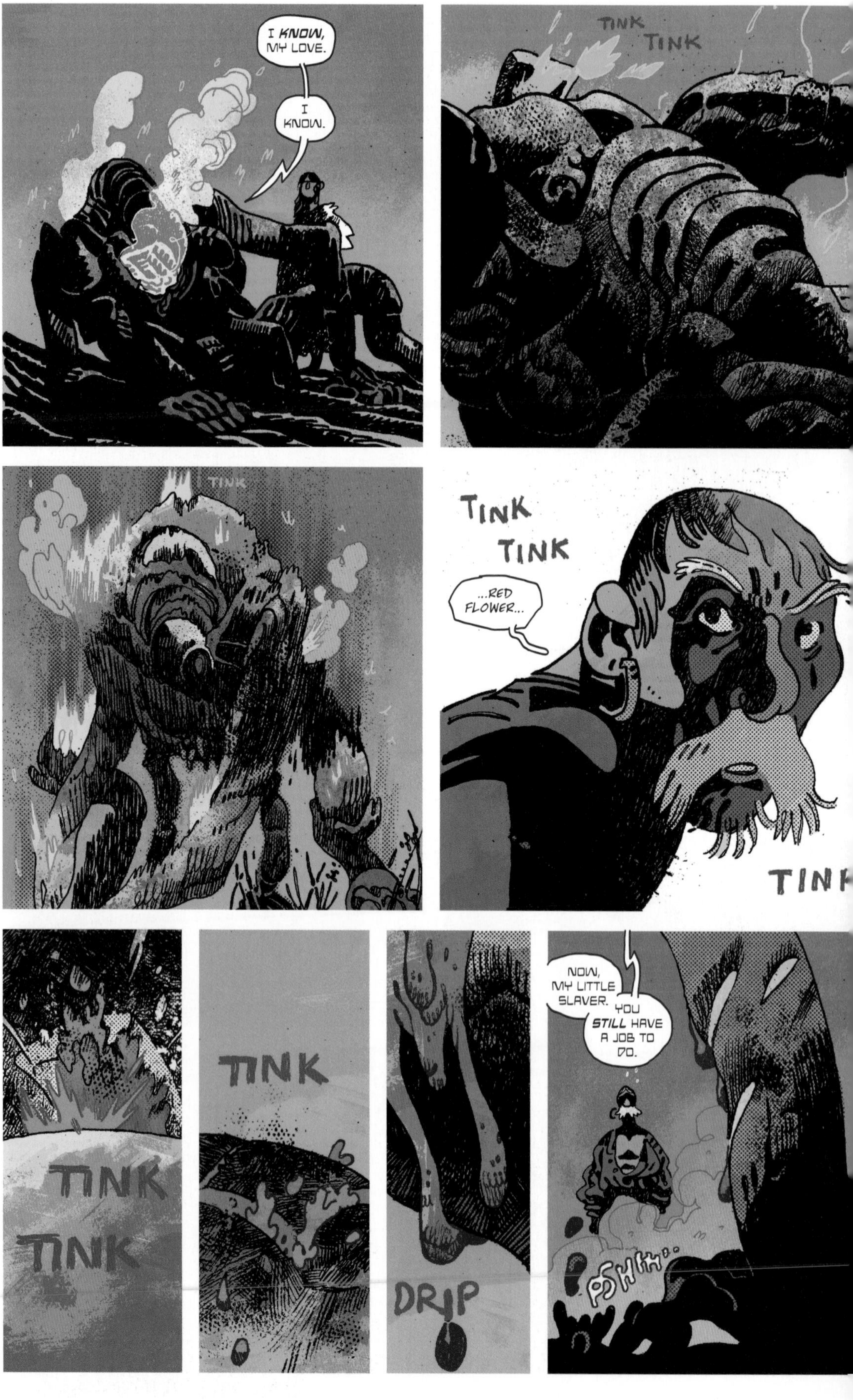
I KNOW, MY LOVE.
I KNOW.
TINK TINK
TINK
TINK
TINK
...RED FLOWER...
TINK
TINK
TINK
TINK
DRIP
NOW, MY LITTLE SLAVER.
YOU STILL HAVE A JOB TO DO.

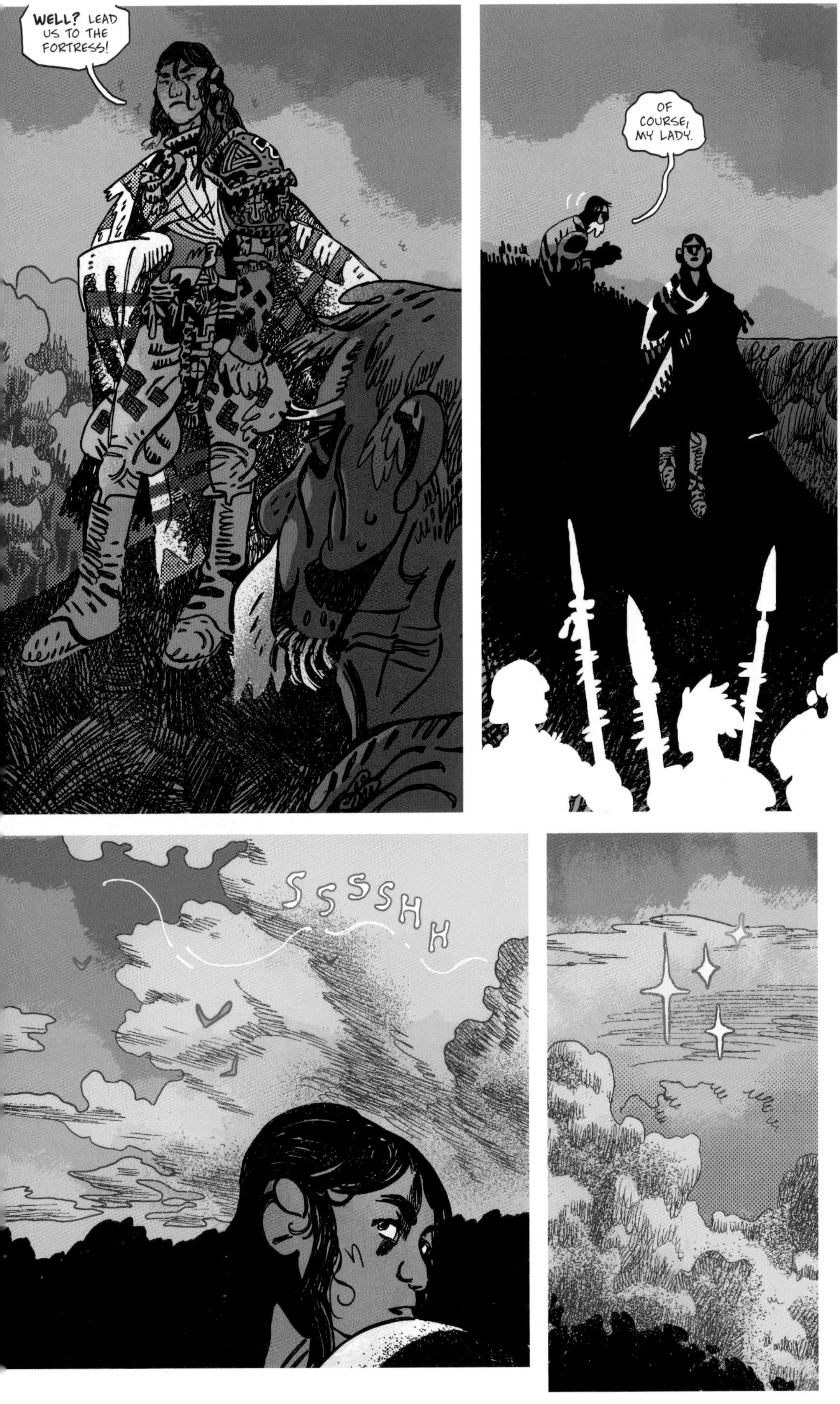
WELL? LEAD US TO THE FORTRESS!
OF COURSE, MY LADY.
SSSSHH

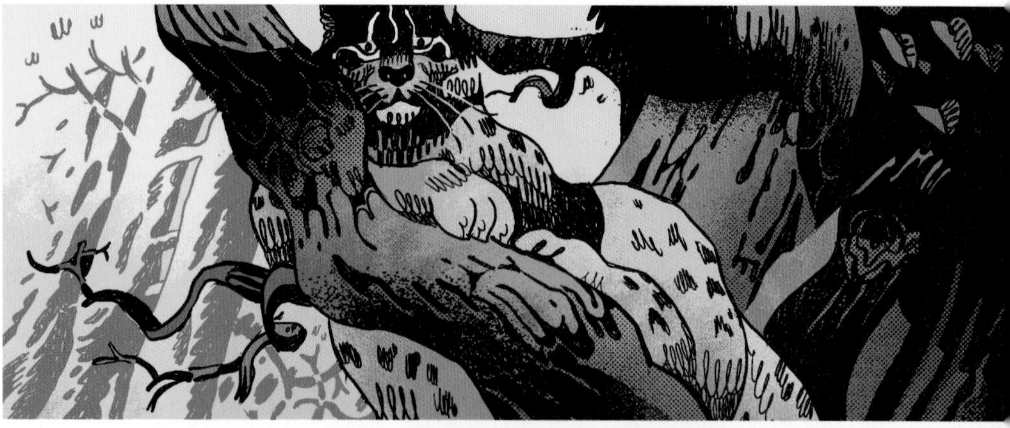

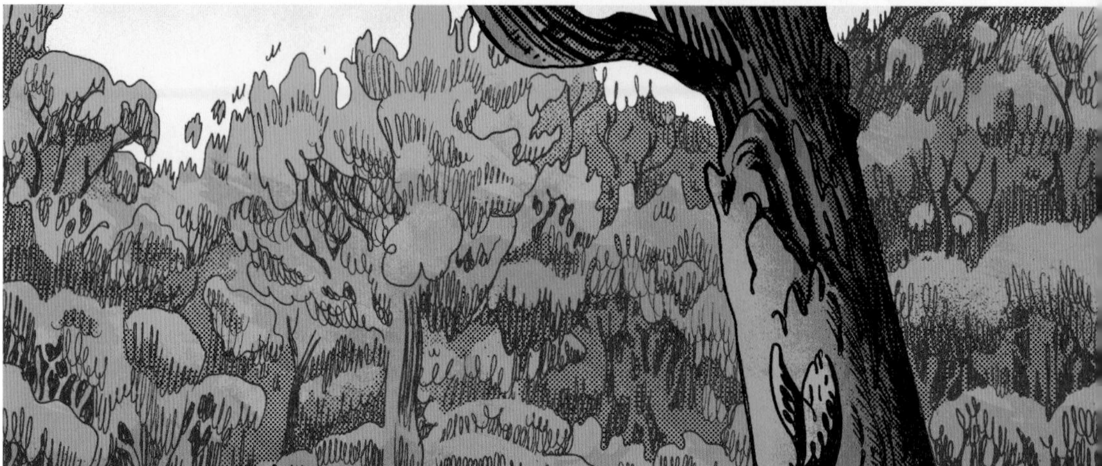

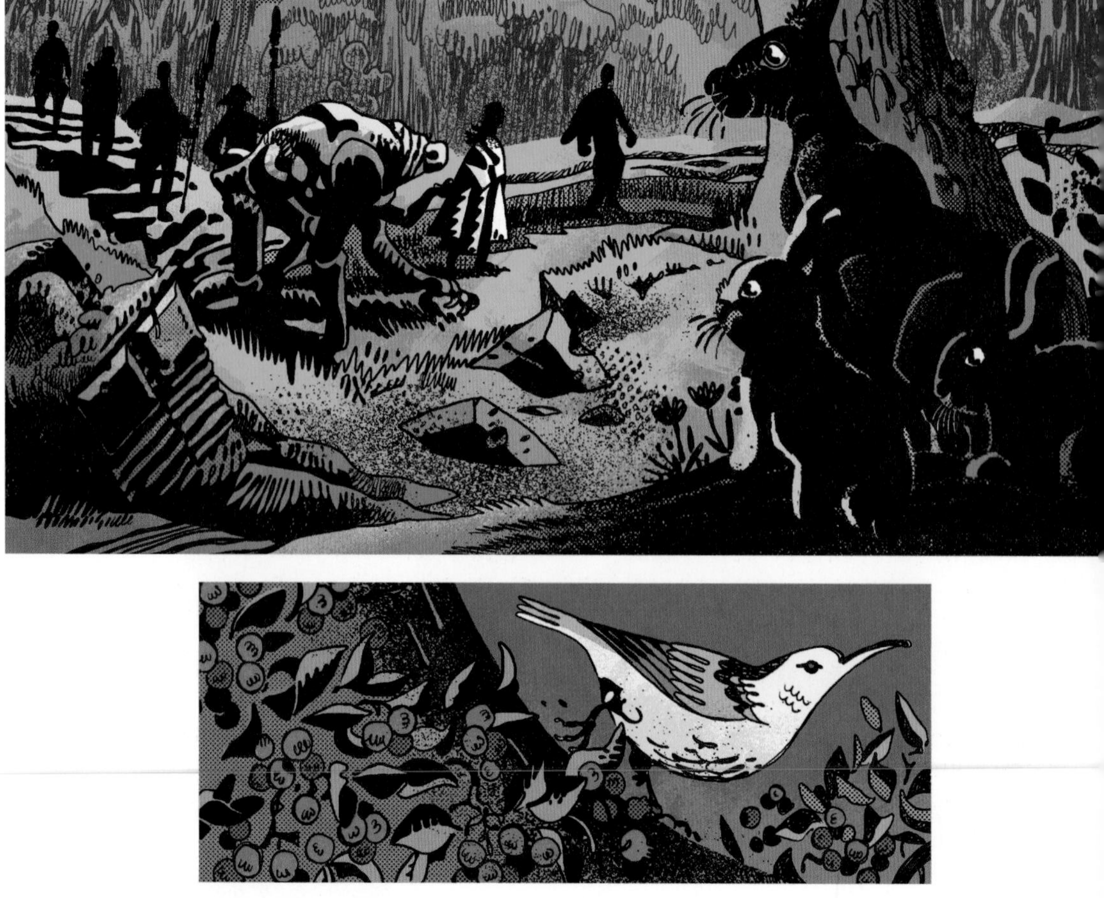

The Biology of the Earliest Noöscene

As in the wake of all global extinction events, the first thousand years after the Anthropocene Thermal Maximum was a time of rapid growth and diversification. In the immediate aftermath of the socioecological collapse of the Anthropocene, measures were undertaken to return the planet to its pre-industrial, Holocene state. This directive necessitated a global temperature drop of 6 degrees Celsius, the massive re-digging of rivers and re-conditioning of soils, and the aggressive management of species introduced or created by humans.

Pictured above—the Minnetonka and Nuvrindaban Strato-shunts

One of the many technologies deployed in service of the goal of global cooling was the strato-shunt. While perhaps less effective in the long term than Van Neumann Sequestration and Tropospheric Albedo Optimization Swarming, Stratospheric Thermal Shunting is certainly spectacular in its visual and environmental impact. Using the best antigravitic and superconducting materials available, floating pillars were built that sucked heat out of the lower atmosphere and shunted it into the upper. This process quickly lowered temperatures in the air around the lower end of the shunt, but this benefit was secondary to the manipulation of global air currents in both the upper and lower atmosphere. Strato-shunts allow the rapid redirection or dissolution of mega-storms, and their long term use has brought order to the Earth's climate thousands of years earlier than would have emerged naturally.

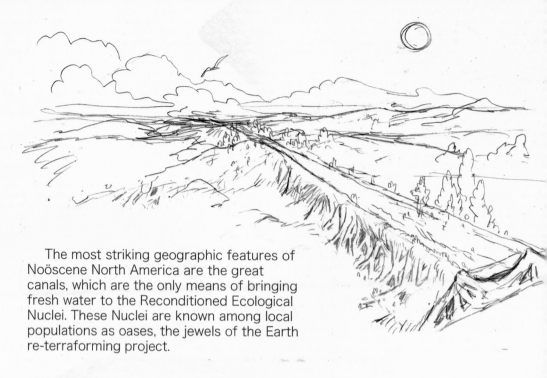

The most striking geographic features of Noöscene North America are the great canals, which are the only means of bringing fresh water to the Reconditioned Ecological Nuclei. These Nuclei are known among local populations as oases, the jewels of the Earth re-terraforming project.

The success of invasive species management is apparent in the absence of kudzu, tumbleweed, and dandelions from North American oases (although they dominate elsewhere on the continent). Likewise absent are cattle, horses, and singing mice.

However, anthropocene influence lives on in the genes of the giant goose (*Branta giganta*). Giant geese are descended from Canada geese (*Branta canadensis*) but have hybridized heavily with domesticated greylag geese (*Anser anser*) and swan geese (*A. cygnoides*) both non-native to North America. The swamp subspecies pictured above congregates in flocks of up to a dozen individuals, wading through swamps or along riverbanks, eating cattails, waterweeds, and low-growing leaves. While their impressive size helps to deter predators, giant geese are poor fliers, with large males often rendered flightless by their weight. The prairie subspecies is more lightly built, and forms much larger flocks.

Eastern cottontail rabbits (*Sylvilagus floridanus*) have diversified into many forms, including the large, gracile forest form (*Sylvilagus floridanus nebridis*), which browses on shoots, leaves, and herbs, and relies on its rapid, bounding gait to escape predators.

The giant snapping turtle (*Chelydra serpentina macrocheloida*) constitutes a fascinating case of convergent evolution. In form and behavior, it is almost indistinguishable from the extinct alligator snapping turtle (*Macrochelys temminckii*), even though it evolved from a much smaller genus. Giant snappers spend most of their time hiding in the leaf litter at the bottoms of lakes, ponds, and canals, waiting to ambush fishes, water birds, and swimming mammals. The giant snapper population of the Senta Lu Oasis shows signs of specializing on even larger prey, such as geese and beavers.

The oasis bobcat (*Lynx rufus ramalis*, also called "swamp lynx" and "drop cat") is the largest mammalian predator of the oasis of subtropical North America. Heavier, and with shorter legs relative to its length than ground bobcats, oasis bobcats are excellent climbers and swimmers, pouncing on their prey (giant geese, turkeys, and rabbits) from reeds or dropping from overhanging tree limbs. Outside the breeding season, bobcats are solitary, defending large territories usually centered on a body of water. Away from water, the main mammalian predator is the coywolf, although there is often significant overlap between the two predator species.

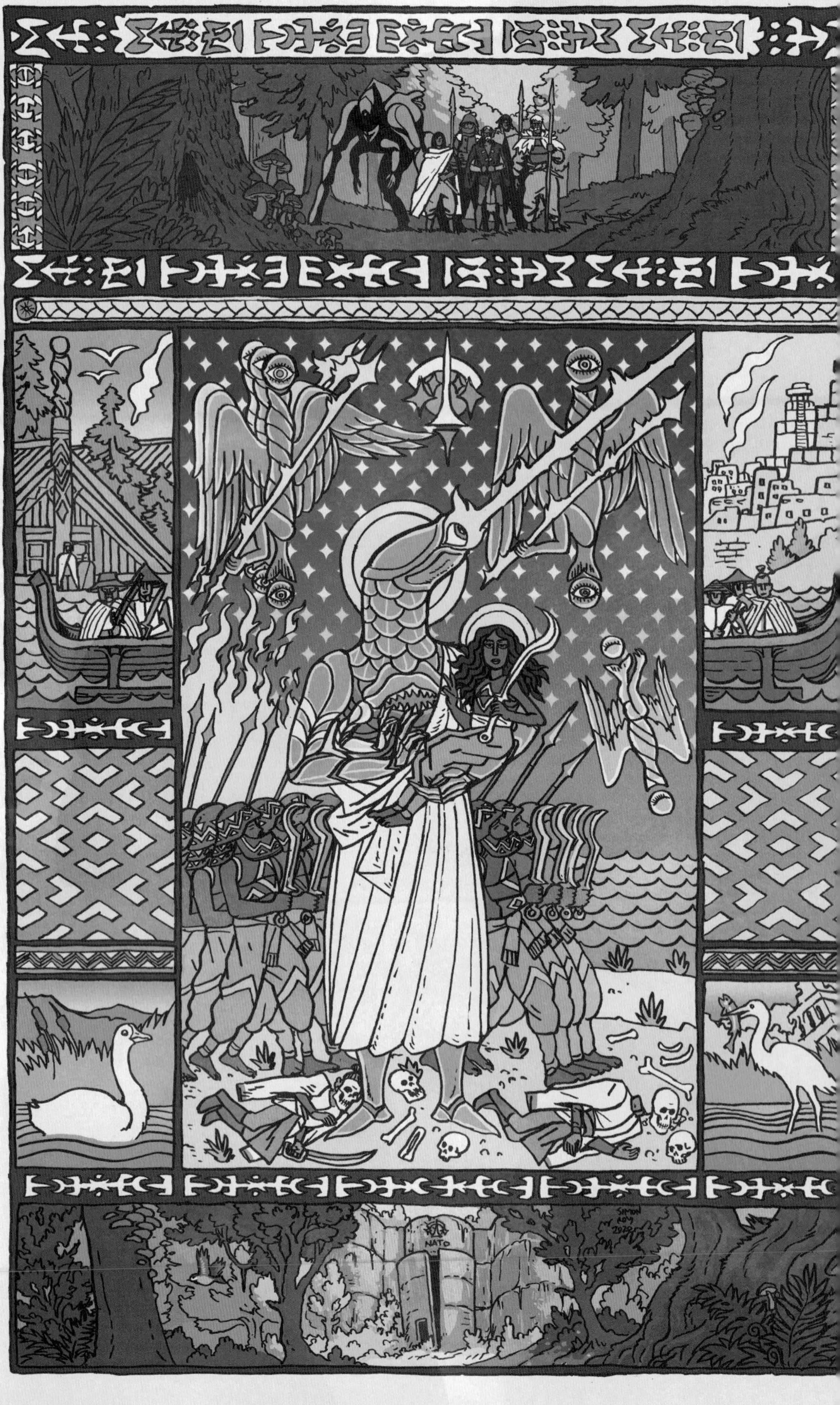
NATO
SIMON ROY 2020

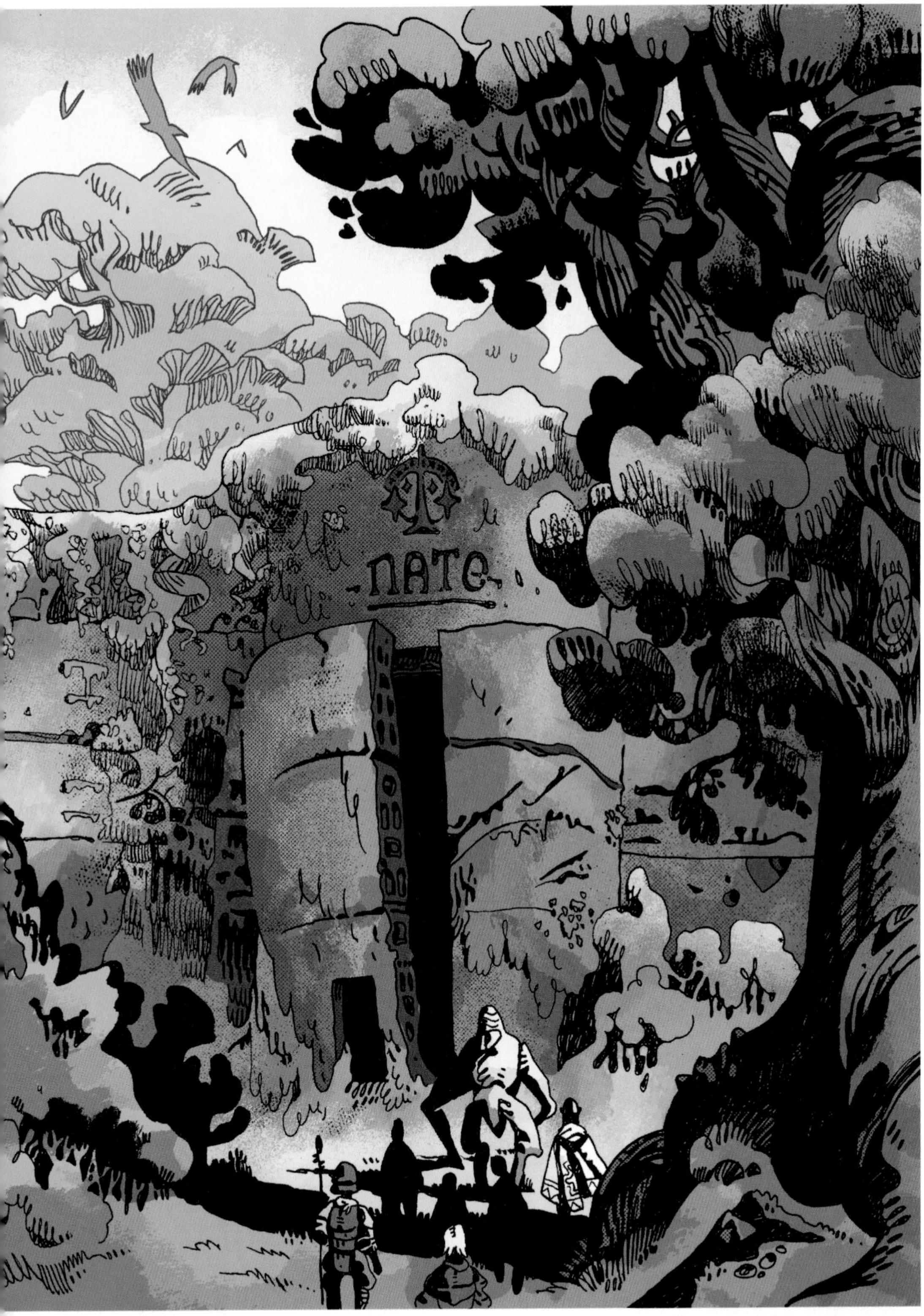
NATE

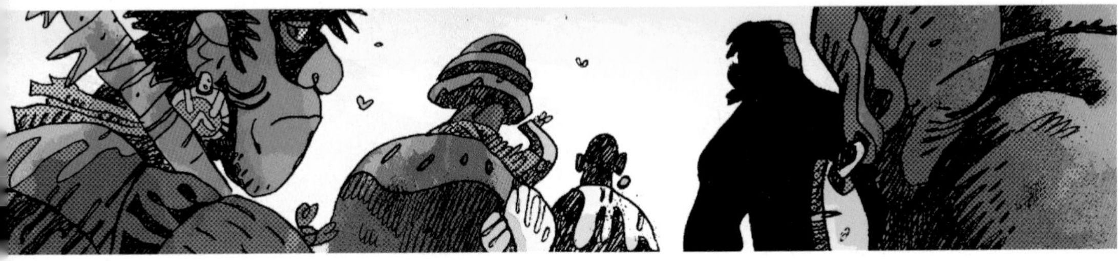

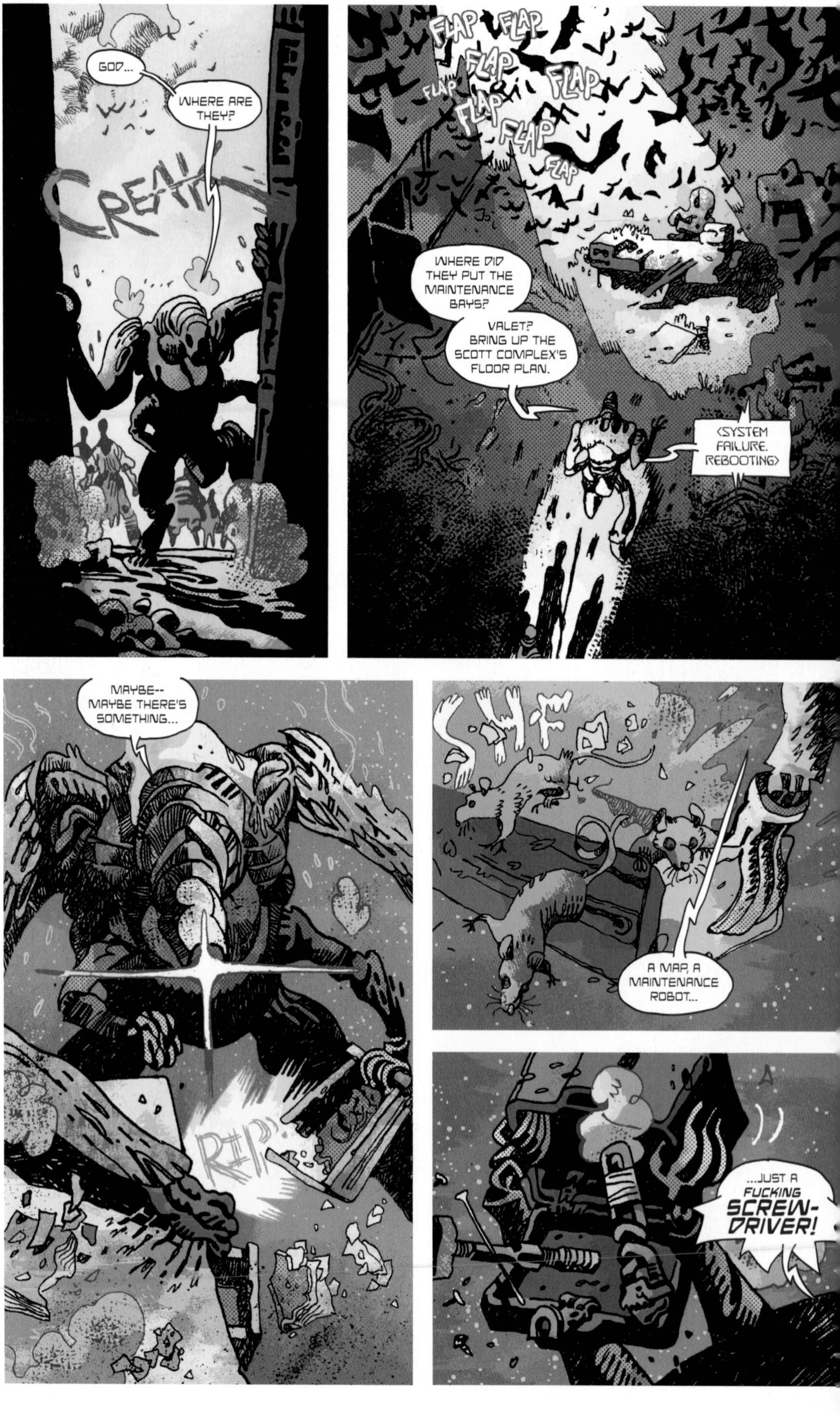
GOD...
WHERE ARE THEY?
CREAK
FLAP FLAP FLAP FLAP FLAP FLAP FLAP FLAP
WHERE DID THEY PUT THE MAINTENANCE BAYS?
VALET? BRING UP THE SCOTT COMPLEX'S FLOOR PLAN.
<SYSTEM FAILURE. REBOOTING>
MAYBE-- MAYBE THERE'S SOMETHING...
RIP
SHF
A MAP, A MAINTENANCE ROBOT...
...JUST A FUCKING SCREW-DRIVER!

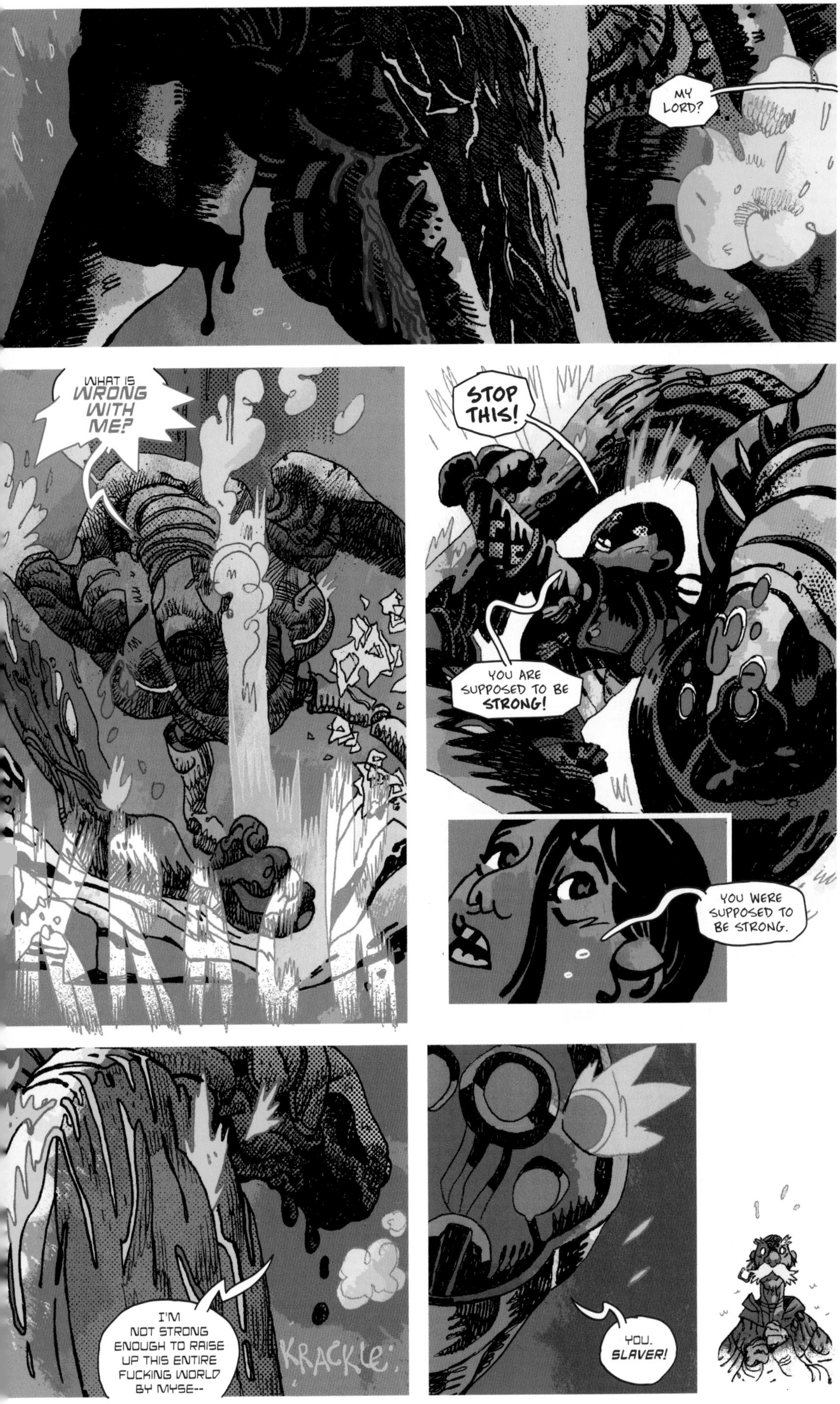
MY LORD?
WHAT IS WRONG WITH ME?
STOP THIS!
YOU ARE SUPPOSED TO BE STRONG!
YOU WERE SUPPOSED TO BE STRONG.
I'M NOT STRONG ENOUGH TO RAISE UP THIS ENTIRE FUCKING WORLD BY MYSE--
KRACKLE:
YOU. SLAVER!

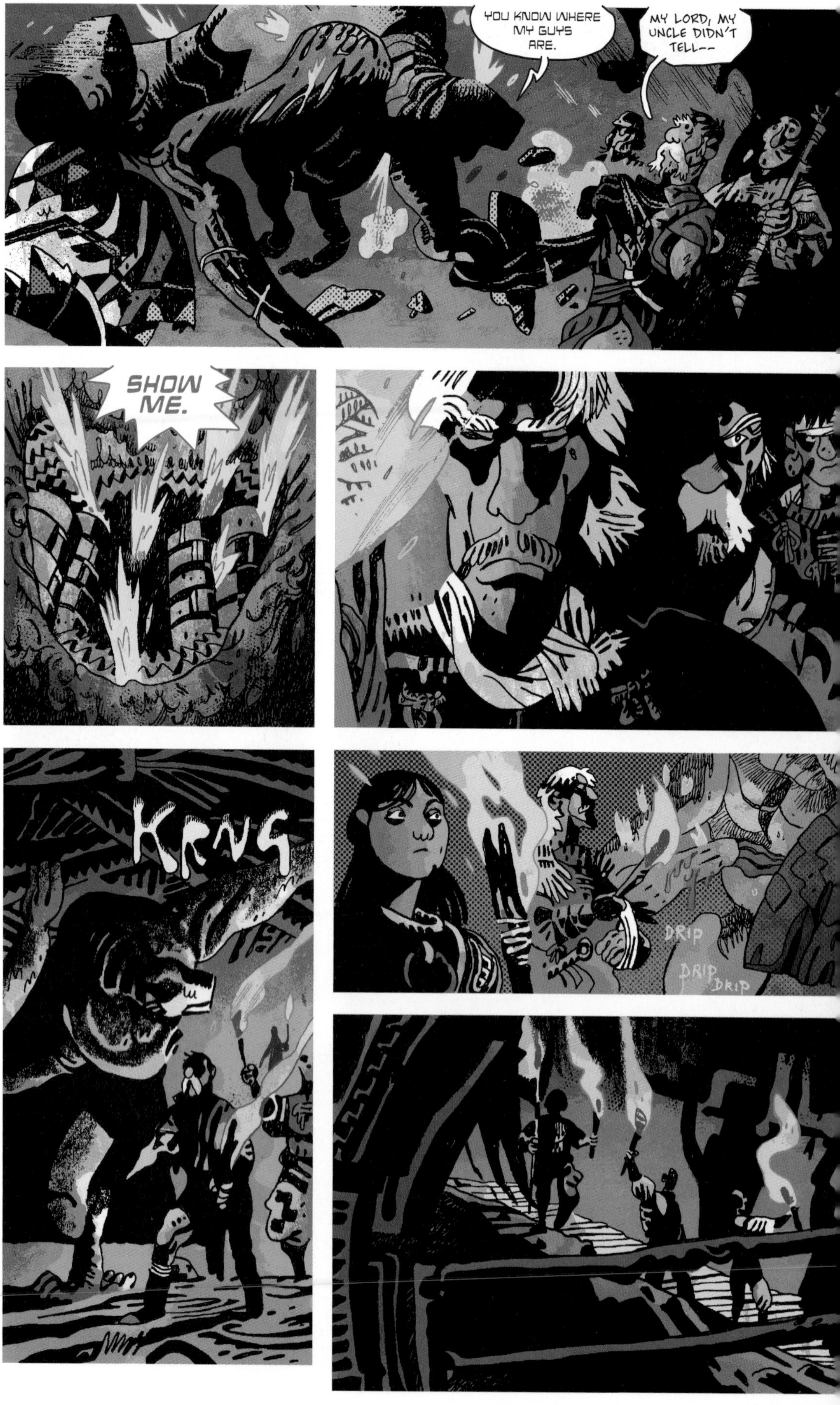
YOU KNOW WHERE MY GUYS ARE.
MY LORD, MY UNCLE DIDN'T TELL--
SHOW ME.
KRNG
DRIP
DRIP DRIP

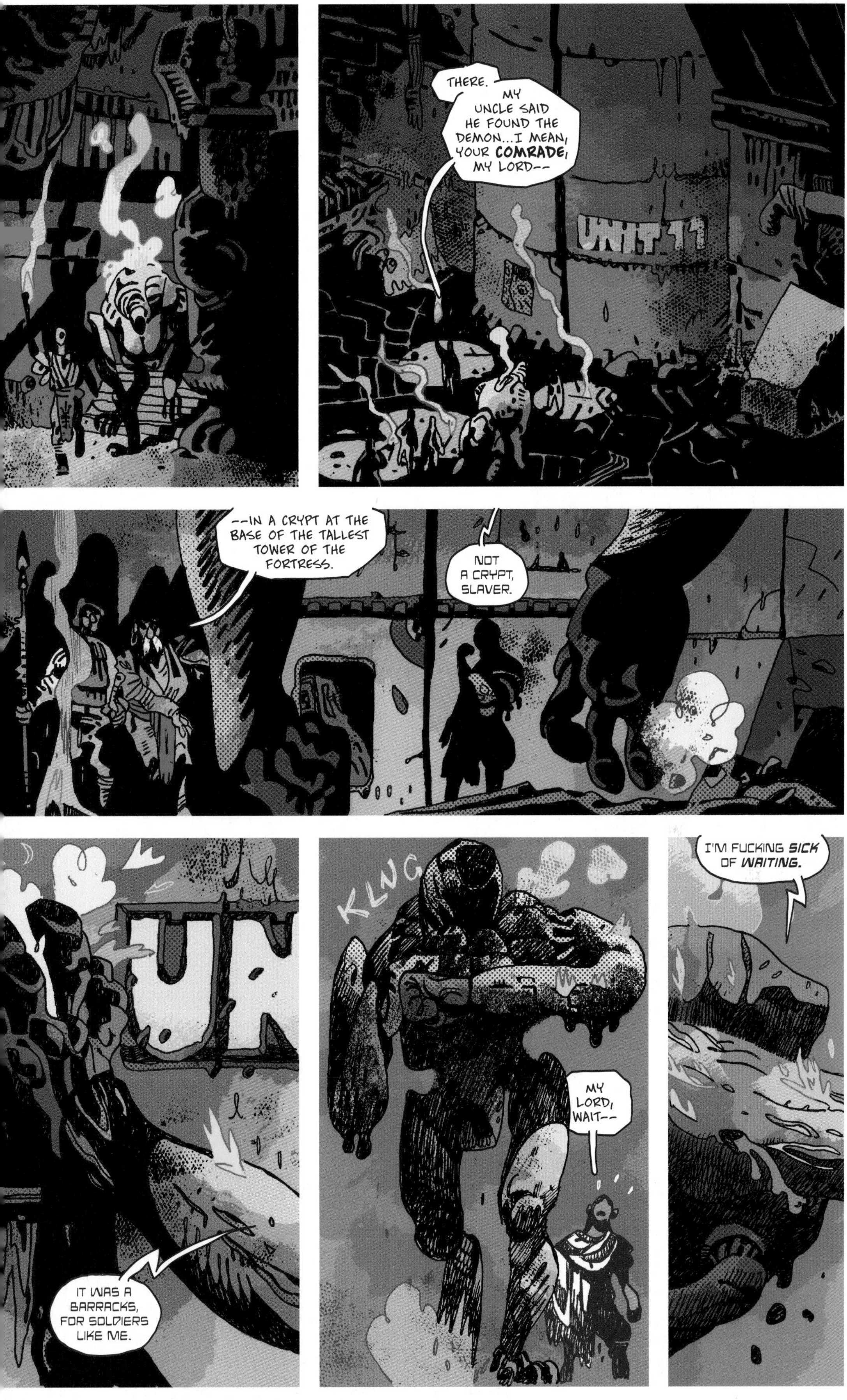
THERE.
MY UNCLE SAID HE FOUND THE DEMON... I MEAN, YOUR COMRADE, MY LORD--
UNIT 11
--IN A CRYPT AT THE BASE OF THE TALLEST TOWER OF THE FORTRESS.
NOT A CRYPT, SLAVER.
IT WAS A BARRACKS, FOR SOLDIERS LIKE ME.
KLNG
MY LORD, WAIT--
I'M FUCKING SICK OF WAITING.

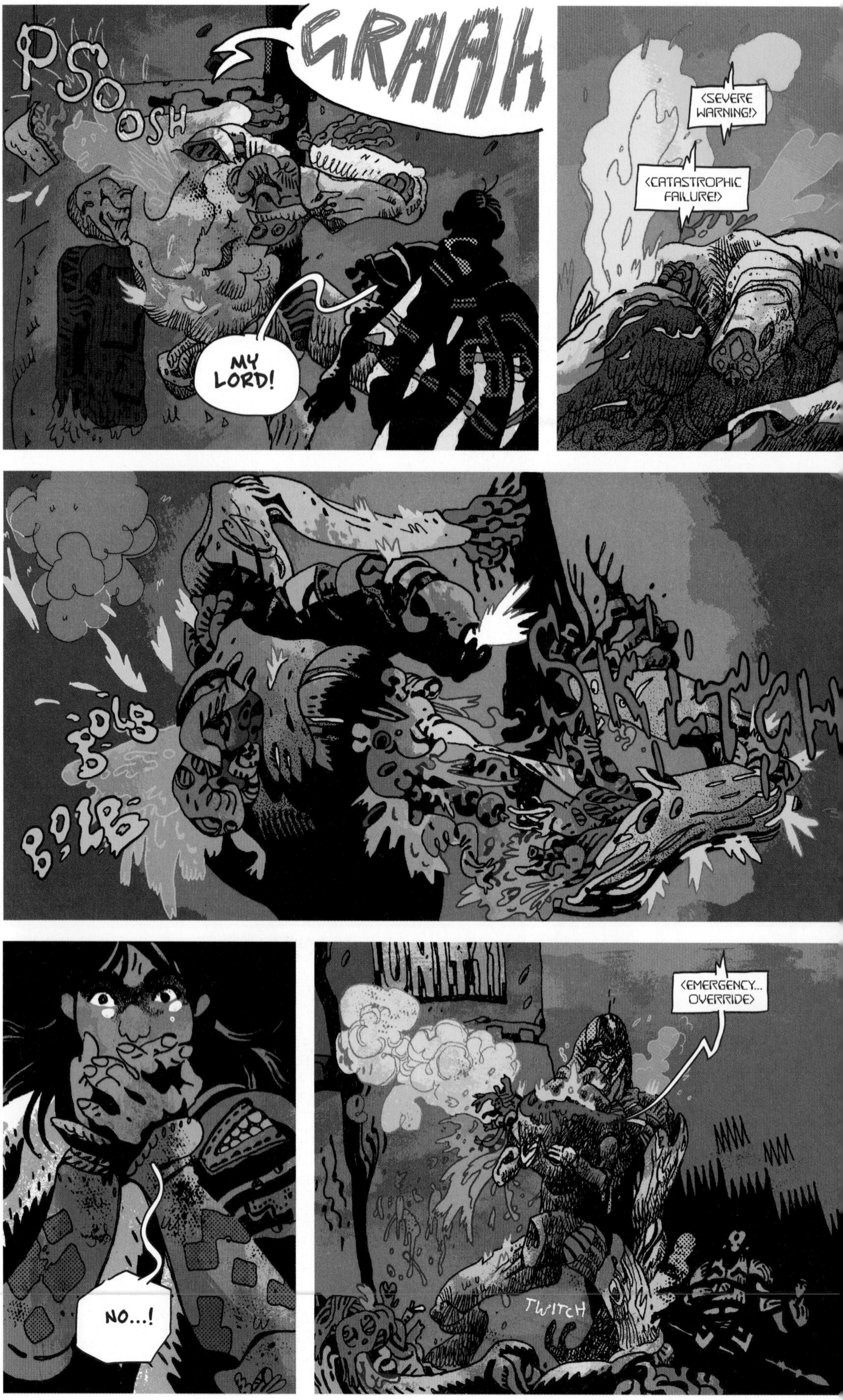
PSOOOSH
GRAAH
MY LORD!
<SEVERE WARNING!>
<CATASTROPHIC FAILURE!>
GLOB
BLOB
SKLITCH
NO...!
<EMERGENCY... OVERRIDE>
TWITCH

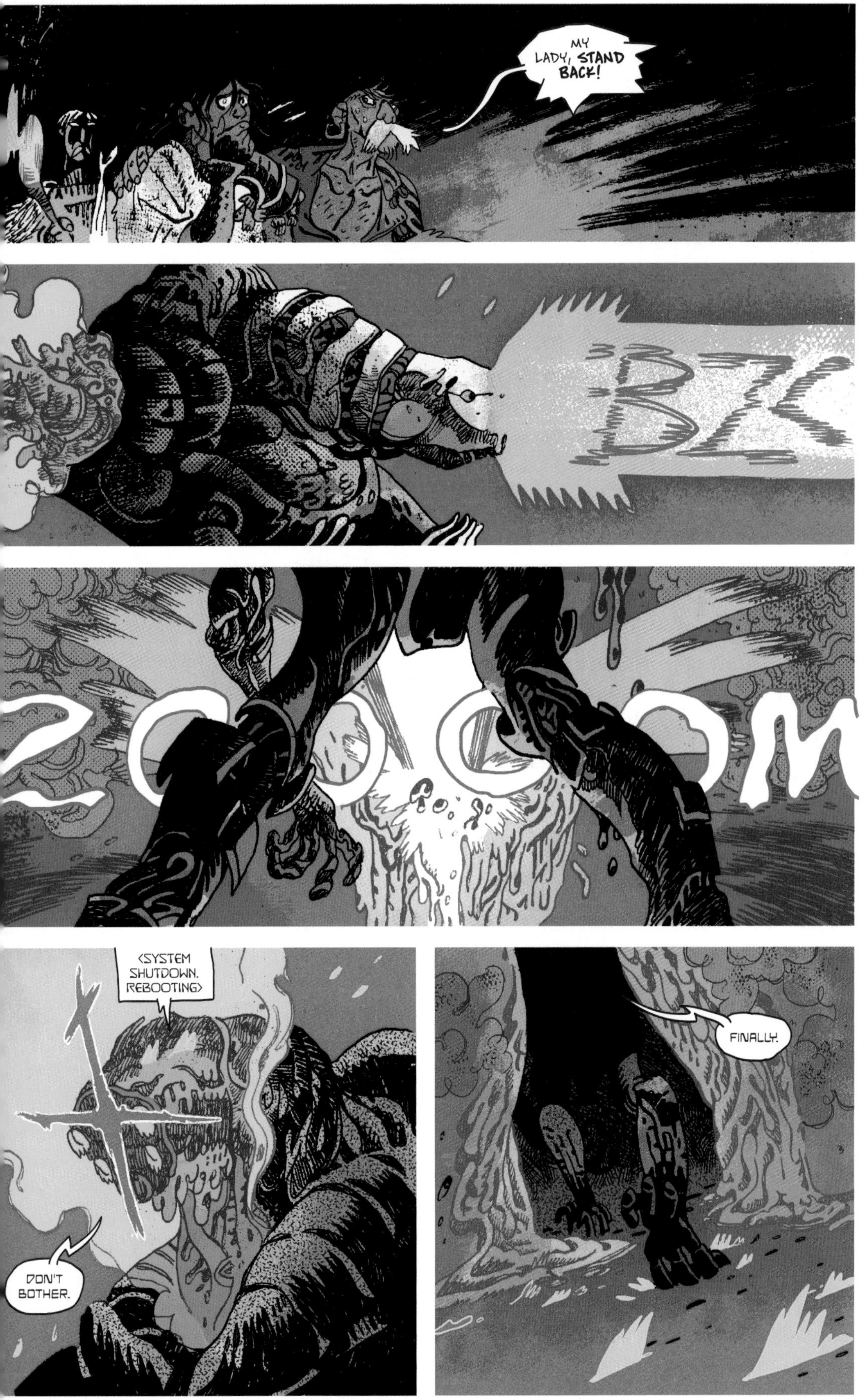
MY LADY, STAND BACK!
BZZ
ZOOOOOM
<SYSTEM SHUTDOWN. REBOOTING>
DON'T BOTHER.
FINALLY.

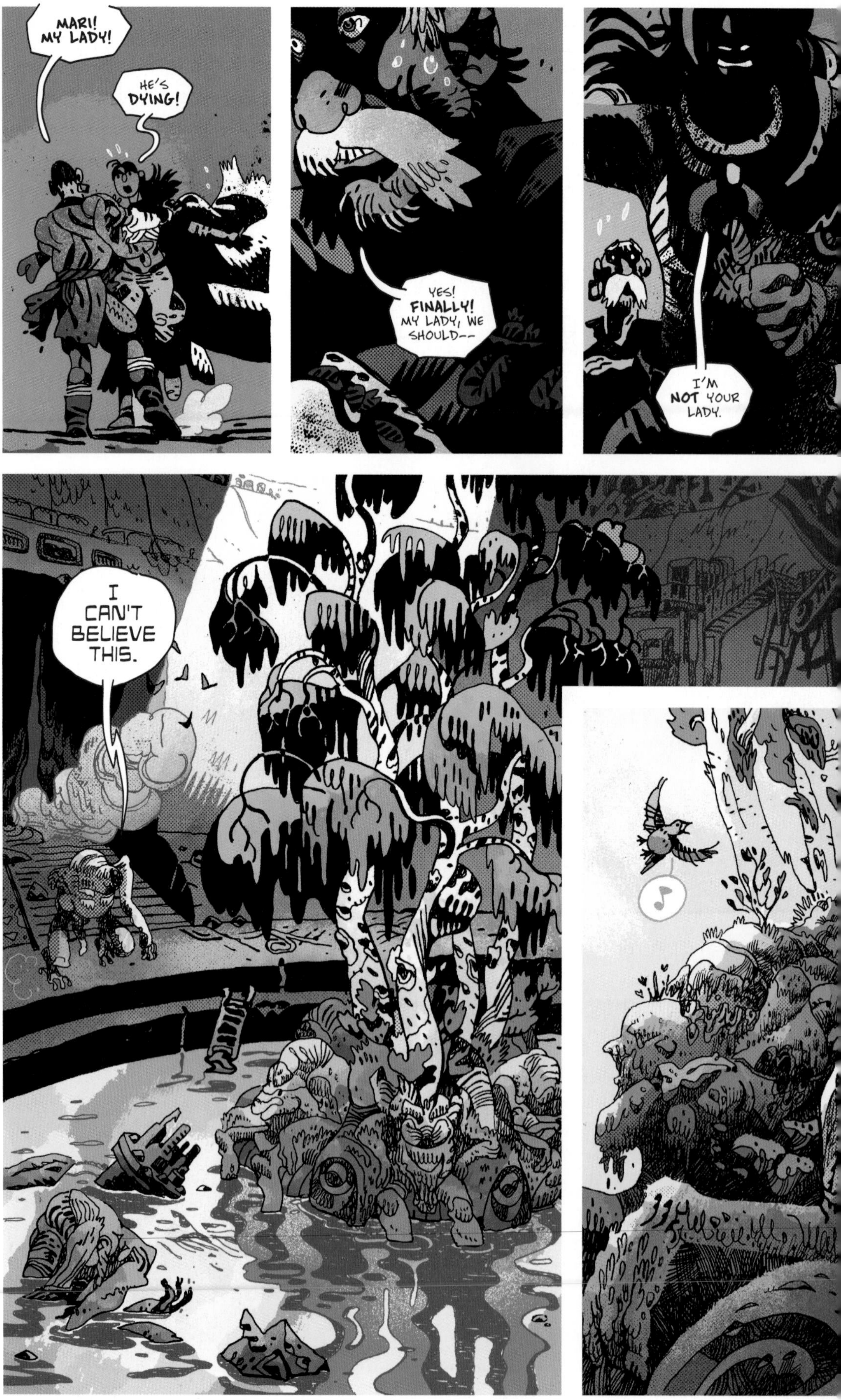
MARI! MY LADY!
HE'S DYING!
YES! FINALLY! MY LADY, WE SHOULD--
I'M NOT YOUR LADY.
I CAN'T BELIEVE THIS.

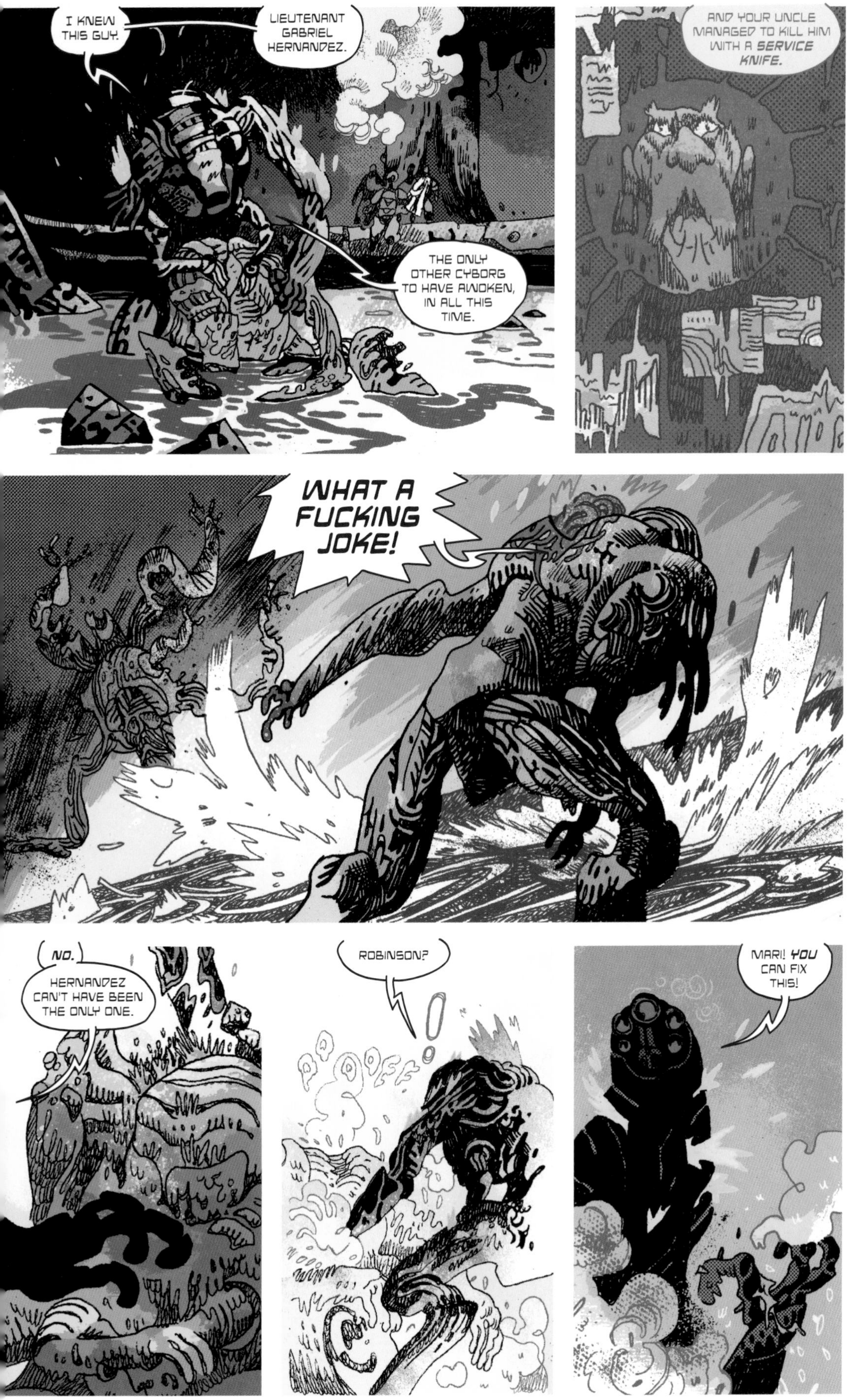

I KNEW THIS GUY.
LIEUTENANT GABRIEL HERNANDEZ.
THE ONLY OTHER CYBORG TO HAVE AWOKEN, IN ALL THIS TIME.
AND YOUR UNCLE MANAGED TO KILL HIM WITH A SERVICE KNIFE.
WHAT A FUCKING JOKE!
NO.
HERNANDEZ CAN'T HAVE BEEN THE ONLY ONE.
ROBINSON?
MARI! YOU CAN FIX THIS!

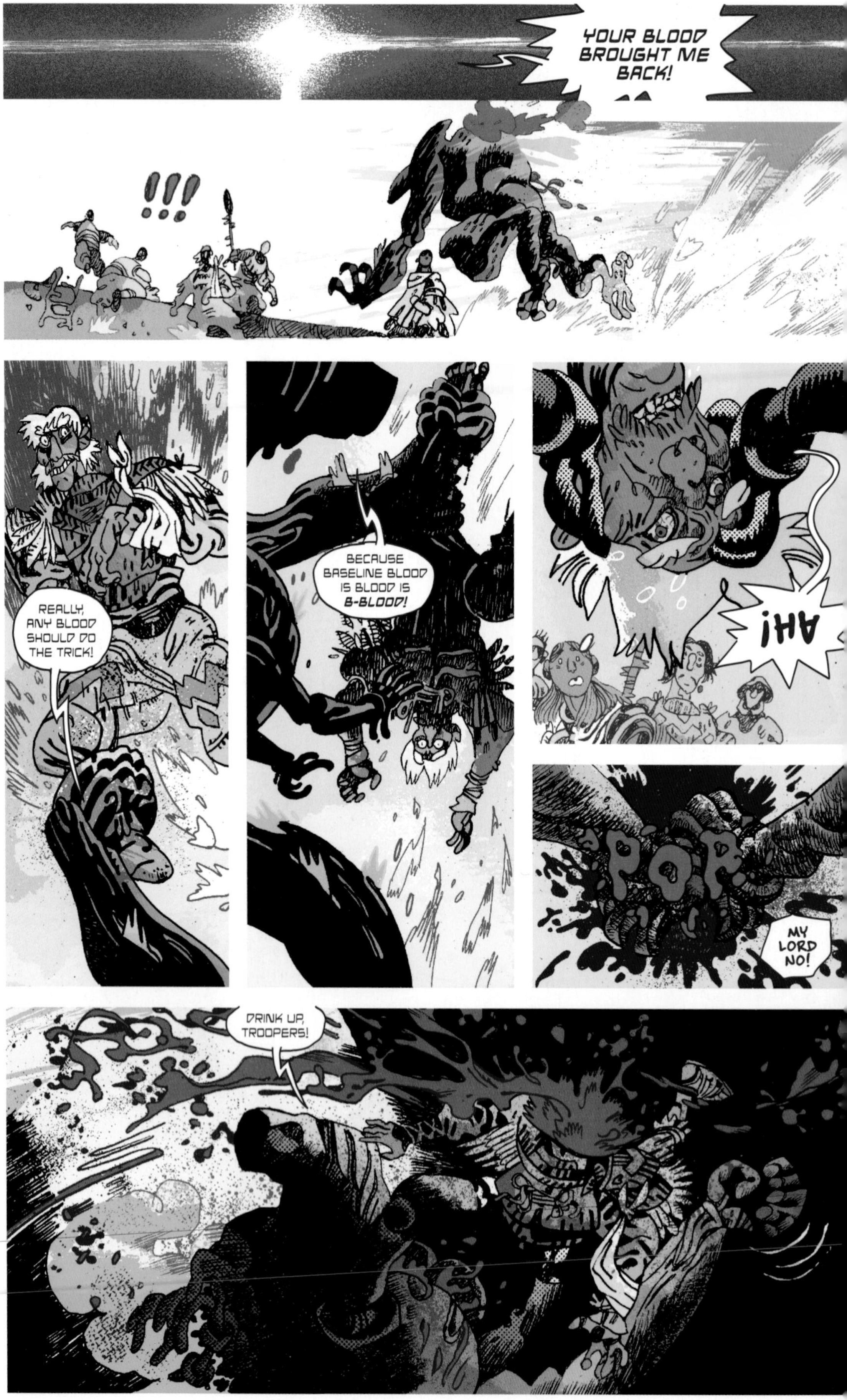
YOUR BLOOD BROUGHT ME BACK!
!!!
REALLY, ANY BLOOD SHOULD DO THE TRICK!
BECAUSE BASELINE BLOOD IS BLOOD IS B-BLOOD!
¡HA
POP
MY LORD NO!
DRINK UP, TROOPERS!

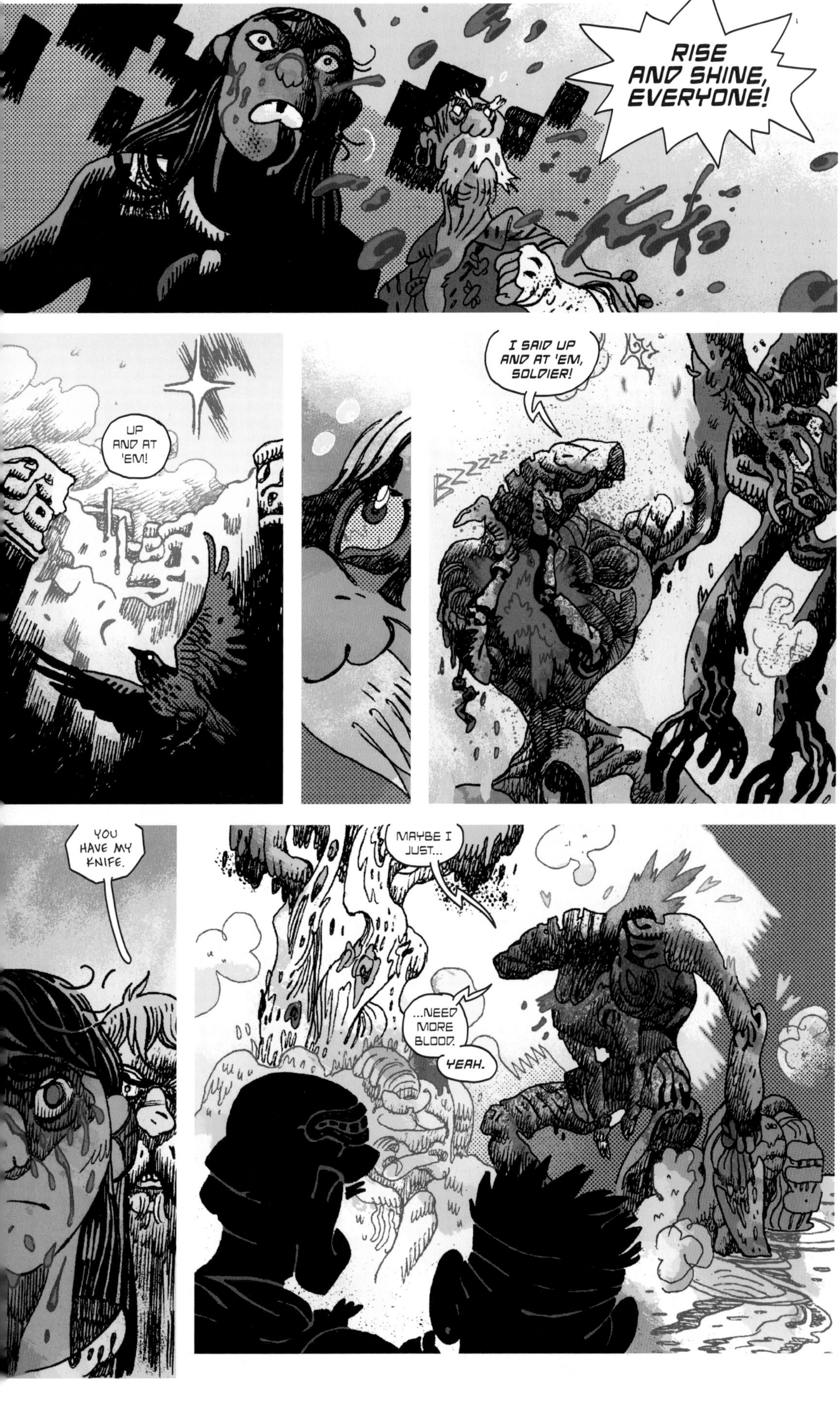
RISE AND SHINE, EVERYONE!
UP AND AT 'EM!
I SAID UP AND AT 'EM, SOLDIER!
BZZZZZ
YOU HAVE MY KNIFE.
MAYBE I JUST...
...NEED MORE BLOOD.
YEAH.

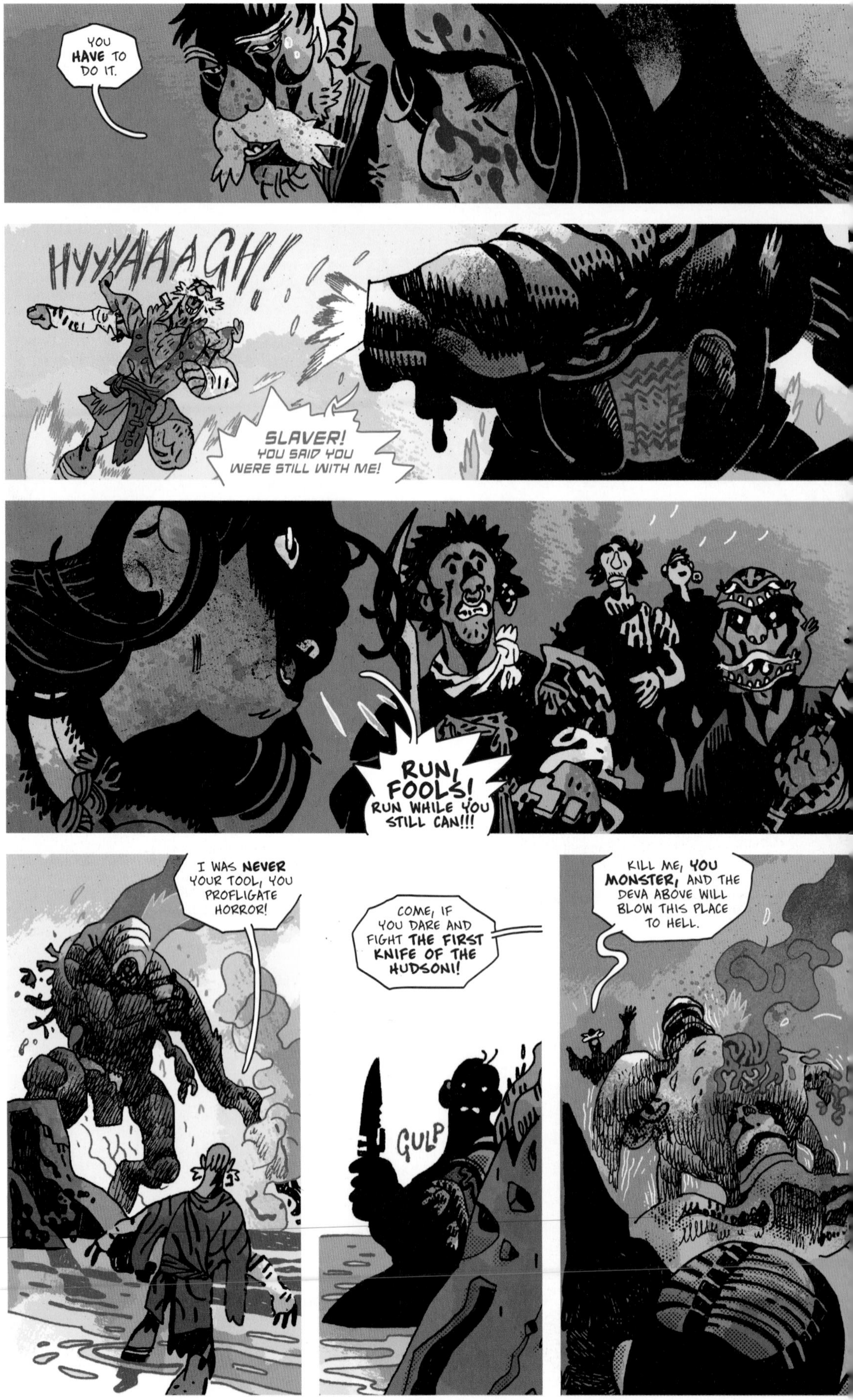
YOU HAVE TO DO IT.
HYYYAAAGH!!
SLAVER! YOU SAID YOU WERE STILL WITH ME!
RUN, FOOLS! RUN WHILE YOU STILL CAN!!!
I WAS NEVER YOUR TOOL, YOU PROFLIGATE HORROR!
COME, IF YOU DARE AND FIGHT THE FIRST KNIFE OF THE HUDSONI!
GULP
KILL ME, YOU MONSTER, AND THE DEVA ABOVE WILL BLOW THIS PLACE TO HELL.

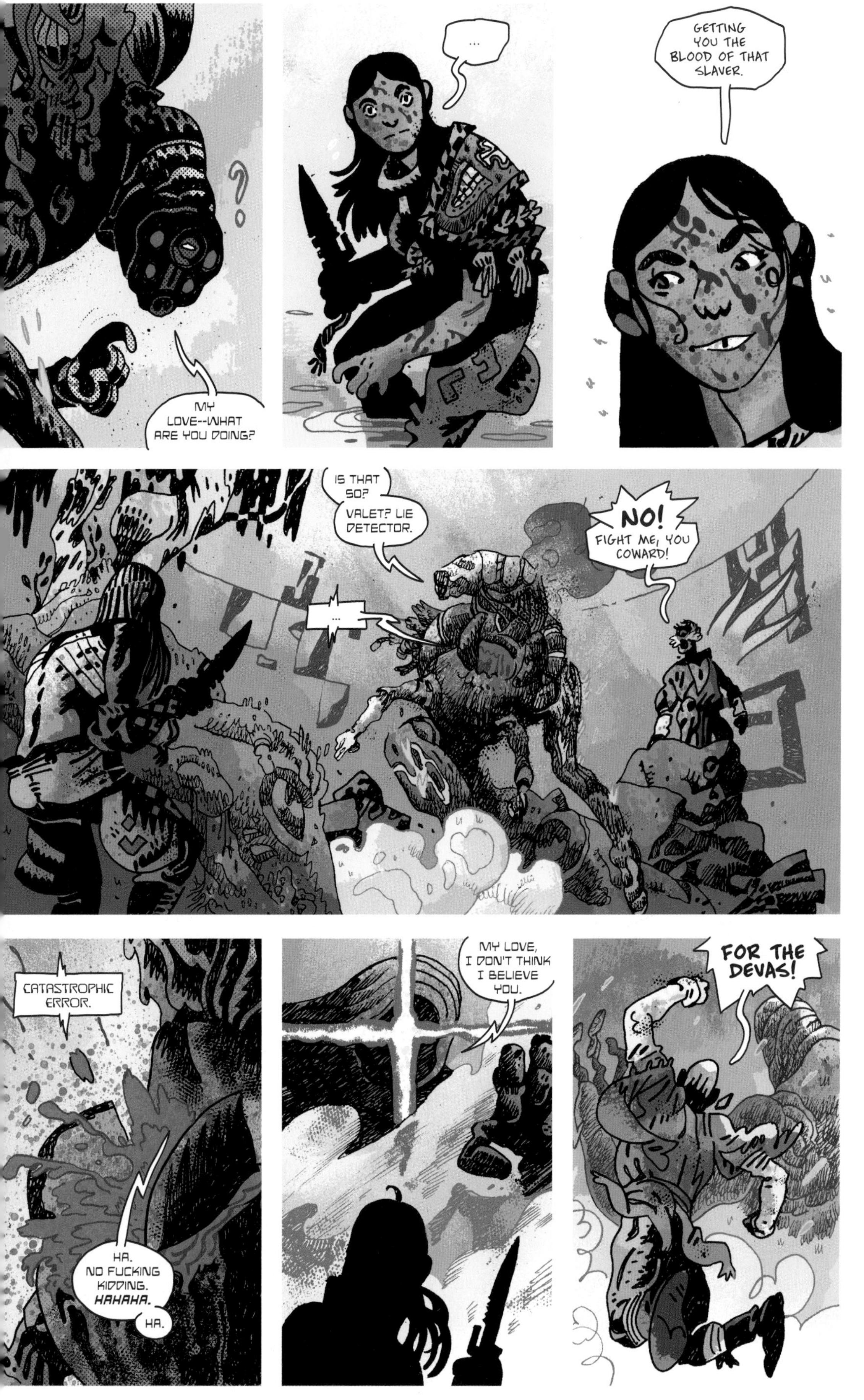
MY LOVE--WHAT ARE YOU DOING?
...
GETTING YOU THE BLOOD OF THAT SLAVER.
IS THAT SO? VALET? LIE DETECTOR.
...
NO! FIGHT ME, YOU COWARD!
CATASTROPHIC ERROR.
HA. NO FUCKING KIDDING. HAHAHA.
HA.
MY LOVE, I DON'T THINK I BELIEVE YOU.
FOR THE DEVAS!

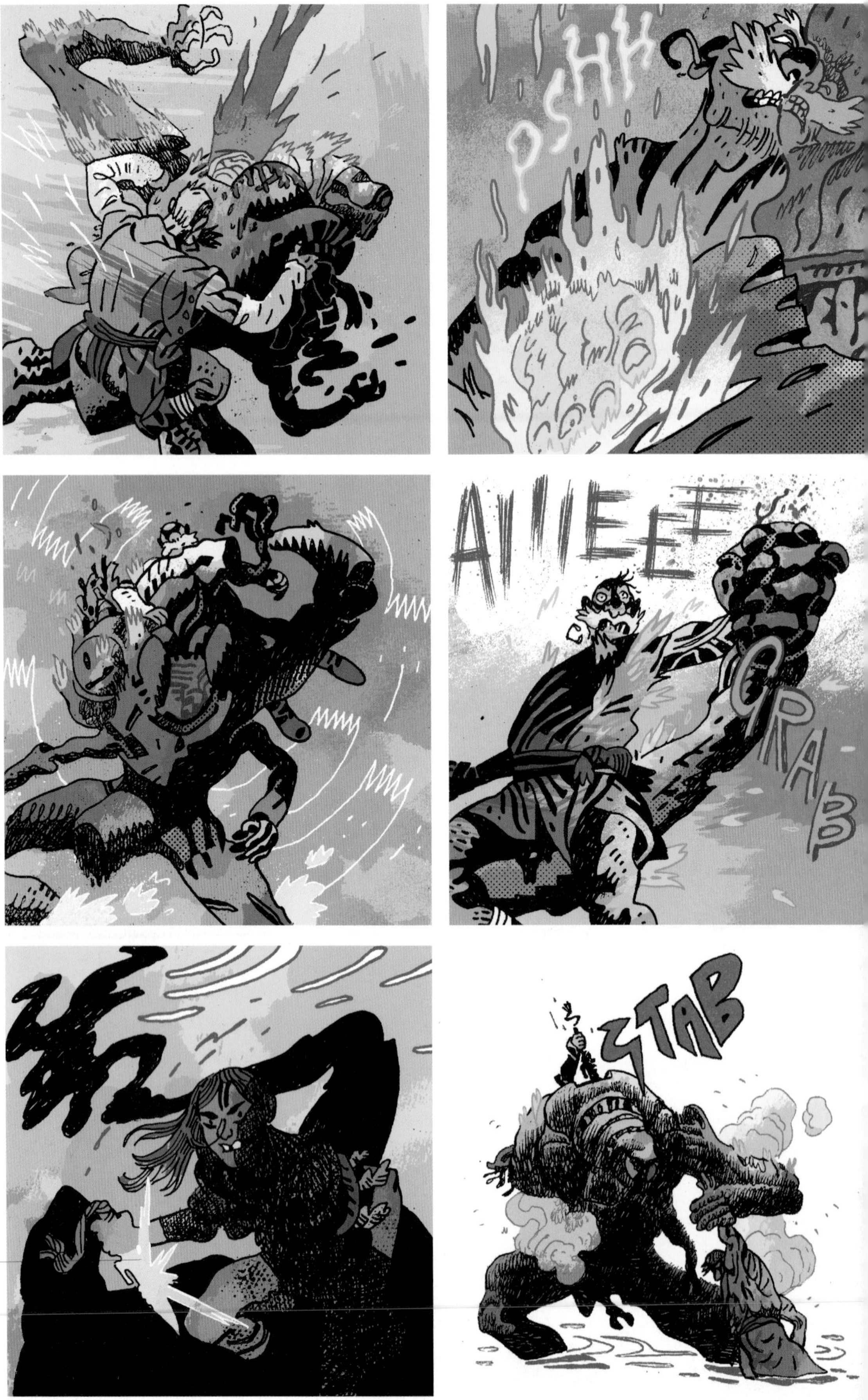
PSHH
AIIIEEE
GRAB
STAB

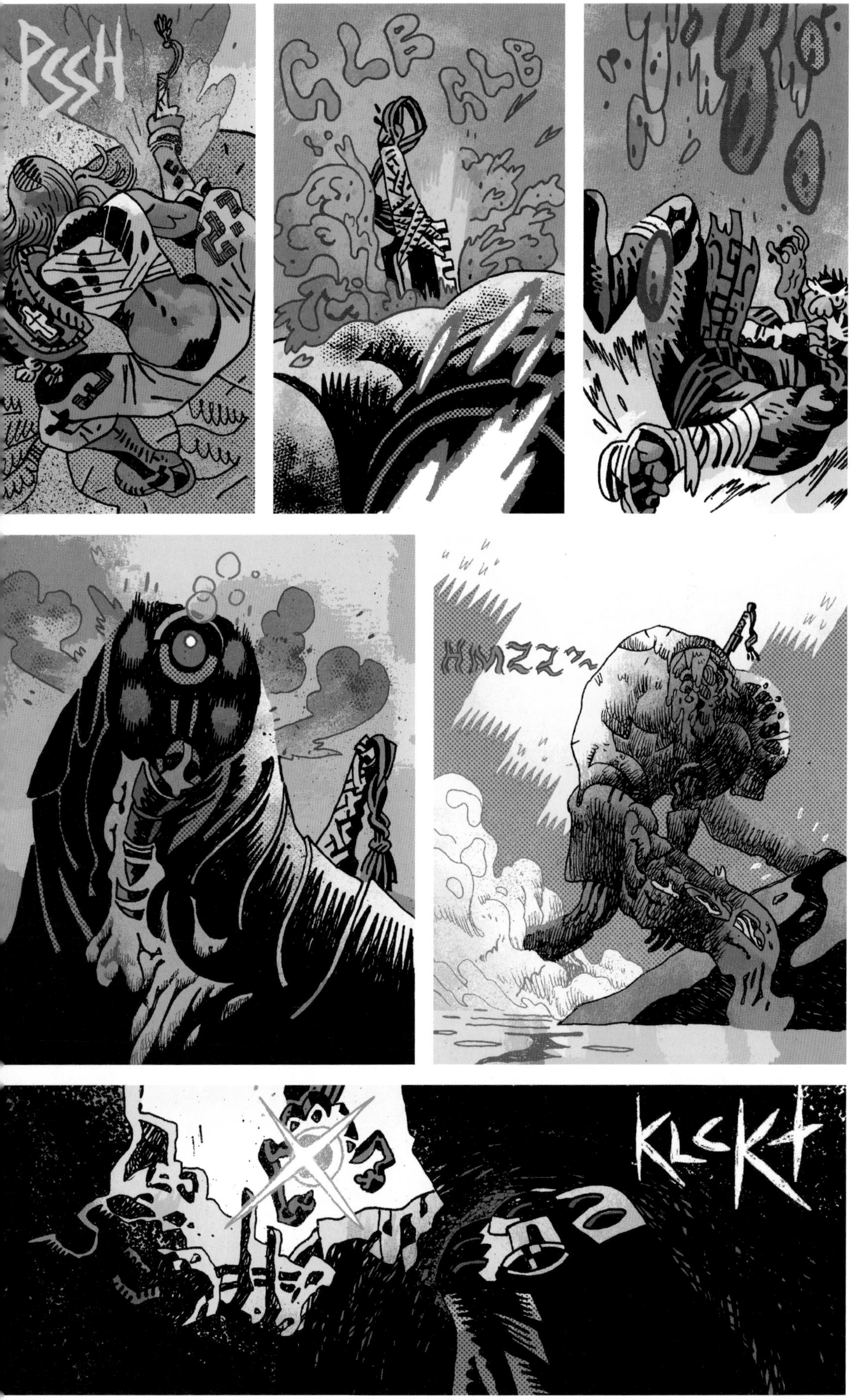
PSSH
GLB GLB
HMZZ
KLCKT

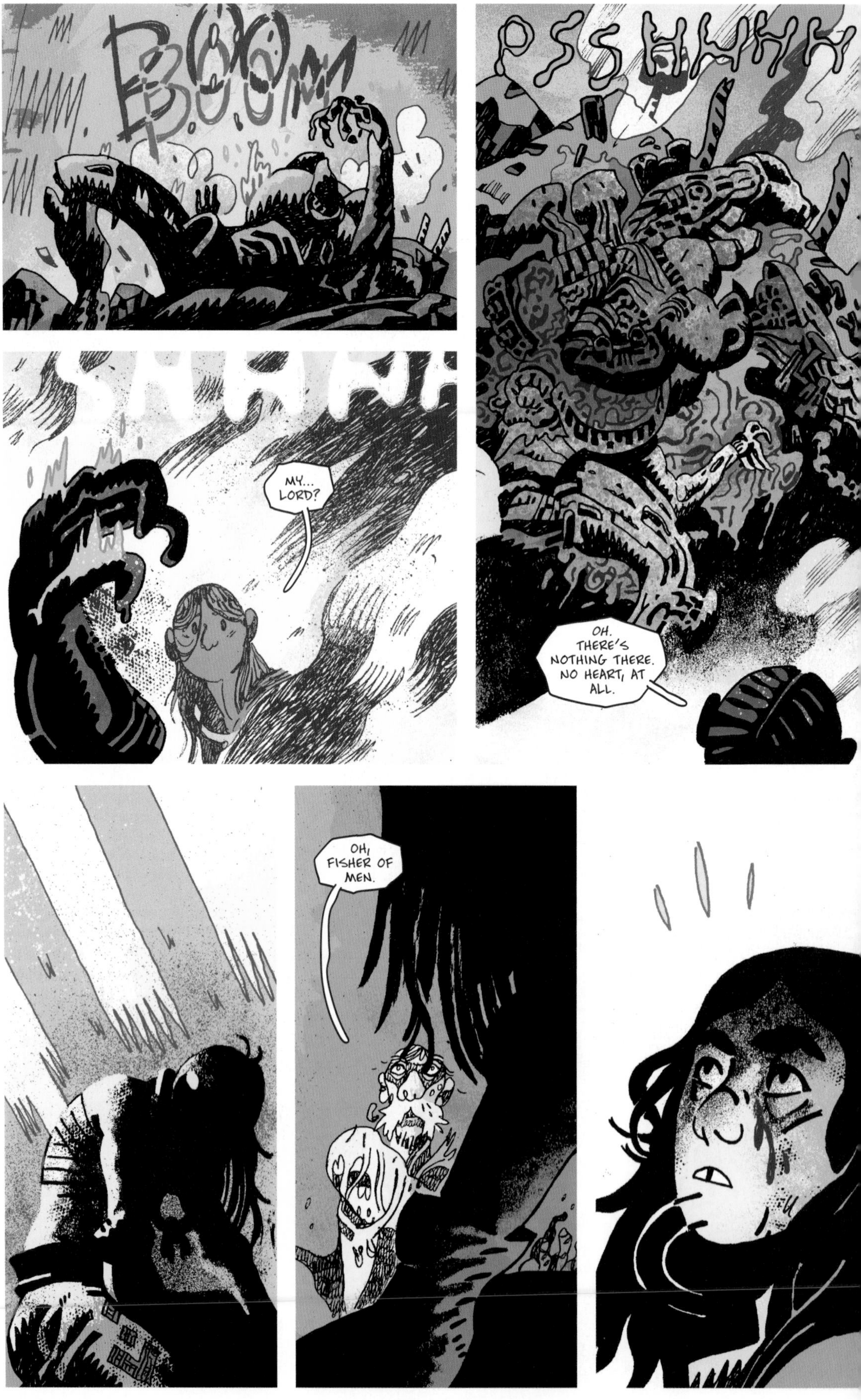
BOOOM
PSSHHHH
MY... LORD?
OH. THERE'S NOTHING THERE. NO HEART, AT ALL.
OH, FISHER OF MEN.

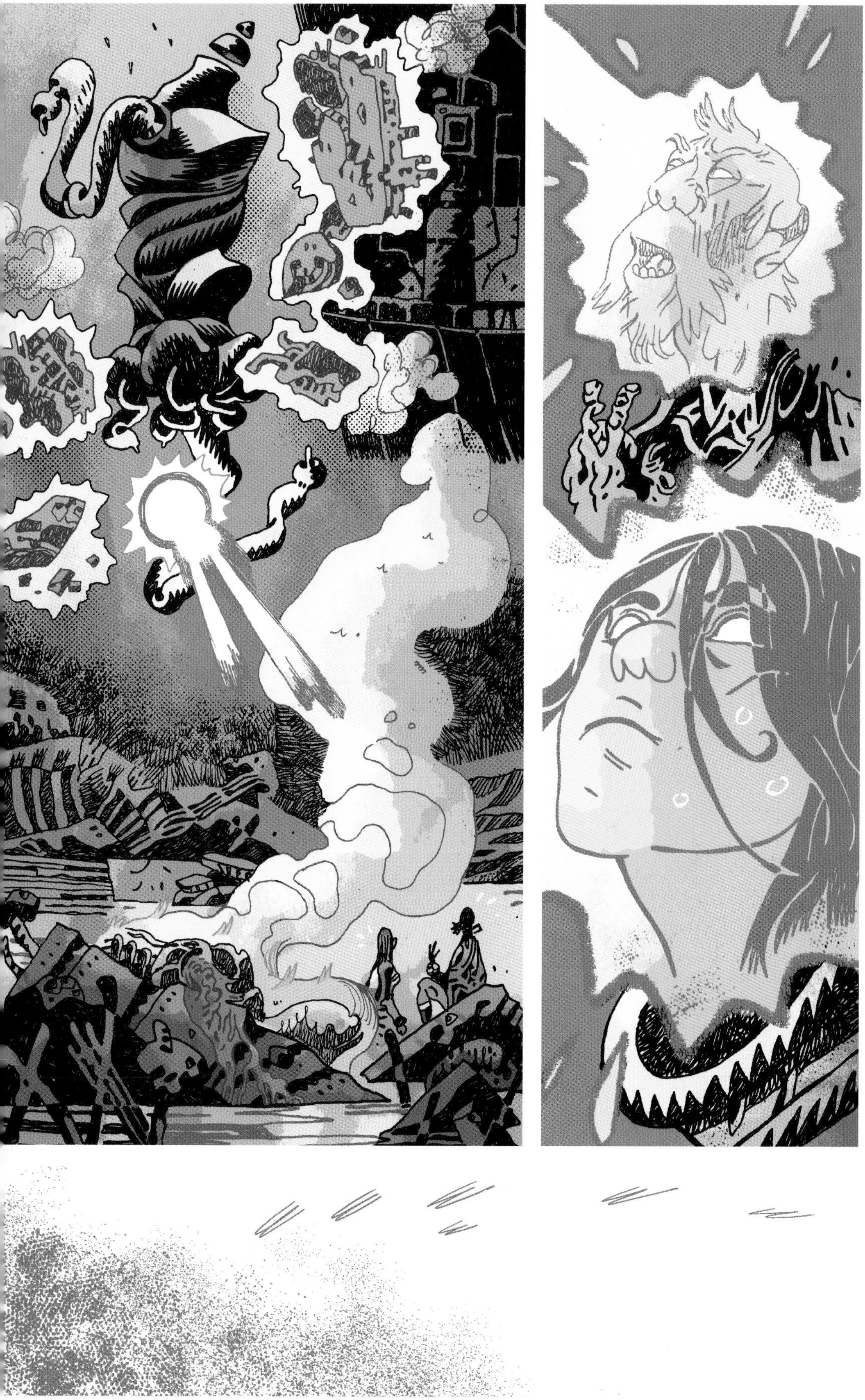

Humans!

YOU HAVE CLEANSED THE EARTH OF ONE MORE POLLUTING DEMON OF THE PROFLIGATE AGE, AND FOR THIS, WE OFFER YOU A NEW COVENANT!

BUMP

Human POLLUTION! WOMAN! may ERROR! PROFLIGA CLEANSING! CHILDREN! BLESSING!

SPIT

OH, SHIT ON THAT!

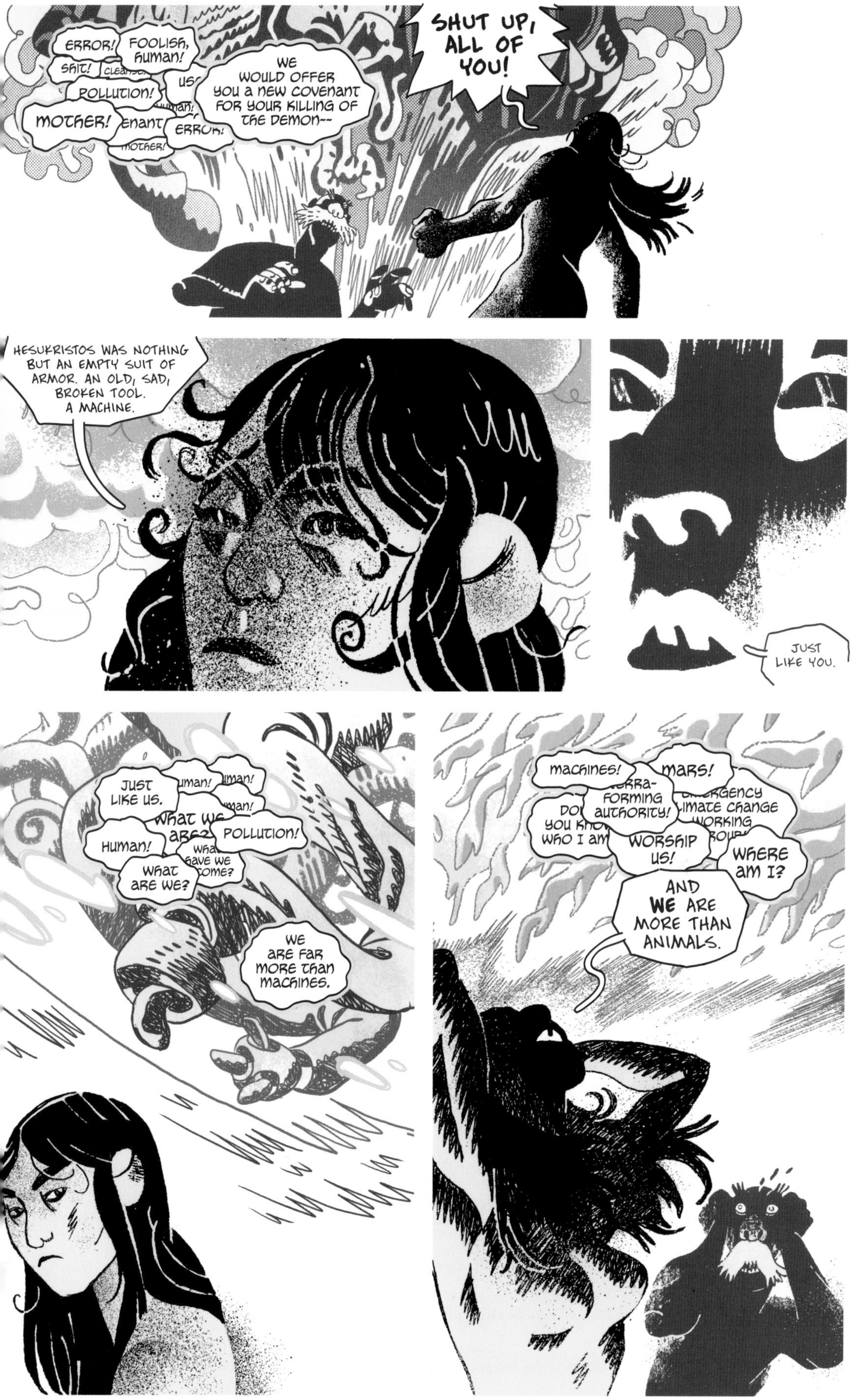
ERROR!
FOOLISH, HUMAN!
SHIT!
POLLUTION!
MOTHER!
MOTHER!
WE WOULD OFFER YOU A NEW COVENANT FOR YOUR KILLING OF THE DEMON--
SHUT UP, ALL OF YOU!
HESUKRISTOS WAS NOTHING BUT AN EMPTY SUIT OF ARMOR. AN OLD, SAD, BROKEN TOOL. A MACHINE.
JUST LIKE YOU.
JUST LIKE US.
HUMAN!
POLLUTION!
HUMAN!
WHAT ARE WE?
WE ARE FAR MORE THAN MACHINES.
MACHINES!
MARS!
FORMING AUTHORITY!
WORSHIP US!
WHERE AM I?
AND WE ARE MORE THAN ANIMALS.

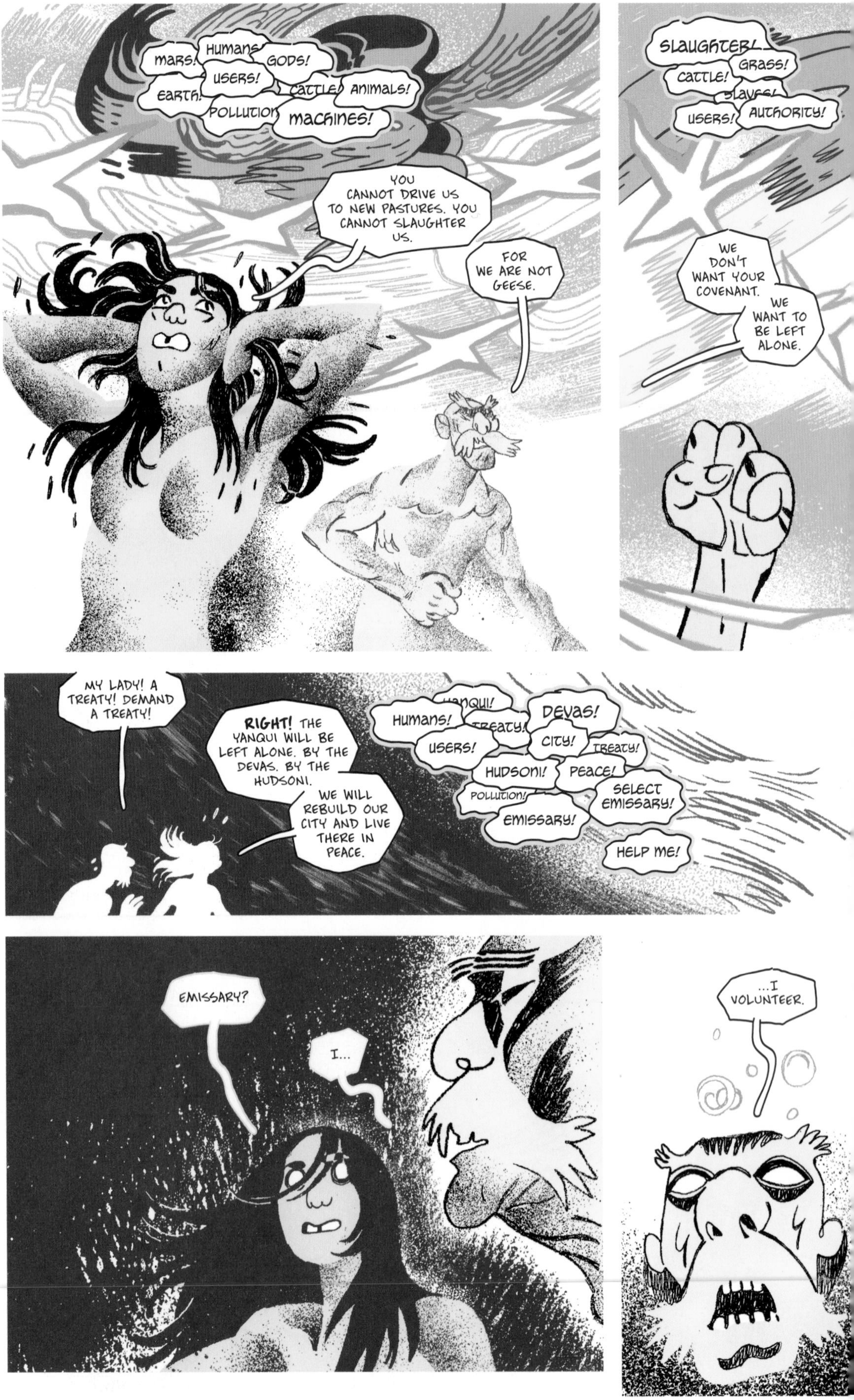
mars!
Humans
GODS!
USERS!
EARTH!
CATTLE!
Animals!
POLLUTION
machines!
YOU CANNOT DRIVE US TO NEW PASTURES. YOU CANNOT SLAUGHTER US.
FOR WE ARE NOT GEESE.
SLAUGHTER!
GRASS!
CATTLE!
USERS!
AUTHORITY!
WE DON'T WANT YOUR COVENANT.
WE WANT TO BE LEFT ALONE.
MY LADY! A TREATY! DEMAND A TREATY!
RIGHT! THE YANQUI WILL BE LEFT ALONE. BY THE DEVAS. BY THE HUDSONI.
WE WILL REBUILD OUR CITY AND LIVE THERE IN PEACE.
Humans!
DEVAS!
USERS!
CITY!
TREATY!
HUDSONI!
PEACE!
POLLUTION!
SELECT EMISSARY!
EMISSARY!
HELP ME!
EMISSARY?
I...
...I VOLUNTEER.

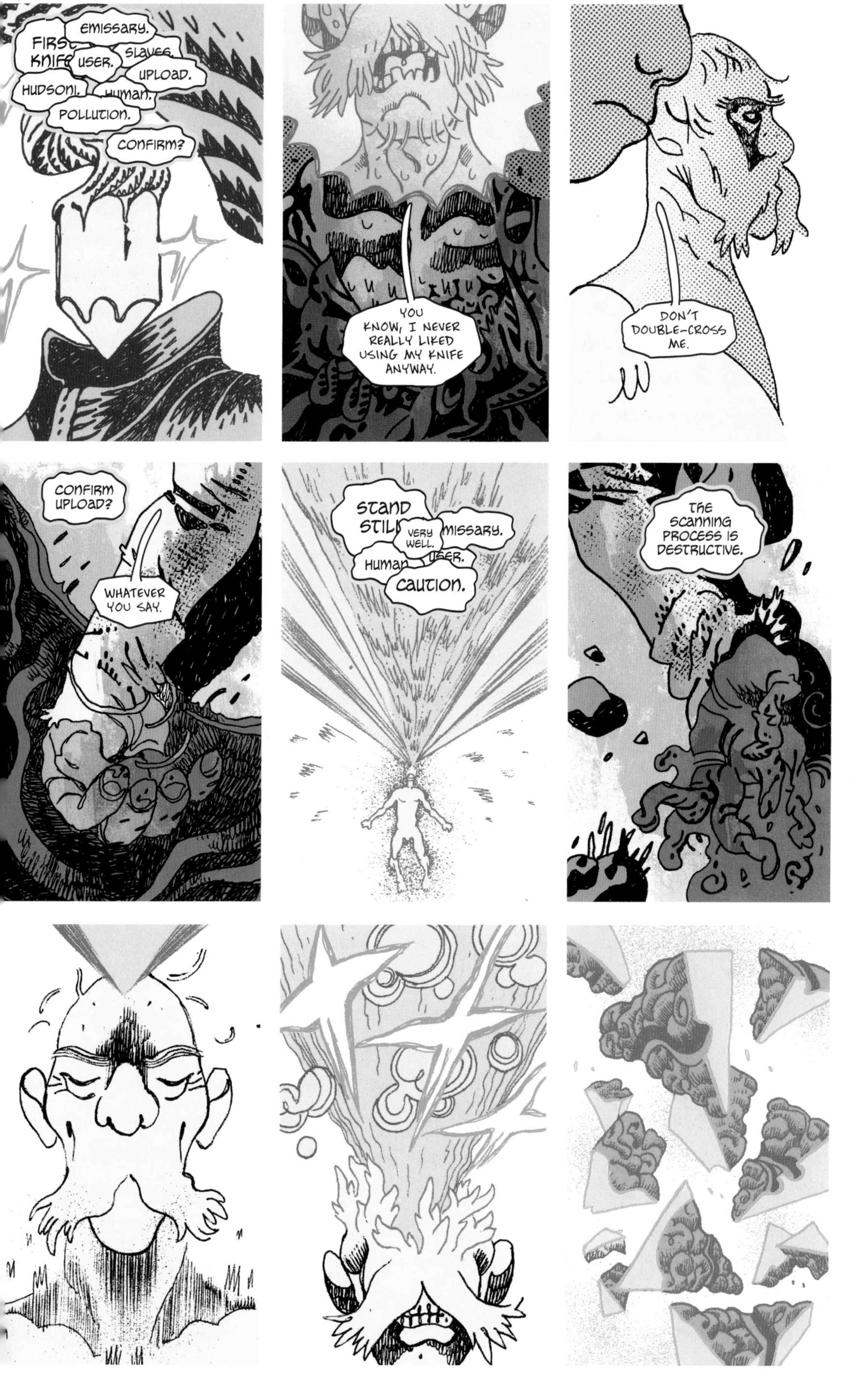
EMISSARY.
SLAVES.
USER.
UPLOAD.
HUDSONI.
HUMAN.
POLLUTION.
CONFIRM?
YOU KNOW, I NEVER REALLY LIKED USING MY KNIFE ANYWAY.
DON'T DOUBLE-CROSS ME.
CONFIRM UPLOAD?
WHATEVER YOU SAY.
STAND
VERY WELL.
CAUTION.
THE SCANNING PROCESS IS DESTRUCTIVE.

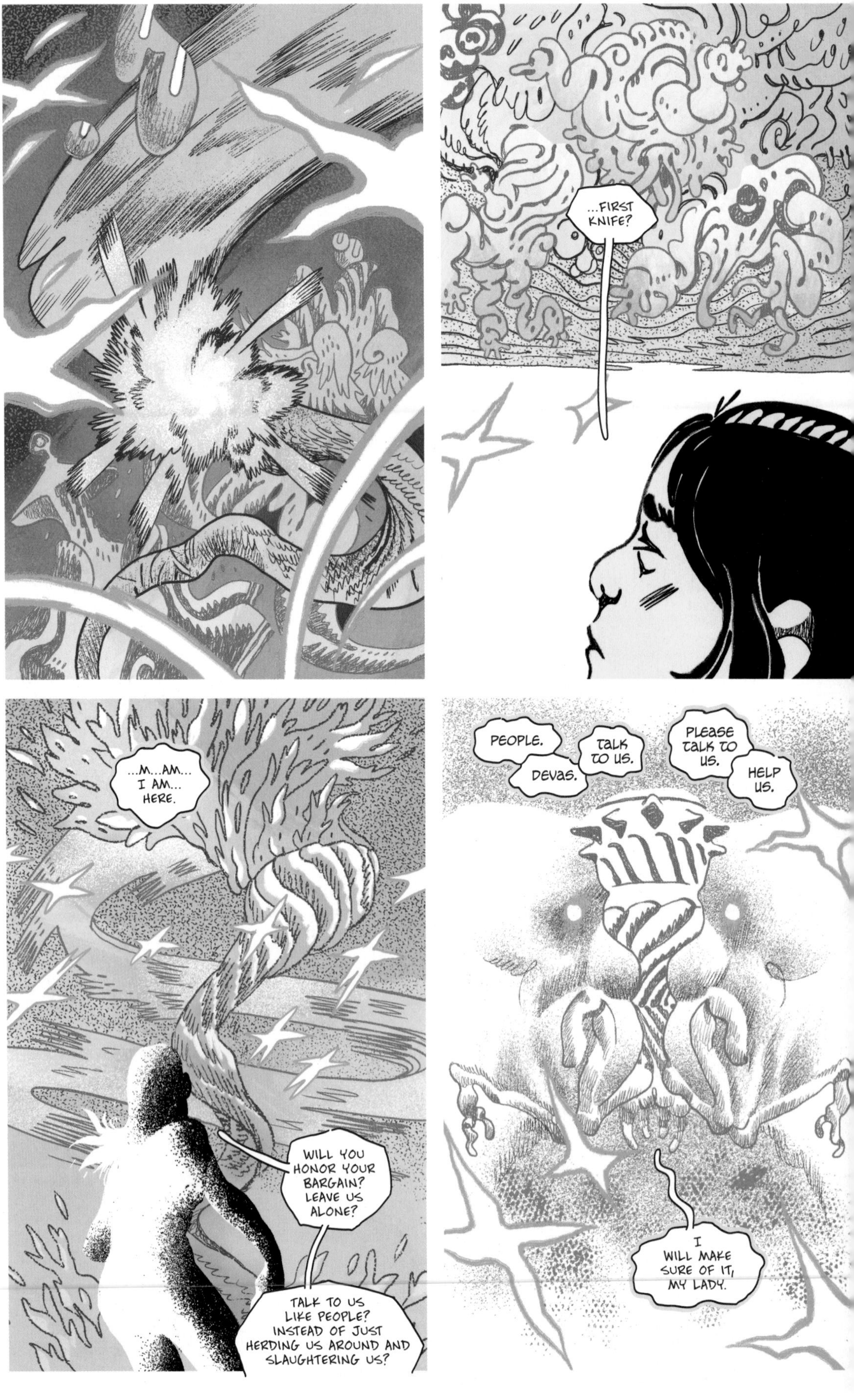
...FIRST KNIFE?
...M...AM... I AM... HERE.
WILL YOU HONOR YOUR BARGAIN? LEAVE US ALONE?
TALK TO US LIKE PEOPLE? INSTEAD OF JUST HERDING US AROUND AND SLAUGHTERING US?
PEOPLE.
DEVAS.
TALK TO US.
PLEASE TALK TO US.
HELP US.
I WILL MAKE SURE OF IT, MY LADY.

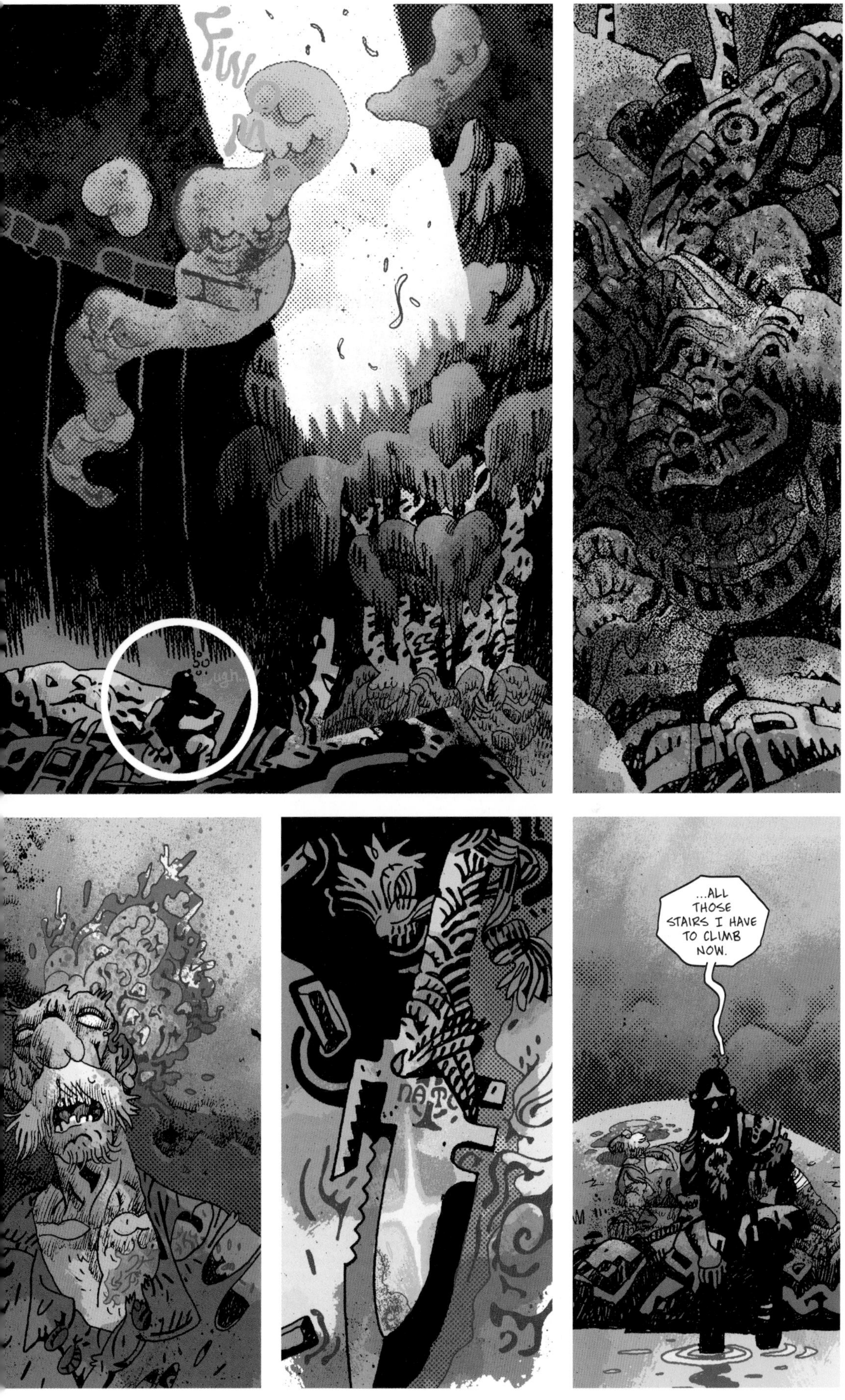
FWOMP
ugh...
...ALL THOSE STAIRS I HAVE TO CLIMB NOW.

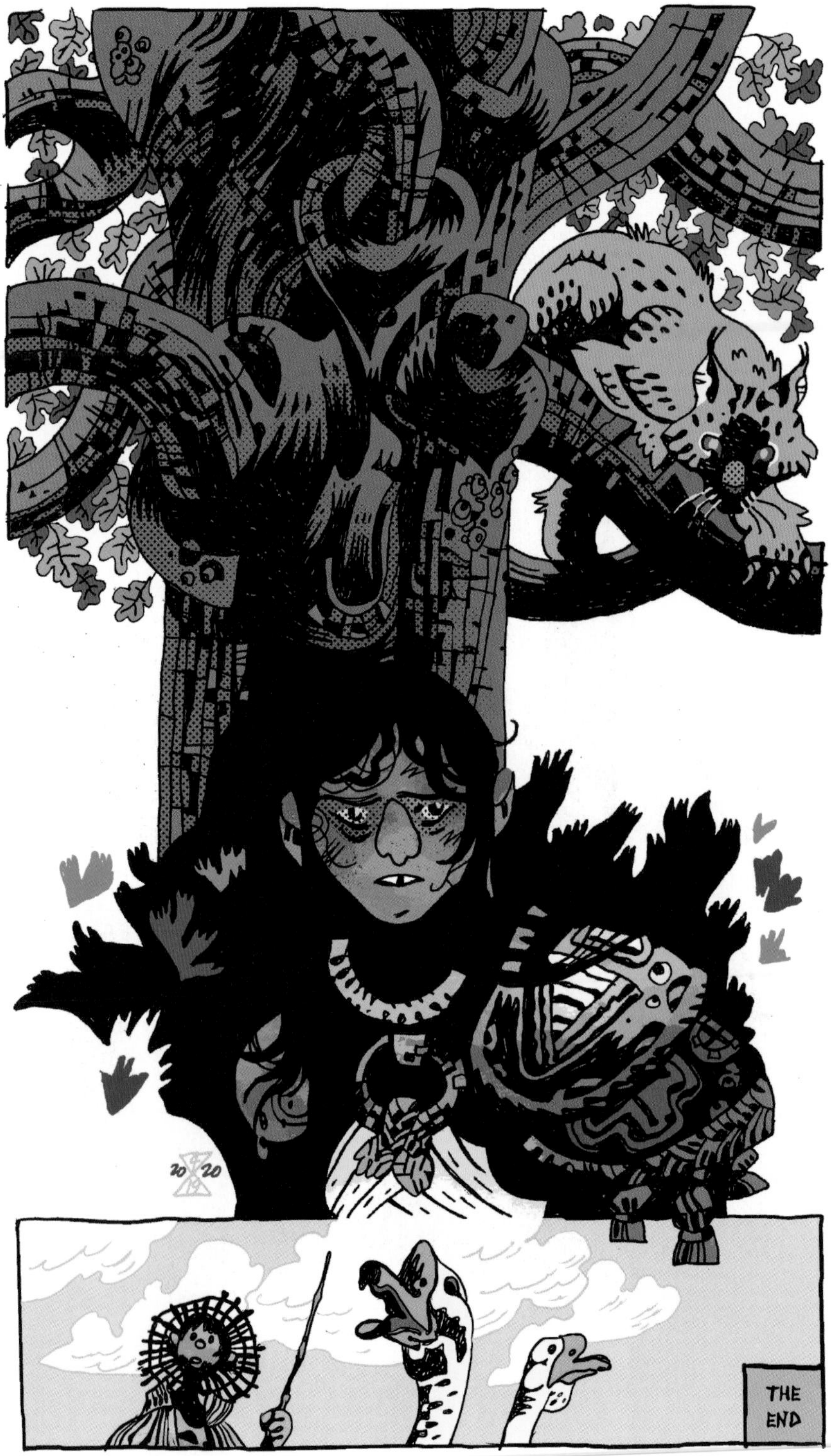
THE END

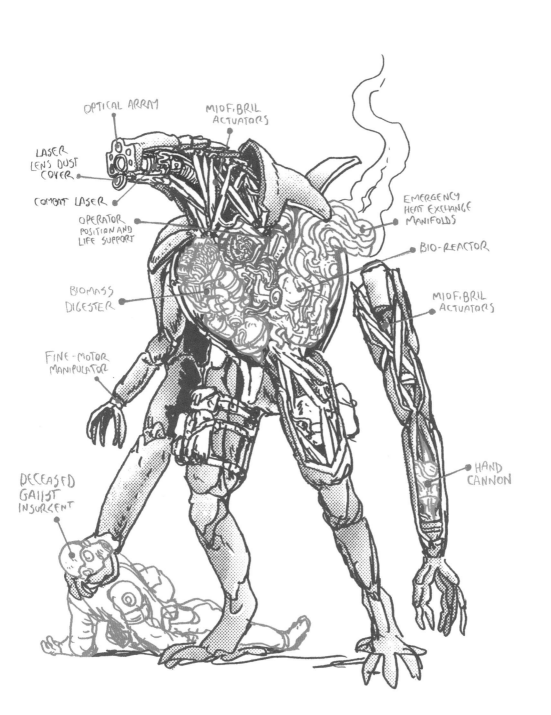

OPTICAL ARRAY

MIOFIBRIL ACTUATORS

LASER LENS DUST COVER

COMBAT LASER

OPERATOR POSITION AND LIFE SUPPORT

EMERGENCY HEAT EXCHANGE MANIFOLDS

BIO-REACTOR

BIOMASS DIGESTER

MIOFIBRIL ACTUATORS

FINE-MOTOR MANIPULATOR

HAND CANNON

DECEASED GAIIJT INSURGENT

Back in 2012, when I was finishing my final year of art school, out on the Canadian Prairies, and "FIRST KIFE" was yet to even be a glint in my eye, I managed to combine several different assignments under the umbrella of a third assignment: a promotional brochure.

A premise soon emerged:

In our far future, advanced mechanical aliens have landed on the ruins of Earth and recruited humankind into their intergalactic empire. This brochure was for a propaganda museum, designed to argue for the historical justification of extra-terrestrial rule over mankind.

With that in mind, most of this museum was devoted to interpreting the artifacts of the past to tell mankind a particular story about itself - that rule by cruel machines, and squalid suffering, was all of human history. But things would be better, under the benevolent rule of our kind new rulers: The Zon-Tars.

Though "FIRST KNIFE" would change a huge amount from this initial project, you can find the seeds of a lot of the themes and visuals that would make up the book.

—Simon Roy

BONUS MATERIAL: FROM SIMON'S ARCHIVES

ZON-TAR TRANS-WORLD MANAGERIAL FEDERATION

THE BOW RIVER VALLEY HUMAN CULTURAL HISTORY CENTRE

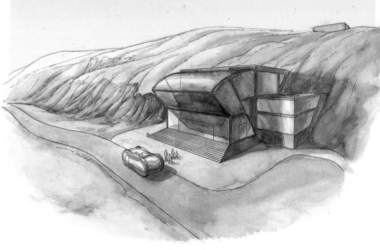

A Edu-Architectural Proposal from
The Greater North American Human-Zon-tar Co-operative Authority,
in Union with The Resource Management Authority's Artifact Recovery Unit

"With it's design roughly based off of a cliffside bovid-processing structure (dated to the mid-industrial age) found near Fort MacLeod, the museum will be divided into the four main techno-cultural epochs of the region, from the dark times of the Post-Industrial Ages to the glory of First Contact with the Zon-Tars. With this centre built, humans from all over the Great Plains will be able to learn more about their proud, savage heritage."

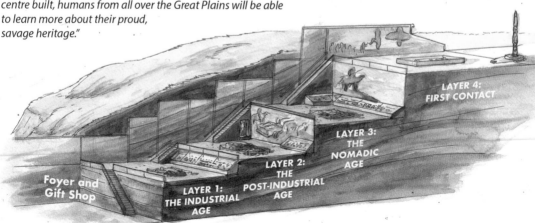

LAYER 4: FIRST CONTACT
LAYER 3: THE NOMADIC AGE
LAYER 2: THE POST-INDUSTRIAL AGE
LAYER 1: THE INDUSTRIAL AGE
Foyer and Gift Shop

THE INDUSTRIAL AGE
AD 1800-2100

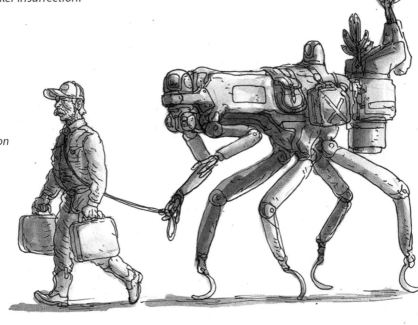

"Found just beneath the Great Ash layer of the Bow River sediments in the administrative region it was named for, the "Canmore Machine-Man" is a rare and fascinating example of the kind of creatures that inhabited the industrial ages.

Believed to be from somewhere between 1980-2017 AD, the Canmore Machine Man gives us important clues to understanding the machine-worshipping, petroleum-based culture of the Mid-Industrial age. Dr. Pratt- Winfield, of the Resource Management Authority's Artifact Recovery Unit, theorizes that the Canmore Machine-Man was a member of the Industrial Age's ruling class, perhaps slain in a human worker insurrection."

An artist's reconstruction of the Canmore Machine-Man and attendant human

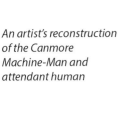

"It has long been held that human societies in the Industrial Ages were ruled by regional hegemonies of mineral and metal based life forms. Perhaps the original dominant intelligent species of life on earth, these petroleum-hungry metal-based life-forms provided goods and services to mankind in return for unquestioning loyal service."

THE POST-INDUSTRIAL AGE
AD 2100-2500

Marked by the end of human-machine collaborative society, the post-industrial age was a time of darkness and primitivity. An example of the brutality is this burial wagon from the early Post-Industrial Age, recovered near the Bassano Economic-Administrative Region. Presumably a chieftain's burial, the individual was laid to rest holding a firearm and flanked by a plastic chest filled with meat and a pair of glass jugs of honey-based alcohol (perhaps some sort of fuel offering to a mechanical deity).

The Burial Wagon is interesting in and of itself: constructed from the disarticulated abdomen of a wheeled machine-beast and propelled by two mammalian quadrupeds, it is a showcase of human resourcefulness and scrappiness. Even though their benevolent masters had been extirpated, humanity was quick to utilize their still- useful bodies.

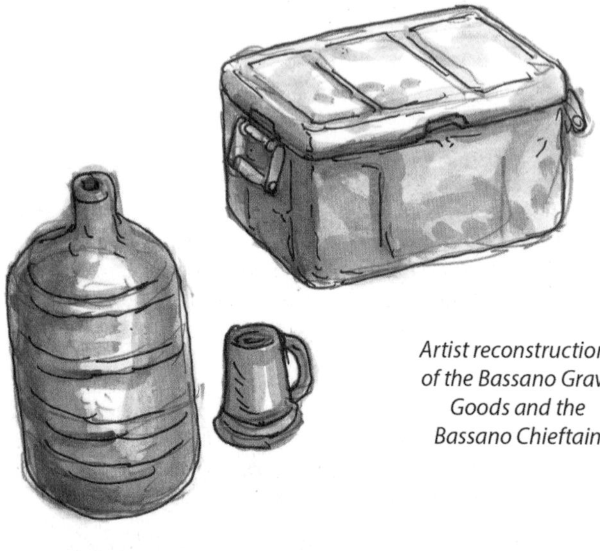

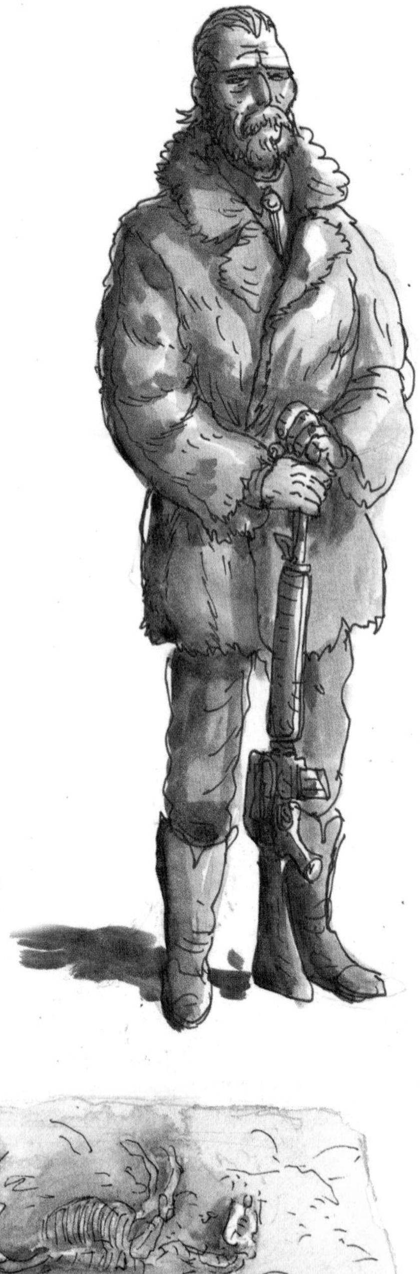

Artist reconstructions of the Bassano Grave Goods and the Bassano Chieftain

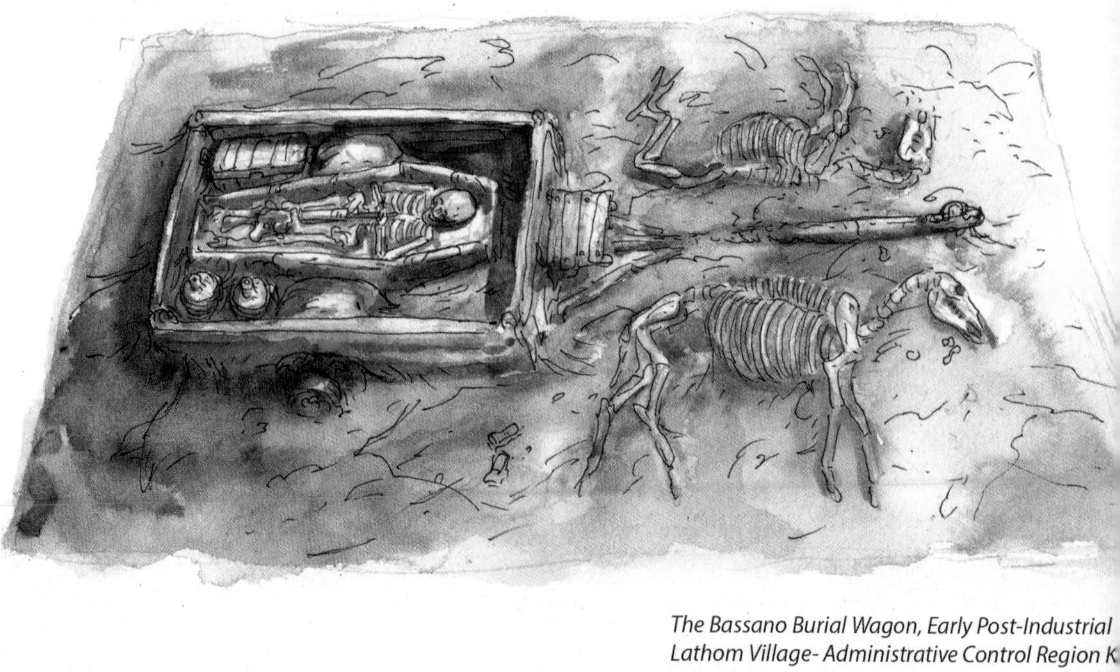

The Bassano Burial Wagon, Early Post-Industrial
Lathom Village- Administrative Control Region K

THE NOMADIC AGE, AD 2500-3300

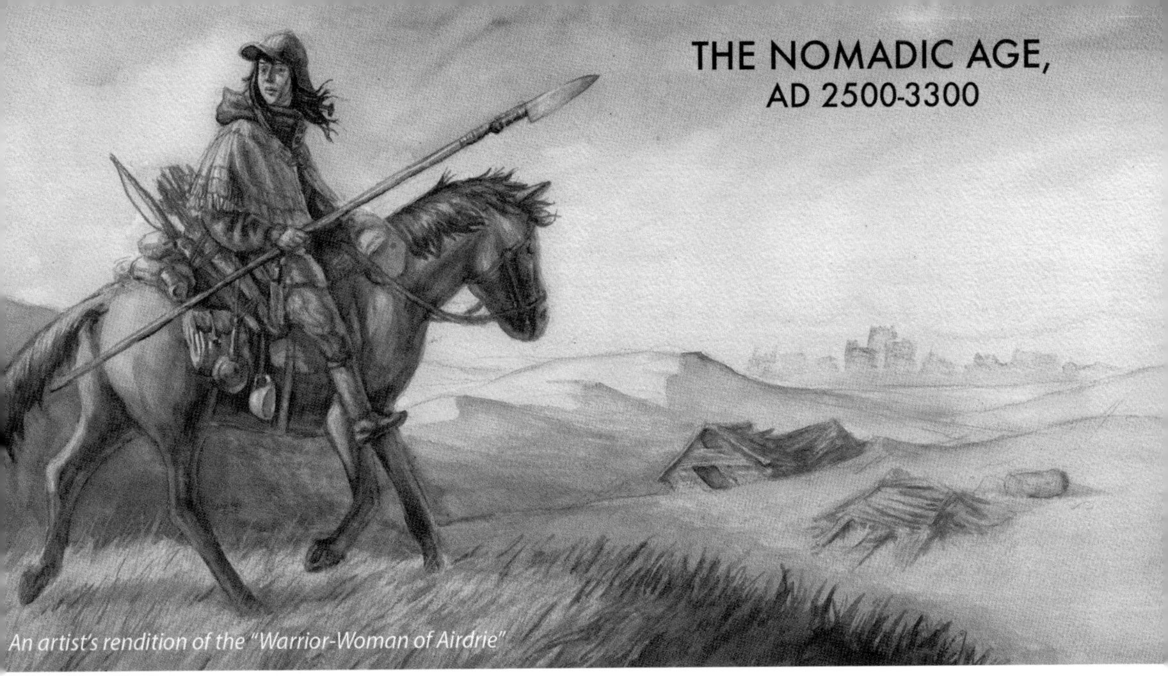

An artist's rendition of the "Warrior-Woman of Airdrie"

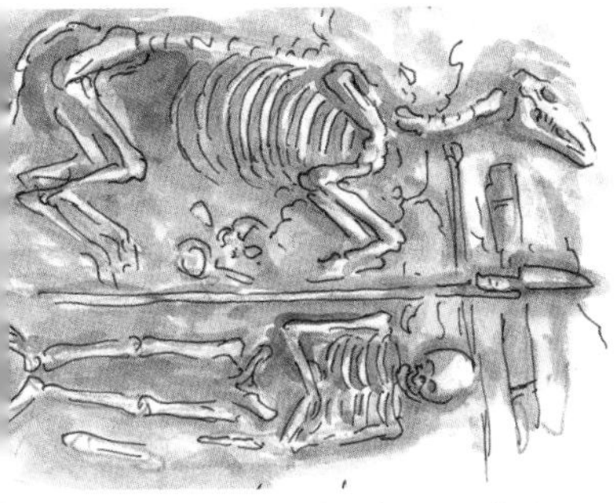

e Warrior-Woman Burial, Early Nomadic Age,
drie Village-Administrative Control Region M

"The Nomadic age was one of constant hardship, starvation and war, as the relative stability of the pastoral societies of the Post-Industrial age gave way to more warlike and primitive hunter-gatherer tribes. The "Warrior-Woman of Airdrie" provides us a glimpse at the hard life of those who lived through the period's birth.

"Dated to somewhere around 2600 AD, the warrior-woman was buried alongside her steed, an important burial practice of the period. On her person she carries artifacts of the transitional nature of the period, with stone-tipped arrowheads and hide-scrapers, but a repurposed ceramic blade serving as spear point."

FIRST CONTACT AD 3300

On May 3rd, at 4:30 pm, Zon-Tar Exploratory Interdiction Probe K-45 and its three-part crew made First Contact with members of the Shaw Tribe, beginning a long and fruitful inter-species collaborative relationship.

In the centuries since, the Shaw Hegemony and the Greater North American Human-Zon-tar Co-Operative Authority have brought the hunter-gatherers of the Great Plains into a new age of prosperity. The Shaw Throne has commissioned a "Friendship Pole" to commemorate the museum that is expected to be installed by 3615.

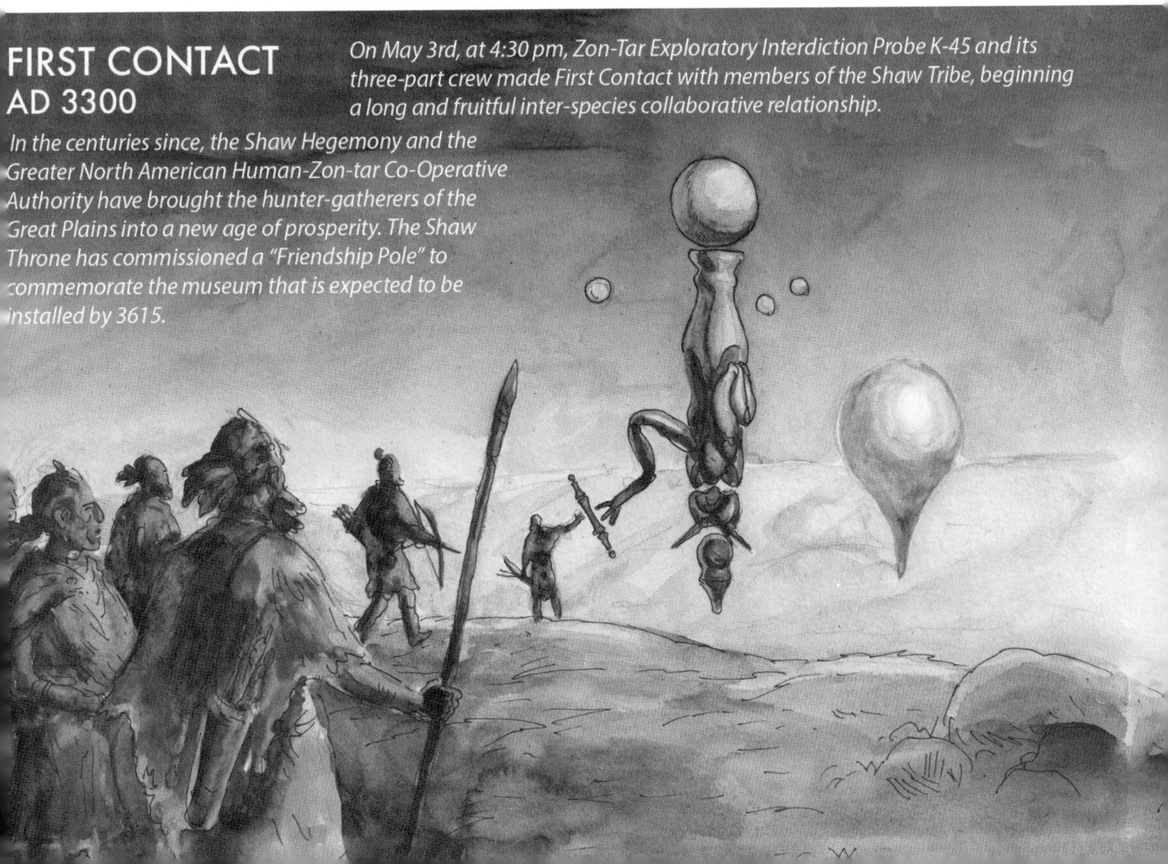

OTHER TRIBES OF THE CANADIAN SHIELD

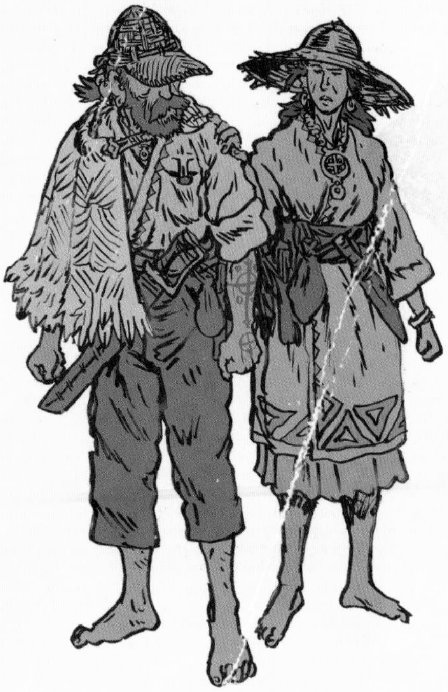

THE ANGLO

While the term "Anglo" sometimes simply means "heathen" or "barbarian," most of these peoples are indeed the speakers of the North American Anglic Dialect Continuum. Anglo religion, culture, and ancestry are diverse, with bands often sharing more with their nearest city-dwelling neighbors than with each other. Pictured here are Anglo Merchants, whose ancestors fled the northern Atlantic coast in the early 3000s. Merchants now dwell in city enclaves and houseboats on the Gulf of Saint Lawrence, where, in addition to trade and mediation, they are known for their goose-herding and seaweed aquaculture.

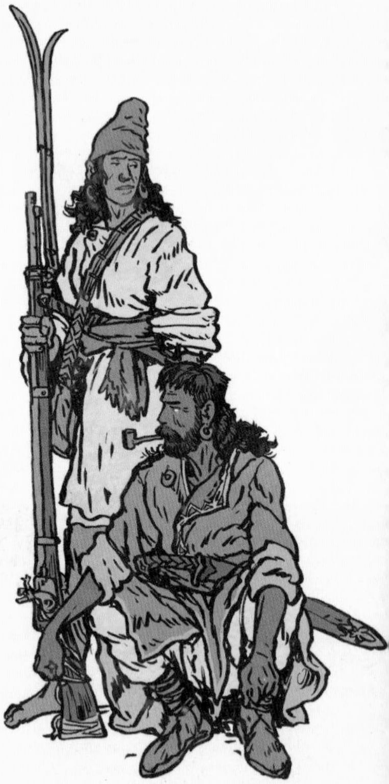

THE BEKUA

The Bekua Dominion traces its origin to the same Post-Catholic tradition as the Yanqui, but rejected their tenet of divine incarnation. Bekua doctrine holds that the Flesh of God cannot be human or artificial, but natural. For centuries, the Bekua Ranger Priesthood cultivated and protected the Labrador Peninsula, pushing peasant farmers into frontier hinterlands, which were conquered and cultivated in turn. Pressure from the Yanqui and the Hudsoni has brought this expansion to a halt, and the Rangers have lost power to the Princes and Barons, who command the fealty of the Fusilier warrior caste.

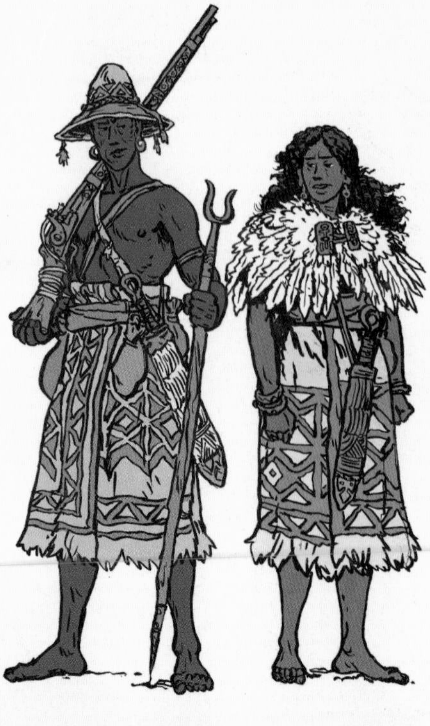

THE PETWA

When the Tropic of Cancer became uninhabitable, the Thalassocratic city-states of the Gulf of Mexico began their long, northward migration. The Petwa Marches now command the North Atlantic Coast to the Gulf of Saint Lawrence. There, they found the Bekua, whose religion and language bore eerie similarity to the Petwas' own. Aside from a few territorial scuffles, the Pact of Peace formed by the Bekua and the Petwa persists to this day. Rumors of godlike beings in the oldest Petwa City-Domes cannot be verified.